BREAK ME
LIKE A
PROMISE

Also by Tiffany Schmidt

Send Me a Sign
Bright Before Sunrise

Once Upon a Crime Family series
Hold Me Like a Breath

ONCE UPON A CRIME FAMILY

BREAK ME LIKE A PROMISE

TIFFANY SCHMIDT

BLOOMSBURY
NEW YORK LONDON OXFORD NEW DELHI SYDNEY

First published in the United States of America in June 2016
by Bloomsbury Children's Books
www.bloomsbury.com

Bloomsbury is a registered trademark of Bloomsbury Publishing Plc

For information about permission to reproduce selections from this book, write to
Permissions, Bloomsbury Children's Books, 1385 Broadway, New York, New York 10018
Bloomsbury books may be purchased for business or promotional use. For information on
bulk purchases please contact Macmillan Corporate and Premium Sales Department at
specialmarkets@macmillan.com

Library of Congress Cataloging-in-Publication Data
Names: Schmidt, Tiffany, author.
Title: Break me like a promise / by Tiffany Schmidt.
Description: New York : Bloomsbury Children's Books, 2016.
| Series: Once upon a crime family ; book 2 |
Summary: When new legislation threatens to destroy her family's
operations in the black-market organ trade, Maggie finds herself falling
in love with Alex, a computer whiz who makes a shocking revelation.
Identifiers: LCCN 2015024930
ISBN 978-0-8027-3783-0 (hardcover) • ISBN 978-1-61963-983-6 (e-book)
Subjects: | CYAC: Organized crime—Fiction. | Transplantation of organs,
tissues, etc.—Fiction. | Love—Fiction. | Sick—Fiction. | Family
life—Fiction. | BISAC: JUVENILE FICTION / General. | JUVENILE FICTION /
Love & Romance. | JUVENILE FICTION / Mysteries & Detective Stories.
Classification: LCC PZ7.S3563 Bp 2016 | DDC [Fic]—dc23
LC record available at http://lccn.loc.gov/2015024930

Book design by Amanda Bartlett and Colleen Andrews
Typeset by Newgen Knowledge Works (P) Ltd., Chennai, India
Printed and bound in the U.S.A. by Berryville Graphics, Inc., Berryville, Virginia
2 4 6 8 10 9 7 5 3 1

All papers used by Bloomsbury Publishing, Inc., are natural, recyclable products
made from wood grown in well-managed forests. The manufacturing processes
conform to the environmental regulations of the country of origin.

For Heather and Marena—
who are always there to keep me from breaking

BREAK ME LIKE A PROMISE

A long, long time ago, back when I had hair as long and shiny as any of the fairy-tale princesses Mama was always shoving down my throat, I made a promise to run away with the boy I'd chosen to be my prince.

Actually, that's not quite true. I made *him* promise *me,* not the other way around. And it was more that I dared and pressured Carter Landlow until he agreed to run away. Just like he'd agreed to drinking hot sauce, licking the inside of his freezer door, and jumping from the tree by his pool. The word "dare" had gravity for Carter—a pull he couldn't escape. *I* had gravity for him too.

Our plan was concocted with a twelve-year-old's simplicity and shoddiness: he would get off his Family's estate in New York and come to my ranch in Texas—then we'd ride off into the sunset. I'm not sure where I thought we'd go, but I had our horses all picked out.

Carter hadn't made it farther than the doughnut shop in his hometown. And I got caught dragging a suitcase to the barn. Our parents went crazy. There were lectures about security and risk. Then there were the airy judgments they tossed about, not noticing how they landed like grenades: *"Bad influences on each other." "Keep them separated." "No more visits!"*

Our parents thought the situation had been remedied. Carter thought we were doomed. But me, I fumed. I hacked off all my glossy-brown princess hair and called that boy, dialed with fingers that felt deliciously deviant and ears that rang with Mama's oft-repeated, "Girls who chase boys prove they're not worth being caught." It was ten digits, two rings, and a *hello* that started an avalanche of connections and conversations and years.

Carter fell as hard for me as he'd once fallen out of that jump-dared tree. This time I caught him. Was caught up in him, in a spell that knitted us into something that felt permanent. Until I was no longer a girl and no longer living on that ranch with its suffocating supervision. Until it was time for us to play with fate again, to plot and place our paths together: face-to-face.

"Garrett Ward? Carter Landlow?" I inflected my voice with the perfect degree of surprise.

Carter took his cues from Garrett. Used his best friend/ bodyguard's genuine astonishment as a model for how to fake his own. "Magnolia Vickers, is that you?" His voice, so familiar from my phone and computer speakers, sounded richer in real life. "What are you doing in New York?" He gestured at the stone buildings that made up his college campus. There was tension in his hand; he curled his fingers into his palms and jammed them in his pocket. I hoped he was having as hard a time not reaching for me as I was not reaching for him.

"I thought you went to college somewhere in Texas?" added Garrett.

"Cross-country invitational." It was the benign excuse we'd agreed upon. One Garrett was unlikely to question, especially if I caught them on their way to his favorite class. "You go here? What a small world."

"Did you win?" Garrett asked politely, but his eyes were drifting to the clock tower behind my head.

Mine strayed to Carter, who was fighting a smile. "You could say that."

"Cool. We've got class, but any chance you'll still be around tonight? We could catch up. Or maybe we shouldn't . . . I promised to keep Carter out of trouble, and you were always so good at getting him into it." Garrett was all oblivious, good-natured teasing—it was almost enough to make me feel guilty about our decision to keep him in the dark.

"Hey! We were just kids—now I'd be *great* at getting him in trouble. But . . ." I forced a sigh. "I can't. The team's leaving. Maybe another time. It was good to see you both!"

Garrett and I exchanged waves, but Carter offered a shrugging, why-not hug. As my arms drifted around his shoulders,

I let my lips graze his cheek and whispered in his ear, "Visitor parking lot."

He nodded and squeezed me tighter before he let go. "Good to see you too."

I had to curl my toes in my sneakers to keep myself still while he walked away. I was much too frenzied to sit and wait in my rental car, so I paced the lot. What if Garrett didn't buy Carter's sudden migraine? What if he insisted on accompanying Carter back to their dorm? What if Carter had changed his mind? Had seen me and decided he liked the long-distance fantasy better than the in-the-flesh reality? Why had we picked a sports cover story? I could've worn a cute dress instead of sweats. A perfect face of makeup instead of bare-skinned vulnerability.

I took a deep breath and reminded myself we'd Skyped through early adolescent skin rebellions and stomach flus and the worst of my piss-off-Mama haircuts. And I'd worn my cutest running apparel—green-striped leggings that were actually long enough for my ridiculous legs and a soft purple sweatshirt with a cowl neck. I crossed my arms over it, over the winged beasts that were swooping in my stomach.

And then he was right there in front of me, hugging me tight. Sweeping me off my feet and into a spin. My head still felt twirly with his coffee-and-toothpaste scent when he set me down. It was so strange to look at him. At *him*, not his pixely image on a computer screen, going spastic when the connection skipped or disappearing with a slammed laptop lid if one of our parents or Family members walked into the room. *Him*, and he was so much more handsome than I'd daydreamed in all of my daydreams of his fingers in mine, his arms around me, his lips on my lips, his breath against my skin.

We stood in the parking lot for hours, but we didn't talk, not right away. We had a half-dozen years of e-mails, messages, and late-night conversations between us. He knew me better than anyone. But it was knowledge from across cellular lines and Internet connections and from the distance of screens and miles. Now was the time for staring our fill, squeezing each other's hands, breathing the same air, and looping the thought "I can't believe we're both here. It doesn't feel real"—until Carter said it out loud and I chased the doubt from his lips with a kiss.

And even though there was a ticking clock hovering over our first rendezvous, and all our rendezvous to come, we'd finally done it. For a moment I forgot that in just a few hours we'd have to say good-bye, and about the waiting and planning and scheming that would be required to sneak away and see each other again. This moment of handholding and gazing and kissing was full of beginnings and potential.

It was supposed to be the start of our *happily ever after.*

But *ever after* was cut short by a bullet when the Landlows were betrayed by Garrett and the other Wards. Killed by those hired to protect them. Carter bled his life into the dirt, and I shattered into a million jagged pieces of grief.

After Carter, I wasn't *ever happy.*

CHAPTER 1

It used to be that my cell ringing in the middle of the night made me think of Carter. Made me think of flirting, of the warm way his voice drifted into my ears and settled in my heart.

Five months after his funeral, it still made me think of Carter . . . but now those thoughts choked me and echoed in the emptiness of his absence.

And when the dark o'clock ringtone was the one I'd assigned his little sister, it added panic to my grief. I threw off my tangled covers, rubbed my puffy eyes, and forced my voice to sound calm when I answered. "Hello?"

"Mags?" Hearing his nickname for me was both a reward and a punishment. It acknowledged that *Mags* had existed, but reminded me *he'd* never say it again.

"Hey, Penny." I blinked at the unfamiliar shadows. These were not the dark shapes of my dorm room with Lupe's bed across from mine and her sighing in her sleep at my too-frequent late-night conversations. No, I'd been yanked from those in early October—five weeks ago. And though I'd grown up in this room, I didn't fit here any more than I'd fit at school. Any more than I fit in my own skin. "Are you okay?"

I winced. She'd asked me *not* to ask that question, because *everyone* asked her all the time. Of course she wasn't. Her life had been destroyed last June when her brother and parents were murdered.

I understood her hating the question. It was the inverse of my craving to be called by Carter's nickname. Pen had artifacts and evidence of her loss everywhere. She didn't need to be reminded. I swallowed against my jealousy of the way her grief was legitimized and acknowledged. "I mean . . . what's up?"

"I need to ask you something?"

Penelope Landlow was all inflected endings and requesting permission to exist. She'd been raised this way, coddled because of a disorder that caused her body to destroy its platelets and bruise easily. Coddled, according to Carter, far more than the diagnosis required. Our roles in life *should* have been similar—we were the only daughters of the three Families that controlled the black market for organ transplants. But while I was all stomp and shout and splash in every mud puddle that stood in my way, she wouldn't even be allowed outside if it was raining. *I'd* never been willing to accept the Families' ideas about how girls should behave, and *she'd* never been given any chance to rebel.

At least not until the moment she was presumed dead along with the rest of her family—then she'd escaped to New York

City, managing both to evade the killers and catch them before they caught her.

If Carter hadn't connected us, I don't know that Penny and I could've found common ground. But now we had an island built for two, fortified with grief and guilt. And a relationship that may have started as all obligation—Carter would have wanted me to look out for her—had developed into real friendship.

Not that this made me any more patient when she went missish. "Okay. Permission granted. Ask away."

"Is it okay that I like school? Like, really like it. Love it?"

"Is 'school' code for something else?" I asked. "Like Char, perhaps?" Then I groaned, because now she had *me* calling her boyfriend "Char" too. I didn't blame her for not recognizing Ming Zhu when they met in NYC last summer—they'd both been in hiding and using fake names. Plus the puberty fairy had been *very* kind to the formerly scrawny and sniffly son of the third Family.

She laughed. "Nope. I mean *school*. I really like it. The people, the teachers, the classes, the halls, the lunchtime . . . everything about it. Is that wrong?"

"Weird, yes. Wrong, no. Why? Is someone picking on you?"

"No. It's just . . . if I like school, if I can handle school, and I've mostly been okay—I mean, there's no miracle cure, but I haven't missed many days and Dr. Castillo says I'm doing fine . . . But that means my parents were *wrong* all those years when they said anything but a private tutor on the estate would be too dangerous for me. And I don't want them to be wrong. I don't want to be mad at them."

"Anger is pretty much what's holding me together." The words were out of my mouth before I'd thought them through.

"Me too," she said. "Apparently my father and Bob used to fight about me. I wish Father had lost or listened or . . . something."

I almost snorted at her casual use of "Bob" for the vice president of the United States. It seemed unreal that Penny *Landlow* lived with the veep. They'd bonded during her efforts to figure out who killed her family and stop illegal organ trafficking— that's what all the news channels said. She never wanted to talk about it.

"Bob always thought I should be in school—believed in finding out my limits, not just setting arbitrary boundaries," she continued. "I mean, where would Kelly be if he'd assumed Down syndrome made her a lost cause like my father decided idiopathic thrombocytopenic purpura doomed me?"

"Your daddy did *not* think you were a lost cause. Sure, he babied you to a crazy degree—and I don't know how you tolerated all those rules and never being allowed to leave your estate—" I paused and rewound my words. My reassurances didn't sound all that reassuring. "But he and your mama thought they were doing what was best for you."

"I know, but it feels wrong—*evil*—that I can finally live my life because they're dead."

I sat up fully and kicked the blankets off my legs. "Carter would've gotten you out. The last time we talked, he was all worked up about you wanting to go to school. He hated seeing you trapped at home. It would've been a done deal if he'd had a chance to—" My throat gripped in the stranglehold of grief. I coughed. "He loved you so much."

Penny sniffled. "He . . . I bet he . . . he *must've* loved you too."

"Yeah." He did. But we'd never told anyone. We were supposed to soon. Carter had insisted, "After I tell my Family about Deer Meadow, we'll sit our families down and tell them about us." I'd argued *we* should come before his secret cadaver clinic—that we'd existed as a couple for years before he and Garrett had schemed and started "Dead Meat"—but I'd given in to his puppy-dog eyes and pleas for patience.

And Dead Meat had gotten him killed.

I looked up into the canopy above my bed at the dark outlines of the only photos I had of him. Two. I was supposed to have deleted them like I had dutifully deleted all the other selfies and texts and e-mails. It was our bedtime ritual. Say good night, then delete the evidence from the day.

These two pictures had defied deletion. And now I was so grateful for them.

The first was years old. A screenshot of a Skype chat where Carter grinned at the computer and rubbed a hand across the slightly crooked buzz cut his dad had given him. It was so vibrant, I still expected fourteen-year-old Carter to open his mouth and flash the silver of his braces as he laughed.

The second was from New York, from our apartment soon after it became *ours* late last fall—bought with money Carter had earned at Dead Meat. It was the day I'd found the brown leather chair-and-a-half, which Carter had to lug up four flights of stairs and squeeze through our door.

In the photo he's sitting in the chair like it's a throne—his cheeks pink and a stupid-proud grin on his face. His feet are up on our coffee table. His eyebrow is quirked, and his eyes are all mischief. It captures the half second before I'd snuggled in beside him.

I wanted to live in the pictures, in the memories they'd frozen.

"Maggie? You still there?" Penny asked.

"Yeah." I yanked my thoughts out of sweat-salty kisses. "I'm here."

"I know it's late. I mean, early. And an hour *earlier* there in Texas than it is here in DC . . . I bet I woke you. Sorry. Want me to call back later?" She rambled when she was nervous, and I added her discomfort to my list of sins.

"No. It's fine." I squinted at my alarm clock. "What else is on your mind?"

"The sentencing."

Of course. If watching on TV as the Wards stood in a courtroom and heard their verdict had kept *me* up half the night, of course it had affected her. She'd grown up with those men. They may have been her *business Family*, and not her blood family, but spend enough time together and those boundaries don't mean much. It'd be like if James or Enzo suddenly pulled a gun and started—

I shuddered at the thought. "How are you feeling about it?" It wasn't a fair question. I didn't know how *I* felt about the sentences delivered to the men who'd killed the Land-lows, who'd attacked the Zhu Family too. I'd hoped it would give me closure, but their punishment hadn't changed a dang thing.

"Multiple life sentences and no chance of parole—I never have to see Al or Mick Ward again. I guess that's the best I could've expected."

"But it's not getting your family back." I winced as my words registered. "Sorry. That was blunt." While I'd heard Carter's stories about Penny for years, I didn't really know *her*. She knew me even less. "I have a horrible habit of using my lips before my neurons."

"Me waking you up so early probably isn't helping."

"Yeah." I slipped gratefully into her compassion. "Me before coffee is pretty much a demonstration of stupidity. Don't lis-ten to anything I say. Well, except for that advice about school. That was solid."

"There's something else." Hesitation hushed her last word.

"You can tell me." The funny thing was, I wanted her to. I'd pushed away most everyone in my life, but she was a piece of Carter and I wanted to keep her.

"Garrett."

One word and my feelings flipped. "I don't want to talk about him."

"I know. It's just—" She sighed. "Char *won't* talk about him. At all. And there's no one else who can."

"Pen, I—" Her inhale sounded like a wince. I'd used Carter's name for her. "Sorry. Fine. Tell me."

"I'm trying to hate him . . . I know I *should* hate him, but . . ."

Her feelings about Garrett Ward—the boy who'd been Carter's best friend, bodyguard, *and* betrayer—were complicated. Mine were simple: blood-rage and hatred. So maybe *he* hadn't pulled the trigger that took down Carter, his parents, or the nurse they mistook for Penny, but his father had. His brothers had. And Garrett had known—if not everything, he'd known enough of their plans that he could've stopped them. And he *should've* turned them in after the fact. Because he hadn't, they'd attacked Char's house, murdered members of the Zhu Family, *and* almost killed Penny.

But Garrett had also saved her life. He'd been hit by the bullet his dad meant for her. And he'd testified against his family. The things he'd said on the stand about growing up with Al Ward as a father made frequent appearances in my nightmares.

"Penny, nothing about this situation is easy," I told her. "There's no *should* when it comes to feelings. We just feel what we feel."

"It's all a mess. And usually I can talk to Char about anything, but he's weird when I bring Garrett up."

"Well, on top of everything else, Garrett was your first love—that's pretty intimidating. I can't really blame hot stuff for not wanting to hear about him."

"I didn't *love* Garrett—at least not like I do Char. It's so hard, though. Garrett's *always* been in my life. He and Carter were my best friends, and I can't make myself not care. He looked awful at the trial. I just want to know if he's okay. *Where is he?*"

"I have no idea." Which was probably safer for him.

"I want him to apologize. I want to understand how he could . . . Maybe if he explained, I'd stop thinking about it so much."

"What could he possibly say that will make any difference? I mean, if *you* have some colorful words you want to say to him, *that* I understand."

"I don't know." She sighed. "I thought he was dead. That no one would tell me, but he was dead. I saw him get shot . . . and then he was just *gone.*

"When I saw him at the trial, I was so mad at myself for being relieved. And he wouldn't even look at me—not once during my testimony or his."

"He probably felt guilty," I said.

"Maybe. His mom left the Family when he was twelve. He always said he didn't know where she was. But . . . he told so many other lies. Do you think he's with her?"

"I have no clue." I only knew Garrett from Carter's stories and rare childhood visits to the Landlow estate. And as an obstacle we had to sneak around whenever I could steal away from my college and security and get to New York. Carter was occasionally allowed to go out without Garrett bodyguarding, but not as often as we liked. Which meant lots of lies and evasion. I'd spent *hours* hiding in the apartment's bedroom closet doing Sudoku puzzles and cursing lost minutes with Carter because Garrett unexpectedly showed up.

Carter and I had argued about the inconvenient Garrett factor constantly—me saying, "If you trust him enough to start a secret clinic with him, why don't you trust him enough to tell him about us?" and him responding, "You'll just have to trust *me* to know my best friend."

"I guess I never really knew him." The overlap between Penny's statement and my reminiscing was jarring. There was so much pain in those words. The way it radiated off her hit me with unwelcome perspective. She had lost *everyone.*

I wanted to feel compassion. To tell myself that mine was the lesser loss, a lesser pain.

But.

Doing that felt like diminishing what I'd had. What was gone. And I had loved Carter. I didn't need to use Penny's grief as a measuring stick to beat myself up.

"I should let you get back to bed," she said.

"Don't ever feel like you can't call me." I meant it. "If there's *anything* I can do, please let me know."

"You could read the Organ Act info I e-mailed you?"

"Penny . . ." I had a whole list of e-mails from her with subject lines like *World Health Organization reverses stance on donor compensation.* I treated them the same way I did school newsletters, e-mails from the registrar's office, and *how are you?* messages from friends—ignored, unread, but not deleted.

"Just read the articles. I'm not saying you *have* to agree with Char and me, but . . . just read them?"

We said our good-byes and promised to talk soon. I *might* have said something about reading the info she'd sent me "later"—a nice, vague word that could mean any time from after breakfast to when I was being fitted with dentures.

I leaned back, staring up at the photos I knew were above me but couldn't see in the shadowy predawn. It didn't much matter. Dark or late-for-breakfast bright, the pictures were burned into my memory.

CHAPTER 2

I woke up well past any hour Mama considered acceptable for a lady to have slept. At some point while staring at Carter and chastising myself about all of the things I should have said to Penny but didn't, I must have fallen asleep. Hopefully, our housekeeper, Anna, would still feed me. For the first couple weeks after I was pulled from college, she'd kept warm plates of huevos motuleños, pumpkin french toast, and jalapeño corn cakes for me. But lately, whenever I missed a meal and wandered into the kitchen, she grumbled and pointed to the cabinet where the cereal was kept.

Still, soggy Cheerios were better than Mama's lectures across the dining room table.

I grabbed an elastic headband from the back of my door and shoved it on as I went down the curved front staircase toward the kitchen. It made my brown hair stick up in fourteen different directions, but it had been weeks since I'd bothered with product or anything resembling a style.

"Are you just waking up?" Daddy's voice rumbled from the foyer.

"Something like that. You're going somewhere?"

As a rule Daddy didn't go *to people*, people came *to him*. That he was palming keys and Byrd was waiting at the front door was strange enough to make me summon up the energy to be curious. Where was he headed with his second-in-command?

"We're going to the meeting with the clinic heads and security." Daddy took in my bed head and baggy clothing, his mouth pursing in disapproval behind his neat beard.

"What meeting? Where? Shouldn't that be *here*?"

And *why*? And *shouldn't I know about this*? He'd been grooming me as his heir since I was fourteen. Even when I was at college, a meeting like this was something he would've brought me home to attend. And since my parents had pulled me out of school, there weren't classes or cross-country meets to schedule around.

"It's nothing for you to be worried about, missy. Go get yourself some breakfast and a shower and do . . . whatever you've been doing."

He *always* shared company problems with me. How else was I going to learn how to handle them when I took over the Family? I tugged sheepishly at the sweatshirt-and-pants combo I'd been wearing for three? . . . four? days. "What's going on? What aren't you telling me?"

Daddy dismissed Byrd with a toss of his keys. "Get the truck; I'll be out in a few." Then he turned back to me. "Maggie Grace, why're you so riled up?"

My heart pounded against my crossed arms. Over the past few months I'd rarely felt anything but hollow and sick. Now I felt rage. "Nothing for *me* to be worried about? Am I no longer your heir? No longer on the Family council? Now what? Want me to go join Mama on the Junior League? Think I can still squeeze myself into those spangled outfits and lisp a poem about flowers? Maybe it's not too late for me to do beauty pageants."

He raised a soap-white eyebrow and held up a hand. "Before you go getting yourself all worked into a good snit, take a deep breath and pause that tantrum, darlin'. That's not what I'm saying at all."

"Oh, I'm 'darlin'' now, and 'missy'? I used to be 'sport'— this change sums it all up perfectly."

"Wait just a minute there, Magnolia Grace. You've *always* been my darlin' and my sport. And if you even think about parading around in a pageant . . . I'll eat every spangle on those old costumes before I let you wear 'em. Now come sit a minute, and let's have this out like adults."

I followed Daddy into his office. My chair wasn't behind his desk any longer; it'd been tucked away in the corner. If Anna didn't run such an efficient household, there would be dust accumulated in the dark wood's ornate carvings and around the brass nail heads that held on the black leather seat. I dragged it beside his and sat, determined to act like the professional I'd always prided myself on being. I met his eyes with a steady gaze. "Please explain."

"I'm closing down the clinic here."

"What do you mean?" My fingers curved into the familiar grooves of my chair's arms, tightening with the anxious stir in my stomach.

"I don't know how I can be any plainer than that. I'm shutting down the Homestead clinic. I'm moving the meeting room too."

"But . . . why?"

"Think." He leaned over and tapped my forehead, but all I could think was how I'd grown up sitting in those meetings, inching closer and closer to Daddy's spot behind the massive, leather-topped oak desk and imagining the day it would be mine. After the raid when I was fourteen, he had bought me my own throne of a chair and placed it beside his. But I hadn't sat in it lately, and I couldn't come up with an answer.

Daddy sighed. He always got a pinched expression when he was about to mention Carter, like it pained him to hurt me. Or pained him to remember how I'd deceived him for so long—had this second life that he knew nothing about until I fell apart after flying to New York and discovering that *one* Landlow, just not the one I'd been hoping for, wasn't truly dead. He sighed again. "This decision's been months in the making. After what happened on the Landlow and Zhu estates . . . the Business should be kept away from where we live. I want you and your mother protected and out of the line of fire."

"I don't need you to protect me." I gritted my teeth and looked around his office. Everything appeared to be in its place.

It was just my chair that had been shoved aside. Would he even bother packing it when he relocated? "Anything else you've decided without me? Any other major changes I should know about?"

Daddy's eyes rested heavily on my face for a long moment, and the echoes of my flip questions sat sour in my mouth. Because clearly the answer was yes to major changes and he was still weighing whether or not to tell me. Finally, he nodded. "I'm flying to DC tomorrow to take some meetings about the Organ Act."

"The Organ Act?" I recoiled against my chair. "No."

"Both the Landlow and Zhu kids are backing it with what remains of their Families behind them. I'm weighing my options."

I didn't want to think of Penny and Char and all their appearances on C-SPAN, smiling and showcasing their romance while promoting a legalized organ trade. "The Organ Act is poison. It's going to destroy the Business. It already destroyed their Families. Mr. Landlow was *killed* by his own Family because he named a pro–Organ Act successor. How can you even consider supporting it?"

"I'm not seeing I have much of a choice." He shrugged like he was powerless, but Daddy was never without a strategy.

"How could you decide this without asking me?"

"When was I supposed to do that?" He leaned back in his seat and raised an eyebrow. "You've been too busy wallowing."

"But—" *But* what? I kicked at the edge of the rug and thought through all the angles of this argument. There weren't any I could win. I lowered my chin. "I haven't been acting like someone who should be consulted in Business decisions lately."

"Darlin', you haven't been acting *human*. I've seen zombies with more life to them."

"You do this and there's not going to be a Business left for me to inherit."

"Do you even want it anymore?"

"Yes!" I sat bolt upright. "How can you even ask that?"

"The Business takes complete focus. It can't be ignored or expected to wait because you're dealing with heartache or want to indulge your emotions."

"Indulge my emotions? Like I'm a little schoolgirl who had a crush and a breakup?" My veins were so full of fury that when I stood to glower down at him, I shook. "The man I *loved* died, and it makes me weak to mourn him? And I guess if anything happened to Mama or me, you'd be able to shrug it off and go about your daily agenda?"

His fists slammed down on his desk. "You are not allowed to even *joke* about anything happening to you or your mama."

"Oh, so it's only *my* loved ones who don't qualify?"

"No one even knew you two were dating," he said. And I wished I'd never told him. I resented every answer he'd dragged out of me after the Zhu's estate was attacked. But I'd been too exhausted, too terrified about Penny's health, too worn down by years of secrets and a month of mourning. When Daddy had shown up at the apartment demanding explanations, I'd cracked and confessed in mangled sobs.

He sighed. "You're young, sport. Give it time."

"While my age might make it easier for you to dismiss, that doesn't make it any easier on *me*." I fought the quiver in my voice. "I've been in love with Carter practically my whole life . . . He was supposed to be my happy ending."

"Oh, Maggie Grace." He stood and wrapped his arms around me. While he wasn't tall—several inches shorter than me—his hugs always made me feel like I had something solid to depend on. This time I felt trapped. "Your ending ain't written yet, darlin'. You're just getting started."

I couldn't talk about Carter anymore. Not with someone who didn't take us seriously. I pulled away from him and squared my shoulders. Made eye contact and kept my voice steady. "Not if you wreck the Business I plan on leading. Let's talk. What would make you reconsider this relocation?" Daddy liked plans of action, concrete facts, and haggling. He was never happier than during ruthless negotiations.

The corners of his mouth twitched. "There's my girl. Welcome back. So let's get this straight. You've got two issues." He held up fingers to count them off. "You disagree with me moving the Business. And you don't approve of the Organ Act."

"Yes."

"And, knowing you, you don't care about the clinic." He rested his round chin in the V between his thumb and pointer finger and stroked his trim white beard. "Your head's all figures and business. Patients aren't even on your radar. Except for when you complain about the way the clinic smells, or having to wait to ask Dr. Ackerman a question, because how *dare* he be busy with one of them. Frankly, I thought you'd be glad to have the clinic gone."

He wasn't wrong. Patients and donors were necessary, but messy and complicated and needy. And where they were, there was *blood*. I wasn't medically trained and had no desire to be. I doubted the CEOs of any of the fast-food chains assembled burgers or patted the cows they came from. The clinics were for patients and donors, not me. I narrowed my eyes. "Make your point."

"So, the way I read it, you're all worked up over that because I didn't consult you and you didn't get to have your say. This ain't my first rodeo, Maggie. It ain't yours either, even if it's been a while since you've been on a horse. These issues aren't unrelated. We go pro–Organ Act, then we need to be on the up-and-up. Getting the Business off-estate helps that appearance *and* keeps you and your mama safer. It's wins all around."

"Except for the part about being pro–Organ Act," I snapped.

"Things changed while you were checked out these past few months. The Organ Act is starting to look like a speeding train—we can get on board, or get run over."

"But—"

He held up a hand. "That being said, it's still possible it'll derail. You still want this to be *your* Business—prove it. You want to come along to DC, get informed, and have a rational discussion about the Organ Act, well, I wouldn't be opposed to your opinion or company. But if you come with me, Maggie Grace, then you need to get your game face on and get up to speed. You need to be able to look at this thing from all angles. Not just numbers, patients. You need to be aware of your biases and weaknesses, or else you're liable to only see what you want and miss the big picture about what this Business *is* and what the Organ Act could be." He paused and leveled me with a look. "You've got twenty-four hours to show me you can pull it together and keep it together. Get dressed. Get read up. Get prepared to do me proud on this trip. I need you to 'man up,' if you'll allow the expression."

His wording felt like a test. Did he want to see me show some moxie and fight him on it? Pull out a lecture on how I'd "lady up" and how he should keep his *good ol' boys* mentality out of this? Or would it be better to capitulate? I tugged on a thread in my sweatshirt pocket, then leveled my chin at him.

"I will *person up*." I wrinkled my nose, and he chuckled. "Okay, I'll *pluck up*. How about that? I'll be the pluckiest person you've ever seen."

"Heaven save us if you're pluckier than you used to be." He kissed my cheek, and I followed him into the foyer. "I've got meetings all day, but I look forward to seeing that pluck at supper, *sport*."

I fought a wince; those meetings were still off-estate, still without me—for now. I raised an eyebrow and said, "Prepare yourself."

Daddy shot me a hopeful wink as he shut the front door behind him. I continued into the kitchen. Anna had a game show on the television and a hand on her hip as she lectured Manuel about something. She had influence—but it stopped and started in the kitchen. The Family men would've guffawed if she tried to weigh in on the Organ Act or whether or not we needed to adjust our donor recruitment or research budgets. They respected her—downright worshiped her cooking and feared her ability to cut off their supply of coffee or sweet tea—but she fit within the parameters of the stupid gendered roles the Family had always followed. Roles I'd been rejecting since the first time I toddled into Daddy's office and refused to leave.

It was amusing to watch her take her brother-in-law to task, but Manuel wasn't really concerned. He was head of Family security. The kitchen may have been Anna's domain, but even here the power balance wasn't tipped in her favor.

I caught Manuel's eye and winked, making him blink in surprise and then grin. Anna cut off midsentence and turned to see what he found amusing.

"I'm starving, Anna. Any chance there's some of your excellent coffee and breakfast left?"

She waved a dismissive hand. "You know where to find the cereal."

"I do," I answered. "But since I'm supposed to be plucking, I was hoping for something a bit more spicy."

"You're supposed to be *what*?" Her hands dropped from her hips, and Manuel's shoulders were shaking with laughter.

"Plucking up," I clarified. "I told Daddy I'd pluck up."

Anna's eyes went soft in a way that only occurred when she talked about her husband, who'd been in jail since an FBI raid when I was a toddler, or her kids—Enzo and my best friend,

Lupe. "Go shower and get dressed. You're stinking up my kitchen with your laziness. When you come back, I'll have a plate of plucky food waiting."

Manuel had used my diversion to slip out the back door, which was *almost* enough to make me smile as I said, "Thank you."

I trudged upstairs to my room. It didn't match the rest of the ranch—no exposed beams, earth tones, or heavy carved furniture. It didn't match itself either; it looked like two different decorators were each pulling on a corner to claim it as their own. Mama's taste was displayed in the canopy bed with its dove-gray velvet, tufted headboard, the matching dressing table, and ice-pink curtains and chandelier. These competed with my college memories from last year—framed group photos of friends wearing orange Longhorns shirts and making "Hook 'em, Horns," my highlighted-to-death business textbooks, and dizzying Escher prints.

But I was haunted by all the things that *weren't* here. Hiding my relationship with Carter had been an amusing rebellion when were young, had felt necessary in the years when I was proving myself to the Family, but since we'd left for college, it had just been aggravating—something he and I fought about all last year. If I'd won the argument—even if he'd still been murdered—at least I'd have souvenirs to keep me company.

It was pure stubborn will that prevented me from climbing beneath my duvet again. Wearing grungy sweats and lying in bed took all my energy. Breathing felt like effort. I hurt. Joints, head, everywhere. And the parts of me that didn't ache felt hollow.

Layered over all this was one thought, one inescapable, incessant thought: *What if it never gets easier? What if life hurts this much forever?*

It felt impossible that five months ago, Carter and I had been kissing in New York. Or that five weeks ago, I'd been back at University of Texas, a month into my sophomore year. I'd had a dorm room, a class schedule, and at least a partial belief that I could be functional.

I'd failed spectacularly at it—but Mama and Daddy yanking me out of school and bringing me home to "heal" hadn't made things better.

My fingers clenched the curtains that ringed my bed, my body retreating before my mind had even realized I'd surrendered.

No. I pried my fingers off the dark-gray, fleur-de-lis fabric and turned my back on my bed and its sanctuary.

I'd do this. I'd playact at being pulled together or plucky or whatever else Daddy required, because I couldn't let him turn the Business over to the Organ Act. I had already lost one half of my "happily ever after." I couldn't lose this too.

CHAPTER 3

The easiest way to start would be to shower and put on whatever dress and shoes first grazed my fingertips, but easy wasn't good enough. I needed to be convincing.

I went for a lilac dress printed with flocks of green swallows that spiraled from the lace at the hem all the way up to the collar. And rather than choosing proper ladylike shoes that matched, I grabbed my orange cowboy boots. Maggie Grace's style was defiant, and if I was being her, then I needed to costume myself with an outfit that flirted with Mama's demure taste, then flipped it the finger. I applied product to my overgrown pixie cut, subtly winged the edges of my eyeliner, buffed my nails, then stacked items around my neck: a pocket watch on a chain, a key on a ribbon, and my grandmama's pearls.

I reentered the kitchen, greeted by the scent of eggs and chorizo and Anna's "Sit and eat before the *second* breakfast I've prepared today goes cold."

"Thank you." My smile was bright, shiny, and fake—like the things Grandmama had called "paste jewels." The term fit this smile. I'd glued it on and just hoped that no one realized it was worthless.

Anna scrutinized me while I ate. When I stood to put my empty plate in the sink, she intercepted me, took it from my hands, and gave me a quick, fierce hug. "You've always been a fighter. I'm glad to see you back in the ring."

I didn't feel like I was even in the arena. But I returned her squeeze, inhaling her soap and flour scent.

"Where's Mama?" I asked.

"She had one of the men drive her to meet a friend for lunch and shopping."

Which meant there wasn't anyone I needed to impress for a few hours. "Okay, I'm going to go . . ." I faltered.

"Get some air," suggested Anna, pushing me toward the door. "You've been inside too long."

I blinked at the sunshine blazing beyond the terra-cotta arches supporting the covered patio. It glinted off the pool in front of me and cracked the dirt around the scrub brush to my left. Beyond that I could see the roofs of the barn and the clinic, and across the pool was the room used for Business entertaining. In less than a minute, my dress felt damp, though that was probably anxiety as much as the heat.

I leaned against the column of one of the arches. I'd made

it this far before since coming home from school—usually at night, when most everyone was asleep and the only people I saw were security on patrol. But this was daylight, and I was going farther than the patio. I crossed the pool deck, passed the fire pit and the grill stations, and kept walking until I reached my old rope-and-plank swing. I didn't sit on it, but set my phone on the seat and threaded my fingers through the frayed string below the knot.

My cell's bright rhinestone case had seemed quirky when I bought it from a street vendor in New York; now it looked dull and cheap. I carried my phone out of habit, and in case Penny wanted to call. She was the one person I hadn't completely failed. Yet. I wasn't the perfect friend or support system, but man, I was trying my best. If she wanted to cry, I soothed. If she wanted to talk, I listened—whether it was about school, Char, or adapting to life in the vice presidential residence, I was two ears and all attention. Except when it came to her Organ Act e-mails.

How hard could it be to read a few articles? It definitely counted as "getting up to speed" and put me one step closer to earning a seat on tomorrow's flight to DC. I focused on the phone on the swing—and tapped on the e-mail icon.

At the top of the list of unread Organ Act articles and the other things clogging my in-box I found an e-mail that forced a sound like torn paper from my lips. Half sob, half gasp. And half my soul flinched and hoped, and then flinched away from that hope.

Subject: Hey . . . I miss you, sexy. From Carter's e-mail address. Dated this morning.

CHAPTER 4

It couldn't be from Carter. I knew that.

Except . . . Penny had supposedly been dead for a few weeks. I'd cried over her obituary. I'd gone to her funeral. If her whole death was a hoax, then his . . .

Why couldn't *his* be? Why couldn't the government have him hidden away? Somewhere safe until the trial was over.

Sentencing was yesterday.

So now he could . . . he could!

The thread my thoughts constantly snagged on was *it wasn't enough*. I hadn't had enough time with Carter. I didn't have enough memories stockpiled. We didn't have enough dates, and I didn't have enough mementos. I should have saved every text he sent. Laminated every takeout napkin he'd doodled on. Videoed and selfied and immortalized every moment of our relationship. Papered my room, papered my life with *proof* Carter and I were a *we*, a dang good *we*, a *we* worth celebrating. A *we* worth mourning.

But if he . . .

Oh, please. Carter. *Please.*

My fingers shaking, I tapped on the e-mail. Tapped and tapped again until I opened it. There was an attachment, but my phone couldn't download it.

Carter.

I ran in the back door, my heels reverberating against the floor like gunshots. Like blanks. Like the blanks that must've been used to fake his death. *Carter, Carter, Carter.* It was a prayer, a hymn, a vow, and it took me half a hallway to realize I was chanting it out loud.

The closest computer wasn't mine. My laptop was somewhere in the back of my closet, but Daddy's office and desktop were right there. And logging in with my network ID would take mere seconds. The mouse was jerky in my shaking hand as I clicked and typed and clicked. The Internet had never been slower. My typing never more inept.

"I'm hurrying, Carter," I said under my breath as I opened his e-mail. "Just a few more seconds and I'll be . . ."

I clicked *download* on the attachment and leaned so close to the monitor that my breath left film on the screen. A progress bar filled, moving left to right in jumps and spurts that seemed to match the racing and skipping of my pulse.

Done.

The screen blinked.

A new window opened. Black background with white text that scrolled and replaced itself. Scrolling so fast I couldn't decipher it. Not even words. A code? Why would Carter . . . ?

The letters and numbers zooming by didn't mean anything to me. Anything but . . . *oh, crap!*

The text box closed and other windows started opening. Internet pop-ups. Three. Six. A dozen. I was closing them fast, but they were appearing faster. Twenty. More.

And *crr-aaaap!* Some of them were playing music. Others showed a whole buffet of skin, and blinked, flashed, moaned. In moments they'd buried the screen under forty, fifty—so many layers of pop-ups. I glanced at Daddy's open office door, but I didn't dare waste time running to close it.

Double deep-fried crap.

I yanked the computer's plug from the wall and watched the screen blink off.

It meant . . . it meant—

I sank to the floor. Dropped my face in my hands, covering my palms with tears and dissolved mascara.

My phone rang with Penny's ringtone.

I sniffled and swiped at my face. "Hello?"

"I hate hackers," she said.

I nodded, then managed to squeeze "Yeah," through a throat that was suffocation-tight.

"For a second I almost thought it could be real. Like, Carter left us those letters, so why couldn't he have set some delayed e-mail too? And then I saw the subject . . . I'm pretty sure my brother would never call *me* 'sexy.' *And* it was sent to a whole list of his contacts."

"It was?" I hadn't even noticed. I was too busy being an idiot. Being duped.

"Char said it had to be a—"

"Virus?" I interrupted, shutting my eyes as my fears were confirmed.

"Yeah."

"Did he say what the virus does?" I rubbed my eyelids, feeling the griminess of makeup mixed with dried tears.

"I don't think you can tell that sort of thing until it's too late. Want me to ask?"

"No, don't bother." I bit the inside of my bottom lip, clamping down on screams and sobs and the shards of hope that were stabbed into all my most vulnerable places. "Are you okay?"

Because I wasn't. I so wasn't.

"Mostly angry. It's cruel!"

"Yeah."

"And I wanted to ask if you knew his passwords?"

"No. Sorry." I'd spent weeks of sleepless nights trying everything I could think.

"Oh. I thought, since you said you . . ."

She didn't need to finish the sentence. Proof. Everyone wanted proof I wasn't making *us* up. They wanted me to offer evidence, to justify my inability to crawl out of my devastation, and since I couldn't . . .

"Can I call you later, Penny? I've got to . . ." I waved a smeared hand in a gesture that expressed a sentiment I couldn't verbalize and she couldn't see.

"Oh, okay. Sure."

I allowed myself a few minutes doubled over. Of silently screaming on Daddy's office floor. Of pressing my face into his deerskin rug and choking on empty sobs, on the hollowness of facing a future I'd dared to allow myself to reinvent.

"If there was ever a person who should be a Luddite for her own safety, it's you," Carter had said after I'd hit myself in the eye while applying mascara using my phone's camera as a mirror. He'd seen me trip over my laptop cord, slam my finger in its lid, get a phone charger tangled in my hair. But he'd never seen me fall apart like this.

I stood. Grabbed a tissue from Daddy's desk and used it to wipe my face. Opened and closed my fists. Grasped at numbness. At control. At any sort of facade I could hide behind.

I held the computer plug in one hand, my phone in the other, said a quick prayer, and dialed.

"Loops, I need a fast favor." I didn't have time to sugarcoat it, but Lupe was Family—and my best friend. "Computer repair person: Do you know any?"

"The people at campus IT are good."

"What about around my place? And one that's trustworthy."

She sucked in a breath, and I could practically hear the way she squinched her mouth back and forth while she thought. Her mama had done the same thing while scrutinizing me over breakfast. "You know the strip mall around where Six meets Thirty-Five? Between your place and school? Oh, I know! It's right after that Dairy Queen where James threw up in eighth grade! My mama brings the curtains next door for dry cleaning, and they fixed Enzo's laptop when he got some virus from nasty websites and didn't want to tell Theo."

Theo, the Family IT guy, would absolutely have squealed on Enzo. I couldn't tell if Theo sucked at his job and tattled about everyone's tech atrocities to make himself look competent, or if he just sucked as a person. I'd committed more tech atrocities than most—he and I were not friends. But the place Lupe suggested could work.

"They were discreet?"

"Enzo's still alive—and he wouldn't be if Mamá knew." She laughed, then added, "Ask for Alex Cooper—his name was on the paperwork when I picked it up. And good brisket."

Lupe was brilliant. She barely glanced at her bio and chemistry textbooks, yet aced her classes. But following her logic required a bit of a road map. This one was easy: the dry cleaner's and computer store shared the same strip mall as a barbecue place.

"You're awesome."

"So they tell me." She said it with affected weariness. "But don't let my mother know you talked to her awesome daughter. I've been dodging her calls so she can't guilt me into coming to visit."

"Deal," I agreed quickly. Our friendship was coming off a rocky couple of months. I'd asked a lot of Lupe last year—for lots of lies and covering for me. She hadn't learned the full reason *why* until this summer when Carter died and I'd had a breakdown in New York. And she hadn't been okay with all the things I'd kept from her. I'd apologized, and she'd said she forgave me—but things weren't as easy between us as they'd always been.

"How are you?" she asked in a careful tone that made me cringe.

"I'm trying."

"That's a start. And I'm glad you called—our room's so quiet without you." She paused. "You know—if *you* need me, I'll come home. I can take a semester off too. It doesn't seem fair that I'm here when you and James left."

"No, Loops. Thanks, but no. You stay. Keep that GPA up so med schools drool over you. I'm . . ."

"Trying," she repeated. "Well, go bug James for me. And, at the risk of sounding like my mama, call me more. Love you, chica."

We said our good-byes, but my thoughts had moved on. How was I going to carry the computer stuff? Disguise it?

I shut the door to Daddy's office, raced up to the storage closet, grabbed a suitcase, then clattered back downstairs. I crammed all the pieces and wires inside, zipped it up, and crept into the hall to figure out the next part of this stupid, stupid plan.

But some of my best memories were the result of stupid plans, and long odds had never stopped me before.

Maybe my instincts weren't dead, just hibernating, because now that I had a goal, I began reviewing my mental Family roster and trying to figure out the *how* and the *who*. I folded a tissue and spit-wet the crease, dragging it under both eyes to catch any remaining mascara streaks, then walked down the hall to lean my head into the room where Family members were assembled in casual conversations over sandwiches and a trio of salads: potato, bean, and macaroni. There were bowls of chips, a blaring TV, and a half-dozen men.

I zeroed in on the one I wanted. "Hey, Manuel. Can I borrow you a minute?"

"Hey again, Maggie Grace." He followed me back into the hall, carrying his plate with him and taking a bite of roast beef sandwich before continuing. "You about gave me a heart attack this morning with that wink. It sure is nice to see you smiling and looking like yourself again."

Smiling? I was pretty sure I was grimacing, but people saw what they wanted.

And maybe my silence stretched a beat too long, because he shifted his grip on his sandwich and cleared his throat. I cleared mine too and gave him the same answer I'd given his niece. "I'm trying."

His grin flickered a little at the corners. He glanced back over his shoulder to make sure the other guys were still busy with their lunches or rehashing whatever sports game had half of them red-faced and shouting while Enzo stomped his foot with laughter. Brooks, taciturn as always, was sitting close to the TV and watching with a focus that defied the others' chaos. He and Enzo were four years older than Lupe, James, and me. Since neither had interest in medical or law school, they were currently rotating through a variety of Family jobs—security, donor communications, pharmaceutical liaisons—to see which fit best.

Manuel tried to shut the door all casual-like. It didn't look casual at all, but they weren't paying attention. "I'm pulling for you. We all are. There's not one person here who wouldn't love to see you raise some hell again. Keep trying."

"Thank you." It was a kindness that felt like an obligation. I wanted to be the hellion they all remembered, but she felt like a stranger.

He put his plate down on one of Mama's foyer tables, not even noticing that it clinked against a vase and pushed it off-center. "You need something?"

"It's nothing big." I watched the lisianthus sway in the vase, then realized meeting his eyes would appear more guileless. "I need to run an errand. It'll take a few hours, tops. If you and I sneak out now, we'll be back before my daddy's even home."

Manuel hooked his thumbs in the belt loops of his jeans and leaned away from me. "I can't."

"Please? I'm really in a pinch—I broke something, and I need to get it fixed before Daddy finds out." I tilted my head and twirled a strand of hair in the way I'd seen Lupe do whenever she thought playing the clueless co-ed would get her further than showing off her crazy intelligence. "It's a computer, and you know I can't ask Theo. I've already gotten the whole be-more-responsible-with-your-belongings lecture twice. Please."

Manuel shook his head. "Drop the act, Magnolia Grace. You're no pouter. *I can't.* Not even if I wanted to. You've got a mandatory two-person detail now."

"Says who? *You're* head of security."

"And your daddy's head of the Family. He pulled rank. And after what you pulled with ducking James and jet-setting, I don't blame him. I'll do my best to get you in and out quietly, and I'm not gonna blab, but I've got to bring someone else along."

"Oh." I guess discovering I'd evaded my bodyguard, not just once or twice, but on *ten* different trips to New York might cause Daddy to change my security coverage. "Well, not James. Maybe—"

"Not James, what?" Tall and lean, with a voice that was often a hair too quiet—definitely too quiet in the ruckus of the TV room—James shut the door behind him and raised an eyebrow as he asked.

James Byrd. Not Jim. Never Jimmy—well, never minus the times I'd wanted to make him spitting mad. We'd been bickering best friends for the first fourteen years of our lives, but now we were kerosene and lit matches.

His father simply went by Byrd and was Daddy's second-in-command. James's older brother, "Hawk," was an anesthesiologist at the Amarillo clinic. His older sister, "Baby Byrd," had graduated from Baylor, married, and was having babies of her own somewhere around Austin.

But James was always just James. And for the past five years he'd been my reluctant shadow. Like Garrett had been stuck going everywhere Carter went, my classes became James's in high school. His college choice hinged on mine. If I wanted to leave campus without Lupe—even just to pick up takeout—he had to come with me. We'd both chafed under the arrangement. I'd frequently ditched him, and he'd frequently pretended not to notice.

But he *hadn't* known about my covert trips to New York to see Carter. And when his lapse in guarding had been exposed during the chaos that followed the attack on the Zhus, Daddy's reaction hadn't been pretty.

Also not pretty—James's response when he learned that my being pulled from college meant he was expected to leave midsemester too.

This time I hadn't intentionally hurt him, but inviting him along on *this* trip . . . I might as well dial Daddy now and hand James my phone, because there was no way he wouldn't tell.

Manuel shrugged. Without missing a beat, he proved why he was my first choice for accomplice. "Maggie Grace wants to run errands this afternoon, and I told her about the double-coverage rule. She asked who was free; I said you were busy. So she said, 'Not James.'"

"I'm not busy. I was supposed to be meeting with Theo to set up the distance ed software, but he called and said something came up. I don't have anything else to do, so count me in, I guess. What errands?"

"Um, the female kind," I lied in a faux-whisper. "Tampons and bra shopping. Since you passed out in sixth-grade health class, you'd better skip it. I'll bring someone else. Want to get Brooks for me?"

"Give me a break, Maggie. It's not like you haven't dragged me along on that sort of thing before." He ground his teeth. "I was on a first-name basis with the receptionist at your bikini waxer's."

"We don't need to bother you if you need to meet with Theo once he's free," said Manuel, and I wondered how deep the Family distrust of James ran. And why none of it seemed aimed at me.

"He's dealing with some network disaster—and said it'd take hours. I can't register for classes till it's fixed. I need something to distract me from my education being derailed—again. If it's got to be bras and tampons, well, that's better than anything I got goin' on here. This coming?" He grabbed the handle of my suitcase and started toward the front door. "Let's go."

CHAPTER 5

The drive was fifty-five minutes of tension. Time crackled like the air before a thunderstorm sets the sky alight. All I could think of were charged conversation topics—and given my history of offending James accidentally *and* on purpose—I chose silence.

"What happened to bras and tampons?" James asked when I directed Manuel to pull into the strip mall Lupe suggested.

"Later, if there's time. I need to drop off some clothing at the dry cleaner's."

"So, that was, what, an excuse because you didn't want me to come?"

I didn't need to turn around to know James's ears would be bright red and his neck blotchy. We'd grown up together, him, Lupe, and me. We were close until he had decided he needed to impress my daddy more than me and turned into a world-class tattletale.

I'd jokingly called him on it when we were fifteen. "Should I get you and Daddy BFF necklaces? Clearly *we* don't need 'em anymore."

And James had calmly replied, "It's just Business. My loyalty is to your father. If you're in charge someday, it'll be to you. Till then, he trumps you."

Daddy "trumped me," and so James and I couldn't be friends anymore. Not without getting in trouble for seeing an R-rated movie at fifteen, or for the flask Loops and I sneaked into prom. Or speeding. Or skipping class. Or any of the other stupid rebellions he'd squealed about.

We still followed the patterns we'd established back then—I evaded him as often as possible, and he returned the favor by telling on me. So there was no point in sparing his feelings now.

"Exactly. I didn't want you to come. Stay in the car. Manuel, can you help me with my case?"

"Nice try, but I can't stay in the car; you're supposed to be double-covered all the time."

"Hold up, you two," Manuel interjected before I could argue. "James will stay here and watch the front of the store and parking lot. He'll call if he sees anything suspicious. It's a dry cleaner's, not some big threat. It'll only draw attention if three of us go in."

"It may be awhile," I warned. "It's a full suitcase. They'll need to write up the slips, and I have to find the stains and make sure they get the instructions for the different fabrics."

"All I've seen you wear lately is sweats; I don't even know how—"

"Exactly, James. You don't know. So stay put." I climbed out and Manuel did too. He grabbed the suitcase from the truck bed, setting it on the pavement before giving me a look.

"Don't be so hard on the kid. He's getting grief from everyone about how he failed you—and from where I stand, he's trying and you're being difficult."

"Isn't that what you wanted?" I asked. "For me to raise some hell?"

He chuckled.

"I'll apologize." I would. But not now. "Come on, before he gets impatient."

I wheeled my suitcase into the dry cleaner's, smiled at the person behind the counter, then walked past him and out the back door. I circled around a Dumpster and a woman smoking outside the back of a frozen yogurt shop, then pulled open the gray door labeled Tech World.

"Why, howdy there." A guy leaned across the counter, scanned me from head to boots, and leered like this was a compliment.

Manuel cleared his throat and shuffled a step closer, but I didn't have time or patience for machismo. "Is Alex Cooper here?"

Howdy frowned. "Yeah, he's in the back." He pointed to a door leading to a fenced area filled with shelves and bins of wires, circuits, and all sorts of electronic things I didn't get along with. "Alex—customer *wants* you."

Manuel *ahemed* at the emphasis. I tapped a drumbeat with the toe of my boot and let go of the suitcase handle to wipe a sweaty palm on my dress. I was running two races—I needed to beat Daddy home and stay ahead of James's nosiness. Losing either one would mean losing Daddy's approval, losing my seat on the plane . . . and possibly losing my Family to the Organ Act.

"Coming!"

I laughed. The voice was so unexpectedly deep. Like a movie trailer announcer. Like the bad guy in a horror film phone call. Like the bass singer in UT's a cappella group.

Laughter didn't feel natural. It wasn't a choice; it was a pinch of the avalanche of emotions coiled inside me. A deep voice? That wasn't funny. I felt volatile, near-hysterical, near-combustible . . . and was giggling like a pigtailed pageant girl. I shook my head, covered my mouth, and almost missed the guy walking from the back of the store.

"Yes?" he demanded, his slight shoulders bent forward as he continued to examine the busted phone he was holding.

One last giggle escaped through my fingers. "You're Alex Cooper?" I gave him a cursory once-over—my height. Almost? Maybe my height if I were barefoot. Dark hair, brown skin, bad posture. Typical greasy tech-teen, too much time in front of the screen, too little in the shower.

"Alejandro Cooper. Do I know you or something?" His scowl made it clear he didn't want to—that he'd found my laugh-attack even less amusing than I had.

Loops, who did you send me to? I shook my head. "I need some computer help."

"That was pretty well established when you walked in the door. Show me the problem."

Anger flowed through my blood, hot and indignant. I desperately wanted to point my finger in his face and demand, *Listen, geekstain, do you know who I am?* Instead, I gritted my teeth, hefted the suitcase onto the counter, and unzipped it.

"There's a virus on here. Fix it." I counted a slow double beat before pinching my lips into a smile and adding, "Please."

I felt Manuel shift behind me. No doubt he'd gotten a glimpse of whose computer was infected and was processing the ramifications. I didn't dare turn and look at him. I held Alex's gaze and watched his lips turn into a sneer. He flipped through the contents of the suitcase and chuckled. It was low, just as deep as his voice, but it felt like an insult, like a joke I didn't get.

"A virus? I'll be sure to trust the diagnostic skills of a girl who packs a keyboard and monitor cable. All I needed was the system unit."

I gritted my teeth as my cheeks burned. Fine, so that was stupidly unnecessary, but it was easier, safer to sweep everything into a suitcase, since I didn't have time to go back home if I'd forgotten something essential.

Manuel stepped even closer and I knew he was a half second from intervening, but I instigated and fought my own battles. Always.

Swears and threats would've been so satisfying, and kindness and flattery would've been the most productive—I split the difference and went for pragmatic. "Look, you come highly recommended. Can you fix this computer or not? If you can't, that's fine, but let me know so I can go somewhere else."

"Take a seat," he said.

"I need it *today*. I'll pay you double, even triple if necessary, but I'll need you to jump me to the head of the line and fix this now."

"Take a seat, princesa. Or take your computer, suitcase, and money somewhere else." He waited until I'd lowered myself onto a plastic chair of questionable cleanliness before asking, "What were you doing when it started giving you issues?"

"E-mail. I downloaded an attachment."

He scoffed again but bent over the computer, so I swallowed my anger and let him work. Manuel was standing beside my chair. I blinked up at him with my guilty conscience on display. "Don't tell Daddy?"

He shook his head ruefully. "I should've known you were up to something, Maggie Grace."

"Can you go check on James? I'd like to keep him out of this if we can." He'd gotten in enough trouble over me—and gotten *me* in enough trouble too. "I'm fine in here—you know I am. I promise not to leave this chair."

Manuel did a slow scan of the room, his gaze pausing on the guy behind the counter.

"He's obnoxious, but he's not a threat," I whispered.

"Promise not to get in *more* trouble?"

"Cross my heart."

He shook his head but left. I pulled out my phone, deleted and scrolled, deleted some more. Weeded through my in-box until I was left with a stack of e-mails with similar subjects from the same sender: *Transplants and organ donors/Penelope Landlow.*

Apparently, if stuck in an uncomfortable chair with nothing to do but watch the clock and the guy fixing Daddy's computer, I'll actually read Organ Act propaganda.

It was *good* propaganda. All about how, if it passed, H.R. 197—the Organ Act—would be implemented in two phases. The first legalized our industry much as it was, just created strict regulations for donor care and payment. But phase two, that's when the government got involved—providing federal compensation for live donors of kidneys and livers. It was similar to systems already in place in Iran and a handful of other countries. And the financials were sound—paying for donors' medical care and a flat fee per kidney was actually *cheaper* for the government than paying for the expenses covered by Medicare's End-Stage Renal Disease program. I almost believed it. But how could the two phases of the act work in tandem? What would happen to *us* in a few years when phase two was implemented and the government became kidney matchmaker? Would there be any room in *that* arena for us to continue playing? Would we be able to survive financially when they dropped the cost per surgery from the six figures our current clients paid to whatever paltry amount they decided to subsidize? Doubtful. Supporting this was shortsighted and suicidal.

I could see how Penny had fallen for it. She was all warmheart and gentle feelings and had never been part of her Family's Business. And Char would follow her anywhere . . . even into a political position that damned us all.

This was one more reason I needed to join Daddy in DC. I'd sit down with Penny and poke holes in the "facts"—point out all the assumptions and slanted logic. It couldn't be too late for her and Char to recant. And once the veep's poster children switched sides, supporters and lobbyists would find flashier causes to latch onto, and the Organ Act could quietly slip away to failed legislation limbo.

Alex made that stupid sound boys make—that clicking with his tongue and cheek. He did it again, and I looked up. He nodded at me and crooked a finger.

I stood and walked over. "Do you always beckon women like they're dogs?"

Alex didn't even look away from his screen. "It's definitely a virus. I'm almost done running the anti-malware program."

"Is there an issue?"

"No, it's actually good news. This type of virus is meant to search for or retrieve data, rather than corrupt by deleting files from the OS, or even worse, rearranging bytes so randomly that recovery's not possible."

"Wait. Retrieving data? How is that *good* news?" I curled my fingers around the edge of the counter. "Wasn't this just some random spam thing I caught?"

"Computer viruses aren't like the flu—they don't spread at random. There's always someone behind them. They always have a goal. It might be to give you pop-ups that make someone money every time you click on one, or spyware like this to steal your identity—"

"Steal *what*?" My stomach had gone into freefall as my head spun with panic. "Can you tell what they accessed?"

"Give me a few seconds. I'll check and see what files have been quarantined. I might—" He stopped talking, and his fingers flew across the keys. He glanced at me and back at the screen. His eyes lingered there a long time, before slowly making their way back up to mine. His hands were resting on the keyboard, but they weren't typing. In fact, they were shaking. When he caught me noticing, he hid them below the counter. "See, here's the thing, it looks like the people behind this virus are after something a little more exciting than old ladies' Social Security numbers. There's some interesting information in these files. I can see why someone would want it. I'm trying to trace the source, but it's got some serious encryption."

"Yeah, well, you'll live longer and happier if you forget anything you just saw in those files." If Daddy could hear the litany of curse words playing in my head, he'd kill me dead this very instant.

"I really don't think that's true." He laughed humorlessly, then swallowed. "Like I said, *interesting* information. Stuff—stuff the government might like to see. Um, lists of paid organ donors and recipients, medication suppliers, clinic locations. I saw on the news what people like you are doing with organs and—"

"Stop." I gritted my teeth and looked around the store, making sure that Howdy was out of earshot. "You're an idiot if you're thinking of doing *anything* but handing over that computer right now."

"Sure. It's still infected, but if you want it back, that's your choice."

"You didn't fix it yet?" The clock above his head glowed with numbers far too close to when Daddy would be getting home.

"I'm working on it." He squinted his weirdly buggy eyes. "Except, you know what, maybe . . . maybe I'm not. Maybe I'm done."

"You're done like you can't do it?"

"Oh, I *can* do it. But I'm—I'm not sure I will."

"I'll double your fee." I'd add another zero on the end if that's what it took, but he didn't need to know that yet.

His face scrunched up. There was sweat dripping off his patchy forehead and as closely as I was studying him, he was also staring at me. Taking me in like I was something miraculous. "I want something a little more rare than greenbacks."

I stepped away from the counter. "I'm not going to kiss you."

"How full of yourself are you?" He stepped back too and curled his lip. "Fix your own computer."

I felt my cheeks heat—clearly I'd misread that one. "I'm sorry. Please. What do you want?"

He swiped a hand across his forehead and dropped his voice to a husky whisper. "A kidney."

"What? Why would you—" I was tempted to laugh. It wasn't like stolen electronics or drugs or whatever. It wasn't something he could turn around and fence. Stupid, stupid Organ Act coverage was making the Business sound simple: *If you can run a lemonade stand, you can sell kidneys for big profit.*

"According to the info on here, that'll be easy for you to get." He leaned in, and while he probably *thought* he looked menacing, his whole body was trembling. "What do you say? Do we have a deal?" He swallowed audibly. "Or should I make copies of these files, then make this virus worse?"

His nervous threats were pathetic, but it'd be faster to play along with his fantasy then point out his plan to Craigslist a kidney was ill conceived. So I pouted. Stomped a foot for effect, and when he looked absolutely gleeful, I sighed dramatically. "Fine. Sure." I reached across the counter and grabbed a pen and a business card. I scrawled ten random digits, throwing in the dashes at the appropriate breaking spots. "Here's my number—call me in a day or so and I'll get something set up."

I was leaning. He was leaning. There was way too little space between our noses.

He seemed to realize it the same time I did. I recoiled, and he sneered. "There's no need to seal our bargain with a kiss, princesa."

You disgust me—it was right on the tip of my tongue. It was on the tips of my nails on the hand I was drawing back to slap him.

"Am I interrupting something?"

We both turned toward the voice.

"James! You've got to stop sneaking up on me." I placed a hand over my hammering heart and continued to blather in the hopes of distracting him. "First at home and now again. Seriously. Do you have on spy shoes or something?"

"Is that your dad's computer?"

"No!" Confound it! I stepped to the side to block his view. "What'd you do?"

"Why'd you assume I *did* anything? Maybe he wanted me to—" That line of lie was hopeless, so I tried something different. "What do you want?"

"To see what you wanted to eat. Manuel went to get barbecue."

"I'm not hungry." How much had he heard? What had he inferred? I turned my back on the second most obnoxious boy in my life to ask the first, "Are we almost done here?"

Alex was removing a USB drive. He carefully put the computer into the suitcase and reverently touched the card with my fake number. "All set, princesa. I'll be in touch."

I threw a stack of bills on the counter—I hated myself for the gesture, but since he *wasn't* getting a kidney, I didn't want to stiff him. "Absolutely no need to rush."

His laughter sounded sarcastic. Sounded sad. I shoved the suitcase at James and stomped out the door.

"Drive fast," I said to Manuel. "And great job keeping James busy."

"I take offense to that," said James.

"You were meant to." But poking the tiger wasn't safe. Not when I didn't know what he'd overheard. "I wasn't doing anything nefarious. I wanted to surprise Daddy with some software upgrades. Call Lupe if you don't believe me—she recommended the place."

"Yeah, and we all know *she'd* never lie to me for you," he said sarcastically. "If that's true—why the secrecy?"

"Did you miss the part where I said *surprise*? And you can't keep a secret or your mouth shut."

The best lies are based in truth and while this was a low blow, James couldn't refute it. Instead he glowered, slumped in his seat, and did me the favor of not talking for the rest of the drive.

CHAPTER 6

It had been a while since I'd voluntarily taken my place at the dining room table. Since I'd worn clothing Mama considered meal-appropriate. Even now, I wasn't perfect. My sundress was wrinkled, my attempt at a hairstyle was droopy, my makeup was smudged from crying earlier, and my forehead was sweaty from the scurry of getting Daddy's computer assembled as his car pulled down the drive.

But we'd done it. Eased out of his office and scattered before the front door opened. I'd left James with the empty suitcase to put away while I slipped into my seat for supper.

As anyone within earshot could report, Mama and Daddy were embarrassingly pleased about the "major milestones" I'd achieved today. The five minutes following grace seemed to be a contest of who could heap more praise on me.

"When I got home and Anna told me you'd gone out to run errands, why, I almost cried." Mama put a hand on my arm and left it there so long her tennis bracelet went from chilly to warm against my skin.

"You still clean up good, sport. It makes an old man happy to see you looking like yourself."

"It's true, honeybee. I was worried you'd lost your shape with all that moping and eating, but you're still pretty as a picture. What do you think about letting your hair grow? Why don't we see my stylist tomorrow? Maybe get you some highlights? And then while we're in town, let's stop in that pottery place I was telling you about—I think it'd be so fun to take a class together."

"Manuel said you didn't give him any trouble about the double coverage. I appreciate that. I know you're used to more freedom."

"I can't wait to call my prayer group. They'll all be so happy. See, I knew Suetta was wrong about you needing pharmaceuticals—not that there's anything wrong if you did."

I blinked at Mama and pulled my arm away—that was more than enough of that. "Daddy, I was reading up on the Organ Act today."

"Hmm? While you were out? Where did you go? Manuel didn't say."

"Oh, here and there." I waved a vague hand and almost knocked over a candlestick. "I was talking to Loops, and—"

"You spoke with Lupe? How is she?" Mama grabbed for my arm again, but I yanked it away.

"If she can stop chasing boys long enough to focus, that girl'll make a fine doctor someday. Does she have a specialty in mind? If not, steer her toward anesthesiology. I can always use—"

I pushed the candlesticks out of the way before waving my hands like an air traffic controller. "Time out. Too much attention. Do me a favor and have another kid. You're smothering this one."

"Egads, the thought of *two* of you," teased Mama.

"I'm just happy to see you being plucky, daughter of mine." Daddy paused to cut a bite of steak. "It's a good distraction after today."

There was palpable tension in the way he'd delivered that second statement. It settled on the table like a layer of dust, making my pulse quicken.

"Did things not go well at the meeting? Are we going to keep the Homestead clinic open?"

"The meeting went fine."

"Is it Organ Act related?"

Mama shook her head and raised a finger to her lips. The gesture was one we saw frequently and meant *no Business talk at family meals*. A rule Daddy and I'd been battling for more than a decade.

"There were problems here—they must have occurred after you went out. Theo called me. The network was—" Mama raised her hand in a slicing motion, and Daddy turned to her with a sheepish grin. "Sorry, Patricia."

"Holt, let's have a happy supper. I'm so glad to see Magnolia

Grace dressed and going out in the world again—let's focus on her."

"No, we really *don't* need to focus on me." If they focused too hard they'd see the cracks in my charade. Besides, panic was growing like mold inside my stomach. "What did Theo say about the network?"

"Not at supper!" scolded Mama. "Now tell me about your call with Lupe."

We all looked up at the sound of soft rapping on the doorframe. James's smile was apologetic, but he had his shoulders back. I tried to catch his eye and find some sort of meaning in his odd combination of hesitant and confident body language, but he refused to look at me. It made my fingers tense.

"I'm sorry to interrupt."

"Sweet heavens above, what is it, James?" Mama's patience was gone. "We're having supper. Haven't we made it clear meals are family time? And after the day Holt's had."

James shifted his feet but didn't duck his head and leave.

"If it can't wait, just spit it out," said Daddy.

"You have a visitor."

Mama looked at Daddy. "Are you expecting guests?"

He shook his head, folded his napkin, and set it beside his plate. "Who is it?"

Now James met my eyes. "Alejandro Cooper. He's here to see Maggie."

I choked on a bite of asparagus. I'd been attempting to look innocent and unconcerned by eating, but now I was spewing bits of green across the table. "He's *here*?"

"Who is he? Magnolia Grace, are you okay? Holt, is she going to faint?"

"Naw, she's never fainted—but you are looking mighty peaked, sport. Here, take a sip of this." Daddy pushed his low-ball glass my way. The amber liquid sloshed and I was tempted to gulp it down, but then it was too late. James had moved aside to let *him* through the door.

"Sorry to interrupt while you're eating. I'm Alex, the IT guy Maggie hired to get rid of a virus. But I only fixed one computer, and if she's reattached it to the network, then it's already been reinfected. I need to address all the computers on your system." Side by side with six-foot James, Alex should've looked young and dismissible, but he had a gravity that held Daddy's attention . . . which was the last thing I wanted.

I shoved my chair back and stood. "And you didn't think to tell me this at the store?"

Alex shrugged. "Call it an insurance policy? I—I can still fix it. I can fix them all, and this way I ensure I'll get . . . what you promised me."

Daddy was standing now too, his fork still clutched in his right hand. "Magnolia, am I to infer that the network trouble Theo's been dealing with is something you know something about?"

"Yes, Daddy."

"I see. And what exactly did you promise this young man— Alex, is it?" Daddy's voice was low—not low like Alex's—but in a way that made it clear his temper was at a simmer and could quickly escalate to a boil.

"A kidney?" My shoulders were creeping up, and I'd inflected the end of that statement. Both of these were unacceptable. I straightened my spine and raised my chin. "But it's not like I meant it. The stupid media and their Organ Act coverage are making people think selling organs is practically the same as Girl Scouts selling cookies. I wasn't planning on—"

"I have autosomal recessive polycystic kidney disease," said Alex. "My last GFR was a six, and I've been doing hemodialysis for three years."

Shock made my legs feel boneless. I dropped back into my chair and really looked at him. Not as an underwashed geek hidden behind a counter and hunched over a computer, but as someone *sick*.

I scanned the table—no one else seemed as thrown by this revelation. Maybe they saw the things I'd missed when I'd been too focused on the computer to notice the boy fixing it. Like how his skin was sallow, a brown gone rotten and cracked and peeling. His chin-length dark hair was lank. If there was a jawline on him, I couldn't see it. His cheeks and face were inflated, puffy, which was odd, because the rest of him didn't look soft. In fact, he was spindly thin. And what was wrong with the boy's arms? I couldn't stop staring at the way his long-sleeve Tech World shirt was tight on one swollen forearm but hung loose on the other.

His eyes, however, were fine. Almost luminous. A brown that was closer to yellow, to green. If I looked just at his eyes—not at the bloated skin surrounding them, then I could get through this. And I'd be assertive. Daddy counseled eye contact as a means of taking command of any situation.

So I stared defiantly into Alex's and realized that he was furious. His yellow-green-brown bulbous eyes glared and his puffy, chapped lips scowled.

"If you'll excuse us a moment." Daddy was standing, gripping my elbow, and towing me out of the room. Pausing only to give James a nod and a look that said *watch him and don't screw up.*

He didn't let go of my arm until he slammed his office door behind us. "What in the Sam Hill is going on, Magnolia?"

"It was an accident. The virus. And he came recommended. I didn't—"

"You realize the type of information in our system? How sensitive that is? And he's *here*, which means he went through the files to locate our address."

"He seemed harmless. Pathetic, even."

Daddy's frown made it clear he thought that adjective fit *me*. "We can't let him leave. Not without containing his threat." He cupped his chin and was quiet for a long moment. "There's no choice. We'd better get him sorted and set up for dialysis ASAP."

"What? You can't be serious."

"You put *all* of the men's futures at risk with this stunt—do you get that? How important it's going to be to keep that boy satisfied?"

"Yes, Daddy."

"And did you or did you not promise him a kidney?"

"Yes . . . but." Inspiration hit, and I smiled. "*Only* if he fixed your computer. Which he didn't."

"Oh, he will. I'll be sending him to Theo next to discuss the mess you've created, then out to Ackerman to start assessing his medical needs."

"We're not going to help him."

"Yes, we are." Daddy's voice was hard. "He's your patient now. And patients aren't just interchangeable cogs we use to keep the Business running. You need to start seeing them as people."

"I know he's a person. He's the computer repair guy." How was I supposed to make the leap from Tech World to transplant recipient? I certainly couldn't reveal I hadn't known. In the Family, cruelty was strength and stupidity was weakness.

Daddy shook his head. "I don't know if you're not listening or if you're just blind to how narrow your focus is right now. Wake up, sport!"

"Oh, I see plenty. First, you want to support legislation that'll bankrupt us. Now you want to give away free kidneys." I curled my toes in my boots to keep from stomping or kicking something. "Do you have some secret offshore billions I don't know about? Or have you just stopped caring about being profitable?"

"Magnolia Grace Vickers!" It was a roar accompanied by a flush of anger around his throat. It meant shut up, sit down, acquiesce, and apologize.

Not my style.

"This is blackmail! Him showing up here, making these demands."

"He wouldn't have needed to resort to blackmail if you'd acted honorably in the first place. *Profitable?*" Daddy practically spat the word. "If that's what you think this Family's about, then I'm sorely disappointed to call you my daughter. We help people, and that boy needs help. You gave your word that you'd supply him with a kidney. Your word as a Vickers *means* something."

"But he—"

"We make a good living. You've never wanted for anything, and we take care of our own. One kidney is *nothing* for us. Our bottom line's not even gonna quiver." His voice was full of the type of solemnity that added weight to judgment, gravity to disappointment. "You need to spend some time reflecting on what it means to be a part of this Family and your responsibility to the patients behind all those profits."

It was anger or tears. There were no other options in my arsenal right now, and the balance between these two was precarious. I ground my teeth. "Fine. I get that I was wrong about him. We'll give him a kidney. Satisfied?"

"Dang right we will. Not only will we get his kidney and provide his care, but *you* will oversee it. This is a problem of *your* creation; you will be responsible for fixing it. Hopefully you'll gain some perspective along the way."

I didn't wait for his dismissal or any further lecture. I slammed his office door on my way out, stomped up the stairs to my bedroom, and kicked my boots into my closet with satisfying thuds that left scuff marks on the wall.

I wanted to cry angry tears. Cry I-really-tried-today-and-all-I-did-was-screw-up tears. Cry because I felt helpless. Cry because the one person I wanted to talk to was still gone.

I couldn't. And Daddy could never find out I hadn't known Alex was sick. Because even if I *had* known, I would've made the same decision. We weren't a charity, and accepting a client without doing all the background checks was a security risk. He'd already tried to blackmail us—what more did Daddy need? Alex was just some random boy who fixed a computer virus—he wasn't *our* responsibility.

And okay, I'd been wrong to emphasize profits—but they mattered. Not just as money, but as what they represented: our ability to provide for the Family men and their families. If Daddy wanted me to prioritize what it meant to be a Vickers, I'd put *them* first.

I sat at my desk and started working through the cost-analysis of different Organ Act scenarios. Best case and worst. I'd done something similar last year for Carter—worked up projections for Dead Meat, the cadaver clinic he'd secretly started with the Wards. I'd wanted him to pick a profit point for when he'd tell his parents about it, because the next step, he'd promised, was telling them about *us*.

But the benchmark Carter had chosen wasn't money. "A hundred successful surgeries. That should convince Father of my Business worth. After that I'm telling them and the whole world how much I love my girl. Deal?" We'd kissed on it. Sealed the agreement in the apartment Dead Meat's profits had made possible.

I'd started a countdown on the desk calendar in the apartment's spare bedroom. We'd toasted every tally mark. When he hit seventy surgeries, he'd started planning what he'd say. He had his speech perfected by eighty.

At eighty-nine—eleven surgeries shy of his goal—he'd been killed.

I was standing by my desk with a shaking hand pressed to my mouth when there was a knock on the door and Mama swept into the room. "Oh, sweetheart, not this again."

She rubbed my back and tried to pull my hand down, but I resisted. My lips quivered against my fingers.

There was a cough from the doorway. Mama hadn't come alone, and the pair of guys standing in the hall looked like they'd rather be anywhere else. I hated the pity in James's eyes, the embarrassment in Alex's. I latched onto that emotion, spun it into anger I could wear like a cloak.

"What do you want?"

"Your father said you have to come with us to get Alex's stuff," James answered.

"I thought we'd settle him in the blue guest room across the hall," said Mama. Her voice was all forced cheer. "It's such a soothing color, and the back stairs lead directly down to the patio—it's just a hop-skip from there to the clinic."

"What are they talking about?" I turned to Alex. "Why do you need things or a room?"

"Wasn't my idea." He scowled like it was *mine*. "I wanted to fix things techwise, then come back when my kidney was ready."

"He's moving in? Oh no, no, no. Why—" I paused and answered my own question, "Because you're a liability. You're a leak risk. We don't trust you."

"Like I trust *you*? You admitted you were lying and were never going to give me a kidney. If anyone here has a reason to—"

"The blue room has great light in the morning, but if you prefer afternoon sun, there's the yellow guest room as well."

Alex broke our stare-off to blink at Mama. "Either is fine. Thank you."

I opened my mouth to protest, but James interrupted, "Can we pretend you argued whatever your point is—and it was brilliant and all—then just skip to the part where you acknowledge we're doing this and get going? Brooks is already waiting on us downstairs."

I rolled my eyes and grabbed a pair of shoes. "Fine. Let's get this over with."

"Oh, and honeybee?"

Mama used lots of nicknames: sugar bean, honey pie, darlin' child. And she said them in a tone so sweet and gentle that you wanted to lean in toward her, like a puppy expecting to get scratched behind the ears. It was then, when your guard was down and you were full of cozy warmth, that she'd let the other shoe drop. I knew this. I'd lived it for nineteen years. But still, I wanted the rest of the sentence to be "everyone makes mistakes" or "we know you're doing your best."

"Yes, Mama?"

"I'm so sorry this means you'll be too busy to go to DC with your daddy."

CHAPTER 7

Alex was shutting the door to his dented beater, and James was already behind the wheel of one of the Family trucks. I assumed we were taking two cars so Alex's could stay at his house and not be an eyesore at mine. And I was supposed to climb in the passenger seat of the Escalade EXT, so I hoped Daddy wasn't watching when I gestured to Brooks to switch spots and ride with James. It might not have been kosher for Alex and me to be without guards, but given the current animosity between James and me, it was safer for everyone.

My whole life it had seemed like he and I were on a see-saw of Family approval. In order for one of us to succeed, the other had to fall from grace. James had been the golden boy for fourteen years—while I'd been the girl who ignored the boys' club subtext that I wasn't welcome. Then his mother had tried to turn FBI informant—and I'd emerged from the carnage like a phoenix while he'd become the whipping boy. We'd jostled each other in and out of favor through high school, but what I'd done our freshman year at college—the way I'd thoughtlessly lied and set him up to fail as my guard—those felt like permanent marks on his reputation.

He'd retaliated this fall by tattling to my parents about how poorly I was functioning at UT, and it had gotten me pulled from school. Today I'd belittled him on errands, so he'd paid me back by parading Alex into supper. He was probably gloating that I'd been grounded from the trip to DC. So, yeah, I wasn't in the mood to be his copilot.

Alex didn't say anything when I sat on his duct-taped seat and clicked the belt shut. He didn't say anything for the next twenty-seven minutes. And either the radio was broken or he was trying to drive me insane with the silence. I could practically see our anger filling up the car, growing and churning with each jolt of the broken shocks, and sweltering and seething in the lack of AC. You'd think some of the rage would've eked out the crack where the door seam didn't seal, but nope, that rattling, whistling sound just wound me up more.

"How much farther?" I finally demanded.

"Half an hour. Do you need to pee?"

"Did you really just ask me that? I'm not a toddler."

"Is that a no?"

I swallowed down a string of curses—that would give him too much pleasure. Instead, I thought about what Mama would say and turned with a saccharine smile. "Why bless your heart, are you trying to be clever? Don't strain yourself on my behalf."

He scowled and mumbled, "I'll take that as a no, then."

I shut my eyes and leaned back against the headrest, biting down hard on the inside of my cheek. He didn't talk again until his phone rang. He answered in Spanish and his low voice sounded almost musical as it climbed with emotion and descended into a feverish argument.

"What did you tell her?" I asked after he'd said, "Te quiero, Mamá" and "cuídate mucho," and lowered his phone. I turned my head toward him and opened my eyes. Alex scrubbed a palm across his face. How could I have looked at his sallow coloring and not known he was sick? "You feeling okay?"

He ignored this. "Now I know how good your Spanish is."

"I took Latin."

He picked at the steering wheel's frayed casing. "You do realize you live in Texas? A state where almost half the population habla Español—so, yeah, Latin. Great practical choice."

"Well, genius, Latin *is* helpful for all the medical lingo in my line of work. Now, what excuse did you give your mom? I need to know if we're going to have to coordinate some sort of cover story."

"I told her I was going to stay with my older brother. I'll need to fill him in soon."

"And she believed you?" As far as lies went, basic was better, but this was barely a story at all.

He nodded. "They'll think . . . they'll assume he's taking me to some third world country for a transplant. Max, my brother, he's been talking about that for a while, but he never figured out how."

"And they're okay with that? They'd let you go? No questions asked?" I looked him over. "How old are you?" I'd guess sixteen, tops.

"Yes, and nineteen. Speaking of 'no questions asked,' we're done talking about this."

Nineteen? This kid was my age? And why the heck did he think *he* could call the shots?

"No. You don't get to tell me I can't ask questions. You want a kidney; I'm going to need to ask questions. And you'll answer them. It's part and parcel of this whole *you blackmailed me* package. Get used to it."

"Does this work both ways? Because I want to know why you're such a huge—" He banged his fist on the steering wheel, and I was surprised it didn't break off in his hand. "You know what, forget it. You're not worth it."

"Excuse me? What's your problem? You won. You get that, right?"

He swerved. Pulled over to the side of the road before he whirled at me and roared. "You *lied*. You were never going to give me a kidney."

"It's a *kidney*, you fixed a computer—and apparently you didn't even fully fix it—they're hardly on the same level. I came to a store and asked for help—I paid you. How was what you did fair?"

"Princesa, you may not have learned this in your privileged little bubble, but life isn't fair. You said you'd get me a kidney. You looked at me and *lied*. Like it was no big deal that I needed it."

"It was *blackmail*. Of course I lied. It's not like I was thinking: here's a great idea, I'll trick this guy and then he'll die."

"That's right, I'll *die*. And if your dad wasn't forcing you, that would still be your plan."

The word "die" had been jagged in my mouth—it shredded the argument and tore at raw feelings. Would I? If I'd known, would I have lied? I felt my shoulders curling in as I mumbled, "It's not like we're the only option."

James and Brooks had pulled over behind us. Brooks's door opened, but Alex waved them back onto the road before pulling out. "You *are* my only option. I was disqualified from the government transplant lists. I can't get a kidney through the legal routes, and I can't afford one on the black market." I watched his jaw tighten, watched his fingers tremble on the steering wheel. "You are my last chance. My kidneys are operating at less than fifteen percent capacity. I *need* a transplant. And I actually thought . . . but it was all a joke to you."

I thought back to the smug way I'd written down that fake number and slapped money on the counter. My ignorance chafed, and hindsight was a grim picture. "No one's joking now. You're serious about it; I'm serious about it; my daddy's serious too. There's a surplus of seriousness. You'll get your friggin' kidney."

"Gracias," he said under his breath.

I was tempted to respond "de nada," prove I knew at least some Spanish. Except it wasn't nothing. It was his life.

"Why—" I had so many more questions, but his eyes were wet and he was trying not to let me see he was wiping them and sniffling. "Why don't we stop here? Turns out I could use that bathroom break after all, and you can call your brother. Just put on your blinker so James and Brooks see us."

Alex pulled into the parking lot of a gas station. Before I could open my door, he grabbed my wrist. Not aggressively. His fingers barely skimmed my skin, and he made no attempt to stop me from jerking away.

"Wait." The hesitation in his touch was in his voice too. "It makes no sense for me to even ask you this, but . . . I can trust you guys, right? I mean, this is a big deal—the medical care and surgeries. But also, I don't—I don't want to give up this time with my family if it's my . . . if I'm not going to get it back."

I'd only known one kind of sadness for the past five months. I'd been steeped so strong in it that there wasn't space for anyone else's. But his voice and expression hit low in my gut—triggered my tear ducts. I blinked furiously. "You can trust us."

I wanted to say more—to confess I truly hadn't known he was sick and, if I had, I wouldn't have been so cavalier. But I couldn't—not without tears spilling. And while Alex may have wanted a kidney from me, I was pretty dang sure he didn't want my pity or sympathy.

"Promise," I added, as I shoved the creaky door open.

James and Brooks stood on the curb beside the truck. "Here's the plan," I said, and they straightened. It should have been gratifying that it only took three words for them to look alert and slip back into the familiar pattern of expecting my leadership. Instead, it was exhausting. I flipped a credit card to James. "Fill his car. And don't bother him. He's got to make a call.

"Brooks, we'll go get bad coffee and junk food. Then you and I will take the Caddy. I'm overdue for some AC. Understood?" I waited for their nods, then headed for the Snack Mart. "Good. Next stop, Alex's house."

CHAPTER 8

Alex had unlocked the front door of a small one-story house and disappeared into it before I'd even unclipped my seat belt.

James, however, had stayed on the driveway. He gestured with the hand holding his phone. "Go on inside. Your daddy asked me to call him when we arrived."

"Of course Daddy wants *you* to call him." I laughed, though my mouth tasted like charcoal. Like my rage had actually burned the lining of my throat. The seesaw had shifted: James up, Maggie down. "Go ahead. Call and report on me and my failings. Then the two of you can buddy it up and talk about how you'll do your secret BFF handshake when you get home."

"For serious, Maggie? You think that's what this is about? You think I care two pins—"

"You care a heck of a lot more than two pins. This is what you *do*. It's the flask at senior prom. It's this fall at school."

His face was bright red and his hand was shaking as he pointed to the door. "Go in the house before I say something I'll regret."

I opened my mouth to go full throttle—all swears and "I hate you" and "*You* do not get to order *me* around," but Alex leaned out his front door.

"Are they always like this?" he asked Brooks.

"Nope."

This was Brooks's full answer. That he didn't find any temptation or pleasure in spilling stories about the rise and fall of our friendship, or take the opportunity to mock our toddler-style tantrum, earned him so much credit with me. Enough so that when he said, "Go on and get him packed, Maggie," I didn't protest or complain.

I pushed past Alex, hovering in his door, and into a small living room. Picking up a wooden statue of Mary from an end table, I turned it over in my hands. He snatched it away and set it back down.

"I don't suppose I get a tour?"

"Doesn't it get exhausting arguing with everyone?" He looked pathetically tired, like the wall he was leaning against was the only thing holding him up. "Being around you is draining. So could you maybe dial the anger down to a nine point nine?" His eyebrows had already converged like he was bracing for my caustic retort.

But I didn't have one. His critique hit with a sharpshooter's precision. Yes, it *was* exhausting. I gave a stiff shrug and turned away from him toward the back of the house. "I'm feeling generous—let's see if you can handle me at a seven."

His laugh was deep, a bullfrog sound that followed me to the short hall back to the bedrooms. It was hung with crosses and covered in framed photos of two boys. The younger one—Alex—hadn't always been visibly affected by whatever was wrong with this kidneys. A picture of him as a toddler—screaming his head off on Santa's lap while his older brother rolled his eyes—made me snort. Alex paused to see what I was looking at and smiled. It transformed his whole face—and I stared for a second, trying to parse out how one expression could make him so much more tolerable. Then, catching myself, I turned back to the wall. Next to the Santa-scream was a photo of what must have been grade-school-age Max holding a baby in a pink blanket. Pint-sized Alex was sitting next to him.

"Sister?" I asked.

He nodded and touched the frame with two fingers. "Gabriela."

"You both look so serious. Were you hoping for another brother? How old is she?" I stepped past him to see if their attitudes changed in future pictures, but my stomach dropped as I scanned the wall. I knew what he was going to say before he said it. There was another baby picture of her on a table with some religious candles, but Gabriela wasn't in any of the frames that progressed down the hall.

"She died when she was a baby. The same kidney thing I have—ARPKD—hers was worse."

"Wait. It's *hereditary*, and your parents chose to have another kid?" He turned away, so he didn't see me wince as I realized how cruel my words sounded. He straightened the frame I'd touched. Then he clenched his fists by his sides.

"You don't get to talk about my sister. You don't get to talk about my family." His voice was a low growl. "In fact, let's not talk. Just stand over there by the table of my mamá's figurines. Decorative, useless, and you get in trouble if you touch them— sounds like a good spot for you." He gave me one last disgusted look, then went in his room.

Before I'd mucked everything up, I'd been planning to suggest he take a break. I'd already chosen my words: "You look tired. Are you up for this? Why don't you just sit and tell me what to pack."

But clearly he wouldn't want my help. Since I was useless and all. Just good for decoration. Screw that. And screw standing in the hallway next a table cluttered with cheap knickknacks. My cheeks were flushed with embarrassment and anger, usually a deadly combination in the Molotov cocktail that made up my temper.

But I couldn't find the spark. I couldn't make myself take that last step from anger to the old me who would've flayed this boy with his own words and twisted any apology into a weapon.

Today had been like trying to swim in quicksand: I couldn't escape; it drained my energy, pulled me under. The stupid clothing, the stupid faked smiles and conversations, and screwup upon screwup . . . It was the type of day where I felt flawed at a cellular level, like I was the opposite of King Midas: everything *I* touched turned to junk.

Carter had been magic at breaking me out of moods like this, making me think maybe it wasn't *me*, maybe I wasn't fundamentally *wrong*. He'd say the tension was because I was bigger than the boxes and expectations on my life.

I raised my hand to cover my mouth and the sob that was snarling in my throat. Bit my palm to try and tamp down everything I was feeling. All too aware I was on the verge of losing it in front of the person who had most recently judged me and found me lacking.

It was several long, slow blinks before I could see the coffee-colored floor tiles that led from the hallways to Alex's bedroom. Several more before I felt brave enough to raise my eyes and see he was standing in the doorway watching me. Everything was still right there between us—his anger, my idiot words, his cruel ones . . . and his exhaustion.

James leaned around the corner, and we both startled. "I brought some boxes from the car. Can you two make it a little more rápido?"

"Oh, don't play that game, güero," said Alex. But he grinned at the "white boy" and moved out of the doorway so James could pass me and enter the room.

"Wait. Since when are you two compadres?" I asked as I tagged along after James. I glanced between them as they exchanged eye rolls, then started shoving the clothing Alex had piled on the bed into a duffel bag. "What, did you bond in the car over your mutual dislike of me? Team Anti-Maggie?"

Alex had leaned into a closet and was pulling out shoes. He paused and turned to James. "I like that. T-shirts?"

"T-shirts," affirmed James. And they did a fist bump.

"If you get T-shirts with my name on them in *any* way, shape, or form, I will make your lives utterly miserable."

"Goal accomplished, Maggie Grace," said James. "You need a new threat."

I'd been angry, but it was that anger of a person who knows she's being riled on purpose. James's last words, with their flat sincerity, killed all the amusement in the room.

Alex was watching us now. James's tight-motioned shoving of pants and socks into the already full duffel and my lowered-eye lack of motion. One of us needed to break the tension, and since James was actually helping . . .

"I'm going to wait in the car with Brooks." Maybe if I left, Alex would drop the bravado and take a rest. Let James do the heavy lifting. "This room isn't big enough for all three of us, and you clearly don't need me."

I almost hoped one of them would throw a good-natured parting shot. But they didn't. They nodded, and Alex began pulling novels out of the milk crate that served as his book-shelf. He flung these over his shoulder at James, who caught and stacked them in a box. Their movements were synchro-nized and efficient, like some well-oiled machinery that I'd jammed up. I paused at the front door and listened; the banter had resumed. Once the toxic element was removed from the room—me—they went back to being besties.

I fingered the phone in my pocket. I wanted to call Loops

and ask if she'd come home. I had no doubt she'd say yes—she'd offered as much earlier today—but then I'd be left wondering if her motivation was friendship, guilt . . . or my last name. And if she ever looked at me the way James did, if our relationship ever became so vindictive and competitive . . .

No. I'd go hypothermic from loneliness before demanding that of Lupe.

CHAPTER 9

"Tell me about Carter," James said quietly.

I'd been mindlessly looking out the window, watching the dust settle and fly and occasionally catching glimpses of the Brazos River though pecan and oak trees. But James's question made me curl in on myself, like crossing my arms across my chest could make me less vulnerable. "What?"

He was frowning at the windshield. "How did you get away with it for so long? Come on. They're asleep, and I really want to know."

I looked in the backseat. Alex and Brooks leaned against opposite windows. Alex snored nasally. Brooks slept open-mouthed with his ball cap pulled over his eyes. His long legs sprawled across more than his share of the backseat.

"What were you told?" I asked, because when I'd come home from my last trip to New York, everyone had clearly been told *something*. But it couldn't have been the entire story, how I'd finally gathered the courage to go back to the apartment and found Penny there—not dead, despite the fact that I'd attended her funeral. And how my arrival and my revelation that her "Char" was really Ming Zhu had started a chain of events that shut down Dead Meat, revealed the Landlows' murderers, and thwarted what would have been a massacre of the Zhu Family.

It wasn't as successful or simple as that—there'd been casualties. Char's dad, the head of the Zhu Family, was in a coma. Pen's call this morning made it clear she was haunted by Garrett Ward's role in her parents' deaths.

And then there was me—when Penny had gone out to save the Zhus and stop the Wards, I'd been left behind in the apartment. It had been a month since Carter died, but it hadn't fully hit me until then. Until I was alone in the space we'd created together. And I—I'd just shattered.

When I'd finally stopped sobbing, I'd made a phone call, struggling to pick out the number through blurry, swollen eyes. And when he'd answered, I'd sobbed some more, barely able to gasp out the words, *"Daddy, can you come get me?"*

"You mean what were we told when you disappeared without telling anyone?" James's wry voice interrupted my memory. "Just a few weeks after Landlows' then-unsolved murder? Well, after a few days of pure panic where no one knew if you'd ended up in the middle of the Zhu-Ward-FBI shootout, we were told Maggie Grace saved the day. I expected you to come home insufferably puffed up with heroics, but you were . . . broken. When you didn't snap out of it, I asked your daddy what was wrong and what I could do. He said you'd had 'a thing with Carter' and were pretty shook up, but you'd be fine once you got back to school."

"A *thing*?"

"No one would tell me more. Believe me, I asked."

"You didn't ask me."

"I just did." He held my gaze for a long moment. "Your daddy made it sound like a fling, but you're grieving like it was more. And based on everything that's come to light—all those trips to New York you took on the down low—I'm guessing it was."

I nodded.

"So, how'd you pull it off? I know I'm not winning any awards for my guard abilities, but I had *no clue*."

"It was easier than you'd guess." My stomach clenched with the need to tell someone our story and make us that much more real. No one had asked—and I resented that, I *really* resented it. "Cross-country helped—I'd tell you I was away for a race with Enzo or Manuel when I really was with Carter in New York."

"It never even occurred to me to check—not once. I was just grateful for the time off."

I winced. "You believed me."

"Yeah, like a fool. But you *did* compete; I came to some of your home meets."

I blinked in surprise. "You did? Why?"

He exhaled in a grumble. "We are friends, Maggie. Why wouldn't I?"

"We are? I don't mean that in a rude way, but *you hate me*."

"I don't. You piss me off constantly, but I don't hate you. And I don't want to talk feelings. So, cross-country meets, what else was a lie?"

"You sure you want to hear this?"

"Yes."

"I didn't have Friday classes spring semester. I know I *told* you it was a crazy day with long seminars, but . . . nope." I paused to think, then ticked other lies off on my fingers. "Loops and I never went away for a pre-finals spa weekend. I didn't 'go home to do laundry.' I never even considered pledging, so all that sorority rush lock-in stuff—"

"That one I doubted." He chuckled. "But I thought you were doing something stupid *on campus*. Not in New York."

"It wasn't stupid."

"That's not what I meant."

"Loops lied for me—a lot. And before you ask, no, she didn't know. She knew I was seeing *someone*—and you know what a hopeless romantic she is, so she was happy to help—but she didn't know who or where, just enough to cover for me."

"I'm not going to turn you in, if that's what you're worried about."

I shrugged. "There's nothing left to *turn in*. Daddy and Manuel grilled me for days after New York." But first Daddy had held me. He'd flown up immediately and scooped me off the floor of that apartment and let my heart break all over his shoulder. In that moment I was his little girl first and Family heir second. I hadn't been able to reverse the order since.

"How long was this going on? You and Carter? I hadn't seen him since we were kids."

I laughed, but it was a sound that pulled from my stomach and twisted in my throat. "It feels like my whole life. Almost eight years."

James didn't say, "Stop effin' with me." He didn't need to, it was written all over his face.

"It was a lot harder for Carter than it was for me. He and Garrett . . . they were close. They spent time together because they *wanted* to. You were always glad for an excuse not to be chained to me, but they . . . they were best friends."

James scowled through my answer, but he couldn't say it wasn't true. "Then why didn't he just tell him?"

"He didn't want Garrett to have to lie to his father. And he didn't want Al Ward having that sort of leverage—he didn't trust him."

"That turned out to be a good call."

"Yeah." I gritted my teeth.

"Why did it have to be secret? That's what I don't understand. Why couldn't you date? I mean, I know your parents were keen on keeping you two separated after the trouble you got into as kids—the running away, breaking his arm, etc. . . . But *now*? Or was the sneaking around what made it hot?"

I wasn't sure whether to sob or slap him. I had given James access to the most sacred and vulnerable parts of me—and he'd made them into a dirty joke. I lifted my chin. "Because I'm a girl—and in this Family that's already a strike against me.

I need to be taken seriously—you see how the men are with Lupe. She has a boyfriend, and they act like she's twelve and tease her mercilessly."

"To be fair, Lupe's got a different boyfriend every week."

"So? She's also got a 4.0 as a biochemistry major—tell me again how being in a relationship makes her weak or stupid?"

James shifted his hands and nodded slowly. "That's a fair point."

"I needed to prove *I* could lead, so all my successes weren't lost in his. We were going to tell. We just . . . ran out of time." Eleven more surgeries. "I can't talk about this anymore."

I flipped the visor down to block the glare from the street-lights, pretending they were the reason my vision had gone blurry. In the reflection in the mirror on the back, I saw two amber eyes. They met mine for an instant before Alex closed them, settled back against the window, and yawned.

To James my pain was a dirty joke. To Alex it was boring.

When we pulled in front of my house, I jumped out. James yanked the keys from the ignition and tossed them in the back-seat to a yawning Brooks. "Can you get this? I've gotta—"

I'm not sure if or how he finished that thought, because I'd already slammed the door. I didn't make it into the house, though, before he caught up and grabbed my arm.

"For what it's worth, I'm sorry about Carter."

I yanked my arm from his grasp. "Nothing. Your pity is worth *nothing*. So keep it to yourself."

His flush changed from embarrassment to anger, his mouth hardening into a scowl that made me feel less vulnerable. "Why do you have to be so . . . ," he growled, fisting handfuls of his hair. "Forget it. Forget I said anything."

"Forgotten." I turned on the heels of my boots and walked away. Someone else could get the boxes from the truck bed and make sure Alex remembered the way back to his room. I couldn't handle one more minute of obligations and failures and feeling like I was a broken doll everyone wanted to examine or fix or discard. I escaped to my room and locked the door, locking out the need for strength and pretense and locking in my sniffles and sobs.

CHAPTER 10

"We were told Maggie Grace saved the day." James's words reverberated through my mind all night while I stared up at my canopy.

I wasn't the hero in any part of that story. I'd known how Dead Meat worked—how it had gotten bodies on their way to morgues, the payouts going to corrupt medical examiners, not the deceased's families—and I hadn't talked Carter out of it. I'd known it was risky, but I'd liked that he suddenly had more money; he could pay for my flights, pay for our apartment, and all without it pinging on our fathers' radar.

It was Penny, fragile, gentle Penny, who'd found the location of Dead Meat, gotten the FBI involved, forced Garrett to confess what his family had done, and then flown across the country to shove herself in the middle of a gunfight.

I'd been left behind in the apartment to cry over pillows and blankets that no longer smelled like us. Over the note Carter had left for me in his sweatshirt pocket—full of apologies and self-doubt, self-blame . . . although part of the blame should be mine because I hadn't questioned Dead Meat's morality either. Hadn't listened when he'd tried. His letter ended:

> Be good. Be brave. Be happy. I miss you. I need you. I love you. Always.

I'd failed at being good, brave, or happy—but missing, needing, loving him? I'd perfected those.

I wanted to ignore the rising sun and stay in bed with my hood pulled up, but if Carter wanted me to be brave, if Daddy wanted to cast me as a heroine, if the Family already believed it—it might be time to try playing one. And maybe, just maybe, Daddy would change his mind and let me go to DC with him. Because talking him out of the Organ Act and saving us from that political mess would definitely qualify as heroic. I got up.

My legs were shaky, like the morning after a flu. I held onto the bedpost until I felt steady.

DC.

Penny. Who missed Carter as much as I did. And while I might not care for her politics, I cared for *her*.

I could do this.

Red. I'd wear red.

It was a power color. One that business articles said exuded confidence and control.

I yanked a red dress printed with navy sailboats from a hanger in my closet and dropped it on my bed. It was equal parts *wow* and classy. The neckline was a demure Peter Pan collar, the hemline swished around my knees, but it was cut in lines that practically demanded double takes. Paired with post-shower hair, red lipstick, and my favorite cowboy boots—the kind whose heels made noise when I walked and announced: *Here I come. Pay attention*—I felt like maybe I could pull this off.

Except that power colors and pay-attention boots couldn't command either without an audience—and Daddy's office was empty. He wasn't in the meeting room. Or the Business entertaining room, which wasn't in the house but in an outbuilding across the pool from the clinic. Not that I really expected him to be out there before eight a.m., but I went in anyway, flipped on the lights, and inhaled the scents of cigars and leather. This room had been a man cave until I'd come along. The year I turned fourteen, Daddy let me in, but my entrance had been met with outcry and reservation. The men suggesting I "run along now, darlin'" and "wouldn't you rather go shopping with Lupe than hang around us old folks talking shop?" I'd had to conquer this room slowly and strategically, winning over the men of the Business one at a time, in the right order. A real-life game of Jenga where I'd either win the whole stack or topple the tower. And I'd won. I'd been a colleague, someone they shut up and listened to, someone they teased like one of their own . . . until I'd walked away from the game after NYC.

Brooks's and Manuel's reactions yesterday proved I still had *some* power and influence. Probably because they'd been told

"Maggie Grace saved the day." I shook my head as I straightened an ashtray on the bar. When I was fourteen and everything with James's mom and the FBI went down, I *had* been a hero—now I was trading on a lie.

I flipped the lights off and headed back across the yard. I paused at the patio door to stomp some of the dust off my boots, then made my way to the dining room and sank into my chair.

"You're here! And dressed." It took Mama a beat to compose herself before she added, "How wonderful."

I cut her off before she could launch into a whole pep rally because I'd accomplished tasks I'd mastered back in preschool. "Where's Daddy?"

"Oh." Her pause made me wish I'd at least said good morning or hello before I asked for him. But I'd never been shy about playing favorites, and she'd never cared. "He's already eaten. I believe he's down in the clinic."

"Thanks." I pushed back my chair.

"Magnolia Grace, you sit back down and eat," said Mama. "Your daddy's not going anywhere without saying good-bye."

I sighed. "Fine."

Mama's fork and knife were lined up in a neat diagonal across the top right corner of her empty plate, but she folded her hands and settled back in her chair, which meant she planned to keep me company and fill the silence with requests for me to work on *this* charity event with her, or go to *that* church fund-raiser. Did I want to join a book club? Take a sculpt and tone class? Stories about all her friends. And what all of *their* daughters were doing. Things that involved engagement rings, or studying abroad, or wearing designer gowns at society functions I cared nothing about.

Still, while she might drive me crazy, I'd never say Mama wasn't strong. She ran this household with the precision of a Rolex. If something went wrong in one of the little-f families within our Family, she was the oasis of calm and organization while the other wives wrung their hands and created emotional chaos. When Daddy railed and moaned that the world was collapsing, she would stand right in the path of his hurricane and talk him down. I might prefer trails and roads, while she spent hours on the treadmill, but I doubted our pace per mile was much different. Mama was one of the strongest women I knew, and if she'd only used that for Business good instead of lunching and spending, then we might have found some common ground.

"I was just thinking about when you were a baby."

I filled my mouth with a spoonful of granola and yogurt. I figured the faster I emptied the dish, the sooner I could leave.

"When you were a little—just a scrap of a thing, barely as tall as the coffee table—you decided to learn to walk. But you didn't learn like James or Lupe. They toddled cautiously, held onto their mamas' fingers, and cried when they fell. You threw yourself into it, were downright covered in bumps and bruises. I was appalled about what other parents must think, but you cried if I tried to interfere or help."

I smiled. That sounded about right.

"Then I overheard one of the ladies put into words something I'd already been feeling. She said I wasn't the right mama for you." My mother looked down at her hands and took several deep breaths. "I know in my heart I've never been the type of mama you needed. You're not the type of girl I know how to handle. You're one hundred percent your daddy and zero percent me."

I wasn't surprised by the truth in the words, but I was shocked she'd said them. I'd always thought she blamed our lack of connection on *me*.

When I didn't comment or protest, she continued, "But *now*, I feel like the worst kind of mama, because I can't fix you or shake you out of this. *This* should be my domain—heartache and boy trouble—but I don't know how to reach you."

"You can't fix me. People can't fix people—life doesn't work like that." I didn't bother to tell her it wasn't simple heartache that had broken me. It was guilt. It was Dead Meat. I should've been less focused on the race to a hundred surgeries and more on questioning the morality of what it *was*. If Mama found it easier to believe I was mopey and heartbroken, then that was fine. I had no need for her to start understanding me now after all these years. But she was right about one thing: I needed to shake out of this. "*I* need to fix me. I'm just . . . still figuring out how."

"I'm glad to see you trying." She squeezed my hand. "And you know I'm always here. If I can help you, just tell me how."

I'm sure this was supposed to be a tender moment. It was practically staged like a scene from a sappy movie. But all I felt was annoyed. More passive parenting—if I wanted help, I had to go to her and tell her how to help me. It was the same hands-off, "you don't need me" bull she'd pulled my whole life. It wasn't a mother bird pushing a baby out of the nest to teach her to fly—it was the mother turning away when the baby came back, lesson-learned and exhausted. The baby being told, "You don't need a space in this nest. Look what you're doing. Keep flying."

Everyone needs a place to land once in a while. Mine had been Carter.

I pulled my hand away.

"Caution and slow aren't words in your vocabulary, honey bun. It's time for you to stop punishing yourself and start living."

I looked up in surprise. Every time—*every* time—I decided she and I were a lost cause, Mama would pull out an insight that floored me with its accuracy. Maybe she did understand. A little.

"What's with all the glum faces in here?" boomed Daddy from the doorway. "Fix those smiles, ladies; I won't be gone that long."

Mama smiled on command, and he said, "That's better. I've just got time to kiss my girls good-bye and then I've got to hustle to make my plane."

He was trying to make one of our old jokes. Except I was no longer young enough to find the humor in protesting, "But it's *your* plane, Daddy. It can't leave without you."

Instead, I said, "I could be packed in five minutes."

Mama raised an eyebrow. "Not well-packed, sugar."

Daddy frowned. "You're not coming, Maggie Grace, and you know why."

Apparently refusing to allow Alex into my headspace this morning hadn't made him magically disappear. "I'm not a babysitter. That's what you've got Brooks and Enzo and James for. You don't need me to follow him around like a ninja nursemaid."

"Ninja nursemaid—" He snagged a piece of my bacon and swallowed it in two bites. "Sounds like it should be one of those anime cartoons."

"Daddy, I'm serious. What am I supposed to do with him?"

"I've left you both directions. You're accountable for making sure he gets your computer mess sorted and all his medical needs. While you're at it, I hope you'll learn a little bit about the other side of the Business. The part where you *care* about the patients you're working with."

"I care about the business parts of the Business. I'll take the numbers and leave the patients to the doctors."

"You can't care about one without the other. It's time you learned that. We're a black *market*, not black-*hearted*. We'll see how this trip goes, but there's a chance, with the Organ Act, that soon we won't be a black market either."

"I can't believe you're even considering this."

"You don't buy a truck without kicking the tires. I want to hear what they've got to say and decide if I want to take this law out for a test drive." He paused. "But that's neither here nor there. Sport, you're long overdue to spend some time in the clinic—and not so you can do a cost-analysis of the supplies."

I raised an eyebrow. "You're keeping the Homestead clinic open?"

"For the time being." I smiled at the small victory, and he shook his head. "It just makes sense. It's where we handled kidneys anyway, so we've got all the equipment here. I know you're not a fan of his, but Dr. Ackerman is a top-notch nephrologist—he'll take care of Alex until it's time to turn him over to our surgeons. Plus, this clinic's the most protected, and if you're going to be spending time there, I want you safe . . . and chaperoned."

"Chaperoned? What exactly do you think I'm going to do?"

Daddy grinned. "I learned long ago never to give you any ideas or guess what you'll come up with next. So, try to stay out of trouble, and we'll talk more when I get back."

"While you're in DC, if you see . . ."

"I'll give Penelope Landlow your best." He wiped the bacon grease off his fingers and dropped the napkin, then bent and kissed my cheek, kissed Mama, and started to leave.

And just like when I was a kid looking for one last bit of attention before Daddy shut me on the wrong side of his office door, I couldn't help blurting out, "If you see Ming Zhu, he's going by Char now."

"Char," he repeated, looking back over his shoulder and giving me a nod of approval. "I'll try to remember that. Thanks, sport."

With Daddy gone, Mama and I eyed each other and then adopted the roles we'd spent our whole lives perfecting. She pretended his job was all sorts of credible and legal, and I pretended not to resent her for this charade. She was strong, she was smart—but she let herself be excluded from the Business.

No, more than *let*, she *chose* the exclusion—practically stuck her fingers in her ears and hummed to keep herself ignorant. Didn't she realize that as the wife of the head of the Vickers Family, she set the standard for how females would be treated? Her game of make-believe meant I'd had to spend my childhood fighting my way through doors that had opened automatically for James, Brooks, and Enzo.

But I'd fought; I'd won. And Daddy's newest test—this thing with Alex—I'd ace this too. In fact, I'd go for extra credit. By the time he was back from DC I'd be up to speed and ready to reclaim my seat beside his.

"Who's traveling with him?" I asked. "Besides Byrd." His second-in-command would obviously go on this trip, which meant he wouldn't be around for me to use as a resource.

"I haven't got the slightest idea," said Mama. "When do you suppose our houseguest will be up? It's a mite rude to sleep so late."

"He's sick—maybe he *needs* more sleep. And 'guest,' Mama, really?"

"It's such a shame he's so . . . unfortunate looking." She shifted her shoulders uncomfortably. "Do you think his hair is like that because of his condition? His skin too. There's got to be something that can be done."

I rubbed my forehead in exasperation. "If it'll make you happy, next time I'm blackmailed, I'll make sure the guy duping me is eye candy."

"Hush now." Mama turned from me to the doorway. Her voice and posture perked up in a manner that should've been a warning, like the beautiful markings on poisonous butterflies. "Good morning, Alex. I trust you slept well?"

"Yes, ma'am. The bed was very comfortable. I'm sure you get no complaints from your *houseguests.*"

Mama's lips pursed for just a second before she pasted on a smile and pointed to a chair. "Please, sit and help yourself to some breakfast. There should still be hot coffee in the carafe, or I can ring if you want something else."

He sat and scanned the table, finally selecting a scoop of scrambled eggs and half a grapefruit.

"That can't be all you're eating. Anna is a fabulous cook."

"Most of this food isn't allowed on my diet."

"Diet?" Mama clucked sympathetically. "But you're so thin. I know that's all the rage nowadays—skinny jeans—but I still think a man should look like one. Have heft and muscle."

"Mine isn't that kind of diet. It's more of a nutrition plan—for dialysis."

"Oh." There was surprise and embarrassment on her face as she toyed with her napkin.

I glared at him. Mama was taking an awkward situation and trying to make him feel welcome—which was more than he should expect from me or any of the men. How dare he treat her as if she were silly or dismissible? I dropped my hands to the tabletop; it was time to take charge of this conversation. "Then we should schedule a time for you to sit down with the kitchen staff and go over what you can and can't eat."

"I already set it up. Meeting's at ten thirty."

"*You* set it up?" It was a power play. Which meant it was

crucial I established my authority *now*. I'd be giving the directions, not following his. "A-plus for initiative, but you should really consult me before attempting these things. Ten thirty's not going to work."

"Really? Your dad said your schedule is wide open and at my disposal." He grinned. "But if you're busy, you don't have to come."

I hoped he choked on his grapefruit. "I'll make it work, but in the future, do me the courtesy of consulting me first."

"Of course, princesa." He gave a slight bow over the table, then pushed his chair back. "Now, please excuse me. I've got to get to a meeting with Theo."

"Wait. What?"

"To come up with a plan for virus removal that minimizes network downtime. It's on our schedule." He pulled a folded piece of paper from his pocket. "Your dad gave it to me when we met this morning. Don't you have yours yet?" He paused for a beat to watch me sputter. "I don't want to be late; I guess I'll see you there when you're done."

I yanked my napkin from my lap. "Don't start without me."

"Because you have insights about network security we'll need?" He was laughing as he left the dining room.

"You wait, Alex Cooper, I'll—"

"Careful there, sugar bean." Mama cut me off by tapping my lips with one perfectly polished fingernail. "Remember, a closed mouth gathers no foot."

CHAPTER 11

Despite Theo's comments about how I was a "liability to anything with a battery," we made it through our first meeting. I ground my teeth and seethed, but I kept my temper.

We made it through our meeting with Anna too. She eyed Alex curiously but didn't complain when he explained he'd need meals with controlled amounts of protein, phosphorus, and potassium. I turned my back and tuned them out. Stole croutons off a baking sheet and reread Daddy's instructions. I was to supervise Alex as he cleaned the computers and accompany him to all meetings/treatments at the clinic.

There was one more thought scrawled at the bottom:

WATCH THE MEN AROUND HIM—THEY'RE NOT HAPPY HE'S HERE. SEE IF YOU CAN FINESSE THIS.

Gee, I wondered which part they disapproved of: his black-mail, or the fact he was living *here*, like the house was a bed-and-breakfast, not the hub of an illegal business—one he'd already stolen files from and threatened. But let's give him a password and access to *all* the computers—really, Daddy, what possible reason could the men have to be unhappy with that?

I frowned, but Anna was all smiles when they wrapped up their meeting, which grated on my ego. She should be loyal to *me*, and her friendliness to him felt like she was choosing his side.

First James, now Anna. Oh, and Theo . . . He'd warmed to Alex about as much as he ever liked anybody. At this rate there'd be no need for me to finesse anything—the men would be voting Alex prom king by the time Daddy returned.

An hour into watching Alex work on our computers, I was feeling claustrophobic. I'd followed him from Daddy's office, through three others, and now we were in Byrd's. I flipped a small screwdriver over in my hand and sighed.

"Can I get that back?" He didn't look away from the computer screen or hide the irritation in his voice.

"Why? You're not even using it. All you're doing is typing."

I tossed it up, and Alex snagged it from the air before it could fall back to my waiting palm. "It's distracting me. Don't you have anything better to do than follow me around?"

"You've got the same marching orders I do." I waved Daddy's directions at him. "Like it or not—and I'm a *not*, in case you're wondering—I'm stuck babysitting you."

"*All* the time? Even after I'm done fixing these?"

"All the time. Think of me as your involuntary stalker."

He huffed out a breath in an unfortunate way that made his bottom lip look more bulbous. "What about—whatever it is you did before I got here? How do you normally fill your wide-open schedule, princesa? You know, when you're not throwing your money around and demanding special treatment and to be skipped to the head of the line at stores?"

Staring at my canopy, either fighting to get to sleep or—post-nightmares—fighting to stay awake. Playing games on my phone because the blur of shapes and colors was stupid and numbing and made minutes pass. Reciting Carter's letter because I knew the words by heart, and the shape they made on my tongue cut in ways that killed the numbness.

"I don't owe you any answers," I snapped.

He mocked me by twirling the screwdriver through his fingers. "Nope. Just a kidney."

"A kidney? Really? Dang, I filled out the requisition paperwork for a liver."

He laughed grimly. "There's a chance I'll need one of those someday too."

Old me would've made a crack about repeat clients being good for Business, but now all I could think to say was, "Oh."

"Don't worry. I don't think you'll give me one. I get it. You don't want to help me, and you're pissed I forced you into it."

"Oh, I see." I nodded slowly, priming my temper. It used to be so automatic, but now I had to coax myself into getting mad.

"You're getting your way, but that's not good enough. Your worldview became simpler once you decided *I'm* the bad guy."

"No, my worldview will be simpler when I have a functioning kidney. *Any* obstacle that stands between me and survival is the enemy. It's nothing personal."

"I'm not your enemy." I clenched my fingers around the bottom of my chair to keep from hitting him. A furniture tack poked sharply from between the upholstery and the frame, piercing my fingertip. I winced and wrapped it in my skirt. I hadn't looked, but it couldn't be more than a pinpoint of blood. It was still too much, and sweat beaded on my forehead.

I needed to get back in bed. I needed blankets around me, pulled tight, pillows mounded on either side of my head. I needed the lines of my canopy above me. I shut my eyes and tried to block the woozy feeling.

Alex cleared his throat.

I cracked my eyes open and swallowed down bile.

He was studying me—his irritation replaced by an emotion I found even less welcome: concern. He offered me the screwdriver. "Let's not talk. That way I can work faster."

I accepted his peace offering, curled my fingers around the red plastic handle. "Sounds like a plan."

CHAPTER 12

Our patients loved Dr. Ackerman, the head of the Homestead clinic, but he drove me batty. He was all slow talk and "let's take the time to discuss." If I stopped by the clinic to ask *one* question about supplier prices, I'd likely be stuck waiting for an hour while he finished his current conversation. Then instead of a straight answer, I'd get a fifteen-minute explanation about why the numbers didn't matter near so much as the people they represented: "How do you put a value on improving the quality of our patients' lives?"

I knew his question was rhetorical, but I'm pretty sure I could do a few basic calculations and come up with a dollars-and-cents answer.

Dr. Ackerman wasn't a bad guy; it was just that he seemed to *want* so much from everyone he interacted with. Having a conversation with him meant sharing and personally investing more than I was comfortable with. This was *Business*. I wasn't in it to be therapeuticized, or to talk about greater good or quality of life. I didn't need a gold-star sticker for every patient we saved.

Give *them* the stickers, and give me the facts.

So I was mentally cursing as I led Alex to the outbuilding where the clinic was housed. It had the external appearance of a barn—though smaller and nicer. "Waiting area, water cooler—or there's one of those single-cup coffee makers if you can stand to drink it after the heat outside."

It was a fall that refused to admit it wasn't summer—the weather closer to September temps than early November. Just walking from the back patio to the clinic had left me damp and irritable.

"I know. I was here last night."

"Right. Okay. Well, wait here." The walls of the clinic were painted in pastels that were probably supposed to be soothing, but made me think of Easter candy. It was strange to be here without all the bustle of nurses and patients, the noise of medical machinery and conversations. Even Dr. Ackerman's sound machine and tabletop fountain were turned off. I walked down the hallway, past framed nature prints and exam rooms. The door to Dr. Ackerman's office opened before I knocked. He beamed out, too-blue eyes, too-white teeth, too-neat hair.

"Hello, Magnolia. I haven't seen you in a while. *How are you?*"

Dr. Ackerman didn't just *ask* that question, he *meant* it. And he scrutinized me when I said, "I'm fine."

"I know you've gone through some pretty traumatic experiences lately. I hope you know it's okay if you're *not* fine."

"Thanks, but I am. I'm fine."

He studied me before saying, "Okay, then." And followed up by nodding over my shoulder at Alex, who apparently hadn't bothered to stay in the waiting area. "Hey, bud. How're you feeling today?"

"A little tired."

"I can imagine. Your whole world's been uprooted, that would tire anyone. On the plus side, the facial edema we discussed last night looks better. I imagine the swelling in your legs and feet has gone down as well?" He paused and waited for Alex to nod. "Great. Then the diuretics worked. Now we need to prevent that from reoccurring. Did you give Anna the nutrition plan we came up with?"

Alex nodded again, and I took the opportunity to inspect his face and neck. They were way less puffy. He'd worn pants yesterday, was wearing them now, but if Ackerman was satisfied with Alex's nods, that was good enough for me.

"Good. I want to stay on top of that—we'll need to really control your diet and fluid intake while we reestablish your dry weight." The doctor clapped his hands together. "So, let's finish up the testing, and we'll get you all set to come back for dialysis later."

"How long will this take?" I was already sick of the kindergarten teacher enthusiasm.

"Today's tests won't take long. Then it's going to depend on Byrd finding the right donor match for our friend here. I'll manage Alex's day-to-day care up to the surgery and during his recovery." He put a hand on Alex's shoulder. "Excuse me, pal. That probably sounded rude—I didn't mean to be talking about you right in front of you."

"No big. I already know all this." Alex didn't actually add any emphasis to his *I*, but I heard some anyway.

I gritted my teeth before asking my next question. "Where are the nurses?"

"They've been reassigned elsewhere. Since I'm focused primarily on Alex, that's not a problem. I've been known to rock some blood samples and run a dialysis machine in my day. So what do you say, bud, should we get to it? Start with blood pressure?"

"Sure." Alex didn't hesitate before heading down the hall. He'd only been here once, but he seemed more familiar with the place than I was. I followed him into a room and hated that I was *following*—I should be leading.

Dr. Ackerman had paused to grab something from a cabinet, but when he entered the room he shot me a puzzled look. "Magnolia, I need to examine Alex in private. You're going to have to wait out there."

I glanced at Alex, who was standing in front of an exam table, all eye-contact avoidance with his hands clutched around the top button of his shirt. I'd really just done that. Accompanied a guy my age into a doctor's room. Like I was a mom and he was my toddler. Or like I was some sort of pervert and wanted to see him get stripped down and examined.

Were my cheeks as red as his? They felt like it. "Oh. Right."

"This won't take too long. You can turn on the TV to keep you company."

I nodded and rushed out of the room, narrowly avoiding running into a supply rack in my haste.

I'd only just stopped blushing by the time Alex walked out of the exam room. He was nervously pulling on his cuffs and nodding at whatever the doctor said. His left sleeve was tighter around his forearm than the right, just like I'd noticed yesterday. Except in today's button-down shirt and khakis, it was less noticeable than in his long-sleeve Tech World tee. Had he dressed up for *this*, for here?

The doctor and Alex shook hands. "You two have a good afternoon. I'll get the machine set up. Want to plan to swing by after dinner? Let's say around seven."

"Sounds good," I said.

Alex laughed. "Maybe to you. But then again, it's not your blood that's being drained and filtered. Thanks, doctor. See you later."

Drained? I swallowed sour saliva as Ackerman said goodbye.

"How long does it take?"

Alex opened the clinic door. "About four hours."

"Hours?"

"Yup. So if you're stuck keeping me company, bring a book or something."

"How often do you have to do this?"

"Three times a week."

"And it always takes four hours?"

"Yeah, give or take a bit, three to four hours."

I blinked and chewed my lip, trying to imagine what that would be like. It wasn't the same as tolerating some awful class. There wasn't skipping or vacation, or time off for good behavior. "How long have you been doing this?"

"Three years."

I inhaled and swallowed, determined *not* to say something insensitive or offensive, but unsure how to respond in a way that was meaningful. "How do you . . . How do you even have the *time* for that?"

I winced. That had sounded so much better in my head.

"Well, it beats the alternative." He started across the path without me but glanced back five seconds later.

I scrambled off the clinic's porch and caught up.

"Death," I mouthed. The word was sharp. It tasted of blood— actual blood from where I'd chewed my lip raw. His eyes were on my red mouth when he nodded.

CHAPTER 13

"Which computers are next?" We were back in the foyer, and it was time to tip the control in my direction. The medical world may be his domain . . . and, well, the computer world may be his domain too, but the house was *mine*. I lifted my chin and squared my heels.

"The ones in the meeting room," said Alex.

"If the virus can start on *one* computer and spread itself over the network—why can't you do the same with a cure?"

He nodded his approval, and for a half second I felt less stupid. "We had to shut the network down. Didn't you notice your phone's on cellular data? We can't put it back up until all the computers have been treated with antimalware. Otherwise they'll reinfect everything."

"Oh, okay." Not that I fully understood, but he didn't need to know that. Especially since he was probably deliberately using tech-speak to make me feel ignorant. *Mission accomplished, jerk.*

Anger was just one more emotion piled on top of all the others today had provoked, but it was the one that tipped the stack. I needed space. I need it *now.* "I going to talk to my mama for a minute," I lied. "I'll see you in the meeting room."

He shifted on his toes. "But I'm supposed to stay with you."

I tilted my head. "Alex Cooper, you don't like breaking the rules."

"Not often. No." His deep mumble sounded gruff and aggravated.

"Oh, the irony of that character trait combined with what you did yesterday and *who* you came to for help . . . that's never going to get old."

"If I'd had other options, I would've taken them."

"Well, I'd like to talk to my mama without an audience, so do you want to come wait in the hall, or do you want to be productive? Weren't you just complaining I was distracting you? Here's your chance to work distraction-free. Go on." I pointed. "The meeting room is past the offices."

"You sure this is okay?"

"I said it is—and since Daddy and Byrd are in DC, I'm technically the acting head of the Family." Six months ago I would've spent their whole trip reveling in that fact from the backside of Daddy's desk . . . No, actually, six months ago there was no way Daddy would have left me behind.

Alex nodded, but he didn't move.

"Are you waiting for me to tell you to behave or something?"

He laughed, but the tone was different this time. It was more amused, less bitter, but just as deep. Like someone had taken a microphone down to a pond late at night and recorded the calls of bullfrogs and set it to music. "I was thinking I should tell *you* that exact thing."

I rolled my eyes and left, wondering if he'd still be standing there dithering about rules when I got back.

Not that I was going far. Just literally around the corner. No one in the house played piano or had a penchant for reading coffee-table books, so the only time anyone went in the parlor was to dust. I leaned against its wall and shut my eyes.

I needed a minute—a few minutes. I needed a reprieve from Alex's attention and expectations, from the way his face had looked when I'd mouthed the word "death."

I slid down the wall and buried my face in my hands.

All I could think of was yesterday when he asked if he could trust us. And I'd answered him, but I hadn't really understood what a *big* question that was. Not like I did after watching him stand in the clinic and talk about his transplant while wearing what was likely his church-day best. So many others had stood there and had similar conversations, but they'd bought their way in with deep pockets and lots of zeros. He had to be feeling *something*, knowing that he hadn't.

And could he trust us?

I'd promised him he could. Then Daddy had said Alex was *my* responsibility. It all felt like too much pressure, something

I could screw up so easily. I'd only managed to start wearing real clothing again in the past forty-eight hours; was it truly a good idea to put me in charge of someone's *life*?

My sundress was sweat-stuck to my back, but my hands felt ice-cold. Here I was worrying I'd screw this up *while* currently screwing it up by breaking Daddy's rule and leaving him alone. And breaking that rule had stressed *him* out, because he was a rule follower, a good boy. Someone this Family could so easily chew up and spit out.

I stood. Forced my feet to take me to the meeting room, forced my voice to be light when I asked, "You behaving in here?"

Alex looked up from a computer screen. "So far."

"Good answer. I can't tell if Daddy truly sees you as a threat, or if you're an assignment to keep me out of trouble."

His fingers froze on the keys. "A threat? This is all so crazy."

"Well, you could be. You're on our computers, in our system. You could do all sorts of crazy, damaging stuff from there."

"What?" He scrunched up his face. It wasn't a good look for him. "Why are you saying that? I would never—"

"I know. Rule follower." I waved off his protests—the boy was about as threatening as a stick of chewing gum. And at least gum could hide behind its wrapper—Alex had *no* skill at concealing everything he felt. Which made the postscript on Daddy's directions all the more ominous—Alex had the Family men disgruntled, and while he "would never," there's not much they wouldn't do if they perceived him as a danger to the Family.

I leaned across the table, shutting the lid of the laptop and staring right into those eyes that were the yellow-green of the first leaves to change color in the fall. I dropped my voice low and spoke fast. "My point is, it's not a bad thing for the Family to feel like you're a bit of a threat. That sense of urgency will motivate them to get your kidney faster."

I shouldn't be saying this. I was siding with my blackmailer and giving him leverage. It was pretty much the Family version of treason. But Alex was so in over his head, so out of his element, so alone.

Or maybe my reasons were selfish, because the sooner he received a transplant, the sooner he was no longer tied to my conscience.

He tucked his hair behind his ears. "I'm not sure if this is some sort of trick or trap, so I'm just going to sit over here and get my work done."

"Fine." I sighed. The boy had no poker face and was about as Machiavellian as a tadpole. God protect him from this Family . . . because I wasn't up for the job.

CHAPTER 14

I pushed my food around my plate at dinner, too nervous to eat, because besides annoying doctors and patients, there was another reason I avoided the clinics. I hoped I'd outgrown it—because it's hard to command respect when you're fainting like a delicate flower—but clearly I hadn't, since once we walked in the treatment room and I saw the needles and tubes laid out on a tray, my vision started to fade and my stomach revolted.

"I'll . . . back. Need air." I stumbled a bit as I left the room, but I made it down the hall and out the clinic door without passing out or vomiting. Little victories.

I sat on the floor of the clinic's porch. There were chairs and even a ceiling fan I could've turned on to move around the evening air, but I felt better down low, where I could trace a finger through the dust that was probably sticking to every sweating part of my body.

I'd never thought of myself as weak until I saw how strong Carter's "fragile" sister could be. And now, here was another in-my-face demonstration of what I lacked and what others had. Gumption. Or courage. Strength of some sort. I had health, freedom, practically limitless resources, and I could barely drag myself out of bed. Alex had none of these, yet he gritted his teeth and endured all sorts of obstacles. I couldn't even handle *looking at* dialysis, and he'd spent how long tied to that machine?

Pathetic—I wrote the word in the dust and added an arrow pointing back toward me.

The clinic door opened. "How's it going out here, Magnolia?" I watched the doctor scan all the chairs before finding me on the floor, hastily erasing those letters with my palm. He crouched beside me. "I'd forgotten you're sensitive to blood."

"I'll be okay now. It's the needles going in that gets to me." Which was a total lie, but it made me sound braver than I was.

"If you'd rather wait out here, I'm sure that would be okay."

I shook my head. "I'm fine."

"Let's have a talk before we go back in."

"Won't Alex need you?" I hoped.

"Not for a while. And if he hollers, I'll hear him. He said he was going to call his mother, so let's give him some privacy. And you and I can catch up." He pulled a chair over, sat, and tapped the tips of his fingers together. "So how are you doing? Truly."

I shrugged.

"I've been talking to your daddy—and while he's real proud of you, he also seems impatient to see you 'bounce back.' How are you coping with that pressure?"

It was one of those questions that was exactly what I needed to hear, but also way too honest to handle. "How long should it take—you know, to get over losing someone and everything else that went down and go back to normal?"

He shook his head. "There's no real answer for that. These types of losses and experiences, you can't walk away from them unchanged. I know I'm not a therapist, but I've taken some counseling courses, and I've got plenty of time and only one patient right now. If you ever want to talk, I'll listen . . . but I can't give you a timeline for grieving or healing."

"Oh. Um . . . I don't want to do the whole therapy thing. No offense." Why bother if it was all going to be vague or talk of feelings, not answers and results?

"One more thing, then we can let this drop for now," Dr. Ackerman said. "I want you to think about your triggers. What are the things that make you feel most unbalanced? Identifying these can help."

"Sure." Well, this whole building was one big trigger—but I wasn't sure how I could avoid it. Unless . . . "Does dialysis have to be done here?"

He tilted his head. "You don't have positive associations with the clinics, do you? Would it help to think of them as places of healing, instead of focusing on the blood?"

"It's not that," I lied. "I just thought Alex might be more comfortable in his bed during dialysis. If that's possible."

"We can absolutely do that. I'll need to be on hand to get him started and then again to take him off the machine—or I could see if he'd like to be trained to do it himself—but that would give him more freedom and privacy." The doctor nodded and made a few notes on a small pad of paper he pulled from his jacket. "There's never been a patient staying at the house before, so it didn't occur to me, but that's an excellent suggestion. I always seek to minimize the ways treatment interferes with a patient's life."

He was so willing to attribute altruistic motives instead of blood phobia that I almost felt guilty about inwardly celebrating.

"If you're ready to head back in, let's go tell him together."

Before I could stand, my phone rang—Penny's ringtone. I wanted to ignore it; I didn't need another conversation that proved her ability to overcome in ways that highlighted my own lack. But I wouldn't. Not now, not ever.

"I've got to take this call. But go ahead and tell him. No need to mention it was my idea." Dr. Ackerman had questions on his wrinkled brow, but I waved them off and he went inside.

"Hey, Penny. How are"—I caught myself at the last second and finished with—" things?"

"Better questions: Where are you? Why aren't you here? I mean, it's great to see your dad and James is nice, but I want to see *you*."

"James is there?" I'm not sure why I was surprised.

"Yup. So, what gives? Your father didn't explain. And when I asked James, he said you were babysitting?"

I guess that was better than grounded, but who deputized him to act as my spokesperson? I gritted my teeth. "There was a situation here. Someone had to stay and take care of it. I got volunteered."

"Darn. It would've been the perfect weekend for you to come. Char's in California visiting his parents."

"You didn't go with him?" Except for school and sleep, I didn't think they ever separated or stopped gazing in each other's eyes.

"I wasn't invited," she confessed.

"Oh." And maybe paradise wasn't as perfect as I thought?

"He doesn't say 'you can't come,' but he also doesn't ask me. I think it's because he's so aware each visit might be the last time he sees his father. I don't want to intrude on that."

"Still no improvements?" Mr. Zhu had survived the Wards' attack, but barely. He'd had a heart attack and then a stroke on the operating table when they were trying to implant one of his artificial heart prototypes in his chest.

"No."

"Oh." I cleared my throat. "So, how's school? Still loving it?"

"School's . . . well, the academics are easy. Nolan apparently went above and beyond in his role as tutor."

"What's *not* easy?" Because her voice made it clear she was skirting around something and her phrasing made it obvious she needed me to ask. And I mentally cursed, because why couldn't it be *easy*? She deserved that.

"I know I told you that I like the people and the teachers and all that, and I *do*, but I'm just . . . I'm not good with kids. I mean, people my age. It's something Carter and Garrett always teased me about—that I was both immature *and* an old soul. I don't know how to do all the gossip and small talk. It feels like there's some secret social dynamics handbook I didn't receive."

"Oh, Pen." I winced at the pain in her voice and then again at my name flub. "In a small private school like that, it's got to be rough. But it's not like you're socially inept. You'll figure it out."

"I'm used to being the *only* student. I've never had to raise my hand—and now I don't know how often I'm supposed to. Or *when* I'm supposed to. Why do some people think it's funny to give the wrong answer? And then I tried counting, like how many times did Rebecca answer a question, and what about Tristan? And how long do people pause before volunteering? Is that normal?"

"No," I answered. "I mean, *I don't know*. I'm sure it is. What about Caleigh Forman?" Little Miss Gorgeous Redhead was portrayed as the pinnacle of academic and social perfection in every media article about the vice president's family. "Isn't she a senior too? Have you asked her for help?"

"I . . . um, I . . ." Her voice changed again, to a hesitant whisper. "I don't think she and I are going to be friends."

"Is she mean?" If so, screw Daddy's orders, I'd be on the next plane out to kick some veep-daughter butt.

"No, she's not mean. She's endlessly polite. Just busy. We don't have much in common."

"You both lost your mamas." I winced. Two points for me in the blunt and insensitive category.

"True . . . but I don't know how I'd work that into the conversation. 'Hey, Caleigh, want to share scars? Tell me about your mom's cancer, your dad's remarriage, and what it was like growing up with a sister with Down syndrome.'"

"Yeah, no. There's got to be something else you have in common."

"We both hate Nolan?" Penny's former tutor was a pompous lickspittle, and he continued to plague her life by working as a lobbyist for the Organ Act.

"That's a start. You could invite her to help you and Char on H.R. 197 stuff."

"Last time Caleigh gave an interview she referred to it as the 'Forgan Act'—cute, right? Forman plus organ?"

"Clever."

Penny sighed. "Her dad *really* didn't think so, and let her know it. Now she wants nothing to do with politics. He doesn't want his name attached to the bill."

"That seems . . . illogical. I thought politicians wanted their names on everything."

"He has his reasons," she said quietly. "So, anyway, no political bonding with Caleigh."

"Well, there's got to be *something*. Keep trying."

"I will. Thanks. And sorry I'm being such a whiner. I wish you were here."

"Me too." I'd never had a pet or wanted a sibling, but it had to be kind of like this. It had to *feel* kind of like this. And not being there felt a lot like letting her down. "'Bye, Penny."

I pressed End on my phone and mouthed, "Carter, I'm try-ing," at the clouds blocking the moon, then gritted my teeth and walked back in the clinic.

Eye contact was the way to do this. As long as I looked only in Alex's yellow-green eyes, I'd be fine. I wouldn't be dizzy. I wouldn't vomit. I'd be the most professional babysitter this Family had ever seen.

Of course, uncooperative as always, Alex was looking down at the screen of his phone. I tried fixating on his head instead, but my eyes skated down his dark hair and down the white lines of the earbuds that emerged from beneath it. Down to his arms, which were now exposed by his T-shirt.

His left forearm was motionless on the side of his chair, two tubes feeding into it—and those were bad enough—but that wasn't what had me desperately swallowing down bile and praying my legs would unlock long enough to carry out of the room before they gave out. The reason one forearm always looked bigger than the other was now clear.

His dark skin was swollen in bumps and knots. Like a snake emerging from his arm. Or a knob. Or something that just looked wrong and torturous and—

A small strangled sound escaped between my teeth.

"It's called an arteriovenous fistula," he said. "They surgi-cally connect an artery to a vein."

I hadn't noticed Alex taking out his earbuds or lifting his head. He studied me, and I tried to hide my reaction, but the sweat along my hairline and my shakiness gave me away.

Along with the fact that I could only clench my mouth shut and nod.

Oh, and I shouldn't have done that. A wave of dizziness hit me hard. I sank to the floor and put my head between my knees.

"Hey, um, Dr. Ackerman? I think Maggie's about to pass out." Alex's voice sounded far away. "I can't come help you, Maggie. Sorry."

I wanted to tell him I was fine. That I didn't need helping, but opening my mouth right now wasn't something I wanted to risk.

"It's all right, Magnolia. It's okay." I felt a cool cloth on the back of my neck and saw the tips of Dr. Ackerman's shoes as he crouched in front of me. "Let's move you. You'd probably be more comfortable in the waiting room."

"No." I swallowed a few times, tasting determination and stubbornness on the word. "I can do this. I'll just"—I raised my head and pointed to a chair on the far side of Alex's fistula—"sit there."

Dr. Ackerman started to protest but stopped to help me instead when I pushed up on unsteady feet.

I sagged onto the chair and glanced at their concerned faces. My own face was a sweaty mess. Probably some splotchy mashup of embarrassment pink and chalky white. "I'm fine now," I lied. My head was pounding, my ears ringing.

"I'm going to get you some water," said Dr. Ackerman. "If you feel faint again—"

"I won't." I hadn't meant to sharpen the letters on those

words, but they sounded like they'd dice his concern into use-less ribbons.

Alex didn't wait for the doctor to be out of earshot before he laughed—it didn't quite echo, but it resonated in a way that made my skin tingle, even as it knocked the chip off my shoulder. I turned toward him, focusing only on his eyes—this time they were looking back into mine, dancing with amuse-ment. "Wait. Let me get this straight—you're part of a trans-plant mafia, but the sight of blood makes you squeamish?"

My lips twitched. "We're not a mafia."

"Human organ crime family? Whatever you want to call it. For real? If I wave some needles in your direction, you'll get sick?"

"I'm fine with my own blood." Sometimes. Not really. "It's just . . . other people's. That machine"—I swallowed and exhaled slowly through my nose—"and that arm thing. Yeah, that's a little hard for me—*not* that I'm saying it's easy for *you*."

He laughed again.

It was so *strange*. Strangely intimate to know that all of Alex's blood was parading through tubes in front of me. I was watching his insides pouring out. Watching them pouring back in. Watching this machine keep him alive.

And I knew it was something he'd probably become inured to a long time ago, but it still felt private. I felt . . . almost *honored* to have a chance to be here, to be a part of it. And when I reframed it like that in my mind, I was able to creep my gaze down his face, down past his short sleeve—at least for half a second before my eyes retreated.

"Need anything? Want anything?" I asked him.

"Nope." His answer probably included me and my company . . . or maybe not, because I caught just the ghost of a smile on his face when I looked back up. "And I'll make sure to stick to long sleeves."

CHAPTER 15

That night I dreamed of Carter. He was sitting on a chair in the clinic. A recliner just like the one Alex had used. His head was tipped back as he studied a framed photo of a waterfall. I loved him.

I cleared my throat, and he lowered his chin, his smile overflowing with joy as he gazed up at me. "Hey, pretty girl. Hey, Mags."

But his grin couldn't hold my attention. My gaze slipped to his chest, which was bare and mercifully free of the fake Chinese character that had been carved there when he was killed— a detail the news had repeated over and over until my mind decided it didn't actually need to *see* it to create a visual for endless nightmares. But not tonight. My eyes flitted over to his arm, which was all corded muscle and tan skin—no fistula or other nauseating sights.

"Hey, you," I told him, then reached to pull the reclining lever on the side of the chair. But before I could join him, there was a whirring noise and a dialysis machine appeared beside him. A line suddenly ran from his arm to the machine, but not a thin one topped by a needle, this was thick as a snake and ended with a large, flat blade. A knife digging into his arm.

And his smile had broken into a million pieces. He grimaced and writhed in the chair.

"Don't move your arm like that!" I shouted, remembering something Dr. Ackerman had said. "It'll hurt you. It'll cause a blowout!"

"That won't be a problem," he gasped. I took a step backward, took in the whole picture: Carter, chair, machine, tube. Tube.

One tube. One tube drawing all the blood out of his body.

No tube putting it back in.

The floor around the machine was red. A spreading crimson that encircled and splashed my ankles. I went up on tiptoe, frantic, dizzy, screeching, "Give it back! He needs that blood. Give it back!"

I woke up with a scream salty on my lips and echoes of the dream floating in the shadows of my room.

"Give *him* back," I whispered to the darkness, pulling my legs from beneath my blankets to make sure they were no longer blood spattered, then tucking them under the front of his sweatshirt as I sat and waited for dawn.

"Did you do one of those wishes things?" I asked Alex as I played with my breakfast, smushing my eggs and grits in ways that Mama would've forbidden if she wasn't off planning some church-charity function with Suetta and the other ladies. I hated eggs without ketchup, but the color had turned my stomach, so I'd hidden the bottle behind the vase at the far end of the table. Silence was equally unappetizing—it provided too much opportunity to remember. "You know what I mean? Meet a baseball player? Go to Disney World?"

"Nope." Alex paused to take another bite of toast, and I noticed his face wasn't swollen anymore. His features were crisp, nice. Maybe even the right side of handsome. Granted he still looked about sixteen, and had skin-hair-personality issues, but kudos to Dr. Ackerman for fixing the face-puffing edema or whatever. "I didn't make a bucket list either. Any other sick teen clichés I can spoil for you?"

"Why not do the wish thing? It seems like you can ask for anything."

He looked at me steadily but didn't answer right away. "They can't give me what I want."

"Can I?" I wanted him to say yes. Not because I was suddenly feeling altruistic, but because I was stuck with him anyway. And I wanted it to be something complicated and time consuming. Something that could swallow big chunks of my days and send me to bed feeling tired and productive.

"Maybe."

"Is it illegal?" He responded by lifting an eyebrow and smirking—a frat boy's expression that wasn't any more welcome sitting across from me in the dining room than it was at a party. "Wait. Gross. I'm not sleeping with you."

Now both his eyebrows were up, drawn together. "Did I miss the part where I asked you to?"

"No. But—" I sputtered.

"It's a diploma from MIT." He said it quietly but with a solemnity that made me pause. "And, yeah, they might be able to get me an honorary one, but it won't mean anything. I want to earn it."

"A diploma?" I choked on the irony. Nope, I definitely couldn't help him there. I'd already flubbed up mine *and* James's.

"If you can get me a kidney, I'll get myself that diploma. It'd change everything—I could apply, and if I got in, I wouldn't have to worry about balancing class and dialysis, or dying and burying my parents under my student loans."

He needed to stop phrasing it that way. *If you can get me a kidney.* Like I had a private storeroom somewhere and all I had to do was go pluck the right one off the shelf.

A diploma.

I wanted him to take it back. To say "just kidding" and change his answer to "pitch for the Rangers" or "meet the Cowboys' cheerleaders." Something more ordinary, something more superficial.

A diploma was a noble thing—and also something I'd taken for granted. Daddy would pay, and I had all the time in the world to get my act together and get my degree.

Time and opportunity and privilege were starting to sit uncomfortably on my skin. They felt like a too-thick layer of sunblock that would leave a greasy stain on anything it contacted. All doors were open to me—I was the one turning my back or slamming them shut.

I needed this done. I needed him to get his transplant and leave. Because while he was the one with the failed kidneys, being around him made me feel like my own insides were rotten and irreparably broken.

"How many more?" I'd chewed through a whole pack of gum and resorted to counting the seconds between his blinks. There was dull, there was boring, and then there was watching someone fix computers.

"A few." Alex didn't look up from the screen. "I'll do yours next."

"What?" I dug my thumbnail into the side of my pointer finger. "Mine's fine."

"Not possible."

"It *is* possible. I haven't used it in weeks. It's not connected to the network."

"I still need to check it." He was maddeningly calm as he drew a line through the entry on his list that represented the computer he'd just fixed.

"It's fine." This *fine* was through gritted teeth. The type that would've made Daddy clear his throat or Mama shake her head. Loops would've rolled her eyes and ignored it. James would've tattled. And Carter . . . he would've teased me back into good humor

Alex didn't notice. He was already walking toward the stairs. "Is it in your room?"

"I said—"

"I heard you. Doesn't mean I'm going to listen. Your wish isn't my command, princesa. The agreement I have with your dad is fix *all* the computers on this ranch. We can't turn the network back on until I have. Even if yours isn't infected yet it needs a security patch. So, either show me the computer or I'll have to call Brooks and ask him to get it. Theo wanted this finished yesterday, and some guy stopped me on my way to the bathroom earlier to let me know he was pissed about the wait and I better hurry up."

"*What* guy?" I asked. "And why can't Theo help if this is so time sensitive?"

"I don't know. A guy. And Theo's busy upgrading the security software for all your clinics."

A guy. That was super helpful because there were only a dozen or so of those around at any given moment, but talking about it had Alex agitated—his hand was drumming on the stair rail. And thinking about it made his agitation contagious. *Watch the men around him.* I didn't want the men complacent, but I also didn't want them intimidating him. Was I going to have to start walking him to and from the bathroom?

"C'mon, Maggie. Please don't make this harder."

I ground my teeth as I led the way to my room. It took every ounce of my resolve to go in my closet and come back with my laptop case. I held it out while looking in the other direction. "Here."

The case unzipping made my shoulders creep up. And the sound of metal on wood as he set it down and opened the lid made my arms break out in goose bumps.

"I need you to log out so I can get on."

He'd put the computer on my desk—and the familiarity of it sitting there made my throat tighten. I typed my password with my eyes shut, then stepped back.

He laughed. "How vain are you? You set a photo of yourself as your background?"

I'd done such a good job of not looking until then, but now I was sucked in. The photo may have been of me, but the memory was all Carter. It wasn't even a flattering picture. I was curled up on the brown chair in our apartment, with crazy bed head and my legs tucked up under his sweatshirt. Right before he'd taken it, he'd said, "I'm gonna marry you someday, Magnolia Grace Vickers."

In the picture, my mouth is wide open and I'm leaning forward. Carter had dropped his phone, then dropped down to catch me in case I fell out of the chair. But I didn't. I ruffled *his* bed head and sassed, "Get off your knees, Carter Malcolm Landlow. Our someday isn't happening just yet."

I wasn't ready for that picture. That memory. To even look at the computer where I'd spent hours—weeks, months of hours—Skyping with him. His memory clung to each key like a residue, and now I was letting someone else press them.

Alex had inserted his trusty USB and opened some sort of window to do who knows what, so the picture wasn't on display anymore. I shivered. Everything about this was wrong. Him in my chair at my desk. That my computer had been on for a whole five minutes and hadn't chimed with a message from Carter. Would *never* chime with one. Alex tilted the screen, and I had to shut my eyes, because the memories were too strong. Too suffocating.

"Angle that camera a little better, Mags. I love your forehead, and what I wouldn't give to see your bedroom ceiling in person, but—ah, there are those eyes! You're so hot when you're annoyed with me.

"Mags, are you—are you wearing a shirt? I'm seeing lots of bare shoulder and neck. Oh yeah. Strapless. Well, can't say that's not a letdown.

"Seriously, Mags, do you see where your camera is pointed right now? Is this your way of tormenting me 'cause I couldn't get away this weekend? You're merciless. God, I love you."

I had to get out of this room, get away from everything that was being stirred up. But I couldn't leave Alex.

I grabbed Carter's sweatshirt and shoved it over my head before I'd even made it to the end of my bed.

"That sweatshirt? Again?" Mama hadn't bothered knocking. She stood in the open doorway and shook her head. "I thought we'd moved beyond that, Maggie Grace. What is going on with you?"

"I—I can't have this conversation right now." That was soul-deep honesty, but Mama and I didn't have much practice in that, so maybe I couldn't blame her for not recognizing it.

"Because you're too busy staring at your canopy? You need to pull it together, honey. I really think you ought to reconsider that kickboxing class I was telling you about. It's supposed to be a good workout, and Suetta says it's great stress relief. Much better than lying around doing nothing all day."

"I'm—I—" I shook my head—but only a little, because my eyes were filling and I was *not* going to cry.

"She's actually helping me with something," said Alex. "I asked her to—to—"

God almighty, this boy was the worst liar on the face of the planet. I sniffled. "I'm counting his keystrokes."

"His what?"

Alex's expression was similarly baffled when he turned away from Mama to look at me lying on the bed. I sat up. "I'm counting his keystrokes. Or I was trying to before you barged in. Now I'll have to start again."

"Why in the world?"

"It's a thing. You know, a measurement thing they use in the computer industry."

Mama looked skeptical. And Alex looked *more* skeptical, but he nodded and I guess that was good enough for her. "Well, it's nice to know you're doing *something*. But ditch the sweatshirt before supper."

Alex kept staring at me after she left. I wriggled my fingers between the strings fraying off the cuffs and pretended not to notice. "Thank you."

"What's the deal with that sweatshirt?"

I shrugged.

"It was the guy's, wasn't it? The one you were talking about in the truck?"

"This conversation is over." I stood up. "I'm waiting in the hall. I'll see you when you're done."

"Hey, I was just asking. I didn't mean to chase you from your room or anything."

"You didn't—you didn't *chase* me from anything. I'm just—" Since my lying skills were suddenly on par with his, I didn't bother to finish the statement.

CHAPTER 16

There was a glass sitting beside the pitcher of tea on the tray on the patio table. Mine was sweating in my hand in a way that felt soul-deep satisfying at the end of this hot Texas afternoon. Alex had finished all the computers and we had nothing to do until our five o'clock meeting with Dr. Ackerman to go over his test results. I was supposedly reading and Alex was actually reading, but I couldn't stop looking at the empty glass he hadn't touched.

I didn't want to pour it for him. I'd spent nineteen years cultivating resentment for anything that resembled being forced into traditionally feminine domestic roles. Enzo and James used to laugh for hours about how peeved I'd get if either of them asked me to serve them something—but then again, they didn't have to sit through Mama's lectures on decorum and social graces.

Not that I'd sat through many. I'd quickly established that tea parties, hostessing, and any task that required a female to wait on a man, apologize for her accomplishments, or demean herself as a way to boost his ego was not my thing. I could open my own doors, carry my own boxes, and change my own oil, thank you very much.

But that second glass was still on the tray. And maybe this wasn't an instance of Alex expecting me to serve him. Maybe he didn't feel comfortable enough here to help himself?

"Are you thirsty?" I asked. "If so, you'd better get some tea now before I drink it all."

"You know that glass you're currently playing with?" He pointed at the straw I was swirling and the smiley faces I'd drawn in the condensation. "That's almost half the total amount of fluids I'm allowed to consume in a day."

"For real? What happens if you cheat?"

"The puffy face, swollen ankles, hands, and that's just the start. Kidneys are what screen the fluid from your blood—mine don't work. And there's only so much dialysis can do."

His words weren't accusations, they were flat with resignation, but my instinct was still to hide my glass behind my back or under the table. I took the slightly more mature approach and asked, "Should I not drink in front of you? I didn't know. I wasn't trying to rub it in or anything."

"Naw." He shook his head and smiled. "I didn't mean to make you feel guilty. I appreciate the offer, though."

"Can I get you something else?" Who was this girl and

what were the words coming out her mouth? But, strangely, I meant them.

"Something to do? I don't know about you, but I'm sick of sitting around. I actually miss Tech World and fixing cracked phone screens."

"You any good at pool?" I asked.

He was.

We played in the semidark, not bothering to turn on more than the track lighting over the entertainment room's bar.

But he wasn't perfect, and once he missed, I had my chance to show him *I* was good too. I'd secretly spent an absurd amount of time practicing pool, darts, poker . . . any skill I thought I might need in order to prove that not only did I belong in this room, but I commanded it.

Of course, thinking about this made me waver, and the five ball I hit ricocheted off the pocket. At least it landed in front of *his* last ball.

Alex grinned. "You had to make it difficult, didn't you?"

I laughed. "I'm pretty sure that should be the title of my autobiography."

He was laughing too—the ridiculous bullfrog melody of it was starting to grow on me—when the door opened. Brooks entered, followed by Enzo, Manuel, and a handful of other Businessmen.

Enzo spoke first, breaking the silence with a grin. "Maggie Grace, I'd recognize your cackle anywhere—it's good to hear you laughing again."

I didn't laugh daintily. I'd long since gotten over the fact that I honked like a goose while other girls giggled like wind chimes. But despite Enzo's teasing, the mood in the room was tense.

I set my cue on the edge of the table. "Gentlemen, those of you who haven't, meet Alex Cooper. He'll be staying here while we sort out a kidney for him. And he's already schooled Theo on the computer system—so if you've got tech questions, bring 'em his way."

I wasn't telling them anything they didn't know, but I was framing it differently, making him a resource instead of a liability. "Finessing," as Daddy requested.

Brooks stepped forward, holding out a hand. "Good to see you again, man."

But the others held back.

"'Bout time the network's back up," said Manuel.

Their postures were aggressive, arms crossed, chins high, legs spread wide. They encircled him, creating a barrier between us. Alex's grip on his pool stick was white knuckled.

Manuel leaned against the pool table beside me. "He giving you any more trouble?"

"Nothing I can't handle."

"Well then, missy, can I give you some unsolicited advice?" He didn't wait for me to answer, but kept his voice low and his eyes cold as he focused them on Alex. "Keep your head on straight. You're acting awful chummy with the guy who blackmailed you. I was there in the store, remember? I didn't like the way he treated you then, and I'm opposed to your father letting him stay here."

So that was why—they were pissed at him on my behalf. Well-intentioned but entirely unnecessary and unwelcome.

"I wouldn't say 'chummy' and I also wouldn't say it's any of y'all's business," I countered.

Manuel shrugged. "You've got a lot to prove right now. I hear you're anti–Organ Act. We need you back in the ring. Boss needs to hear your voice in this fight. And if he thinks you turned this assignment into a playdate . . . well, you're smarter than that."

He pushed himself up and turned to the other men. "Let's leave the young people to their fun. I'm sure Anna's got cold drinks in the kitchen. We can rustle up something to eat too."

I blinked. *We need you back in the ring*—the words sang in my blood. I turned my back on Alex and hung my cue on the rack. *You're acting awful chummy.*

"No, y'all stay. I need to get him back to Ackerman's office— I've got to check in with Byrd and the big man later, and I need to be able to give them a timeline for this . . ." I paused to draw their attention, then frowned and tipped my chin in Alex's direction, "*interruption.*"

I hated myself for discarding Alex's regard like trash, but it was the right call Businesswise. I had sacrificed a pawn to save the queen. Manuel nodded his approval. The others relaxed onto stools and started filling glasses.

"Maggie Grace, *you* come back out and join us if you can." Enzo, who'd been jocular two minutes ago, paired his invitation with a scowl for Alex.

I'd failed at finesse but had won back this group. It felt like a stupid victory. Their esteem—which I'd spent so many years courting and enjoying—didn't hold its usual appeal. I had no desire to join them tonight.

"If you're lucky." I sassed, because I was supposed to. And they howled, because they had no clue how I really felt.

I didn't want to see how Alex—the pawn I'd just sacrificed—reacted. So I held my chin up, squared my shoulders, and made my way across the room without looking back.

I was halfway around the pool when he caught up. "Since I'm an 'interruption' and all, can I interrupt your brooding and ask *what the heck was that*?"

I was hit with an urge to apologize, which I swallowed down. "I need them to take me seriously. If we look chummy, they won't."

"Do you ever give yourself whiplash? Yesterday, you tell me to make sure I'm seen as a threat. Today you position me as their new tech-buddy, then thirty seconds later, I'm an 'interruption.' There's something to be said for picking a strategy and giving it a chance to work."

I gritted my teeth. I didn't need him to point this out or teach me how to run the Business. Or maybe I did, since my own instincts were either atrophied or hibernating.

"When you decide what role you're gonna have me play, you let me know, okay?" he said. "And, hey, compared to them, you're practically warm and fuzzy."

"Shut up," I answered, but like his, my words didn't have any anger in them. He laughed and held the clinic door for me. I was smiling as I greeted Dr. Ackerman.

We settled into chairs in his office, and the doctor tapped

a pen on a file folder on his desk. "Alex, we've got all of your results back. There wasn't anything unexpected or that conflicted with the data in your records."

I wondered if Alex was thinking the same thing I was: the past two days of testing had been a complete waste of time.

"Our next step is looking at potential donors and finding the one that's most compatible. You probably already know about the different factors that go into making a successful pairing between you and a transplant organ—"

"He may, but I don't. So explain." I swallowed down my impatience and added, "Please."

Dr. Ackerman smiled. "I was planning to, but it's nice to see you invested. Alex, I know this may sound old hat to you, and I'm sure you've been working with an excellent nephrologist, but I want to make sure we're using the same terminology."

"Please, go ahead." The look in Alex's eyes made my chest tighten. It was stripped-down, raw, unvarnished vulnerability. And his deep voice had gone quiet and thin in a way that suggested it might break.

"Okay then. There are several factors we need to look at when screening our potential donors—the first, and easiest to measure, is blood type. Alex is type A, so he can best receive transplants from donors who are type A or O. Once we've eliminated all donors without the right blood types, we move on to looking at the results of your PRA." Dr. Ackerman turned to me. "That stands for 'panel reactive antibodies'—it's a screening that's a fairly accurate judge of how difficult it will be to find a compatible organ. The more antibodies a person has in his blood, the harder it can be to find a suitable donor."

"How many does Alex have?" I wanted to cover his ears until I knew if it would be good news or not, which was ridiculous. It's not like Alex didn't know the answer already. This was another reason why I stayed out of the clinic: It was full of numbers I couldn't control, things that made me feel helpless. Stories that clogged my throat and made it difficult to swallow.

As if to prove my point, it was Alex who replied. "They test it every month. I'm not unsensitized, which would be ideal, but I'm not highly sensitized either, which is extremely hard to match."

I nodded.

"And the final factor is HLA—that's 'human leukocyte antigen,' Magnolia. This is where we look for histocompatibility—tissue that'll get along. With all the improvements we've seen in immunosuppressive medicines, these are often considered less of a factor these days. It doesn't much matter if an organ matches the donor on zero out of six measures or five out of six, the prognosis is just about the same."

"Just about? That doesn't sound too exact."

"Well, we're not dealing with exact—because every patient is different. But since we *are* dealing with living donors, we're already ahead of the norm—a zero match from a live donor is better than a six match from a deceased. The longer-term survival rate of the graft—that is, how long the donated kidney lasts—improves with a higher match rate, but when comparing quality of life on dialysis with a transplant of a kidney with

a lower HLA match . . . the match isn't significant. It's typi-
cally more of a deciding factor if there are multiple potential
donors."

"And what about six out of six?"

Alex gave me a slight nod of approval, and for the first time
since entering the room, I felt a little less like an ignorant out-
sider.

"Six out of six . . . that's a different story. A perfect six-
antigen match does increase the long-term survival of a graft
and reduces the amount of anti-rejection medications needed.
But it's also extremely rare—especially among people who
aren't related. And Alex's parents and brother have been ruled
out as potential donors for him."

"Six out of six. That's what I want."

"In an ideal world, that's what we'd get, but six out of six
might be out of our reach. There are billions of HLA combinations. The odds of finding a perfect match . . . they're something like one in a hundred thousand."

"My father left the management of this case and all decisions pertaining to it in my care. I'd like for you to pursue a
six-out-of-six match before dismissing this out of hand."

"I hear what you're saying, and I really respect your inten-
tions. I think we can reasonably assume we'll be able to get a
four or five match, but—"

"Are you calling me unreasonable? Because I don't think it's
unreasonable to want Alex to have the greatest quality of life
or the longest possible success of his transplant. Or less meds—
don't those have lots of side effects?"

I turned to Alex for backup. After all, shouldn't *he* be the one leading this argument? He was grinning.

"What?" I asked him.

"You're a born CEO. Or a lawyer. I'm starting to get why those grown men were practically snapping their heels to attention by the pool table."

I snorted to cover my startled smile. "*That's* what you're thinking about right now? And no, thank you. I'll settle for someday running the Family and defeating the Organ Act."

Both Dr. Ackerman and Alex reacted to my statement with a tightening of their postures and expressions. Daddy said a leader had to know when to let a topic derail and how to get it back to the station. Well, I'd put us back on the tracks, but the mood in the room felt like we were headed in the wrong direction.

"You'll look into a six-out-of-six match," I restated.

"I'll do everything in my power to provide Alex with the best transplant outcome," said Dr. Ackerman. "And once we have some potential donors, we'll do what's called a crossmatch, where we'll mix some of Alex's blood with theirs. If his cells fight the donor's, then they're not a suitable match, but if they get along—then we're in business. Of course, there are methods and procedures to get around some of this—plasmapheresis—but I don't think that'll be necessary." He shut the folder in front of him. "And those are the basics. Questions?"

"I have one. Not about my transplant, but—" Alex swallowed. "How do you, you know, get away with this? Finding donors? Paying for the organs?"

"That's more of a question for Byrd. He handles all transplant coordination—contacting potential donors and facilitating the arrangements of testing and payments."

"Is he also the one to ask what we have in our database?" I asked. "Because I'm sure we have records of blood types and the HLAs. I want to see them."

"He is, and I'm sure you'll set up a meeting with him soon. But, as you know, he's currently in DC with your father."

I turned to Alex. "How are your hacking skills?"

He blinked. His eyes started going buggy as he said, "Um, I— Well—"

Dr. Ackerman held up a hand. "I'm going to pretend I didn't hear that and remind you they'll be back tomorrow."

It wasn't a *reminder*, it was the first time I'd heard it. I'd called Daddy last night, but he'd responded to my voice mail with a text message: We'll talk when I'm home. Stay focused on the task at hand.

Oh, I was focused all right. I nodded. "I suppose it can wait until then."

CHAPTER 17

I hadn't realized it was Sunday until I saw one of Mama's church hats sitting on the table in the foyer. Even then the day might not have registered if Alex hadn't been carrying a well-read Bible under his arm, in the same position I was carrying fashion magazines. We'd agreed to get something to read and meet in the hall, but seeing him with the Bible filled me with all sorts of questions that were probably too rude to ask.

"Are you mad at God?" I blurted.

"Right this second?" A wrinkled-brow smile stretched across his face. "Not particularly."

"I mean, for making you sick. For what happened to your sister. And I'm sorry for being a completely tactless imbecile about that at your house. I'm just . . . I'm sorry."

"Thank you." His smile faded, but the brow wrinkles only got deeper. "I've been mad, upset, just about every emotion you can be . . . It doesn't help. Medicine does. Faith does. I'm not one for subscribing to a 'vengeful God'—I don't think being sick is punishment."

I nodded like this made sense to me, but it didn't. If there was a God (Daddy would have me over his knee no matter how old I was, just for indulging that doubt), but if there was, how could he stand by and let people like the Wards do what they did? How could he allow people to be born only to break pieces of their bodies so they died in slow suffering?

I couldn't hold both "life's not fair" and "God is love" in my head at the same time. Lately I'd been drenched in the first and filing the second away with the Tooth Fairy. Because if God was love, why did he allow the man who'd loved me to die?

"Do you need a ride to Mass?" I asked. "I saw all the crosses at your house, and your reading material is a hell of a lot more pious than mine."

He grinned as I replayed my statement and winced at my choice of language. "Isn't there a chapel here?"

"Yeah, it's a couple minutes' walk past the barn, but it's not Catholic. It's not really anything. Mama uses it sometimes, but I think it was built more to be like, 'Look what I'm building.' She and Daddy go to services in town. You can go with her if you want. I do sometimes." When she made me. I'd gone voluntarily when I was little. Tripping over myself to be the first kid down the aisle when the minister called us up for the children's sermon. Finding way more than my fair share of eggs at the Easter hunt, then stealthily dropping them into the youngest kids' baskets. I'd stopped going when Carter and I got started.

When church time became the perfect chance to Skype without anyone interrupting.

"The chapel is fine. I'm supposed to be keeping a low profile, and all I really need is a place to pray. The pomp and ceremony and stuff don't matter."

"Really?" I snorted, and his glance narrowed. "I don't mean anything against *you*, but it seems like the whole reason my mama goes to church is to show off how Christian she is. And flaunt her clothing and handbags."

"I'm sure she'd love to hear you say that."

I rolled my eyes. "It doesn't mean it's not true."

"Faith doesn't need an audience to validate it. For me, it's about taking time to be quiet and reflective. Give respect to God. Right now I've got a lot to be thankful for."

The hope that glowed in his expression was nearly painful to witness. I turned away. "I'll show you where the chapel is."

I walked him all the way to the door, but I didn't step inside. As impressive as his faith was, it wasn't contagious. I wanted there to be a heaven. I wanted Abigail, Malcolm, and Carter Landlow to be in it. But the closest I could come to a prayer was the refrain that spun through my head in an endless chorus: *I miss you. I need you. I love you.*

Daddy found me at the clinic after dinner, where I was sitting on Alex's right side, playing poker and fixedly ignoring the dialysis happening on his left.

"Hey, sport. Alex."

"Daddy." I put down my cards. I hadn't expected him yet. Last I'd heard, he wasn't supposed to be wheels down for another hour. I stood and kissed his cheek. "Welcome back."

He gave me a smile. Recently it felt harder to differentiate between paternal smiles and Business ones—these used to be so distinct. "Alex, I'm going to borrow Magnolia for a bit."

"That's fine, sir."

"Do you need anything?" I had to look back over my shoulder to ask because I was being steered out of the room.

"I'm good. Thanks."

Daddy waited until the clinic door was shut behind us. "I didn't expect to find you in there."

"You said to watch him." I didn't know why I had to justify following his orders, but if so, I'd do it well. "What if he took pictures of the clinic or something to show the Feds?"

"Ah, good point." He reopened the door and leaned back inside. "Hey, Hal, could you go sit with Alex?" When Dr. Ackerman called back an affirmative, Daddy headed toward the house and his office. I followed him like a duckling. "Do you have any reason to believe Alex plans to take pictures or sabotage us?"

"No. Not at all. He just wants a kidney."

"Has he been giving you trouble? The boy's got no fans among the men."

"All he's done is fix the network. They have no reason to dislike him." Except that I'd encouraged it—alienated *him* as a way to promote myself. I swallowed. "He's not here to cause trouble."

"Well, here's the thing—" Daddy shut his office door. "He's going to be some trouble."

I narrowed my eyes. I wasn't ready to come out and ask what he meant, so I asked a question I hoped was perpendicular, not parallel. "In the interest of maintaining what's left of my sanity, how long is organ recruitment taking these days? When do you suppose we'll have a match for him?"

"I can't rightly say." Daddy looked down. "Now, I know there's some hesitance in the Family about the Organ Act."

I pointed to myself. "There's some hesitance in your lowercase family about it too."

"That's unfortunate. See, I'm counting on you to bring the others around to see our position."

"*Your* position." He always did this—assumed his rank made him right. Assumed everyone else would fall in line. Normally rounding up the stray dissidents and persuading them was a challenge I enjoyed, but this time . . . "I'm not changing my mind."

He shrugged. "Then we seem to be at an impasse. Why don't you sleep on it, and we'll talk tomorrow?"

"What?" I screeched the word. There was no other way to describe it. If Mama had heard that tone come out of my mouth, she'd have me dissolving sugar cubes on my tongue and practicing parlor conversation. "You didn't—I need—um, *answers?*" I sputtered, "Could I have some? Like, what any of this has to do with Alex or how the trip went? Daddy, you are being infuriating right now."

"Both those topics relate to the Organ Act—if you're not

willing to discuss that with an open mind, then there's not much point in continuing the conversation."

"I didn't say I wouldn't discuss it—I said I wasn't going to flop opinions because you told me to. Last I heard you were still 'kicking the tires'—I wasn't expecting you to come home indoctrinated."

"Then let's discuss. The problem we have with transplants in this country isn't a medical care one. Or even a financial one. It's a supply issue. There aren't enough organs to go around. H.R. 197's compensation and donation incentives will help with the shortages. And while our Family does just fine with recruitment . . . we're *illegal*, sport. You're asking donors to risk their health *and* the law. We're asking the Family to live with that threat always looming. I don't know about you, but I'd like to see what we can do without these restrictions."

"We'll go broke. Look at phase two, do you really think the government is going to offer a hundred fifty thousand subsidy per kidney? And what percent of their payment will even go to *us* after they compensate the donor?"

"You're right—we won't be earning six figures per transplant, but we'll make up for that in lower overhead costs. Do you know the percentage of our operating budget spent on security?"

It was rhetorical, but I *did* know. "Thirty-four."

Daddy grinned at me. "That's my girl. Halve that. Less than half. Plus volume. We'll be doing so many more surgeries. The math works, sport."

"Please explain what any of this has to do with Alex."

Daddy leaned forward and put both hands on his desk. "I've been asked to stop all transplants. It's part of the deal we're brokering with the attorney general."

It took me a few breaths to absorb that. Another few to wrestle my stampeding temper so I could ask, "Broker-*ing* or broker-*ed*? This is going to make things so much harder for Alex's kidney."

"No." He shook his head and leaned forward. "You're not getting it. Stop focusing on the one boy—this is so much bigger than him. And I'm telling you this in confidence, sport. You've got to keep this under your hat for now. If I sign this deal, I can't break it. As soon as the terms are set and the ink is dry—he's got to go."

"Go? Where? He doesn't have any other options. How long do we have until everything is signed?" I wanted to think that *we* encompassed the whole Family, but it felt a lot more like it only applied to Alex, Ackerman, and me.

"Not as long as I'd anticipated when I invited the boy to stay."

"Then call the veep—get him to put Alex back on the government list. Or could he be grandfathered in?"

"I'll ask, but . . . I think you've got a right challenge on your hands."

I shook my head and paced the length of his office, tempted to sweep a whole shelf of books and trophies to the floor. He didn't get to do this. Present some impossible task like it was a test. A right challenge? Screw that. This was Alex's life.

I turned around and marched back over to his desk. "What

happened to all your talk about my word and the Family name? I *promised* him a kidney."

"Sometimes there are extenuating circumstances." Daddy's hands were in his pockets, and he was shuffling his feet. "I'm not saying I'm any happier about it than you are. But the reality of the situation—"

"The reality of the situation *sucks*." I slammed the door as I left, but the bang did nothing to dislodge my words from the air. Did nothing to change the fact that if Daddy accepted this deal, we were no longer doing transplants or recruiting donors. And I needed both of those to save Alex.

Alex was fixing his sleeve when he found me on the clinic's porch. He had the right one rolled up to the elbow, but the left was buttoned at the wrist. It was hot as brimstone out tonight, and I knew that he was covering up his arm for me. The thought that I might not be able to do anything for *him* made the edges of my vision blur.

"Everything okay?" he asked. "You're looking like you did before you took a seat on the clinic floor."

As he sat down I forced a smile. "No. No, I'm fine."

"I don't believe you. You're all dead-eyed again."

"Dead-eyed?"

"At first I assumed it was some designer cocktail of prescriptions that made your privileged life bearable."

"Excuse me?" That got my attention. I blinked and crossed my arms.

"I said *assumed*. Past tense. You were . . . glazed and empty—I don't know. You'd get angry and there'd be a spark, but then you'd go back to being . . . dead-eyed. Like now."

Daddy had compared me to a zombie the other day, and he used to say I was a "spitfire trouble-magnet." Carter had once said, "Mags, your eyes are always full of mischief—I can see it even on my computer screen."

Now he was dead . . . and so were my eyes.

And if I didn't pull off some sort of miracle, the boy in front of me would be too.

I blinked and blinked because no way was I letting Alex see my dead eyes fill with tears. "Pretty stupid assumption about the way meds work. But I'm not drugged *or* dead-eyed. I'm just distracted. How'd it go?"

"Okay. Dr. Ackerman said they'd move the machine to the house tomorrow. How was the meeting with your dad?"

You can trust us. I turned away from him and headed across the lawn, but I couldn't outrun the lie in those words. "It's politics and Business—I don't know that Daddy and I are ever going to see eye-to-eye on it. And disagreeing with him always makes me hungry."

Alex put a hand on my arm as I reached the kitchen door. "That's why you're upset? A fight with your dad?"

"Yeah. Nothing like a good dressing-down to work up an appetite." He was studying me—his eyes were the color of fresh-cut pine boards, and they were far from dead. They crackled with life and concern and curiosity.

Tomorrow I'd go all warpath and figure out a strategy to convince Daddy this deal was a mistake wrapped in a trap attached to a catastrophe. Tonight I needed to regroup. I needed chocolate.

"Anyway, I'm not sure if you're allowed to eat this, but I always make Anna buy huge bags of Halloween candy, even though we don't get any trick-or-treaters out here. Want to help me get rid of the leftovers?"

"What kind of candy?"

"Twizzlers, Skittles, M&M'S, Snickers, Milk Duds, Sour Patch. You know, the good stuff."

He nodded and his mouth twitched into a smile, one so warm that mine slipped from artificial to authentic without me noticing. "I could go for that. It's been a while since I've had a grade-A sugar high."

"So, you were really DQ'ed from the government list?" I was sitting on the kitchen counter in a pool of wrappers. And even though my glass was full of nothing stronger than tea, my head and blood felt buzzy. Grade-A sugar high, indeed.

Alex shook his head and smiled ruefully. "I was."

"Why?"

"I'm not telling."

"But you're such a little rule follower, what could you have possibly done?" He shrugged and looked away. On any other night this kitchen would be full of Family and I'd have some serious competition for the chocolate. Alex worked like pest control; the men peeked in, then kept right on walking. And since Alex was avoiding the chocolate in favor of Sour Patch and Hot Tamales, I had it all to myself. I unwrapped a Snickers bar and ate it in two bites. "If I guess will you tell me?"

"If you guess? Yeah, okay."

"Hmm. Is there a mug shot of you somewhere?"

He ducked his head and his hair swung forward. "Yes."

"No way! For real? I was totally joking. Ha! I don't think you'd look good in orange."

"Are *you* really going to give *me* grief about criminal activity?"

I'd kicked off my shoes more than an hour ago, around the time the lights in the main part of the house had clicked off. Instead of going to bed, we'd decided to open the Skittles. I poked his knee with my bare foot in an effort to get him to look away from the legs of his barstool and up at me.

"Orange doesn't look so hot on me either. But, man, a mug shot? I wouldn't ever have pegged you for a deviant, Alex. I'm surprised, and impressed, and incredibly intrigued as to *what* you did." I nudged his chair so it swiveled a few inches in each direction. His arm brushed my knee when he reached for some more Sour Patch Kids. "Can I get a hint? Please?"

"Is this flirting?" Alex lifted his head and examined me with a puzzled expression. "You guessing what my criminal record says?"

"No." My cheeks flushed, and I yanked my foot off his leg. "Of course not."

"Oh. Sorry." His head was back down, that curtain of wavy hair back in place. "I shouldn't have—I wouldn't know."

"What do you mean?" I leaned over to my left and pulled out the miscellaneous drawer, grabbing the ball of rubber bands. Peeling one off, I handed it to him and tugged a strand of his hair.

He rolled the elastic in his fingers for a minute before nodding and using it to pull his hair out of his eyes. "I wouldn't know what flirting looks like. I was a kid before I got sick—a total geek who was more interested in computers than girls. And then I was the sick kid who was always absent and looked funny. And then I was the guy who dropped out before seventeen and got his GED because it was too hard to do both school and dialysis."

My mouth was dry, but I didn't lick my lips. I didn't dare do anything that could be misconstrued or add to our awkwardness. "I can't—I mean, even if I had been—which I wasn't—I can't possibly have been the first person to flirt with you. You just didn't notice."

"Maybe. I'm clueless about girl stuff. When I get my kidney and my second chance—I'm going to have to learn."

"How to flirt?" I smiled at his earnestness. I'd spent my whole life steeped in agendas and duplicity—stark honesty was a refreshing change.

"Yeah, and dating in general. When to hold hands. Signs she wants to kiss you. What you're supposed to do when a girl cries."

I was tempted to ask if he'd truly never held hands or been kissed, but the third one was safer. And my head was drifting in a different, dangerous direction as I realized that I was going to have to relearn to flirt too. It'd been so many years since I'd done it with anyone but Carter.

"Not that I'm planning on making girls cry," he clarified.

I cleared my throat and shook my head. "If she cries, you get her a tissue. Or apologize. Or pretend not to notice. Or give her a hug. Or leave her alone. Sometimes you call her mama. It really depends on why she's crying."

"You're no help to me."

The elastic I'd been toying with snapped back against my finger. I yelped and dropped the ball. It bounced across the kitchen, but I ignored it. He didn't know how true those words were.

No, I couldn't help him.

But I wanted to.

Stupid Organ Act.

"It's late. We should get to bed."

If he noticed a change in my mood, he didn't comment on it. He was still smiling and chattering as we headed up the stairs. He said, "Sleep well," in the hall outside our rooms, but I just nodded. I was practically sleepwalking already.

Sleepwalking, yet too hyped up on sugar and stress to truly fall asleep. I considered the sleeping pills Mama had helpfully left in my bathroom. I'd never taken them, though I'd held the bottle more than once and imagined dark and dangerous possibilities. On a few of the bleakest nights right after I got pulled from school, I'd even brought them to bed with me. Curling the bottle in my fist, holding it close to my chest, had been the thing that allowed me to drift to sleep.

Now, lying on my bed, beneath my covers and wrapped in Carter's sweatshirt, I rolled away from the bathroom door, rejecting the idea. Instead, I stared up at his pictures.

"I wasn't flirting," I whispered. "Carter, I miss you. I need you. I love you. Always."

CHAPTER 18

At breakfast Alex volunteered to reinforce our firewalls, then shrugged self-deprecatingly. "I noticed a couple easy ways to strengthen them . . . if you want. I've got nothing else to do, and I don't have much practice with downtime."

I wondered if Daddy felt guilty accepting this offer from a boy whose future might be collateral damage in his government deal. His smile was tight as he clapped Alex on the shoulder. "That'd be fine. I'd sure appreciate it." Then he hadn't eaten another bite.

I hadn't either. Daddy and I sat with full plates and averted eyes while Mama prattled and Alex finished eating.

Normally I would work in Daddy's office, but I wanted space and privacy to craft the perfect, double-spaced, fact-checked, irrefutable argument. So I dragged Alex out to the entertainment room.

"Still sore at your dad, huh?" Alex asked as he held the door for me.

I froze on the threshold and blinked at him.

"Last night you said you'd had a fight—and you were both quiet at breakfast."

"Oh, right. Yeah. And preoccupied. I've got some work to do today."

"Good, then maybe you won't be so distracting while I do mine." He spread his things out across the cover of a poker table: two laptops, a notebook, a pen he was drumming like a piston, and some sort of book on code that looked duller than dull. Of course, he'd said the same thing about the governmental policy and business books I had strewn across the bar top beside the notepad and laptop I'd snagged from the meeting room.

And it wasn't that I was bored or I didn't know what I was doing, but it was hard not to be overwhelmed by the task when the consequence of failure was sitting a few feet away, humming an off-key melody while tapping his pen to a beat that didn't match.

He caught me watching him and pulled off his earphones while lifting an eyebrow. "¿Qué onda?" He tapped the pen another time or two before shaking his head and adding, "What's up?"

"Nothing. I was taking a break."

"And decided to spend it staring at me? Weirdo." He grinned and shook his head, put his headphones back in place.

I hadn't actually been staring before, just spacing out. But now I was. Trying to figure out when in the past five days I'd stopped paying attention to the ways kidney disease and dialysis had wrecked his body and started noticing the guy within it. And when had he stopped feeling super self-conscious and defensive whenever I looked at him for more than two seconds? He'd even pulled his hair back instead of hiding behind it.

"Stop it," Alex grumbled, but he was smiling around the cap of the pen he was chewing.

"You're going to get lead poisoning."

"Lead poisoning? What exactly do you think is in pens?" He laughed, and as the sound floated over me, I couldn't help but smile. Not that I wanted him to know it. I turned away and got back to work.

I rolled my shoulders and my neck, clicked Print on the document I'd spent the past two hours drafting, and shut the laptop's lid.

Alex pulled off his headphones, proving I wasn't the only one super aware of the other person in the room. "You done working? Because I could definitely take a break and kick your butt at pool."

"Actually, I'm starving. Let me go grab some snacks, then I'll give you a rematch."

"Sounds good," he said with a smile.

And it did—it sounded like a perfectly reasonable plan. But Daddy intercepted me on the way back from grabbing my pages from the printer in the meeting room. The tone of his "Magnolia Grace, come in here," made it clear the snack tray, the pool game, and life in general would have to wait until he and I had it out.

"I've been waiting for you to come see me," Daddy said when I entered his office and shut the door. He was seated behind his desk, a position I'd never found intimidating before. But then again, I'd always sat beside him. Now I was on the other side of its wide expanse in a chair that was an inch or two shorter than his. Mine was shoved in the corner, and I couldn't make myself drag it across the room. "What've you been up to? I don't like not having tabs on you when you're in a sulk."

A sulk?

I'd wanted to do another read of my pages—to poke at all the facts I'd stacked into an argument and make sure none of it would topple—but I was out of time. "Here." I passed the papers across the desk and spent the next five minutes trying to interpret his expression.

Daddy paused and looked at me. "You're shying like an unbroken foal. Want me to come get you when I'm done reading?"

I took a deep breath and forced myself to sit still. "No. I'm fine."

He *uh-huh*ed and flipped to the next page. Too soon after that he tapped the edges together and put the stack down. "Maggie Grace, these are some mighty fine notes, but I signed the deal right after breakfast. I'm telling you first. We'll inform everyone else tomorrow."

"What? Already? But . . ." I hunched forward in my chair as if I'd been hit across the abdomen, because it certainly felt like it. "I'm too late?"

"I get it. You're teed off, and I get why."

"Do you get *all* the reasons I'm angry right now? You seem to be ignoring that *this* issue divided the Landlow Family from the inside and led to their *deaths*. You just made a decision that affects *all* our men. Including the ones whose jobs will be obsolete. If you think *I'm* mad, how will they feel when you get around to cluing them in?"

"That's why I *need* you on my side when I tell them. I can't give them any guarantees. I'll do my best to repurpose everyone and avoid as many layoffs as possible, but I can't make any promises. This is a dangerous time to be in our Business." He tapped the pages in front of him. "All this research you did, all these facts and stats, you're missing the bigger picture, sport."

I gritted my teeth. "Care to fill me in?"

"Profits and efficiency and all that? Well, they were a bit damned if we did sign, but they're a helluva lot more damned if we didn't."

I raised my eyebrows but didn't unclench my jaw to voice the question.

"Amnesty. That's why I signed the blasted deal. They know too much, and they're gearing up to prosecute."

"Because of Char and Penny?"

"Because the world's a lot smaller these days. A lot chattier. No one keeps their dang mouth shut. Not just those kids, who mean well, but patients. Donors. We can only plug so many leaks at once, and the Families are starting to hemorrhage. It was a matter of time."

Time. Because the trigger had been pulled on our own

extinction this morning and time was wasting. While all this sucked and made me furious, the topic he was avoiding was the one that mattered most right now.

"And Alex? Is he back on the government list? Prioritized?"

Daddy paused for so long I didn't even need his answer. "The government can't seem like they're granting favors to our Family. He had his shot at the list . . . and he blew it."

"So, we'll do one last transplant and they'll pretend not to notice?"

He sighed and wouldn't look at me. "I'm afraid not, sport. I hate this. I hate that we gave our word to the boy and we're going to have to rescind. For now, he'll have to stay here. I can't risk him going to the media because he's angry. And we'll continue to give him all the best medical care we can. Once the act passes, he can be the first transplant we do."

"How long will *that* take? What if he can't wait until all the bureaucratic tape is cut?"

"The second he starts to go downhill . . ." Daddy rubbed his beard. "If it comes to that, I'll pay for the best hospice care there is. Promise."

I stood up and stepped back. My hands up at my mouth. I was biting my knuckle, shaking my head. All of me was trembling—like my individual cells wanted to shake off those words. And if they couldn't, then I might vomit right on Daddy's rug to purge that thought from my body. *Hospice?*

"I know it's not ideal . . . and that's an understatement. But we'll do right by the boy. And for now I need you to continue to, you know . . ."

"Keep it under my hat?" I snarled.

"Just until the governmental folks make it official and public." Daddy stood as if he might reach for me, but there was no way I could tolerate any sort of touch right now. I took another step backward. "You understand, don't you, sport?"

"Of course I do," I said loftily. "I've always understood the Business." It was the patient part, the most important part, I hadn't gotten until now. *Now*, when it was too late.

I ignored that my eyes were growing increasingly wet as I stormed from Daddy's office, through the kitchen, and out the back door. But when I almost tripped over a planter, I set the snack tray on a patio table and swiped at them.

"Too heavy? You getting weak now that you're not doing those crazy cross-country workouts?" James was sitting at the other end of the patio. He put down his phone and stood. "Where're you headed with that?"

I turned away and pointed toward the outbuilding, trying to sniff surreptitiously.

He grabbed the tray. "I'll be the muscle. You be my arm candy."

I snorted. "You *do* get stuck with that role alarmingly often for a person who hates going to the gym."

"Well, when I'm official Family 'muscle,' I'm not allowed to carry heavy things—my hands have to be ready to react."

"React *how* exactly? Jazz hands? High fives? Opening doors for me?" I *used* to be funny. Now I didn't care how lame or haughty I sounded so long as it kept him from noticing I'd been crying.

"How's your ego today? I haven't schooled you on the targets in ages. Fancy some humiliation?"

"I'll take a rain check." I opened the entertainment room door, then turned and grabbed the tray. "Thanks," I added, before it shut in his startled face.

"Was that James?" Alex asked.

"Yeah." I took a deep breath and handed him a plate of sugared, frozen lemon slices. He blinked at me and shoved aside a computer to make room.

"Wow. Thanks. How'd you know?" He gave me one of his rare smiles—the kind that made him look like a whole different person. I took a step backward. His joy, his gratitude felt like they were turning a knife in my gut—which made no sense, since he was the one being stabbed in the back.

"Contrary to popular belief, I'm not a hundred percent computer illiterate. I can use a search engine." I'd spent an hour early this morning researching dialysis diets and recommended snacks. "And from the way you were stealing all the yellow Sour Patch Kids last night, I thought you might like these."

"I do. Thanks." His voice was a deep rumble, like when you feel a truck approaching through your bones long before it appears on the horizon. And then his smile faded as he studied my face. "Hey, you okay?"

It wasn't safe to let him in at a bone-deep level. It wasn't safe to let him in at all. I nodded and swallowed, bit my lip to ward

off a second round of tears. "I've got to . . . I've got to talk to
James for a second, be right back." I stumbled out the door, the
sunlight stinging my eyes.

"James!"

He hadn't made it far, just to the pool deck. He stopped when
I called and turned around with a scowl. "What?"

We'd done hundreds of staring contests when we were little
and I'd won them all, but this time I knew I'd be the one to
blink first because his gaze was steady anger and mine was a
heartbeat away from spilling down my cheeks. "I need to talk
to your daddy. He's in his office?"

He gave me a short nod. "Yes, ma'am."

"Thanks." I had a tentative plan, and I needed to start it
now—this second—before I lost my nerve.

"Maggie?" James reached for my arm, and his anger cooled
into concern. "You okay?"

I shook my head.

"Then what can I do to help?" His offer—so soon after I'd
literally slammed a door in his face—only added to the pressure building in my tear ducts.

"Go stay with Alex in the entertainment room."

He frowned and slapped his palm against the thigh of his
blue jeans. "Why do I even bother? Every time I try and help
you, you use it as an opportunity to put me in my place. Fine,
I'll go sit with him and stay out of your way."

I wanted to tell him this was a real request. That the Family men's animosity toward Alex wasn't pretty and especially
now—especially when news about Daddy's deal might leak

and cause tempers and trigger fingers to look for *any* target—I didn't want him alone.

But explaining would take time I didn't have and break my promise about keeping Daddy's deal under my hat. Though, in light of what I was about to do, that minor betrayal seemed inconsequential.

"Please," I added belatedly. "And thank you—this is a bigger help than you know."

James tipped his cap and spit out another angry "yes, ma'am" before walking away.

CHAPTER 19

"Byrd, we need to talk."

Daddy had taught me not to ask permission, to use declarative sentences, and assert my right to others' time and wisdom. I shut the door to his office and planted myself in the chair across from his desk.

"How can I help you?" Byrd was just as tall as his son. His desk was extra high to accommodate his long legs. He tapped the toe of his boot against it. "Has James done something?"

"You know about the deal with the attorney general?"

The boot tapping stopped. "We're not telling the rest of the men till tomorrow."

"I'm not here to talk about the men. I'm here to talk about Alex." I sat up straighter. "It's one kidney."

"Now, Maggie Grace, your father—"

"*One* kidney. How many of those do you match in a normal year?"

"Lots, but—"

"It's not a heart, or lungs, or anything the donor needs to be dead for. I'm not asking for something that's hard." I hoped recruiting Byrd would be the hardest part and finding a donor would be as easy as opening a few files on his computer.

Byrd shifted in his chair. "True, but—"

I held up a hand. Alex wasn't anyone to him, so I needed to hit him with the bigger picture. "Talk to me about what happens to our reputation when the Organ Act fails to pass and clients hear we've let patients die on our watch."

"That's a fair point, but *if* the Organ Act does pass—"

"If the Organ Act passes, we're out of a job. I don't care what rhetoric you're being fed by politicians, there's no way we'll survive in a legal market." Byrd tipped his hands up, and I leaned forward. "Come on, you really think the attorney general and the surgeon general are going to want to play in our sandbox? Best-case scenario: They let us operate legally while milking us for info on how to organize their transplant industry. Then they'll either run us into bankruptcy or assign everyone a court date and a jail cell."

Byrd whistled. "You should've been on this trip."

"I know. If James hadn't—"

"James is interested in this?"

I frowned. I was the one doing the interrupting and steering this conversation. But then again, Byrd was letting himself be steered, which meant he wasn't Camp Organ Act. So for him to break pattern was significant.

"Well, James—" His eyebrows lifted when I mentioned his son's name. Interesting. "He's with Alex right now."

True.

"Your daddy inviting James along to DC—I'm hoping that means he's starting to regain some confidence in him after the way my boy bungled guard duty and let you down last year . . ." Byrd swallowed. "And you two are patching things up? Over *this*?"

"He told me where to find you. And asked what he could do to help."

Also technically true, but man, I was going to hell.

"And he said—" Okay, James hadn't said anything I could use to complete my sentence, and manipulating Byrd with his concern for his son was making me ill. "Look, you're good at your job. And you've got willing donors at your disposal. Does my daddy need to know about *every* transplant? We're talking *one* more patient, and I'll personally pay all expenses."

Adding a *please* would make me look like a teenager wheedling for a curfew extension, but that didn't stop the word from burrowing its way onto my tongue.

I could practically see Byrd absorbing the risks of this plan—realizing he'd be defying a boss who didn't give second chances. He rubbed the back of his neck. "I reckon I can poke in some files and make a few calls."

I exhaled a rush of giddy gratitude. "Thank you."

"I'm not making any promises, Magnolia."

"Give me your word you'll try your best and I'll be satisfied."

I held out my hand, and Byrd studied my face for a moment before reaching across his desk to shake it. "Let's be clear about something here. This isn't about the Organ Act, or that boy. I'm glad to help the boy, and you know I like my government keeping its hands to itself, but I'm doing this for *you*, Magnolia Grace. For the way you saved this Family from my ex-wife's betrayal, for the way you're giving James a second chance. I owe you more than I can ever repay. If you want a kidney, I'll get you one."

If a heart could wince, that's what mine was doing. And how could I respond? I couldn't commend his loyalty while I committed sedition. If I insisted he *didn't* owe me anything, would I undercut his reason for helping? Our clasped hands felt so heavy as we lifted them up and down to seal our treasonous agreement.

"Thank you. That's a right nice thing to say. You let me know when there's news." I got up to leave, stopping before I opened his door. "I assume you know this is more discreet than even your usual discretion. You report to me. I'll coordinate with Ackerman."

First I needed to *recruit* Dr. Ackerman, but I'd deal with that next.

"Who else is inside?"

"James, of course." I figured I'd start with the name I'd used like currency, then state the next person I'd be asking—"I'll bring in Brooks too."

Byrd whistled. "I didn't just agree to participate in a coup, did I?"

I shook my head and left his office, diagramming that last question as I walked to the clinic. It wasn't a statement. He hadn't said: *I didn't agree to participate in a coup.* There was such a significant difference between those sentiments, and I wasn't quite ready to think about what that meant or what I'd started. Or how, when the Landlow Family had divided against itself, it had ended in their murders.

Getting Ackerman on board was easy. Brooks didn't hesitate either.

But I did. I think world records for slowness were set with how long it took me to walk back to the entertainment room and push open the door.

James and Alex both had expectation written on their furrowed brows as they put down their pool cues and looked over at me.

Alex picked up a plate. "I saved you a—"

I cut him off. "Sorry, I need to talk to James for another minute. This won't take long."

Alex nodded, and James ambled over and out the door.

"Can I trust you?" I asked as soon as the door was closed behind him. "Like, *really* trust you. You can't tattle to my daddy. Heck, I'd prefer you didn't even look at him."

James whistled. "I don't know. Can *you*? I've always thought you could, but you've spent the past year proving you don't."

My voice and eye contact didn't waver. "I get that you're sore about the guard thing—I do, but *this* can't become a tattling game. Not like what you did at school."

"I think it's past time you and I had a sit down and hashed out what you think went down at UT." His calm felt like condescension and rasped against emotions that were already raw. All the anger and hurt from five weeks ago came hurtling back at whiplash speeds. I'd told Byrd James was on board, but I'd figure out some other way.

"Never mind. I don't need your help." I started to walk away, then whirled back around, unwilling to let his statement go unchallenged. "What I *think* went down? I know. You sold me out." There were only three traits that mattered: respect, honor, loyalty. What he'd done . . . he'd shown none.

"I *sold you out?*" James's posture mirrored mine: raised shoulders, locked jaw, hands fisted.

"Of course you did. You're just like your mother."

"Don't you *ever* say that." His finger was in my face, and it was trembling. He turned his back and slumped his shoulders, walking away from me into the small tangle of trees and brush we'd called "the wild" when we were small and only allowed to go this far unsupervised. "Dang, Maggie, is that really what you think? *I* sold you out?"

"You called my parents! Told them I couldn't handle school." I followed his footsteps, my boots crunching twigs, my arms dappled in sun and shade.

"No. The dean did. Apparently when you've been in school for a month but don't show up for class, turn in work, or return any calls from your adviser or RA, they do that."

"The *dean?*" I froze.

"Yeah, *I* didn't call. But go ahead and blame me. Your daddy thinks it's my fault you weren't in class. For some reason it's okay Lupe couldn't get your butt out of bed, but I've failed him, and you, and the whole blasted Family because I didn't act as magical life coach guru on top of bodyguard and my own class schedule."

"Daddy said . . ." But what Daddy had said just amounted to a whole lot of blame—for this fall, for failing to notice the times I took off last year. He held James responsible for the results but hadn't ever said he was the *cause*. "The dean?"

That was on my head. This was *all* on my head.

"Sweet heaven, Maggie." James turned around slowly, his hands still raised, but palms instead of fists. "I'm not your enemy."

"You're not my friend either."

"I used to be. That's *your* choice, not mine."

Daddy always said, "Being in charge means never saying *I'm sorry*," but he wasn't right. He wasn't right about the Organ Act either. And definitely not about Alex's kidney being an acceptable "extenuating circumstance."

I reached up and squeezed his hand. "Sorry I've been such a . . ."

"I never expect you to stop being such a . . ." He raised his eyebrows and grinned. "But to answer your question: you can trust me. I'm Team Maggie—all in. Now what's the plan? 'Cause I can tell from that smirk, you've been scheming."

CHAPTER 20

James and Alex were watching a movie in the den. I was supposed to join them when I finally escaped from Daddy's office—where I'd spent two hours after dinner helping him strategize how to tell the Family about the deal and trying not to crack and confess what I'd planned. I paused at the door and listened to their chatter and laughter, but instead of going in, I sneaked outside and headed for the hayloft in the barn. The *actual* barn, not the clinic that looked like one.

This was where Loops and I always sat when we smuggled drinks out of the entertainment room's bar, or if we were hiding from some sort of punishment. It was strange to be there without her, so I dialed her number. When it hit voice mail I said, "Call your mama . . . and call me. You can actually go ahead and call me first, I promise not to tell."

Then I hung up, and it was just me and the thought I was avoiding: Byrd's wife.

James's mama had wanted to be called "Lady Byrd"—after the wife of some president who served before she was even born. It didn't fly. At all. The other wives smiled politely and said, "You're so funny, Linda!" and Byrd straight-up refused.

But she wasn't a Lady Byrd or any other type of lady. She was—to go all mafia slang—a stool pigeon. A rat. Someone willing to give evidence against the Family in order to save her own neck.

Her big crime she needed saving from? Shoplifting. Apparently she had a taste for designers that exceeded her bank account. It's not like she faced years in prison. Not a decade like Dr. Santos had been sentenced to, or six years like two of the nurses, or even the year and a half one of our patients endured before dying in prison from complications of renal failure. All those families were growing up without their aunts, sisters, sons, fathers.

Fourteen-year-old James—a mama's boy through and through—had lost his mother when she took off. Last I heard she'd headed to California. Her betrayal and abandonment had changed him. His whole focus became proving to my daddy that he was loyal. That he wasn't like her.

That's when he and I drifted. He went from friend to snitch practically overnight. Plus, there was the guilt aspect—*I* was the one who'd figured out what his mama was up to. It wasn't much more than a guess strung with a hunch and tied together with luck, but it was what *made* my reputation in the Family. It opened doors and minds, broke down the barriers I'd spent my whole life crashing into.

Now I was in charge. Or close enough to it. And James's "all in" was validation I hadn't known I'd needed. It went a good ways toward combating my doubts.

I didn't move when the barn door opened. The creek of its hinges interrupted the low sounds of the horses shuffling and breathing. I didn't move when the person backlit in the doorway crossed over to the ladder and began to climb. I'd seen the rebellious whorl that remained of his cowlick. I'd known he'd come.

"Where's Alex?" I asked.

"Gone to bed. I figured your babysitting services stopped at good night, but if there's a whole tuck-in process, you go right ahead and do that."

"I can push you off here."

James crested the top of the ladder and sank down on the hay bale beside mine. "Eh, maybe just ask me to leave before it gets to that point. I wasn't sure if it was me you were avoiding, or him."

Him. I was hiding from him and the word "hospice" and the fact that the two combined felt like being stabbed with all the needles in the clinic.

"Both. I don't know. Not *you*, but . . ." I shifted backward. The ends of a hundred pieces of straw dug into my thighs, but that wasn't nearly as uncomfortable as the conversation I was about to start. "Your dad brought up your mama earlier."

James rapped his knuckles against the floor, stirring up some dust. "Can we—can we put that conversation on pause?

At least for tonight? We already kumbayaed about school; I don't know that I can handle rehashing my mama too."

I fiddled with some straw, and he studied my face and then swore. "Fine, what about my mama?"

"This thing we're doing . . ." I swallowed and wondered if my next question was going to put us right back on opposite sides of a fence we'd so recently torn down. "I need you to tell me it's not wrong. That we're not being . . . well, that we're not being like your mama when she betrayed the Family."

He inhaled and stiffened. His face pinched with hurt. "I hated you for a long time after that."

"I know."

"It was really *me* I hated, but I turned it on you. *You* figured out what my mama was doing. That should've been me. I should've noticed and talked her out of it."

"You couldn't have. She wasn't asking you the same types of pointed questions she asked me. I just happened to be an inconvenient roadblock between her and my daddy. And I don't know, the questions, combined with the way she was so concerned with sitting close to me and fiddling with that necklace . . ." I'd changed seats in the living room twice only to have her come up with reasons to relocate beside me. "You didn't see that behavior, and that's what tipped me off."

Thank God. Because I'd been able to slip into Daddy's office and whisper in his ear: "The fence is down in the far field." His face had gone gray. It was the catchphrase I'd known since I was little—the one that meant we'd been infiltrated.

He'd gripped my shoulders in his hands. "You're sure?"

I'd nodded and swallowed. Twice before I found my voice. "Mrs. Byrd. I think the wire's in her necklace. I swear on Conniption."

"Listen carefully. Tell your mama you two need to go down to Austin. Now. Pack a bag and go. Bring Manuel. Stay the night, and I'll call later."

He'd sent out one e-mail. A one-word e-mail to the upper echelon of the Family: *brushfire*. There hadn't been time to ask then, but later he'd told me it meant destroy anything incriminating, get ready for a raid.

Daddy's last words to me as I left were, "I'm trusting you, sport."

But his trust had only lasted two days. Two torturously long days of Mama dragging me through Austin's shops and galleries on an epic stress-fueled spending spree. Two nights of lying sleepless in a hotel room.

Two days and his trust ran out and he brought us back home.

The raid hadn't occurred till day three.

Four a.m. Pounding on the door. Feds with guns drawn. Shouting and barreling through the house. A vase had gotten broken and one of Daddy's hounds had cut his paw on the glass—adding barks, howls, and blood to the melee. Mama had tried to cling to me, shield me as I gaped at the sight of Daddy in handcuffs. She'd gripped me so tight my shirt tore when I yanked free of her grasp to run to him. I'd yelled at the officers not to take him, but I hadn't cried. I'd made sure Daddy's last glimpse of me involved my chin up, my shoulders back.

And when he came back home on bail, and through the proceedings where charges were made . . . and his lawyers got the charges dismissed, I made sure he only saw me defiant and angry.

He'd noticed. The other Family men had noticed too. It was what had gotten me entry to their clubhouse. It was what had bought me my chair in their meetings.

It was what had made James hate me.

I reached across the hay bales and grabbed his hand. He blinked, easing himself out of whatever horrific memory had him trapped. I mentally counted another slow three beats before I let myself pull my hand back.

James sighed. "This isn't the same, Maggie."

"I'm betraying Daddy. I'm betraying the Family."

"No." James straddled his hay bale as he turned to face me. "If you want to fit that scenario on this one, then your dad's the rat." I stiffened, but James continued, "He's the one who's turned informant for the government—you're the one who's staying steady. I may not have seen what you did as heroic when we were fourteen, but I sure as heck do now."

Daddy's deal and my countermeasures meant I wasn't going to get to do a lot of things. I'd never lead the Family. I'd never take my spot in the chair on the other side of his desk. I wouldn't get to see the next generation of enforcers and doctors grow from toddlers in dusty rompers to men and women my own age.

But I would save Alex.

Heroic.

"Thank you," I told James. "That was exactly what I needed to hear."

"I don't hate you anymore," he added. "In case you were wondering."

"And I only ever pretended to hate you," I said as I stood up and made my way to the ladder.

I'd long ago mastered the art of creeping across the patio, in the back door, and up the stairs in the dark. Hallway lights—who needed them? I certainly hadn't all the high school nights I'd sneaked in and out so I could talk to Carter while stargazing.

"Are you avoiding me?"

My throat tightened in a painful clench. I was too busy gasping to be able to scream, which is the only reason I didn't. I clawed at the doorframe and used it to steady myself before turning toward the room across from mine and the boy standing in it. "Sweet Lord, Alex! Are you trying to give me a heart attack?"

"Sorry." He flipped on his room light as he stepped into the hall. It lit us both in a soft glow—him, sleepy face, comfy clothing. Me, creased sundress, crumpled me. "But are you avoiding me?"

"No." Yes. Absolutely.

"Really? 'Cause if I did something, I'm sorry. I can't think of what, but you've been . . ."

"Oh, Alex." My heart had just dropped back to its usual position, but now it was seizing with guilt. I'd dodged eye contact and conversation since my meeting with Daddy. "It's been a crazy day. Business stuff. I'm not upset or mad. I promise."

"You were crying."

"I've been known to do that from time to time." I gave my best attempt at a flippant smile. "I'm okay. You don't need to worry."

"There's one more thing I need to tell you." He scrunched his face. "When I was working on the firewall today I noticed something. There was an attempt to gain entry to your network from an IP address that I'm pretty sure is a subnet of the one behind the virus."

"What does that mean?" I understood it wasn't *good*, but how *bad* was it?

"It means they're trying to get back in—get more information. They didn't succeed, but they tried."

"You're sure it's the same people?" I squeezed my phone in my now-sweaty hand. "Like, you're *sure*, you're sure? There's no other explanation?"

"I'm pretty sure. I think I'm remembering the IP address behind the virus correctly."

"I can't go to Daddy with 'I think.'" And right now I wanted Alex completely off his radar. I chewed my lip. "You said they didn't get in. Is the network safe?"

"Yeah. I put a lock on all IP ranges close to the one from today. It'll send me an alert if anyone in that range attempts to breach the network and then shuts down Port 80 to all traffic."

"I don't . . ." Everything after *yeah* had gone over my head. "An alert? So you'll know if it happens again?"

"Right away. And they won't be able to breach my safeguards." He stood up a little taller. "They didn't get in now, and they won't if they try again."

"So maybe let's wait and see?" Because the last thing I needed was for Alex to cause more drama or draw attention to his presence here. And was there a reason to cry wolf—or hacker—if he'd fixed the problem?

"You really think that's best?" His disagreement was there, but woven with uncertainty.

"We're gonna wait," I said. "I don't *think* that . . . I *know* it."

His shoulders slumped, and I hated myself for being cruel, but I was in for a penny, a pound, a ton. "If there were really a problem, Theo would know. If you *think* you see anything new, or get an alarm or whatever, be sure to tell me. In the meantime, get some sleep. Stay rested and healthy, so you're ready when we get our donor."

Because I was only getting one shot at this, and in the aftermath—when I was dealing with the repercussions of this mutiny I was leading on his behalf—I needed to believe Alex would be healthy, happy, off living his life.

CHAPTER 21

Breakfast petered out slowly. Mama was happy to have Daddy back and was recounting everything she'd done while he was gone and her plans for the week. "I was thinking, let's all run a 5k together. I know I won't be able to keep up with Maggie Grace, but it'd be fun to do as a family. Though not one of those mud races Suetta was telling me about. Or the ones with the zombies."

"Zombies?" I shook my head. "Never mind. I don't want to know."

And then I felt guilty, because she was *trying*, and she was the only person in the dining room doing so. I was struggling to sit at a table with Daddy. Struggling with my guilt and my anger and how to handle them while seated across from the boy who'd caused both. And that boy was squirming in his seat and avoiding eye contact. Basically doing a piss-poor job of hiding

his own discomfort, which had me confused for a minute—
since he didn't know about my disobedience on his behalf—but
then I remembered how tangled our web of deception truly was
and his firewall fears.

Daddy looked equally uncomfortable, which probably
explained why he'd distractedly agreed to Mama's plan for him
to start jogging.

I needed somewhere to hide out and something to fill the
hours until I heard from Byrd.

What if it wasn't today? Or tomorrow? How could I possibly sit through this afternoon's meeting about the deal and
convincingly fake my support?

"Are you *okay*, Magnolia Grace?" Mama asked, and I looked
up to see all three of them watching me.

"Yes. Why?"

"You just groaned like your appendix was fixing to pop.
You sure?"

"Oh. I thought of something. I forgot to e-mail Lupe. I'll go
do that now—if you'll excuse me."

"Sure, sugar bean." Mama pressed a hand to her heart. "But
I swear to the Lord, you're going to send me to an early grave.
Don't you ever make that noise again."

"Noted." I stood. "Coming, Alex?"

"Yes." He bobbed his head at my parents as he pushed in his
chair, then followed me out to the foyer. "An e-mail?"

"Did you want to hear about Suetta's new dog for the
second—no, *third*—day in a row?"

"Good point. Now what?"

"Now we . . ." Why didn't I have hobbies? The Business, classes, Carter, and cross-country had pretty much been my entire life. "Um . . . You play horseshoes?"

"¿Cómo?"

"You heard me. Come on. The pits are way out in the middle of nowhere. Down by the creek—it's shady, there's a breeze, and—even better—there's no one around to eavesdrop, because I have some questions."

His eyebrows went up. "Lead on."

Alex was all sideways glances as we made our way to my truck for the short drive to the creek that cut diagonally across our property. He waited until I'd parked beneath a sugar hackberry tree and gotten out before he asked, "Questions?"

"Why do you have a mug shot?"

"What? No, seriously, *what*?"

I'd been thinking about the government list since Daddy's comment yesterday about him having blown his shot.

"You're a rule follower. What could you do?" There was no way he could mistake *this* conversation for flirting. Not with my arms crossed and the toe of my cowboy boot tapping on the dry ground.

His face was red and as he tucked his hair behind his ears and practically growled. "Wait. You made me come all the way out here—"

"The whole five minutes?"

"—to ask about my *mug shot*?"

"Why were you kicked off the list? I think it'd have to be

something bigger than underage drinking. Unless, did you DUI? And hurt someone? Or violence? Gangs?"

"None of your business."

"It *is* my business because you're in my house and I'm putting my neck on the line for you. If they disqualified you, it'd have to be something major." And if he hadn't done whatever cracked thing it was, then I wouldn't be a barbed-wire ball of nerves, worn out from planning behind Daddy's back.

"No, it doesn't have to be 'something major'—not at all." He walked around the truck to stand in front of me. "There aren't enough organs to go around; the wait on the list is barely better than a death sentence—the government *wants* reasons to say no."

He wasn't that close, but I felt crowded by him, by his words, by the way his health problem unsettled me and kept me up all night. He'd blackmailed his way into my life, and it was tearing my whole world apart. *And* he hadn't answered my question.

"You've got a mug shot. Your room is across the hall from mine. You were waiting in the dark for me last night—should I be scared?"

"You're scared of me?" All the anger hissed out of him, and he took a step backward.

"Well, no. Not actually. But sometimes I'm reckless. Mama says I'm not frightened of half the things I ought to be."

"I'm not . . ." He scraped his hair back from his face. "Don't be scared of me."

"I know!" I held up a victorious finger. "Hacking. Was that it?"

"No. Drag racing. Happy now?"

"Drag racing?" I spoke the words to see if they'd change meaning once they'd rolled around my mouth and off my incredulous tongue. They didn't. "Did you hurt someone? I mean, if it's on your record and got you disqualified . . . Oh God." I pressed a hand to my lips, wanting to push back the words and the fears brewing behind them.

"No. No one got hurt." He held up a hand and waited until I'd nodded and lowered mine. "But you're right, they could've."

"If no one got hurt, why'd they throw the clichéd book at you?"

"Because I laughed."

"You what?"

"I laughed. The cop who pulled me over said, 'You want to end up dead, boy?' And I laughed."

"That's a rather grim sense of humor . . . I don't think it's funny."

"Neither did he. And he was less amused when I wouldn't give him any other names."

"The other driver didn't get caught?"

Alex shook his head. "Just me. It's a Class B misdemeanor. I paid a fine, delayed my license by a year, and lost my chance for a legal kidney."

"Couldn't you have traded the other drivers' names for a lesser sentence?"

He snorted. "I could live without my license. And in my world, people don't snitch."

My cheeks flamed as I realized what I'd suggested. "They don't here either. Not without consequences."

"It wouldn't have changed the list decision anyway." He shrugged and turned to face the creek. "If you're done playing inquisition, can we throw some horseshoes?"

"Fine."

Alex picked his way down toward the creek bank. "Are you satisfied that you're safe in your bed yet?"

"I wasn't scared." At least not *of* him. *For* him . . . That was a different story. "But you should be, because I'm about to whup you."

He laughed, and I let myself drift into the sound of it. He reached over and snagged a pair of horseshoes from the pit. "Maybe I'm also not frightened of half the things I ought to be."

CHAPTER 22

Alex took a nap after lunch.

I'd taken plenty of naps in the past couple years—after pulling all-nighters studying, gossiping, partying, or . . . usually, talking to Carter.

But when Alex rubbed his eyes and said, "I need to rest before dialysis and dinner," all my naps suddenly felt indulgent. He *needed* a nap. Because he was sick. Because his body was working too hard just to function—his veins and arteries circulating blood that wasn't being cleaned by his stupid broken kidneys.

Maybe I'd pushed him too hard? His stress about the firewall, staying up too late, this morning's shouting match—if every one of his actions took a toll, what was the cost of him living behind enemy lines?

Once his door was shut I called Pen. I had twenty minutes until *the* Family meeting where Daddy would break the news about his decision. I'd have to convincingly feign support for the Organ Act, so I was hoping to borrow some enthusiasm from her.

She answered breathlessly, "Perfect timing."

"Hi. You okay?"

"Was doing a workout video. With Caleigh. Man. She's in shape. Thanks for the excuse to quit!"

"Are things better with her? And is your boy back?"

"A little, I think. And, *yes*! There's no change in his father's condition. I hate how upset Char is when he comes home from these trips. He pulls away from me, and it's . . ." She sighed, and I wished I could reach across the cellular waves and hug her.

And since I was the opposite of a hugger, this urge made me stiffen. "You sure you don't want to go finish your workout?"

"A hundred percent sure. You don't think Char blames me, do you?"

"No. I think he's . . . It's got to be hard seeing his dad like that. I doubt it has anything to do with you."

"You're probably right, but it feels like it does." She sighed again. "Anyway, you called me and probably not because you wanted to play relationship counselor. What's up?"

"If I asked you why you supported the Organ Act, what would you say?" I grabbed a piece of paper to write down her answer.

"That's easy. Because everyone who needs an organ needs a better chance of getting it. Not just those who can pay, or who qualify for government lists, or who are stubborn or lucky enough to live long enough to outlast the wait time. *Everyone.*"

"Good answer." Its sincerity was as profound as her lack of hesitation. "But what about when people say the Organ Act only benefits the wealthy—allows those who have money to take a shortcut and buy an organ to avoid waiting?"

"That's what's already happening—not just in our Families, but globally. Often in unhygienic clinics in third world countries where the donors get no follow-up care. H.R. 197 didn't invent the organ trade—it's seeking to provide safeguards so donors aren't exploited. And in the second phase of the act, it levels the playing field by providing federal funding to compensate donors. By that point, I don't even think there'll be a list—well, maybe for those who would be donors, but recipients will pretty much be 'step right up.'"

"But you admit only the rich recipients benefit during phase one?"

"I admit no such thing!" I could hear the smile in her voice. That she was enjoying this debate as much as I was made me like her even more. "Legalizing donor payments equals more organs. More organs available is better for everyone. If the wealthy choose to purchase them privately, then they're not taking up spots on the government list."

"Another good answer." I'd never considered it that way.

"Next question? This is fun."

"I think I'm good for now."

"What's yours?" she asked, "Whether you're for or against the Organ Act, what's *your* why?"

"I—" Because I didn't want my life to change more than it already had. Because I still wanted the merged-Family future Carter and I had planned—Vickers-Landlow or Landlow-Vickers, depending on which one of us you asked. Because of Alex.

But all those reasons felt hollow.

"I'm still working on my *why*."

"When you figure it out, I can't wait to hear."

Me neither.

The meeting went every bit as badly as I'd imagined.

Yelling.

Swearing.

The Family men were arranged around the meeting room wearing expressions that ranged from skeptical to outright hostile.

Manuel stormed out, then stormed back in. "Holt, I don't know what you're thinking lately—letting that blackmailer stay here, cutting deals with the attorney general—but it's supposed to be my job to keep this Family safe, and your erratic decisions are making that mighty hard. Or, now that you've decided to go legit, maybe you don't need me anymore? Is that what this means?"

Daddy looked at me, and I knew this was my cue. When we'd strategized last night, he'd agreed to let the men rail and bluster for a while, then said *my* role was to step in and settle them so they'd be open to hearing him and Byrd explain the particulars.

"Now, Manuel, sit down," I chided with a grin. "Of course he needs you—you're the only guard I haven't managed to give the slip." His begrudging smile turned to outright laughter when I tapped my lip and added, "Hmm, on second thought . . . you're fired."

I waited for the men's ribbing to die down, then made eye contact with each of them as I lied, "This is a *good* plan. I know you're surprised—believe me, I was too. And I did the whole tantrum thing"—I winked at Manuel—"but when I stopped to listen, this makes sense. So save yourselves the pouting and stomping, and skip to the listening part. You'll see."

I wasn't sure if they *saw*, but they did sit and listen. I didn't. I tuned out as soon as Daddy pulled out a marker and started writing on the whiteboard.

The false enthusiasm was exhausting. The tiny headshake Byrd had given in response to my searching glance was discouraging. I stood gratefully when the hour hand finally kissed the edge of the three.

"Where you going?" asked Enzo in a faux whisper. "And can I come?"

"I—um . . ." Alex's dialysis was about to start, but it didn't feel smart to offer this as an excuse. I raised my arms then sat back down. "Just stretching."

I cringed every time his name came out of the men's mouths—accompanied with "What are we going to do with him?" or "What if he talks?" or "He's a loose end. I don't like loose ends."

And defending Alex *now* when I hadn't before would only instigate suspicion, so I hid my fear behind a scowl and watched the clock. How long could I live in this place of betrayal and grief and stress before I crumbled? Because I wasn't all that steady on my feet to start with.

I knocked and Alex's deep "come in" echoed from the other side of the door.

"Sorry I'm late. I got away as soon as I—" The white noise whoosh of the machine made me recoil. Apparently Dr. Ackerman had already come, done his needles thing, and gone. And apparently I was wrong: dialysis *outside* the clinic was no less scary. "Dear God. Four *hours* on that thing?"

Perhaps it was tactless, but it was better than what I'd been thinking: For heaven's sake, will it never become easier to see you hooked to that machine?

"Well, a little less than three at this point. Boring, but I think I'd rather be bored than dead." He was smiling, but I could feel the blood draining from my face. It was crashing toward my toes as stars rushed up to fill my vision.

"Maggie? Maggie! Sit down. I can't come catch you if you pass out, and your lips are *white*."

I stumbled to the edge of the bed and sat. Alex reached his good hand for one of mine, but I pulled back. "I'm fine. I don't know why I'm such a shrinking violet about blood." And since we were both embarrassed, I barreled into chatter to fill the silence between blushes. "So, what are you watching? If I was stuck sitting, I'd totally binge on TV shows I never had time to catch up on at school."

I tilted his laptop toward me. He blushed, and for the space of a second I worried maybe he'd been watching something more Enzo's tastes than mine. But it wasn't nudity or skimpy outfits; it was a middle-aged Middle Eastern woman standing in front of a whiteboard full of numbers and symbols. I tilted my head and raised an eyebrow.

"Computer science lecture. MIT shares their classes online."

"Why? I mean, why would people watch them? For fun?" The woman's face wasn't particularly inviting—at least not in the wrinkled-brow studious expression captured on the paused screen. And the whiteboard full of equations that looked like they'd baffle NASA . . . It looked about as enjoyable as dialysis.

"Yes. Or because they're interested in the subject and want to learn. This is the closest I'll get to MIT anytime soon."

"Oh." And like every time Alex held a mirror to my privilege, the reflection glaring back wasn't flattering. "I didn't mean to interrupt, I'll let you—"

"No! Stay. I mean . . . if you want. Pick one of those TV shows you said you'd binge on. There's only so much cryptanalysis I can handle. It's making me stress the Port 80 attempt. You sure we shouldn't tell someone?"

"Yes." They wouldn't believe him anyway. And if I left this room, I'd have to go back to that meeting and sell lies and indifference. Blood felt easier.

I picked up his laptop, signed into my online TV account, clicking over to my Watch List. I scrolled past reality shows and that sitcom with the robot. Past movies that were perfect for watching and rewatching with Loops and a pitcher of something sweet. We'd giggle ourselves into stomachaches as we competed to see who knew more of the dialogue and stole each other's punch lines.

"You're not going to like any of this. Let's watch your lecture. And if I fall asleep—no big deal. Some of us didn't nap."

Except . . . had I just said I'd be okay sleeping on his bed? Because the only boy I'd ever slept next to was Carter . . . and probably James or Enzo when I was small, but that didn't count. I sat up and eyed the eighteen inches of comforter between us.

Alex took the laptop, and I scooted farther away—then realized what I was doing and how it must look and shifted back. If he noticed my hokey-pokey indecisive maneuvers, he didn't say. He didn't click back over to his lecture either. Instead he scrutinized my Watch List. "How about this?" The pointer hovered above *Quiz Show*.

Carter and I had once talked about simultaneously watching the game show while on Skype—playing along to see which of us knew more answers. I waited for the emotional blow of that memory, but it was more of light slap.

I swallowed. "That's fine."

"Get ready for me to kick your butt."

I laughed, forcing the sound to be louder than my tight throat wanted. "Okay, big talker. Like that butt-kicking that did *not* occur in the horseshoe pit?"

"Hey, you get beauty and brawn. I'd like to think I bring brains to this equation." He smiled over at me, and for the first time since I'd entered this room I didn't have to *try* to keep my focus away from his arm and all that bloodiness. It was easy to see the summer lightness in his eyes and in the shape of his full lips, stretched wide in a happiness that felt like an injection of oxygen after holding my breath for too long.

Alex and I—as an equation? Probably one just as tangled and confusing as those in the MIT lecture.

If so, what did we equal? What was our solution?

CHAPTER 23

Hayloft?

I texted James since I hadn't seen him all day. At dinner Daddy mentioned he'd sent him off to the Abilene clinic. I wanted to ask if this errand was a show of confidence *or* if having him miss the meeting was proof of lingering disappointment—but Mama shut down the Business talk. And it's unlikely Daddy could've elaborated in front of Alex.

James was grumbly when he and I met up on those hay bales after Alex had gone to bed. "The men all think *their* day sucked with the deal news, but I was shuttering a clinic and furloughing doctors. I win. It doesn't seem right. We promised people we'd help them and now it's all adios, and bonne chance."

"Exactly how many languages are you gonna slip into this monologue?" I teased, hoping to irritate him or shake him out of the mood that had his brow furrowed.

"It's crappy in any language."

"I know. Yeah, it's great *we've* got immunity, but what about all the patients?" I squirmed on my hay bale. "Well, at least you got off-estate. Next time, take me with you. Being around Daddy and Alex is awful. Every time they look at me, I feel like they're going to guess."

"Maggie, you've got how many years of experience hiding things? That poker face of yours could win awards."

"That was different. It only affected Carter and me. If Alex learns the Family wants to renege, it'll crush him. And when he's transplanted and Daddy finds out I went behind his back, there'll be consequences. You, your daddy, Brooks, and Dr. Ackerman—y'all get that, right? He'll be furious, and I don't know what he'll do."

"We get it." James slid forward on his hay bale, eyes serious and locked on me. "We know the risks. Team Maggie, remember? I'm working on a secret handshake."

"I'm no hero, James. You told me Daddy said I saved the day in New York—that's a lie. My only role was courier. I delivered a letter to Penny from her brother. Then I stayed in Carter's and my apartment while she crashed an FBI raid. That's it. I was a glorified mailman."

James trailed the toes of his shoes through the dust and straw on the floor. "Why were you so different when you got home?"

It was a fair question. I'd been withdrawn but functional between Carter's death and the rest of the Landlows'. After NYC I'd been a grief-stricken shell. "Because . . . the trip made it *real*. When I was here, I could pretend he was still alive—but being *there . . .*" I shook my head, remembering how my self-deception had crumbled like a sandcastle. I'd crumbled with it.

And there was the letter Carter had left for me with his sweatshirt. All the words in it that made me realize how little attention I'd been paying to the subtext of his rambling conversations about Dead Meat. I was too busy counting down the surgeries in our deal to realize how much it was straining his moral compass, or consider how dangerous his questions would seem to those determined to make the rogue clinic prosper.

I miss you. I need you. I love you.

I failed you.

I'd failed James too—betrayed him badly with my lies and casually trashed his reputation because having a guard was inconvenient.

"I'm sorry." I forced myself to make and maintain eye contact. "I really mean that—I shouldn't have sabotaged you and your job. And when it all came out, I should've taken the blame instead of letting everyone skewer you."

"Maggie, it's . . . well, it's not *okay*, but I appreciate your apology."

"This Family has not been kind to our friendship."

"It hasn't been kind to a lot of things. It's not exactly gentle. It steamrolls."

I frowned. "But we save lives."

"And destroy them. Sometimes if feels like a one-to-one ratio." He was pulling pieces of straw out of his bale, folding them between long, thin fingers.

"Oh." I didn't want to hear this. I didn't want to go down the path of the Families' casualties, because that route led to Carter and led to me wanting to hide. I'd just found momentum—but it would be so easy to fall back into inertia.

"We're solid, Maggie. Don't stress it." James flicked a piece of straw at me. "I'm gonna head out and get some sleep."

"'Night, James."

"'Night."

We traded smiles with these farewells—and they were the first in such a long time that didn't feel burdened with baggage or agendas.

Maybe power, competition, and rivalry had corrupted and corroded our friendship. And maybe he was right about the Family destroying things. But maybe it was up to our generation to repair them.

Maybe someday, if luck fell squarely on our side, I'd lead the Family. James would succeed in his father's footsteps as my second-in-command, and Loops would be head doctor at this clinic. I realized with a pang there wasn't a role for Alex in this idealized future. Because if everything went according to plan, the guy who'd taken me to school at *Quiz Show* earlier today, grinning when his lead stretched to four figures and laughing when I tilted the computer screen away from him to give myself an advantage, would be off living his own life somewhere far away from here.

CHAPTER 24

Playing double agent for one kidney shouldn't have been so exhausting. But it was. It meant avoiding Brooks's and Byrd's eyes in meetings. It meant sitting on my hands while Daddy explained what the Organ Act timeline might look like— using legalization of marijuana in Colorado or the reopening of bars after Prohibition as incredibly shaky models. And since no one expected me to sit quietly, it meant getting fiery in defense of positions I didn't believe.

But not *too* fiery—because when we took a break for lunch, Byrd sought me out. "I'm still looking for a match for that boy, right? You haven't changed your mind?"

"Of course not," I answered. "Look fast."

"Then that whole speech was decoy?" He whistled. "I'm not sure whether to be impressed or intimidated."

I smiled and excused myself. I'd done enough Business for the day; it was time to go find Alex. He was training with Dr. Ackerman on how to run his own dialysis. A skill that would soon be unnecessary, but it kept him busy while I was in meetings and kept him away from conversations I didn't want him over-hearing—the ones about the Family's transplant freeze, *and* the ones about "Then why is that dang boy still here?"

"Maggie Grace, I need a minute." Mama stopped us on the way back in from the clinic.

I looked at Alex.

"Go on," he said. "I need to change shirts—I got blood on my sleeve." Which explained why he'd been walking with one hand awkwardly clasped around his other arm—covering the spot so I wouldn't see.

"Meet back here?" After he'd nodded, I turned to Mama.

"Bless his little heart, I think the soap and shampoo are working."

"What?" I asked.

"I stocked the guest room bath with spa-quality acne wash, lotion, and clarifying shampoo, and they're making a difference. His face looks clearer, his hair has body, and I don't feel like his dry skin is going to shed all over the furniture anymore. You haven't noticed?"

I hadn't. But then again, I hadn't noticed I'd stopped noticing his skin or hair or any other piece of him I'd once criticized. Now I watched to see if his smiles reached his eyes or stayed only on his lips. If he was hiding behind his hair or meeting my gaze. If he looked tired and was too stubborn to admit he was overdoing it.

"I wouldn't have guessed it, but he's practically handsome. Don't you think?" It wasn't really a compliment for *him*; it was Mama discounting the effects of medical treatment and nutrition and congratulating herself on a successful makeover. "Now, if only he'd cut that long hair."

"Yeah, he looks great. I guess. I don't care."

"Yes, you do."

"Excuse me?" I squinted at her. "I have no idea what you're talking about."

"You weren't always so blind, Magnolia."

"And Carter wasn't always so dead. Play matchmaker with someone else, Mama. My love life—or lack of—is off-limits. Now, did you need something?"

"Just to tell you I'm glad you and your daddy are agreeing and that this act looks like it'll pass."

I raised my eyebrows. "Are you talking *Business*? Should I alert the media?"

"Magnolia Grace, be still! I know you had your reservations, but this is a *good* thing. I've spent my whole life worrying your daddy would end up incarcerated. That *you* would call to tell me you'd been arrested. If this Organ Act ends that danger, then I'm all for it."

"Well, Mama, I could still end up calling you for bail money. There are plenty of other illegal things that might be fun to do." I tilted my head and sassed, but my stomach was tight with guilt. I hadn't known that this was something she worried about. I'd assumed her Business ignorance was *real*, not pretense.

She gave an exasperated sigh. "One of these days I'm going to lock you in your room and throw away the key."

"Then it's a good thing I figured out how to climb out my window when I was nine."

She laughed. "Run along, dear changeling girl—because you can't possibly be *my* daughter. Alex is waiting. Just, please, *try* and keep out of trouble."

"Yes, ma'am." I dropped an impish curtsy, then just before I twirled past her to where he was coming down the stairs, I added, "Please don't worry, Mama."

She touched my cheek and smiled wistfully. "Sweetheart, that's my job."

CHAPTER 25

"You okay?" Alex was pinching the bridge of his nose, shutting his eyes. It'd been several minutes since he looked at the laptop resting on the bed between us. "Should I call Dr. Ackerman? Did something go wrong?"

None of the alarms on the machine were chiming, but he'd set it up by himself today—under Dr. Ackerman's supervision. There had been high fives and proud smiles when I arrived forty minutes ago, but that smile had been absent for at least twenty. Replaced by a hard set to his jaw and sharp breaths.

"Headache. I get bad ones while dialyzing."

"Can I get you anything?" I turned down the volume on the laptop and dimmed the lights.

He shook his head. Then winced and inhaled sharply.

I reached over and squeezed his hand.

His head jerked up and he stared wide-eyed at me, then our hands, then me. And I was suddenly so aware of our ten fingers, everywhere they touched, the way mine were now sweaty— the way he would interpret this.

"This isn't flirting," I said. "It's friendship." Even that felt like a milestone I hadn't known I'd reached.

"In the best-case scenario, wouldn't it be both?" he asked with a soft smile.

I pulled my hand back, crossed my arms, and stared at the computer screen. He didn't say anything, but he didn't look away either. I flushed under his scrutiny. My one hand felt different than the other—sensitized. I was tempted to wipe it on the comforter, but I just gripped my shirtsleeve more tightly and told myself the reason I wasn't marching out the door was because I should be here in case something happened. Medically. In case something happened medically.

His stare abruptly changed to a wince, a groan. And when he tipped his head back against the pillows and grimaced, my hand returned to his without my permission.

I fit my fingers in the spaces between his. He didn't open his eyes or speak, but he lifted our hands to his thigh and squeezed mine tight.

I let the computer auto play through three more episodes of the spaceish-sciencey show he'd chosen. I had the volume down so low I couldn't hear any of the dialogue and had no idea what was happening. But I knew every time Alex held his breath, sighed, or winced. I knew when his fingers tightened against mine, and when they unclenched with relieved exhales.

I kept waiting for the moment when I'd get restless. When I'd have the urge to yank my hand back and get out of this room—but I felt useful. Peaceful.

And I *didn't* notice the moment his fingers went slack against mine—because I fell asleep first.

When the machine alarm went off at the end of his cycle, we both jumped, then traded sheepish, sleepy grins. I unlinked our fingers, stretched my arms up. He dropped his hand to my far shoulder and tugged me back against him.

"Thanks," he whispered against my hair. And, pulse racing in twelve types of panic, I nodded, shrugged out of the hug, and practically threw myself backward off the bed.

"I'll go get Dr. Ackerman. He needs to supervise this next part, right?"

I didn't wait for his answer.

I didn't walk.

I fled.

When Penny's ringtone blared through the dull monotony of after-dinner conversation, I excused myself and slipped out to the patio. "Hello?"

"Did you ever read *The Secret Garden*?"

"Do you ever start conversations at the beginning? Like, with a greeting and some context?"

"No, not really. I think it's all those years of trying to make sure I got whatever answer I needed before whoever I was talking to rushed off to their big, important meetings.

I used to wait outside Father's office to ambush him. Sorry. Is it annoying?"

"Nope. Endearing." And easy to picture. A pale girl with Carter's eyes and blond hair sitting outside her daddy's office, hoping someone would have time for her. The way his Family overlooked and underestimated Penny had infuriated him. "But *hello*. How are you?"

"Fine. And hi, and I hope you're well too. But have you read *The Secret Garden*?"

"I may have seen the movie? Why? Homework? I bet my mama—"

"No. Not homework. It's just . . . the book's about this girl who's sent to live with relatives after her parents die, and I don't know . . . with Thanksgiving coming up, I—I just relate to how cranky and homesick she feels." Her voice broke and so did my heart.

"Want to come here?"

"Thanks. It's not that I *don't* feel welcome here. I do. It's just . . . I want to go *home*. Except, not really. I don't *ever* want to go there again. Miles Banks took care of getting my things shipped to me—but he couldn't find Rumpel—that was my teddy bear—Rumpelstiltskin. And sometimes when I can't sleep, I lie there thinking he's all alone in that house."

I shut my eyes like I could block out her words. I had the same struggle with the apartment. How could I go back there? But how could I let it go?

"And apparently there was an attempted looting a few days ago."

"What?"

"They barely got in the clinic before the alarms and police chased them off. Bob says they were probably looking for narcotics. It feels like such a violation . . . another one. That was my *home*."

"I know, darlin', I'm so sorry."

"And Thanksgiving's going to be my first holiday away and without them. All these firsts are going to hurt, aren't they?"

"Yes." Sugarcoating or lying wouldn't make it less true or painful. "I keep thinking tomorrow will be easier than yesterday . . . but it's not really linear like that, is it?"

"No. And when I do have a good day—and realize I'm having a good day—I end up feeling guilty about it. Which is *stupid* because none of them would want me to be miserable. But they're having *duck*, Maggie. Duck. And shouldn't the vice president, of all people, be having turkey? And I want Mother's holiday silver, I want her mother's apple-cranberry relish. And I don't know the recipe."

She was crying. I could tell from soft pauses and gentle sniffles. When I cried, I sobbed and honked, but even Penny's tears sounded tentative and fragile. "I want Carter to get yelled at for checking football scores at the table, and Father to threaten to take his phone—wait . . ." She sniffed a few times and took a wavering breath. "It was you, wasn't it? Not football. Or fantasy baseball. Or the weather, or whatever excuse he gave. *You* were the reason he was always on his phone—even during Thanksgiving."

"Yeah." My voice was thick with the memories she'd stirred up. Carter had talked about that relish. About getting yelled at for texting at the table—that his mama had gone so far as to make a no electronics rule because of it. And if my secondhand memories of their lost holidays were painful, I couldn't imagine what Pen was going through. But some selfish sliver of me felt validated that she'd figured out a way to include me in her holiday narrative—connect me to him. "If you want to come here, say the word. If you need me there, I'll get on a plane. If you want us both to meet somewhere—then we can do that too. I hear November is lovely in Vegas."

She laughed. It sounded soggy but sincere, and her voice was brighter when she said, "Thanks, Maggie. Have you given any more thought to your question from the other day? About the Organ Act?"

I snorted. "I think it's safe to say I have done little *but* think about it."

"There's another reason I support it," she said softly. "It's a selfish one, but . . . if our Families weren't running a black market, *my* family wouldn't have been killed."

I didn't know how to begin to scrape together a response to that.

"There are *lots* of casualties in this industry, Maggie. I'm just trying to figure out how we can effect the greatest good."

"Me too," I said. "I really am."

CHAPTER 26

Alex was on the phone when I opened his door. I mouthed "no rush" in response to the finger he held up, then stood by the bed and clicked curiously through the lecture notes on his laptop screen, snorting at my inability to understand them *or* his Spanish conversation.

When he hung up I asked, "How's Max?" He and his brother talked daily.

"My dad, actually."

And though his lack of elaboration should've been a hint, I pushed on. "Do you miss your parents?"

He shrugged. "I do, but . . . it's easier being here. I mean, your men are pretty intense—but there's nothing emotional about their scrutiny. It's hard at home. My parents care, but they're . . . detached. They watch everything I do, but if I eat bananas or avocado or come home with fast food, they won't say anything about the potassium or sodium. They're resigned to the inevitable and waiting for it to happen."

He sighed and stretched out his legs. "It's like the world's longest good-bye. They've been pulling away since the day I was rejected from the list. I think they have to. They already did this once with my sister, Gabriela. Burying her . . ." He shook his head.

I was scared to move and break the fragile strength of his honesty, scared to open my mouth—because who knows what I'd blurt out. Kindness and impulsivity rarely coexisted on my tongue.

Alex lifted his eyes and met mine. "I can't do that to them, make them go through that again. That's why I blackmailed you."

I was cursing the heck out of my tear ducts, the attorney general, and Byrd's lack of speed. We needed to save this boy and reunite him with parents who then wouldn't be scared to love him.

Alex snorted. I sniffled and demanded, "What could you possibly find funny right now?"

"Just that my two real rebellions—one got me kicked off the transplant list, and the other one . . . well, it got me here."

"You better stop while you're ahead," I said. "But *why* drag racing in the first place? It's so un . . . *you.*"

He laughed. "That was the point. My nephrologist told me I'd need to start dialysis, that it was time to apply for the government list, and all I could think was that my future was *this.*"

He gestured to his tubing and the machine beside his bed. I winced. "That I might die and I hadn't done anything that felt like living. They called to schedule the surgery to build my fistula, and I just lost it. I knew where some kids raced. I stole my brother's car keys. I talked my way in. One cop, one Class B misdemeanor, and I got a letter saying that because I showed 'reckless disregard for my life and personal safety,' I wasn't a candidate for a transplant."

"They can really reject someone for that?"

"There are all sorts of crappy, flimsy excuses they use to reject people. They don't even have to disclose the reason."

I absorbed this fact carefully. I'd assumed the people who weren't on the government list didn't *deserve* to be there. But what defined undeserving? A violent criminal past? A history of disregarding doctors' directions? Age? I shook my head, not wanting even the imaginary responsibility of choosing who was worthy of a chance at life.

Alex was studying me, one eyebrow up, his mouth pursed like he'd heard some private punch line. "I can practically smell your brain cells melting."

I pulled on a smile. "How's this for lighthearted? I had two men offer to cover for me to watch you, but I wouldn't be persuaded. Not even with talk of budget reports, and I love budget reports." Which was all one hundred percent true, and since that was rare lately, I was ready to revel in it. I grinned as I kicked off my heels and finally bounced onto the bed beside him. "I picked blood over budgets—you should be feeling mighty special right 'bout now."

He pressed his lips together like he was fighting a grin, and his cheeks went red all the way to the tips of his ears. "Thanks?"

"You're welcome." Granted, the offers had been, "You hate that boy and I hate budgets, let's switch," and "It's not right sticking you with him all the time—you stay, I'll go take a turn watching the bastard." But he didn't need to know that. He definitely didn't need to know I hadn't defended him because it would be suspicious. And suspicion might lead to questions, which might lead to everything unraveling.

My smile had flipped back to fake. I compensated by forcing more cheeriness into my voice. "I think my budget report sacrifice should be honored by letting me choose today's entertainment, so hand over the laptop."

"It's taking this long because he knows I want six matching HLAs, right?" I was pacing the length of the hayloft, ducking the eaves and kicking loose straw out of my way. It stirred up dust, and I sneezed three times before I could continue. "Bless me. Your dad must be going for six out of six."

James was sitting on the edge of the loft, dangling his legs by the ladder. He echoed my "Bless you," but didn't answer my question.

During dinner the vice president had called Daddy personally to share that the Organ Act had passed in the House of Representatives. It was a vote we'd expected to occur almost six months ago, but then Carter had happened, and Mr. and Mrs.

Landlow, and then everything Zhu and Ward. I'd gotten used to the delays and foot dragging. I had gotten used to *soon*—I wasn't prepared for now.

Yet I'd had to cheer when Daddy dragged me from the table to his office and put the vice president on speakerphone. I'd had to sit calmly and smile as they talked about which Senate committee would be assigned oversight. Meanwhile I was googling on my phone and wishing I'd paid more attention in school when we studied how the U.S. government worked.

"Hopefully you and the Speaker will be signing that sumbitch and delivering it to President Martorano quicker than a hiccup," Daddy had drawled, his Texan coming out stronger 'cause he was so worked up.

"One can hope," said Vice President Forman. "I'll keep you posted."

Hoping was about all I could do right now. No, that wasn't quite true. Since James was too busy dissecting a piece of hay to answer, I could continue thinking out loud.

"Maybe time's more important than a hundred percent match. Five out of six, that's"—I did a quick estimate—"about eighty percent. Would you be happy with a B-minus kidney? Maybe we'd better wait for six."

"You're fixating again."

"I'm what?"

"Fixating." He folded his hands behind his head and lay back, looking at me upside down. "You fixate. You mono-focus on one goal and don't see the bigger picture. Call it stubborn, or pigheaded, or mulish, or obstinate, or whatever you want. I call a spade a spade; you fixate."

I scowled. "Who died and named you psych major?"

His laughter rang off the rafters, startling a few of the horses below so they moved restlessly in their stalls. "Maggie, I *am* a psych major."

"Wait." I dropped beside him and stared, trying to decide if he was messing with me. "You are? I assumed you were something business."

He shook his head. "Your dad made it clear my schooling was purely decorative. Something like, 'I don't care if you major in interpretive dance, so long as you keep Maggie Grace out of trouble.'"

"And you picked psychology." I mulled this over. "Well, two and a quarter semesters hardly gives you enough expertise to diagnose me. I don't fixate."

"Oh, but you do." He laughed and swung himself onto the ladder. Once his shoes hit the floor he called up, "Guarantee you'll fixate on this all night long. Have fun."

CHAPTER 27

I cursed James and his game of amateur psychologist as I frowned at my ceiling, my walls, my pillowcase. No matter how I tossed and turned, I couldn't stop thinking that this whole process was taking too long.

And when I finally fell asleep, I woke to a knocking on my door. My sweaty sheets told me I'd had nightmares. My clock told me I'd overslept. It was well past the time Mama and Daddy left for church.

My pajamas weren't indecent, but that didn't make it any less awkward to open the door and face Alex while I was in Longhorns sleep shorts and an I♥NY tank, and he was dressed in a pressed shirt and neat jeans.

"Um, hi," I mumbled, all too aware I had bed head and morning breath.

He looked equally uncomfortable. "Sorry to wake you."

"It's fine." I stretched and attempted to finger-comb my hair. "What's up?"

"There was another attempt at Port 80 from an IP address in the range I flagged."

"Blast it!" My hand snagged in tangles that only added to my frustration.

"We need to tell someone there's a person or people trying to infiltrate your network."

"But they're not succeeding?"

"No. But they might eventually, and I don't want that on my conscience."

"What if I volunteer to have it on mine?" I joked.

He didn't smile. "Your Family is *saving my life.* I can't repay that by—"

"Fine." His gratitude was one more piece of shrapnel in my sanity. "We'll call Theo—but I definitely need coffee before that. He's in my contacts. Want to get started with the technical stuff and I'll be back in two minutes to deal with strategy?"

"Sounds good. Thanks." He took my phone and was dialing before I'd even left the room, which made my stomach prickle. If Alex was *this* worried, maybe I should be too.

When I came back up with a mug of coffee and a plate of Anna's honey-drenched sopaipillas, Alex was off the phone and pacing my room. "Theo didn't answer?"

"No, he did. But he thinks it's no big deal. He said, 'You're creating a conspiracy to make yourself look important.'" Alex stopped pacing. "I swear I'm not."

"He said *what?* Give me that. I'm going to—"

"Maggie, don't." Alex held the phone away from me. "Hear me out, okay?"

I nodded, and he put my cell in my hand, then curled his fingers around both. I froze. Stared at the combinations of our skin tones and the rhinestone phone case. My cheeks were hot, but my fingers felt hotter, like those few square centimeters of shared skin were combustible. He rubbed his thumb across the back of my palm, and I stiffened.

"I gave him all the facts. I forwarded him the alert. Your calling right now won't help. He needs to take a minute and accept I caught this and he didn't, that his system's not infallible."

My instincts were to be all ruffled feathers and reactionary alpha dog, but everything Alex said made sense. "Theo is ninety-five percent ego—I guess this would be hard for him."

"So eat your breakfast. I'm going to spend some time in the chapel, and if Theo hasn't called by lunch, let's talk to your dad."

"We'll tell him at supper," I countered, needing control over *some* part of this situation.

"Okay." He squeezed my hand and gave me a small, hopeful smile as he walked out of my room, leaving me alone with my breakfast and a new problem to contain.

None of it lasted long, though—not my coffee, my sopaipillas, or my solitude. Twenty minutes later, I'd just finished getting dressed when Daddy banged on my door.

"What kind of ruckus are you letting Alex stir up? Where is he?"

"The chapel. And ruckus?"

"Theo called me all disgruntled. Said the boy's telling tales about security breaches."

"They're not tales, Daddy. Theo's just not smart."

"Did Alex say someone hacked our system?"

"No, he said someone's *trying to*. They're not succeeding because of him. It's the same people as the virus."

"That was *spam*, Maggie. Theo assures me our network's secure." He sat down on my vanity. "Look, I was coming to talk to you about him anyway, but this makes my point more pressing—Alex's clearly trying to create new reasons he's needed here. He's got to suspect . . . It's time you and I figured out an endgame for this boy. He's divisive enough without inciting panic about fake hackers."

"They're not fake." Fear was hardening my breakfast into nauseating lumps. I'd underestimated Theo's ego and had inadvertently given him time to go on the offensive.

Daddy ignored me. "With the Organ Act already through the House of Representatives, we'll soon be going public with our support. We need to start closing our fence gaps, and he's a pretty big one. Any ideas on what we should do?"

"Give him a transplant." I lifted my chin and tucked my shoulders back until the blades touched.

"We've discarded that plan. Be reasonable and consider other options. Now, there's hospice care, but the boy doesn't look near ready to hear that suggestion."

"What's plan C?" Because I'd voluntarily work in a blood bank before I'd go to Alex and say the word "hospice."

"Plan C's your job, sport. If you don't like my idea, come up with your own."

"I need—I need some time." My voice wavered, and Daddy studied me. I had to look nonchalant, like this was a point of ego and not emotion, but man was it hard to meet his eyes and steady my voice. "You assigned me this task, and I want to do it right. I need time to come up with an acceptable option C. Who knows, maybe Alex overlooked some relative who'd be an altruistic donor match."

"Unfortunately, we don't have much time. Things are tense enough within the Family right now, and he only causes more controversy. Last night one of the men offered to 'fix the Alex problem' for me and another was right behind him, volunteering to 'punish the boy' when I'm done punishing you by having him here."

"What?" I gasped.

"I told them to stand down and calm down—but emotions are high, and he's an easy target for their frustrations. He's got to go." Daddy shook his head. "Tell you what, take today and do some thinking. Ask him some questions— maybe he'd like to be relocated somewhere else, or wants us to do right by his parents, or has some goal he wants to achieve."

"MIT," I said.

"The school?" Daddy chuckled. "Their admissions office might be a little outside our reach, but if he can get himself in, we could do tuition and medical costs for as long as he's capable of attending."

I wanted to respond, "So, through his PhD? *Three* PhDs? Five? A lifetime's worth?" because I wasn't ready to accept anything less. And as long as Byrd did his job and the doctors did theirs, I wouldn't have to.

"Tomorrow, sport, you and I will sit down and hash this out. I'd like to be moving forward with a plan within the next forty-eight. Understood?"

"Perfectly." I understood Theo needed his butt kicked and Byrd needed to get his in gear.

As Daddy walked away, my fingers were already typing frantic texts.

Byrd called back within a minute, but before I could start hollering, he silenced me with four words.

"I've got a match."

CHAPTER 28

My conversation with Byrd consisted of a whole lot of me: "Can you say that again?" and him: "Maggie girl, are you listening?"

I was trying, but I was also floating somewhere above the stratosphere.

"Repeat this back to me," Byrd said. "When I call you this afternoon to let you know I'm done meeting with the donor, you'll get your boy to the Abilene clinic for a crossmatch blood test."

"You'll call. We'll come. Got it." I did a little dance in the hallway. "Thank you, Byrd. I knew you could do it!"

"It's not *done* yet. This is just the start—but it's a dang promising one."

"One more question: is it a six-out-of-six match?"

He laughed. "How'd I know you were gonna ask? It's a stop-whining, eat-your-peas-and-like-'em scenario. I promise you Alex won't be complaining."

No, he wouldn't. And I couldn't wait to tell him. I grabbed keys, ran for a truck, then floored it to the chapel.

I beeped when I pulled up, which, on second thought, probably wasn't the most respectful way to interrupt his prayers. But I was betting he'd forgive me.

I popped my door and stood on the running board, smiling across the roof of the truck at the boy coming out of the chapel and blinking his tortoiseshell eyes at the sunshine. "Hey there."

"Things settled with Theo already?" Alex asked.

"No. But he and I have a call later." Theo just didn't know about it yet. I'd give him two choices: fess up or get out. There was no room in the Family for someone who prioritized ego over security.

"That's good." Alex studied my face. "Is that good?"

"Get in."

I drove us out to the creek. I didn't want him in the house— I didn't want him anywhere near anyone until I'd had time to strategize with Brooks and James about how we'd keep him secure and safe until the transplant was completed.

When I parked the truck, I didn't turn it off. Alex looked from the keys dangling in the ignition to my face. "Are we getting out?"

"In a minute." I'd played with a hundred ways to tell him, because how often did people get this sort of news? I wanted to do it right. I wanted it to be a memory that would make him smile long after I was just a memory to him. My stomach soured at the thought, but I forced myself to focus.

"I still think MIT's dull as a penny dropped in mud, but you might want to start working on your application."

"I impressed you that much with my *Quiz Show* dominance? Yeah, baby got brains."

"You did *not* just refer to yourself as 'baby.'" I snorted and rolled my eyes.

"Don't hate the playah. Anytime you want a rematch, you know where I hang."

I could laugh at Alex trying to sound gangster all day, but . . . "Funny you should say *match*— "His eyes went wide as mine went wet. "Because we think we found you one. And I'll do as many *Quiz Show* competitions as you want while you're recov—"

The word was choked off when his shoulder hit mine as he dove across the console to hug me. "Gracias. Muchas gracias. Muchísimas gracias."

Before I could respond, he got out of the car, leaving behind an afterglow of body heat.

I watched through the windshield as he planted his feet wide, threw back his head, and whooped in that deep voice of his that hit low in my belly. He grabbed a handful of rocks and skipped them in rapid-fire succession. Then he turned back to the truck with a look of pure wonder on his face, shining wet in those amazing eyes. "Get your tail out here and celebrate with me."

I'd been waiting for an invitation. I'd fully absorbed how precious and rare this moment was—and hadn't wanted to intrude. Even watching his raw demonstration of joy and relief had made me wonder if I should shut my eyes and give him privacy. Except I couldn't turn away. Couldn't stop my eyes from filling or make my mouth relax out of a megawatt smile.

This was what my Family did. Had done for forty-odd years. Alex opened my door, and when I still didn't react, he reached across and unbuckled my seat belt. The brush of his hot skin against the inside of my arm made me jump.

"Come on!" he said. "¡Vámonos!"

How many Family members had gotten to see this? This moment when a patient has been given back his future? How many of them got to dance along a creek bank with a guy whose grin looked like he'd swallowed the moon and who sang in Spanish as he twirled in dizzying, giddy circles? Got to lie side by side on the dust and the rocks, shoes off, feet soaking in the cool water as he whispered deep-toned prayers of thanks up through the clouds in a perfect blue sky to the God beyond?

If I lived to be a hundred, I didn't know that any privilege could compare to this.

I'd wasted lots of time seeing patients as profits, not people. I'd missed out on lots of histories, lots of victories. Though, as much I regretted all I'd done wrong, there was something profoundly *right* about this boy being the one to teach me this lesson.

When Alex fell silent, I pressed up on an elbow and looked down at him. He was grin and glow, his eyes shining with all the emotions and colors of seafoam mixed with sand. I had the urge to hug him, to press my face against his chest or in the crook of his neck—have him wrap his arms around me and cocoon me in this mood, which felt so foreign and addictive. So far from hackers and Family members' threats and Daddy's ultimatums.

Instead I tightened my fingers around a river-smooth stone. "You ready for some procedural information?" I hated asking. It felt like I'd just given him a cactus and told him to cuddle. "I don't mean to—I just . . . We have to be ready."

"Yeah." He sat up, his hands folded in his lap. "Of course. Go."

"We need to tell James and Brooks. They'll be accompanying us to get the crossmatch blood test."

"They don't know?"

This is when I started lying. The idea sat uneasily in my stomach, like I was about to serve something putrid at what had been a holy feast.

"I wanted to tell you first. So far, only Byrd, Ackerman, and the doctor at the Abilene clinic know. James and Brooks will need to because they're coming with us—but for now, we'll limit the knowledge to the seven of us."

"Is it always so secret?" he asked. "Is it a security thing?"

"Not security. Just superstition." I forced the slimy lies off my tongue. "Until your new kidney is out of the donor and into you, the less people who know, the less chance we jinx ourselves. Even my daddy always says he doesn't want to hear anything till the sutures are tied."

Alex swallowed. "Do lots of transplants not work out?"

"No." Panic had started to creep across his features, but I beat it back with my word. "No, Alex, no. Especially not after the donors see the money and meet the recipient—you'll meet today when we do the crossmatch."

"I will? Wow." He shook his head, a dazed, openmouthed grin on his lips. "You know how there's that stereotype of little girls growing up and imagining their wedding and their prince, or whatever?"

"That wasn't *me*, but I know what you mean."

"Yeah, I wouldn't think so—you waiting around for a prince to come?" He laughed. "No way. You'd be the one out slaying the dragon. But, anyway, that *someday* imagining? That's how I've always been about my donor. Wondering what he or she would look like. Why they'd donate their kidney. How old they'd be. All those things."

"It's a guy."

"I can't believe I'll meet him today." He shook his head, whistled low, and stared up at the sky with starstruck eyes. "Today."

"Yeah," I agreed, then repeated my message in case his feverishly excited brain had been too busy to process it the first time. "But we don't tell anyone until it's done."

"Got it. 'Not till the sutures are tied.'" He repeated the motto I'd made up with such solemnity I had to look away. "Does that mean my family too? Max can keep a secret."

"I'm sorry," I whispered toward the creek.

"I'm not complaining. Okay, not much. I'm going to be choking on this news with no one to tell. It doesn't feel real. But I get it."

"Tell James then." I held out my phone. "I know it's not the same, but . . . want to?"

Alex snatched it from my hand. "Hells yeah."

I could hear James's exultant cry from several feet away. The exuberance of their conversation, proof of their friendship, made me grin. Just before I started to feel left out, Alex hung up. "He said to stay where we are. He'll be right out."

Alex was telling me all the things he'd want to do posttransplant when James's truck rumbled across the dry ground. He'd brought provisions and parroted my mama's comments: "A picnic? How nice. Do you have sunblock? Magnolia Grace gets shamefully freckled; see if you can wrestle her into the shade."

I liked that he was there to celebrate too. To join in when we toasted with glasses of sparkling lemonade. Alex's small, careful sips were the only indication he wasn't getting too far ahead of himself. I was already dreaming of the day when he could chug a whole bottle without thinking of fluid-intake restrictions.

And maybe he was thinking the same thing as he drew a smile in the condensation on the bottle. But those dots and that curved line had nothing on the grin stretched across his face.

Stomachs full, we spread out on the blanket James brought. On my right, Alex staring at the sky. On my left, James lay on his belly watching the sluggish drift of the creek. Midafternoon sunshine fought its way through the tree branches to paint us all with glowing polka dots.

"I could take a nap right here," James mumbled.

Alex grunted his agreement, and I sat up—looked at the time on my phone. I wasn't fretting. Not really. But Byrd had called me before eleven. How long did a donor meet-and-greet last?

Alex tapped my knee with a cluster of blue mistflowers and smiled lazily up at me. "If I doze, will you wake me when it's time to go?"

"We certainly can't go without you. *I'm* not supplying the blood sample."

James laughed. "Not unless it's in the form of a head wound from when you pass out cold."

"Hey, I'm getting better about blood." James's grin stretched as he looked past me. I turned to catch Alex shaking his head and mouthing, "No, she's not."

I stole the flower from his hand and whacked him on the nose before tucking it behind my ear. "Take your nap, sleeping beauty. James can play sentry. I'll head back to the house and get security set for our drive."

"Brooks?" James asked, and I nodded as I climbed into the truck and started the ignition.

I waved out the window to the two guys tossing pebbles in the water. I needed an excuse to tell Daddy that would get Alex and me off the property. Or maybe I wouldn't tell him?

Carter had always been big on "ask forgiveness, not permission." And these days forgiveness was more than I could hope for.

CHAPTER 29

All thoughts of escaping under the radar evaporated when I walked in the front door and conversation stopped. There were a half dozen men standing around the suddenly silent foyer, and none of them were smiling.

"She's here, Holt," Manuel called into Daddy's office.

He stormed out. "Where in tarnation have you been?"

"I—a picnic. Mama knew."

"A picnic?" He hadn't lowered his voice or softened the scorn. He snagged the flower from my hair and dropped it to the floor. "You've been off having a picnic?"

"If you needed me, you should've called. Why? What's happened? Is it the hackers? I told you he wasn't making it up."

Daddy grabbed my arm and pulled me into his office, slamming the door behind us. "Do you know what you've done?"

I shook my head, stunned by his anger. He gripped the back of my chair with white knuckles.

"Why don't you ever, ever listen to orders? Or think about consequences? This time, Magnolia Grace, you've—" He pushed the chair over. It fell with a thud that echoed on the floor, and a crack as one of the arms splintered off.

I cowered from my daddy, who'd never so much as spanked me or slapped my hand. "What—what I—" All the buoyancy of the morning felt like a cruel joke as I tried to find the questions I knew were going to hurt.

"Byrd got his fool self arrested this afternoon. Because, despite my orders that transplants were to stop immediately, he was out interviewing a kidney donor."

"No. Oh no." I lifted a shaking hand to my mouth.

"Damnation and hellfires! I don't know how I'm going to get him out of this. I don't know how I'm going to get *the Family* out of this. The ink on the agreement isn't even dried."

He kept ranting, and I shook my head, nodded, tilted my hands, then shrugged. A confused array of gestures that matched the tangle of emotions and questions spinning inside me.

"This has your fingerprints on it, Magnolia."

I didn't answer. Couldn't answer, not with the weight of these consequences pressing against my windpipe.

"It was a setup. Start to finish. Wire taps, the whole deal. He's not walking away from this. And that's on your head."

"I—I—"

"Where's the boy?"

"Why?" I asked. "What are you going to do to him? He didn't know. He still thinks the Business is running the way it always did. He has no idea you—or that I—" My voice trembled into a hiccup.

Daddy stiffened at the sound. Lowered his head and closed his eyes when he saw the tears in mine. "Maggie Grace . . . darlin'." He sighed.

"I'm sorry. Tell me what to do to fix this," I begged, scrubbing the back of my wrist across my eyes.

"I wish it were that easy. We're in triage, sport. We've got to keep the men from seeking retribution against him. Keep Alex from talking to *anyone*. We need to get Byrd legal help, but we also need to make it clear to the Feds that he was acting alone. That the rest of us are unified in support of the Organ Act."

"Are we?" I hadn't meant to ask it aloud, but Daddy took it as a logistics question instead of self-reflective.

"We'd better be if we hope to weather this. So, where's the boy?"

"He's by the creek with James—" My stomach flipped, and every bite of that idyllic picnic revolted. I reached behind me, knocking over books and knickknacks as I tried to find something to lean on. "Oh God. James doesn't know. I've got to tell him."

Daddy's face looked ashy. "It might be best coming from you. I don't think I'm capable of telling him without calling Byrd the fool idiot he is."

I nodded. James deserved to hear this from me. He deserved the chance to flay me for it.

"I don't know how to trust you right now," Daddy said, and I flinched. "Go pick them up then. Get Alex to the clinic. I'll tell Ackerman to get him out of here. Keep him someplace until the dust settles."

I nodded and stared at my chair toppled and broken on the floor. What words could I possibly use to make this less painful for James? And Alex . . . I crossed my arms over my stomach because everything inside me was cramping and breaking.

"Go on, sport. We've got to get ahead of this before we get plowed under." Daddy kicked the arm of my chair as he marched across his office. He paused before he yanked the door open. "And I hope you're thinking about what you've done. I'm disappointed in you. Never thought there'd be a day when I'd say that."

I heard the words. Felt the burn of their meaning, but it was absorbed among all the other pain. I was swimming in a swarm of jellyfish—what was one more sting?

But worse than that, worse than the knowledge that this was a disaster of my own creation, was the awareness I wasn't the only casualty.

"I know, sir," I whispered. But Daddy was already gone. And when I exited his office I was confronted by stares of judgment from men I'd known my whole life.

"How could you, Maggie?" asked Enzo.

I paused at the front door and turned to face them before slipping back outside. "How could I *not*?"

CHAPTER 30

I parked the truck farther back from the creek, not wanting to step into the footprint of a time when we were so much happier and hopeful and unaware we'd already been thwarted and damned.

Alex was asleep on the blanket. I stared at him through the windshield for a long moment, soaking in the way he had thrown his arm across his face, the crook of his elbow resting above his nose. I'd failed him. I'd failed the other guy sitting on the blanket too, and the knowledge made it so hard to look at him.

James had a hand up in a wave. When I didn't wave back, he lowered it to shield his eyes, then stood and walked over. He yanked the passenger door open and climbed inside. "What's wrong?"

The news poured out of me in sobs and gulps, in a torrent of apologies and incoherent half thoughts. I didn't have much in the way of facts, but I had enough remorse to fill all sorts of gaps. James's leftover summer tan turned the gray color of overly milky coffee as the skin tightened around his mouth.

"Maggie. Maggie. *Maggie!*" He reached across the console, grabbed my arms, and shook me, but I couldn't stop blubbering.

"I just . . . I'm rotten. And I—I—I didn't mean—"

"Shh, Maggie." When I didn't, he put a hand over my mouth. "Will you shut up a minute and listen?"

My instinct was to bite him, but instead I nodded slowly.

"Okay." He moved his hand. "Sorry about that."

I didn't trust myself to open my mouth without unleashing another flood of apologies, so I nodded again.

"Can we sit quiet a minute so I can process? Do you want a tissue? I can get one from my truck. Or want a napkin? We've got those in the picnic basket."

I made a messy sob-laugh noise and sniffed. "You don't get to wait on me."

"Maggie, settle. It's not your fault."

"Cut the crap. It sure is!"

"He's had his job since before you were born—he knows the consequences of getting caught. You didn't make this industry illegal."

But I was fighting against legalizing it. Was that the same thing? "I shouldn't have asked him to go against Daddy. Your dad did this as a favor for me."

"And you did it for Alex." He tightened his hands into fists. "Am I supposed to be mad at you for wanting to save a guy's life? I like him. I want to save him too. Or should I be mad at my dad for doing his job? At the Family for being involved in the Business? Or the government for making this industry illegal in the first place? If that was a multiple-choice question, I think I'd choose the last one."

"What about *all of the above*? He wouldn't be in jail right now if he hadn't said yes to me."

"Say what you want, but I won't blame you."

"You should," I whispered.

"I think you should blame yourself a little less, Maggie." I looked away from the empathy in his eyes. Why did his kindness hurt more than hatred?

"I have to tell Alex." I leaned my head against the window. "But I can't tell him everything. Not about the deal, or that we can't help him—not good-bye. Just 'not today, not this donor.' And then I have to get him to Ackerman, so the doctor can shuffle him off somewhere to hide. I hate that this feels like we're playing a game of lives—his versus all the men I'll destroy if I keep pursuing this."

"Did I ever tell you I don't want to work for the Family?" he asked quietly.

"What?" I rubbed both hands on my face, smearing tears and snot. I turned to James and he grimaced, digging through my glove box and handing me a few crumpled fast-food napkins.

After I wiped my face and blew my nose he continued. "I don't know what I want to *do*, but I know what I want."

"What do you want?" I asked. There was a time when I would've followed up with 'I'll get it for you,' but my hubris lay buried in a graveyard in Upstate New York.

"Choices," he said.

"I don't understand." And I was so tired of not understanding. Even when I was following a clear path, it always headed in the wrong direction. I skipped toward trouble while others ran away . . . the others I didn't drag along on my road to self-destruction.

James drummed his fingers on the dashboard. "I know I have some choices. I could be a doctor *for the Family*. I could be an accountant *for the Family*. Or work on the ranch, or transplant coordination, or security. There are all sorts of Family jobs open to me. But those aren't real choices."

"Then choose not to work for us. People leave. Your sister left."

"Baby didn't have private school tuition. She didn't have a college education paid for by the Family. Or a car. Or all those things given to me over the years."

"There weren't strings attached to those. Or, if there were, you've already paid for them by putting up with *me*—because that's why Daddy bankrolled them."

"Maggie, maybe you don't see the strings, but they're there. They're getting braided into a tighter and tighter leash, and it's going to strangle me."

I stared at him. I'd thought *James* was the one with freedom. I was the one with guards to duck and evade. I was the one whose actions were watched and reported back to Daddy.

"When you left school, they sent movers to my dorm and handed me withdrawal forms to sign. They don't *need* me here, but it was my punishment for allowing you to falter." He shook his head. "My whole education was a convenient cover story so I could serve the Family by watching you—'interpretive dance,' remember?"

"I've spent my life shouting for Daddy's attention and approval and trying to force my way *into* the Family's inner circle. I don't know what I'm doing anymore." I reached over and grabbed James's hand. "But I promise you if you want out, I'll get you out. You don't owe the Family anything."

"It feels like I owe them *everything.*" He squeezed my hand. "I think it's time we talk to Alex."

I choked back a sob. Oh God, it had only been this morning that we'd been toasting and dancing. And now . . .

"It's not hopeless." I said the words for both our benefits. "Not yet. I'll call Mrs. Zhu. I'll look at foreign markets. I'll get tested myself and give him one of mine. I'm not giving up."

"Now there's the Maggie Grace I know." James got out of the truck. I swallowed and copied him, gritting my teeth as I walked to the groggy boy blinking up at me from the navy plaid blanket.

Alex rubbed his eyes and asked the same question James had, "What's wrong?" The languid sleepiness of his posture stiffened as he pushed himself upright.

I looked at my hands. Wondering what kind of coward I was that I couldn't meet his eyes or find the words. I knew he had to be thinking what he thought was the worst—but the reality was greater than his imagination.

"The donor chickened out," said James. "We're really sorry." He was shielding me from words I was too weak to say—but my debt to him was already a tsunami and these legs of mine needed to stand on their own. My hands needed to start doing good, and I needed to be brave enough to voice my own lies and face the consequences of my own failures.

Alex hadn't responded yet. I lifted my head and saw he'd taken a step backward. He was on the far side of the blanket. I kicked at it because I couldn't stand the visual mockery of it still spread out and separating us like a cruel joke where the punch line was our hope.

"Look, man," said James. "It sucks, but these things—"

"You can trust me." My voice was steady as I echoed the words I'd said to him that first night. And I meant them. Maybe not to tell him the whole truth, but he could trust me with his life. I was built of guilt and remorse, but it was being kiln-fired into resolve. "This is a setback, not a disaster."

I kicked more of the blanket out of the way as I walked to him.

His head was bowed and his hair swung forward, but I reached a hand out and tucked one side behind his ear, lifted his chin. "Trust me."

His lips were a line so flat and tight it felt impossible they'd ever stretched and beamed in a half-moon grin. His eyes were dull—dead eyes—maybe mine were contagious. And they wouldn't look at me. He left his chin up, but his gaze stayed on the dirt.

"I need to take you to the clinic," said James.

"Why?" His voice was as flat as his eyes. A roadkill voice stripped of emotion and inflection.

"Dr. Ackerman needs to do some test." James shifted his weight and palmed his keys.

"What test?"

I wanted to open my mouth and give him a proper good-bye. Give him a promise I'd find wherever they squirreled him away and not give up on getting him a kidney. Instead I offered more dishonesty. "The blood for the crossmatch. They're going to take a sample now and store it so they're ready for the next donor."

"They can do that?"

I'd seen the way his expression had shifted when I'd pushed the words "next donor" off my tongue. His smile tentatively reappeared, and my throat closed. All I could do was nod and lift a limp hand in farewell as Alex got in James's truck and they drove away.

I didn't want to go with them and see Alex learn about our betrayal. I didn't want to stay here, in the mocking remnants of our ruined celebration. I definitely didn't want to return to the house and face the judgment and questions waiting there.

But despite what James had said in his pep talk, this was my disaster, these were my consequences. I steered my truck toward the house.

CHAPTER 31

I faced a wall of blame and questions the moment I walked in the front door.

"You chose that boy over the Family?"

"You went behind our backs to plan this?"

"Everything you were saying in those meetings—was it all lies?"

I kept my chin up, made eye contact, and accepted their condemnation as I answered *yes* to each.

I had no doubt they'd have plenty to say later, but for now the men were speechless with disgust. The way Manuel glared made me grateful for the first time that I was a *girl* in the Family, because I had no doubt otherwise he'd have punched me. Instead he spat at my feet. He stomped out of the room and the others followed.

I stayed in the foyer in case they came back with more questions or accusations. I wouldn't run from this responsibility, even if it felt like a stoning from the people I'd spent a lifetime trying to impress.

Anna came out of the kitchen. "That's enough of that. This Family doesn't need you playing martyr. Now, what do you want for dinner?"

"What?" I laughed at the absurdity of having a preference or even an appetite.

"Something funny, sport?" asked Daddy from the doorway. "Because I'm failing to see any humor right now."

"No, sir."

He dismissed Anna and brought me out to the entertainment room. "I've told Ackerman and Brooks to take Alex to the hunting cabin for a while. He can't see the papers or the news, because Byrd'll be in both. Along with the amnesty deal we just violated. Not exactly how I wanted it announced."

I gritted my teeth and nodded, letting him rage on until he got to the words "major liability—if Alex got it in his head to go to the media—"

"He's a *person*, not a liability. And if he were to go to the media and tell them we promised him a kidney and then screwed him over, well, I'm not sure we don't deserve that. I'm sorry if saving his life is a speed bump in your plans, but come on, Daddy, how about some perspective?"

He blanched. "We'll do right by the boy in some way, Magnolia."

My hands were shaking so I folded them into fists. "Clearly my presence isn't welcome in the house right now, and I think you probably have more pressing work than standing here arguing with me, so maybe just go." I turned my back, shrugging off the hand he put on my shoulder. "Seriously, Daddy, *go.* If you stay, the conversation's not going to be civil."

"We'll talk later," he said.

I didn't reply. Just cursed and threw dart after dart as the door opened and closed and opened again.

There was a long whistle behind me. "Ladies and gentlemen, the girl's got a tongue in her head that would make the devil blush, but good thing she's pretty, because her dart skills . . . not so much."

I gave James a wilted smile and handed him my last dart. He winged it across the room and it stuck dead center.

He bowed low to an imaginary audience. "Thank you. Thank you." It was easy to see beyond his showboating and glimpse the motives beneath: He was trying to cheer me up. Trying to help us both forget.

"Want to stay here tonight?" I asked.

"Here? I'm not sure a pool table would be comfortable as a bed."

"I mean, at our place. In one of the guest rooms. You don't have to go home, if . . ."

"Naw. Hawk's driving in. I'll be fine. Unless . . . *you* scared? You want a sleepover?"

"No." I laughed. Oh, I was terrified of sleep, but no, that hadn't been why I was asking. "Manuel spit at me."

"What?" He dropped a dart.

"The men are pissed, James. They have every right to be. I used to know this Business so well, but God, everything is changing. You and Carter were my constants. He was my hero, and I was always so quick to make you the villain—and that was *wrong*, I'm not saying it wasn't—but it was how it was. And now I'm the villain, and I'm about to lose you too."

"I'm not going anywhere right now."

"Thank you."

If I were a hugger, I would have leaned my head on his chest. If he didn't know me as well as he did, he would've put a hand around my shoulders. Instead, we nodded at each other, and he set my half of the darts down on the bar in front of me. "Rematch?"

"How'd it go . . . with Alex?"

It was the first time I'd ever seen James wholly miss the board. "What I just did . . . It's gonna haunt me. I'm pretty much delivering him to be kidnapped, and he's talking about us saving his life, practically composing sonnets about you."

I winced.

"Ackerman's furious about being ordered to play kidnapper. I know we're painted in a corner, but—"

The door slammed open, and James and I jumped. Alex was standing on the threshold with a murderous expression.

"You weren't supposed to get me a kidney."

My tongue was tangled with shock and guilt. All I could manage was a shake of my head. Where were Brooks and Ackerman? Why was he here?

"Alex, it's a little more complicated than that," said James.

"Yeah, I heard. Dr. Ackerman followed up with 'But don't be too angry with Magnolia; she's still really heartbroken.' So, because the princesa had a breakup, we're all supposed to be okay with her lies? Even when she's playing with my *life*?" He whirled toward me. "You're about as selfish as they come—I'd imagine after enough time with you, any guy would be begging someone to kill him."

"Dude, no." James shook his head. His eyes looked huge as he stepped closer, but he knew better than to touch me. Not now. Not when I was gasping, trembling, hands hugged across my chest. *Any guy would be begging someone to kill him.*

"You can't say it's not true. How could *any* guy possibly like you? You take and you lie." His voice faltered. "You make them believe . . . and then you destroy. Did you ruin his life like you've ruined mine?"

"That's enough," said James. "You're out of line."

I'd bitten down on my knuckle, as if by putting something between my teeth, I could will myself not to vomit or cry or scream. I pulled it out and swallowed a shaky breath. "I am so sorry about what happened today. But you're wrong—use your whiz kid computer skills to google 'Carter Landlow.' Then tell me I'm not allowed to be broken up about losing the guy I've loved since I was twelve."

CHAPTER 32

I raced in the house and up the stairs to my room. Moving faster than I had since cross-country, but it wasn't fast enough. My eyes were brimming before I touched my doorknob. I told myself if I could get into Carter's sweatshirt, get in bed, then I'd be able to stop these tears from tumbling. I'd be able to re-center and focus and figure out . . . something.

My hands shook over zippers and clasps. I let the clothing fall to the floor and left it in small puddles on my rug as I slid gratefully into yoga pants and a tank top. Carter's sweatshirt.

But the trembling didn't stop. Not even after the bed curtains were closed, the only light filtering in from the open circle at the canopy's crown.

I was so aware of the sleeping pills in my bathroom cabinet. So aware and so haunted by that awareness. One or two wouldn't be bad—one or two might mean postponing this pain until the morning. But if I broke that plastic seal and shook out two pills, would I be satisfied leaving the rest in the bottle? The temptation horrified me—even as I rejected it and curled into a tighter ball.

There was a knock on my door. I ignored it. I counted in the silence and figured whoever had given up, but one hundred and eighty-three seconds later, there was another knock.

"Maggie, can I come in?"

I swallowed. If I said no, would Alex go away? Or would he knock in three-minute intervals all night? Where could he even go? The plan to put him in lockdown in the hunting cabin clearly wasn't happening, but was it safe for him out there or anywhere else on this property? And what had he been told? What questions did he have and reassurances did he need? I was probably the worst person to answer or give them, but who else would? I prayed to Someone I wasn't sure I believed in that James was heading home to deal with his own version of today's fallout.

"Fine," I said.

I heard the door open and shut. Could sense the way Alex's presence changed and charged the room. Could picture him hovering by my door looking awkward and uncomfortable.

"I can't come out," I said.

The tips of his fingers appeared on the edge of one of the bed curtains, but he hesitated a long moment before asking, "Then can I come in?"

"Okay."

Alex parted the curtains and took in the sight of me huddled against the headboard with the hood of Carter's sweatshirt up and tied tight. Comforter pulled over knees that were pressed to my chest. He studied me, and I tried to measure his gaze—it wasn't thunderous like it had been in the entertainment room, but it wasn't anything like the comfortable companionship we'd spent all these days building. It was straight-up confusion, shot through with hurt.

"I'm sorry," I blubbered. "I'm so, so sorry."

He climbed on the bed and drew the curtains, then crawled across to sit next to me.

"We've got a lot of things to talk through," he said. "But first, perdóname. What I said was cruel. James filled me in on what happened to your Carter."

"This is the only place it feels real," I whispered. "We, *I* . . . no one knew we were together. And now he's gone and that huge part of me is too. I've heard so much doubt, so many comments that make light of us. And if the only place where it feels like our relationship existed is in here—" I pulled at my disheveled hair with one hand and placed the other on my heart "—I'm starting to doubt too."

"Tell me about him." Alex plumped one of my pillows and stuck it behind his back. He was sitting parallel to me, looking straight ahead like he knew I wouldn't be able to do this if I had to meet his gaze.

"Why do you want to hear about Carter? We need to discuss—"

"Because you need to talk about him . . . and I'm not ready to talk about the other stuff yet."

I nodded. Not that he could see it. "What do you want to hear?"

"Whatever you want to tell me."

"I don't know where to begin. Carter was a part of my life for so long. And I hate that I feel like him being gone broke me. I want to be stronger than this. I want to be braver and better. And it's not that he *was* my identity, but I don't know who I am without him. Not because I need him to feel complete, but because he was the only one who saw me clearly. Who helped *me* see me clearly."

"Like a mirror?"

"Exactly. Carter was the best mirror. Whenever I was defeated or depressed, he managed to reflect the best parts of me, making sure I saw them. And now . . . it's like I only see my flaws and my mistakes. And I miss him for so much more than that. I miss the way he made me laugh. I miss the way he valued my opinion—he'd Skype just to ask if his shoes matched his shirt, or for advice on a situation with his father. Or to say, 'I've got two minutes until I need to get to an exam, but I wanted to see your face first.' And I'd smile, and he'd exhale and say, 'Okay, now I'm ready to ace this thing' and hang up. That was it, the whole conversation. And it was fine that was the whole conversation, because our whole days, our whole lives were a continuous conversation. And I can't get my mind to believe the conversation is really over."

I turned toward Alex. "They carved him. That's what all the news reports said. Not only did they shoot him, but they *carved* his chest. And I—I can still remember the texture of his skin and what it felt like to lie with my head above his heart. And they"—I had to mouth the last two words because, while I couldn't stop thinking about it, I couldn't say them again— "carved him."

He reached over and gave my fingers a quick squeeze before pulling back.

"And if we're going to go all-in with my damage, I might as well admit there's not a single person in this world I wouldn't trade to have him back. Not my parents, not my best friends, not anyone. It's selfish as all get out and I'm not even pretending to deny it."

"Except it's not," he said. "You don't actually have the power to trade a life for another—not even the mighty Vickers can do that. So it's just . . . natural. You think I don't have thoughts like that about my own life? Or I didn't try and make bargains with God when Gabriela was dying?"

Now I was the one reaching across the duvet for his hand, holding on as my tears began to spill. "Alex, when I made that deal at Tech World, I didn't understand the kidney was for *you*. If I had . . ." I still couldn't fill in that blank. I knew what I'd do *now*, but looking back on the girl I'd been two weeks ago, I just didn't know.

His fingers tightened around mine. "Do you need me to finish that statement for you? You're a good person."

"You, of all people, have a right to doubt that. Today I sent a man who's known me since before I was born to jail. Plus, my Family . . ." I couldn't stop thinking of the betrayal in all their eyes. "I don't know that I am." I squeezed his fingers gently, then removed mine. "What did Dr. Ackerman tell you? I want to make sure you know everything."

"That James's dad was arrested while meeting with a donor, and I might hear some comments or perceive some hostility from Family members. And that you had been told *not* to get me a kidney."

"There was a deal—my daddy made it with the attorney general while in DC—we stop all transplants until the Organ Act, and they give us immunity."

"You're not doing *any* transplants?" His hands had tightened on fistfuls of my covers. "At all?"

"I thought I could get around it. Daddy told me to stop your kidney search. I ordered Byrd to keep looking. I'm sorry I lied to you. I didn't want you to worry more than you have to. I was doing a stellar job of worrying for the both of us, and I just couldn't handle seeing that fear on your face. I'm so sorry."

"So it's over." It was a low, hesitant whisper, like the words scraped at his throat and he could barely get them out.

"No." I knelt up on the bed and shook my head. "I won't let it be. James says I 'fixate.' And while James is usually full of all sorts of crazy, this time he's right. I know it doesn't sound good, but there are still options and other channels I can work through. You're not supposed to know any of this—Daddy's worried about you going on the news and bashing the Family and undermining their support for the Organ Act—but I won't lie or keep things from you. Not anymore."

He shook his head slowly. "Will your Family's endorsement of the Organ Act help it pass?"

"Supposedly." I shrugged. "Penny and Char are both Family kids—and them being advocates for the bill caused a huge boost in its popularity. Pen says the wording of the bill is almost tweaked, and they could call for a Senate vote in the next couple weeks. But, Alex, I'm not going to let that stop me from—"

"Do you know there are currently about four hundred fifty thousand people on dialysis in the U.S.?" He paused and waited for me to look at him before continuing. "And dialysis doesn't 'fix' anything—it treats the symptoms. Some people, they're on it for a decade. More. You know how many legal transplants took place last year? Less than seventeen thousand."

"Why are you telling me this?"

"If this act passes it'll change everything. Compensating donors and making it legal—that would be . . . Do you know how many of those four hundred fifty thousand would instantly have a better life expectancy? A greater chance of getting a transplant?"

"Now I really don't get what you're saying." But that was partially on purpose, because my stomach was churning over where this might be headed.

"Stop," he said. "Stop looking for a kidney for me. Stop doing things that jeopardize your Family's endorsement of the bill. I'm one. One versus four hundred fifty thousand on dialysis. Versus the more than a hundred thousand on the transplant list. And what about livers and everything else covered in this act? Maggie, I'm just one guy."

I bit my lip hard. Harder. Shook my head until I felt dizzy.

"Don't *fixate*." His smile was a blur because my eyes were wet and my head spun, but I knew the expression was forced. "Look at the bigger picture here. I'm a speck in the bigger picture."

There was a banging on my door, but neither of us moved or looked away.

"Maggie Grace?" Daddy called. He knocked again, then let himself in. "You asleep? Didn't mean to wake you, sport, but I'm looking for Alex. Ackerman, the idealistic fool, told him about Byrd before they were even out of the clinic. He took off, and he's MIA. I gave the men strict instructions not to hurt him, but I'm worried if they find him first—"

"I'm right here, sir." Alex pushed back my bed hangings, revealing Daddy in slack-jawed astonishment standing beside my vanity. Revealing us sitting against my headboard.

Daddy shook his head, and his stupor disappeared behind converging eyebrows. "What are you doing in my daughter's—" His face changed again, from fury to concern. "And why is she crying?" He stepped closer, his fists ready. "*Why* is Magnolia crying?"

"I was telling him about Carter."

Daddy grabbed the chair from my vanity and sank onto it with a confused look that would've been comical—him in my boutique chair of powder-pink leather with curlicue legs—if today hadn't consisted of disasters and tears.

"Magnolia, you . . ." He shook his head. "You don't *ever* talk about the Landlow boy. And you won't even talk to this one across the dining room table. You've done nothing but complain about Alex . . . Yet you defied me for his sake and now you're *confiding* in him? You better explain what's going on right quick."

"Daddy, you *had* to believe I didn't like him—that I resented being assigned to watch Alex—otherwise I couldn't have pursued a kidney. And it was true, at first." I made an apologetic face at Alex. "Before I got to know him. Before I understood what we *do*—the patients part of the Business. And then I wasn't going to—I'm still not going to—stop looking for a donor."

"The heck you are," he roared. "I can't believe you're sitting there calm as a breeze telling me this. Telling *him* this. Exposing us and risking everything."

"I'm not a threat, sir," said Alex, but I doubted Daddy even heard him. He was too busy with his tirade, and I was too busy realizing I'd botched this—badly. That my honesty sounded like insubordination.

"He deserves a kidney." I scooted beside Alex to the side of the bed and turned so my feet dangled off.

"Then he shouldn't have wasted his shot at the government list. I had Bob look up his file: 'Reckless disregard for life and personal safety.'"

I bristled at his condemnation. "That's not the whole story. I'm getting him a kidney."

"No, you're not!" It wasn't Daddy this time; it was Alex. And it stunned my father into silence. Alex grabbed my hand, and the action made me pause long enough for him to continue. "I'm not the only one who deserves functioning organs, and

I'm not going to jeopardize other peoples' chances by making the Organ Act look bad."

"What are you proposing, son?" Daddy's elbows were on his knees, his shirtsleeves rolled up and his hands clasped loosely in what I knew to be his bargaining pose.

"Maggie wanted to go to DC the night I arrived. I think she should. The sooner the better. If Penny and Char are powerful symbols of their Families' support for the Organ Act, then Maggie should be there to be yours."

Daddy nodded. "And it would draw attention from Byrd's arrest. Get her far from here and whatever ramifications."

"Y'all are forgetting something," I drawled. "I don't *want* to be an Organ Act ambassador. I don't support it."

"That's irrelevant," said Daddy.

Alex grinned. "You do. You just don't know it yet, fixator."

I smacked his knee, and he laughed. Daddy cleared his throat. "And what's in it for you, Alex? What do you want to get out of this? We can't give you a transplant right now, but whenever the Organ Act passes and things are up and running—you can be at the top of the list."

"And depending how long that takes, that'll either be mighty fine and I'll appreciate it, or . . ." Alex shrugged, and the gesture felt like a kick to my throat.

I wanted to slap him. For real this time, not playfully on the knee. "No." They ignored me, so I said it again, louder, "No! Dammit, Alex. You always do this—always take control of situations. And can't you just let me be in charge? No! No to DC. No to you waiting."

He touched my cheek, turned my head to face his, and left his hand there. It burned hot against my skin, but his voice was a cool rush, a deep whisper. "*Yes*, Maggie. *Yes*. This time I need you to trust *me*. And, God, you're strong, you're so brave, and you're a natural leader, but . . ." His thumb stroked my cheek. "Me waiting is the best thing for everyone. Trust me."

I'd been fighting and scrapping my whole life—but so had he. I didn't do trust nearly as well as I did self-reliance. I'd never had much practice following someone else's lead, and this seemed like a horrible time to start.

Still, I nodded and said, "I trust you."

Daddy scraped his chair closer. "What can we do in the meantime? To show our appreciation for how accommodating you're being."

Alex dropped his hand from my cheek. "I don't need to be bought off. I'm not going to talk to anyone."

"Then let's work on getting you home. The sentiment here . . . It's best we get you home. I'm sure your family will be happy to have you back for Thanksgiving."

"But—" The idea of him leaving gouged at my chest and I sought any sort of protest or excuse. "What about treatment?"

"Dr. Ackerman can see to that transition and continue to coordinate Alex's care. We'll send you home with your own dialysis machine if that'll help."

"Thank you, sir. I appreciate that. My family will be relieved to see me." Alex hesitated, then added, "Also, sir, you really need to have Theo or someone look into the targeted attempts to infiltrate your network."

Just ten hours ago, Daddy had dismissed this idea, accused Alex of causing trouble. Now he nodded slowly. "You and I should meet in the morning to discuss this further." He patted my knee. "You and I will also set up a meeting . . ."

"Yes, Daddy," I said meekly.

He harrumphed in a way that let me know he may love me, but he wasn't fooled by my compliance or pleased with my behavior. "Get some sleep, Magnolia. You too, Alex. In fact, why don't I show you back to your room on my way out."

Alex turned sheepish at the same rate I went indignant. "Daddy, you're overstepping. Put away your Virtue Police badge; it isn't needed. Might I remind you, we were having a conversation when you came in? When Alex and I are done talking, I'm sure he'll be able to find his way across the hall all by himself."

"You're sounding mighty close to uppity. It's a welcome change from mopey—but don't take it too far, little miss."

"Love you, Daddy." I stood up and kissed his cheek. "Now, good night."

"Lord help the boy who ends up married to you. I'm going to go write myself a note so I remember to stay mad for what you've pulled today." He chucked my chin. "I'm sending someone around in an hour—everyone better be done chatting and asleep in their own beds by then. In the meantime, Alex"—he shot a pointed look at the red-faced guy beside me—"you'll be much more comfortable sitting down here in this chair."

"Daddy!"

"I'm just saying." He made a short bow as he exited the room.

CHAPTER 33

I'm pretty sure Alex might have died of mortification right then or followed Daddy out the door, but I clamped a hand on his wrist so he couldn't slink away.

"I heard what you said. I heard what he said, and I *do* trust you, but . . ." But I didn't know how to finish that thought. I only knew today had been a gauntlet and I'd lost every battle. This one hurt most.

"You have to stop, Maggie." He was so close I could feel his words on my skin. On my nose and on my lips. "I know you care, but you can't fix me."

"What? I don't—" But I *did*. I cared and that was stupid and . . . God, what if something happened to him? I covered my mouth with my free hand and bit my palm.

He blushed and shifted away, pulled his hand out from

under my wrist. "I don't mean romantically or anything. Just, you care if I die . . . I hope."

He was talking. I was clawing at the strings tied at my neck.

"I'm not *planning* on dying. I mean, yeah, who knows and another year or so on dialysis will suck, but—"

"I can't—"

I can't care. I can't have this conversation. I can't go down this path where I'm responsible for your life. And we can't be talking about death, because you can't . . .

"I can't—I can't—*breathe.*" I yanked the hood off, and when that didn't help, pulled the whole sweatshirt over my head. But I was still doubled over, fighting to get air in paralyzed lungs.

"Maggie! What do I do?" Alex moved backward off the bed. He stood beside it, tucking his hair behind his ears and looking terrified. "Want me to get your dad back? Or your mom? Dr. Ackerman?"

I shook my head. Air was stuttering in and out in a way that was dizzying and painful. I lay back on my pillow, letting the weight of all the oxygen that wasn't getting in my lungs sit like a bull on my chest. Carter smiled down at me from the pictures, his eyebrows quirked in ways that seemed to say, "What are you doing, Mags? You've been breathing just fine for nineteen years. Why quit now?"

He would've laughed and made me laugh. And then it would've stopped.

Now, *I* had to make it stop. I pried my eyes away from the pictures. Alex looked like he was a half-second away from having a breakdown of his own. He'd gotten me a glass of water from the bathroom, but his hand shook and he was spilling it all over my rug.

And it was suddenly too much in a different way. I was sobbing and sniffling and snot was all over my face for the second time that day. Only this wasn't James. This wasn't a kid who I'd seen cry far more often then he'd seen me. My cheeks burned.

I glugged some of the water, then set the glass on my nightstand. I sniffed a few times and wiped my face with the sleeve of the abandoned sweatshirt. "Mama always says a gentleman shouldn't watch a lady cry."

"What should he do instead?" Alex asked.

"I don't know. Didn't we already have this conversation over some Twizzlers? Give her privacy? Pretend not to notice?"

"I don't know how I was supposed to pretend not to notice that. But I'll pass you a tissue so you can stop using your sweatshirt. Gross."

I snorted and accepted the tissue. He waited until I blew my nose to continue. "I'm not sure what just happened, but I feel like I should apologize for causing it."

I shook my head. "Want to hear something funny?"

"Yes. *Please* tell me something funny."

"Dr. Ackerman told me he was concerned I didn't express my emotions enough." I started to giggle and had to fight to get the rest of the words out. "He gave me 'homework' to try and release some of my feelings."

"Um, well, A-plus, gold-star work." Alex sat down on the edge of my bed. "You okay?"

"Yeah." I touched the snotty sweatshirt. There was no way it could avoid the washer now, but maybe it was time. "I'm tired, but okay. I bet you're tired too. It's been a long day."

His face settled into sad lines, and I wondered if his thoughts mirrored mine—remembering the happiness of this morning, our hands linked as we twirled on the creek bank. It was such a perfect moment.

"Get some sleep. I'll see you in the morning." He stood up, and I did too. Which made him pause and raise an eyebrow.

"Bathroom. Brush teeth." I pointed and mimed.

He nodded. "Oh, right."

"And maybe this too—" Before I could hesitate or talk myself out of it, I reached over and hugged him. It was awkward, all bumping elbows and hitting my cheek against his. I pulled back before he could react. "Thanks."

Alex cleared his throat. "Yeah, um, sure." He banged into the doorframe and fumbled with the knob before pulling it shut behind him.

CHAPTER 34

The next morning, I was a mess in every sense of the word. I'd only halfheartedly removed yesterday's makeup, so there were gray smudges around my eyes from rubbing them all night. It was a look Mama would call trampy, and Carter used to say was sexy.

Carter.

The reason I was a mess.

Or half the reason, at least.

The other half had just knocked and was standing awkwardly in my doorway.

"Did I wake you?" asked Alex. "I'm sorry."

"It's all right." It felt too hot in my room. My head was filling with all the battles I'd lost yesterday. The sequel to last night's hysterical meltdown was brewing in my stomach. I wrapped an arm around it. "Actually, if you don't mind, could

I have just a minute? I'm terribly sorry, but if you'd step in the hall, I'll get myself cleaned up right quick."

He blinked at me. "Sure." Closed the door behind him.

I sounded like Mama. I looked a mess but sounded like my mama. And part of me wanted to dress the part too. Put on armor in the form of a very structured, very pastel, very floral sundress. I had pearls somewhere. And while my hair wasn't long enough to set with rollers, I had clips or head-bands.

Except that sort of getup wouldn't protect me from the men—in fact, it'd be an invitation for mockery. I grabbed a black dress printed with thorny vines and quickly put it on.

Alex looked wary when I stepped into the hall and leaned back against my bedroom door. "You sounded like a Magnolia Grace."

"What?"

"It was really the first time I could see it. Maybe a little that day at the store. But just now you sounded pure deb, like you were liable to tell me 'bless your heart,' or 'you poor, sweet thing,' as you shoved my feelings in a blender."

"Protective instinct." And dang it if I didn't find my hand creeping up to my throat like I was going to clutch at pearls I wasn't wearing.

"What are you protecting? And from what threat?" He took a step closer, leaning one shoulder on the wall beside where I was against the door. It made me want to lift my hand, or turn my body toward him, or open my mouth and say something.

But I was a coward, so instead I shrugged.

He was supposed to be just a guy, a patient, a blackmailer. And sometime in the next couple of days he'd leave—and go back to being a stranger. "I hate that you won't let me keep looking for a kidney." I ground my teeth. "I *need* to."

"*Why?* There's got to be a boundary, Maggie—a line that's not worth crossing. Right now I don't think you have a sense of the bigger picture. I'm not worth four hundred fifty thousand people. And all the ones who'll come after."

I refused to say *You are to me*. Refused. Buried those words under twelve layers of stubbornness and denial.

"I was flirting." The words slipped from my tongue—a confession I hadn't planned to confess. Truths I hadn't realized were true. "That day in the kitchen and so many times since, I was flirting."

His eyes were filled with questions. They wanted me to say more, but I'd already sacrificed a piece of myself with that honesty. And I bet he didn't see it, the rope that tied those topics together, wove them into a net that ensnared me, and made all of this a trap.

If I was flirting.

If I had feelings.

If I failed . . .

I couldn't go through another good-bye. I wouldn't survive another funeral.

"Why are you telling me this?" He leaned toward me, reached out like he might touch my cheek. I tilted my head and closed my eyes. When he sighed, I opened them to see him fold his fingers into a fist and drop it by his side. "What do you want me to *do* with that statement?"

"I don't know." Which was honest, but not helpful. Not fair. Alex studied me—his eyes tracking my headshake, my raised brows, the lip between my teeth. "I swear, I don't have a danged clue what I want."

He laughed, a deep sound like he'd swallowed the whole bayou. "Of course not, because you're you . . . which means you have to make it difficult." He scrubbed his palm across his face, a smile spreading beneath his fingers. "Maggie, as much as I'd like to stay here and see if I can convince you to flirt some more—your dad sent me to get you for a meeting."

"Oh, right." I fiddled with the belt of my dress.

"But I'll take a rain check. On the flirting."

My attempt at a smile felt like a grimace. "Think the men are more or less angry now that they've had time to process what I did?"

Alex put his hand on the small of my back as we headed down the stairs. "I think anyone who manages to stay mad at you must have superpowers."

I'm not sure if it was his touch, his words, or just *him*, but it was enough to make me lift my chin as I headed for Daddy's office.

After a short meeting—more of a briefing, really—in which Daddy laid out the reality of our current situation and the men alternated between silently fuming and pairing curses with their scowls, he and Alex left to talk to Theo about IT security.

I'd followed them from the meeting room to the foyer, not really sure where to go next. Daddy told me he'd have someone deliver suitcases to my room so I could pack for DC—so I guessed that trip was really happening. And maybe packing was as good a way as any to spend my time. But Byrd's office door was open. And instead of heading up the stairs, I froze on its threshold.

"I overreacted. I shouldn't have done that yesterday—spit," Manuel said. I'd been so busy staring at Byrd's empty desk and letting my stomach fill with guilt that I hadn't noticed him and the other men coming up behind me. "But I'm still ticked at you, Maggie Grace. You're better than this. You owe us more than choosing some punk kid over Family."

"Alex is *not* a punk kid. He doesn't deserve to get caught in the middle of our amnesty deal or any of your anger. I'm not saying Byrd deserved this either. He didn't. And that's on my head." I paused to look at each of them, lifted my hands in a shrug, and let them slap against my thighs. It was a gesture of helplessness and exasperation. "I screwed up bigtime. And I'm sorry. I'll be doing everything I can to fix the damage."

"That's real nice and sweet," said Enzo. "But Byrd's still behind bars."

Which was where Enzo's daddy had been since he was six, so the pain in his voice cut deep. "I know."

"You're gonna have to earn back our trust, little girl."

Manuel's "little girl" was such a slap in the face that I stepped back. All those years turning myself inside out to prove gender was irrelevant—and here we were. But the rest of that statement was fair, so I kept my voice steady and repeated, "I know."

"You know what I *don't* know?" Enzo asked. "Where you really stand on any of the issues that matter. I know what you've been saying in meetings. I know what you've been doing behind our backs. But what *you* actually believe—I don't have a clue."

"Me either," I admitted.

"Maybe that's where you need to start then," said Brooks. I didn't miss the ring of extra space around him or the pointed looks he was receiving. Penalties he'd pay for agreeing to help me, even though he hadn't actually contributed anything to my scheme.

"I reckon you're right," I said, before shifting my gaze to the larger group. "And if y'all will excuse me, I'll get right on it." I pushed my way through the group to Daddy's office and shut the door behind me.

I called James—for once not because I needed *his* support, but because I wanted to offer my own. And I would've if he'd answered. Since he didn't, I fiddled with my phone and figured if I was going to hide in Daddy's office, I should at least do something productive like clean out my e-mail in-box.

As I scrolled through and deleted old e-mails, I came across one that made me pause in every sense of the word. I held my breath, my heart skipped a beat, I think even the neurons in my brain stopped firing because I had to read the subject at least four times before I could process it: *Inactive Account Recovery notification regarding Carter Landlow.*

It was probably spam. Or another virus. I knew I should delete it. Fool me once and all that. But I'd been a fool for Carter for so long and my fingers ignored any sort of synaptic warnings. They saw his name and tapped on the e-mail.

And when it opened, I didn't read or absorb much of the form letter at the top—Carter had set this up/requested I be notified/months without account activity/granted access to . . .

There were directions and links and words. I'm sure they were important words, but not as important as the ones at the bottom of the e-mail.

The ones from *him*.

Mags,

Here's a dirty little secret for you: I didn't delete anything. I couldn't. Instead I forwarded everything to an e-mail address I set up just for this purpose.

My plan was always to turn over this account name and password the day I proposed, but if you're reading this, then that didn't happen.

If you're reading this, then no one's logged into this account for five months.

If you're reading this, I'm dead. Man, it feels so morbid to even type that—I'm dead.

I'm sorry.

I hope by the time this gets to you, you've found closure.

I hope you're giving them hell in your Family's boardroom.

I hope you've found peace.

I hope you're happy.

I hope you know, Magnolia Grace Vickers, that you are the love of my life.

I will always miss you, need you, and love you so damn much.

Carter

CHAPTER 35

I ran. Past a smirking Brooks, who asked who was chasing me, my feet pounding up the stairs and into my room and to the bottom of my closet where *shoot! Where was my laptop?* and grabbing it and flinging off the case.

I hit the power button before I'd even placed it on my desk. And then it was infinite moments and near-hyperventilation while it loaded. I logged in and followed the links. And directions. Everything about me was wavering and tremulous and then I was there. Looking at rows of e-mails and an endless screen checkerboarded with photo thumbnails.

On his campus that very first day. Me in decoy workout clothing. Him in what I now knew was a shirt he'd spent thirty minutes picking out and another forty attempting to iron.

A teary-eyed selfie of our farewell on the same trip. I'd never seen it before, and in it he looked about *thisclose* to losing it too.

So many screenshots from our Skypes.

And there were all those e-mails. Seven and a half years times at least two e-mails a day. Usually many more. Enough words and pages to get lost in for weeks, months. I could watch us fall in love all over again. Read our clumsy attempts at flirting and seduction and revisit the raw moments of revealing small pieces of ourselves and our offerings of honesty and vulnerability—ones that were received and cherished and reciprocated.

But clicking, scrolling, clicking—they weren't a substitute for him. These pages felt too small for all the truth they contained.

I wanted those files in my hands, because technology felt jealous, greedy, unstable. All those pictures had been there all these months and I hadn't known. I didn't ever want to be cut off from them again.

I needed something to hold—something to point to and shove in Mama and Daddy's hands. To say, "Here. This is why I'm broken. This is what you didn't get. This was *me*. This is what I *lost*."

I pressed Print. Print all. Then grabbed my laptop and headed down to the meeting room, where my relationship with Carter was being re-created, one sheet of paper at a time.

I read fast, but not as fast as the printer spit out pages. And I didn't want to rush. They were letters and words and punctuation to linger over. I didn't even cringe at the overwrought angst of twelve-year-old me bemoaning that rash decision to chop off my super-long hair.

> Mama says I look like a boy and that now none of them will look at me. How mean is that? But I don't care if they ignore me—as long as you don't hate it.

Carter's response was pure boy. Pure him.

> It's just hair. Dye it green, shave it off, get a Mohawk—I'll still think you're pretty. And yes, tell the other boys to ignore you—I like that plan.
>   P.S. Sorry your mom said that. Sometimes parents suck—like mine who are crazy-nosy about why I'm suddenly on my computer all the time.

I wanted to hug those kids, because we'd just been kids. I wanted to steer them onto a different path, a safer one. Or, if there was no preventing Carter from making the choices that ended at Dead Meat, then I wanted to tell eleven-year-old Maggie to turn away, choose a different boy. Save herself.

Except, how could she when Carter was sharing the sincere, and sincerely terrible, poems he wrote about her during an eighth-grade English class assignment? Or complaining his little sister had a crush on his best friend and what should he do? He didn't want to exclude Pen—because, really, she was his second best friend—don't tell her he said that—but *gross*, and would Garrett be annoyed when he finally figured it out?

Oh, thirteen-year-old Carter, I should've told you to exclude her, to keep those two so far apart they forgot each other's names.

The printer beeped and "low toner" flashed on the screen. I blinked at the pages I was clutching, at the places they were already smearing with tears.

I set down a stack and lifted another page off the top. It was a picture Carter had photoshopped of us together from our senior proms. We'd promised we'd find dates and go and not get jealous—but I'd been miserable and spent the whole three hours of rubbery food and outdated music creating a mental list of the ways my date didn't measure up to my boyfriend. I'd wanted to see Carter look like James Bond's hotter, blonder, younger brother. I'd wanted to be on his arm for photos and in his arms for slow dances. When he'd sent me this picture I'd cry-laughed.

It looked so real. It had hurt to delete it.

It hurt to hold it.

I was still holding it when I called Theo. "I need more toner for the printer in the meeting room. As soon as possible, please. And paper too. A couple reams."

I'm pretty sure he agreed, but I wasn't paying attention. I was sucked into a drama-filled back and forth from junior year when Carter and I debated whether or not we could get away with attending the same college.

I thought *yes*, he thought *no*. We'd compromised and left it up to fate. Agreed to apply to Notre Dame—if we both got in, we'd go. Otherwise, we'd follow expectations and attend the close-to-home schools our parents wanted.

He hadn't gotten in.

I had.

But I'd lied and said I'd been rejected too. It was one of the only times I'd lied to him. I'd wanted to spare him from the truth—he'd let me down.

It wasn't a fair or logical thing to think/feel back then. And now, standing beside a conference table that was rapidly disappearing beneath piles of papers, I felt the echoes of those buried and bitter sentiments.

It'd been five months. I'd survived almost half a year without him. And while all this was amazing—while the romance of the gesture he'd planned for this in-box made my knees weak and my chest ache—it was a broken promise. It didn't change anything. He was never coming back. If I went down this rabbit hole of memories, would I ever let myself consider other futures and possibilities?

"Hey."

I jumped at Alex's voice. At his appearance in the doorway carrying toner boxes and reams of paper. "Hi."

"I was finishing up with Theo when you called. Does the name *Offal* mean anything to you?"

"Awful? Like, *bad?*"

"With an 'O.' O-F-F-A-L?" He paused, and I shook my head. "It's the only identifier I can get for the IP address behind the network attacks. That, and they're in Vermont."

"No clue, sorry."

"What's all this? You prepping for the strategy session your dad's planning? We've got to make you sound like a real

Organ Act-or." There was such a confidence and lightness in his expression and voice as he dropped his provisions on the table—probably a combination of finally being heard by Theo and whatever conclusion he'd drawn from my flirting comment this morning.

It dazed me for a moment, making me react far too slowly when he reached for the latest stack from the printer. "Don't!"

The sound he made was somewhere between a gasp and choking.

I took the pages from his hand. On top was a photo of me. I was wearing one of Carter's shirts, sleeves rolled up, collar popped, all of it thoroughly rumpled. The buttons on the front weren't fastened, just clutched together with one of my hands. It's a photo of long, bare legs, of motion. I'm throwing my head back, I'm laughing, and one of Carter's hands is blurry in the bottom left corner. He was either reaching for or tickling me. My own free hand is reaching back.

There was so much *life* in that photo, and it wasn't just him that died. That girl, that carefree, careless girl, she died too. I flipped the picture upside down. Alex just stood there staring at the piles and piles. His shoulders slumped; he shook his head.

"Alex, I . . ."

He turned his back on me, facing the printer and swapping out the color cartridge with stiff motions. "There's still ink in the black—call Theo if that runs out too."

The machine was already humming back to life, spitting out pictures on top of where he'd rested his hands.

He picked them up and handed them over with a laugh as

humorless as dried leaves—one that settled in goose bumps on my skin. He paused at the door and asked, "How could anyone compete with this?"

I looked between the print tray where my past was accumulating and the closed door where a possible future was fleeing.

I'd handled that badly—no, that was an understatement. I hadn't handled it at all. If a picture's worth a thousand words, how many rejections had Alex just absorbed?

I couldn't stay where I was any longer— with one foot in the past and one in now. Hopping back and forth between memories and guilty moments.

Hurting a boy who was alive because of one who wasn't.

Saving a boy who was alive because of one who wasn't.

And the confession I'd thrown at him this morning . . . He'd been right to question how I wanted him to respond. I might not be ready to admit the answer, but my gasping, gut-punched reaction to his exit spoke volumes.

I shoved the door back open.

"Alex. Alex, *wait.*"

CHAPTER 36

Alex wasn't in his room. Or Theo's office. Or Daddy's.

When he wasn't in the entertainment room or the clinic, I sent him a text. Then two texts. I hit Send on the third—a rambling agreement to respect his space and the fact that he didn't want to be found, while simultaneously begging him to look for me when he was—as I opened the front door to head back in the house.

"There you are! Finally!" Lupe was a five-foot-nothing bundle of energy, brains, and loyalty. And all five feet were sitting on the table in the foyer. "I've been waiting *forever.*"

"Loops!" I ran over to her. "What are you doing here?"

She knew I wasn't a hugger, even though I might have allowed it this time. Instead she hopped off the table and shrugged. "I'm here to see you, crazy."

"Your mama told you to come home, didn't she?"

"Um, because I missed my bestie? Seriously, even watching shirtless Frisbee is dullsville without you."

"Your mama totally called, and you're full of it."

"Fine, she might've mentioned something about you setting speed records for alienating people and self-destructing. I'm paraphrasing, but something like that." Her glibness was totally undermined by the look of concern she was wearing. "Anyhow, so I'm here. Yay!"

I hugged her. Almost knocking her over in surprise but letting go before she recovered enough to get sappy or clingy. "I'm so happy to see you—but did you see a guy go by?"

"You mean, did I see the infamous Alex? Sadly, no. Who would've thought passing along the name from Enzo's computer repair slip would cause such a tempest? When can I meet him?" Her grin was pure delight. So long as she didn't have to lead the way or take the blame, she was always willing to follow me into trouble. But a Lupe interrogation was the last thing Alex needed right now.

I notched up the volume on my phone and put it in my pocket. "He's busy."

Loops wrinkled her nose. "Later then." She swallowed, and her pink lips weren't *really* smiling as she asked, "So, where's Lames? Can we get him to bust a move with us tonight?"

I snorted. "Lames" had been my brilliant retaliation when James had invented "Naggie." "He's at the jail meeting with Byrd and his lawyer. Baby and her family are up too."

"I'll call him later and make sure you're keeping him on his ever-righteous toes." But I knew she'd really offer her support and empathy. She had plenty of experience with seeing a parent behind bars. She smiled with forced enthusiasm. "Okay, so if he's out, who's our paid purse-holder? I mean, 'protection.' You need a night out."

Before I could decline, Manuel appeared around the corner. "Night out?"

"Hola, Tío Manuel."

"Come give me a kiss," he said. "And call your mamá more often so I don't have to hear about it. But you girls aren't going out tonight. Find a backup plan."

There was no warm smile for me. No cheek presented for my lips. It'd been years since I'd been teased about crushes or new haircuts or clothing. No one made comments about my spending or called me "boy crazy." To Loops those were signs of affection. But back when they'd been aimed at me, I'd hated them; they'd been indicators I was being othered and excluded from the Family.

Right now easy affection sure looked sweeter than harsh accountability, but I kept my chin up as Manuel tapped Lupe's pout. "Put that lip away. It's wasted effort. And I've seen those grades you bring home—you're more than smart enough to know it." Whatever Loops responded in Spanish made him laugh and swat at her. "Remind me again which of you is supposed to be the good influence?"

"James," we said simultaneously.

He shook his head. "Run along and *be good*."

Loops grabbed a bag from beneath the table and pulled me up to my room. "I did my mamá time earlier, so I'm yours for the night as long as I get up crazy early and have breakfast with her before I head back to school. And I figured we'd be on lockdown, so I came prepared." The bag clinked when she set it on my floor.

"Loops, I . . ." This didn't feel *right*—having a girls' night with everything going on. I sent another text to Alex. A simple **please.**

"Don't even, Maggie. Don't. Even. You *need* this. When was the last night you did something *normal*?"

"But my daddy—"

"He knows I'm here, and you heard my uncle sign off on it. Seriously, you're nineteen. Let the grown-ups be grown-up. For once in your life, just act your age." When I hesitated, she frowned. A true frown, not a pout. "I came here to hang out with you, but if you don't want . . ."

I swallowed past guilt and looked at my still-silent phone. "No. I do. But—"

"Good. Then dig your makeup out from wherever it's hidden. Just because we're a party of two doesn't mean you don't have to dress to impress."

I sighed and obeyed. The more she laughed, joked, fought for control of my speakers, and danced around my room—the easier it was to play along. To pretend the makeup was a mask—preparation for a character I was about to perform: me circa six months ago.

I let Loops pick out my outfit—a denim skirt that had been short *before* my last growth spurt and a sequined strapless top from her bag. "Stupid dorm dryer shrank it—it'll never fit *my* chest again."

The sequins ranged from bronze to ivory. It made her skin glow, so I figured it'd make me look extra pasty. But while it didn't exactly make the four exposed inches of my stomach look like I'd spent a week in Cancun, the colors pulled out the natural highlights in my brown hair. It made my eyes pop, especially after Lupe doubled the amount of shadow brushed on my lids.

She disappeared into the bathroom to use asthma-inducing amounts of hairspray. I switched the music over to one of my playlists, twisting and spinning like we had on so many Friday and Saturday nights, hoping that moving, that pretending, would keep me from thinking.

"Whoa! White girl's got some moves." I jumped at Alex's voice, dropped a bobby pin. "I hear you were looking for me. Actually, 'she was tearing through the house and bellowing your name' were Enzo's exact words." He was leaning on my doorframe, his eyebrows quirked in amusement, but the eyes beneath them were intense and slightly guarded.

"That's pretty accurate." I glanced over my shoulder at the closed bathroom door. My muscles melted with relief that he'd come, but my stomach still twisted with uncertainty. "Did you get my texts?"

"Yeah. All of them." His serious expression faded into a wolfish grin as he took a step into the room and swung his hips in a way that suggested my moves were amateur compared to his. In a way that made me swallow. "So, you can dance, but I can't say much for your taste in music."

"Alex—"

"You said to come look for you—*Please, please come look for me.*" His eyes were everywhere—my styled hair, my bare legs, stomach, shoulders. My face. They lingered on my mouth, until I wasn't sure whether to smile and laugh or wipe off the red gloss I'd just applied. "I'm looking. Believe me."

My cheeks felt hot. I wanted to wash the makeup off my face, replace these ridiculous clothes with cozy sweats, and hide under my blankets. Except my sweatshirt was in the wash, my best friend was in the bathroom, my foot was tapping in time with the beat, and my eyes were fascinated by the way he continued to sway. I'd thought he'd want to talk, but maybe my frantic search and begging texts had said enough.

Alex flicked the gray beaded fringe on my lampshade, making the strands tinkle against the clear glass body of the lamp. "With the right dance partner, I could definitely become a fan of this music."

My mouth was bone dry. I licked my lips. "If we were going out dancing, I'd invite you to come."

The words sounded so much braver than I felt—and the courage on them must've been contagious because Alex took a step closer. And he was still half a room away and I was still half naked, but I swear the way he was looking at me made me sweat. Made me want a fan, some iced tea, and a time-out so I could regroup.

His voice was gravely when he asked, "Where *are* you going?"

I'd dropped the bobby pin again and this time it could just live on my bedroom floor. "Um . . . the hayloft?"

"Is that a club?"

"No, like the actual hayloft of the barn out back . . . with horses and stuff."

He laughed. The bullfrog melody of it made me smile. It made Lupe open the bathroom door. "What is—*oh!*"

I wanted to shove her back in and barricade the door. Instead, I forced a smile. "Loops, this is Alex. Alex, meet Lupe. She's actually the one who gave me your name. Did you know you de-porned Enzo's computer at some point?"

He laughed and said, "Hey." She gave him a once-over and a wave before changing the song to a Lilah Montgomery pop-country hit.

"Do you like this better?" I asked him. "And what are you doing tonight? We need to talk."

"Talk tomorrow when I'm back at school." Loops danced between Alex and me, grabbing my hands and spinning me around and around. With each rotation Alex's eyes met mine. "Work, bad. Dancing, good. We told Tío Manuel we'd be good."

"You're making me dizzy."

She let go, calling me a wimp before heading into my closet and tossing out a pair of high-heeled wedges. I picked them up but looked at him. Looked at him looking at me. "You busy?"

"Actually, yeah. I'm meeting with Dr. Ackerman. We're going to talk about treatment options and my transition back home."

I flinched, wobbled one-footed as I shoved the other shoe on. "Don't make any decisions without me."

Alex bent down and plucked the bobby pin from my rug, throwing it up and catching it before placing it on the corner of my vanity. "Yes, ma'am."

"I'm serious."

"*Too* serious." Lupe linked her arm through mine. "No more serious."

"I think that's my cue to leave," said Alex. I opened my mouth to protest, but he just offered a smile and a wink. One extinguished my fears while the other set my blood on fire.

"Later," I said.

"Later," he echoed. "Have fun, ladies."

Lupe narrowed her eyes at the back of the door and kept them narrowed when she turned to me. "You ready? You're ready. Come on." Pulling a bottle of cheap sugar wine from her bag and tucking it under her arm, she led the way down the stairs and out the back door.

She climbed the ladder first and claimed the hay bale where I'd spent so many recent nights fretting and heart-to-hearting. This left me to use James's bale or haul another one over. But those things were dang heavy. I sat on his.

As usual, our conversation flowed all over the map. Loop's physical chemistry class that might be her first-ever B. My fence-mending powwows with James. The side dishes we wanted at Thanksgiving. Things on our Christmas lists. Boys she'd dated, rejected, kissed. As the level in the bottle dropped, the topics skipped from superficial to serious and back again.

Finally, she leaned toward me and waggled her eyebrows. "So *that* was Alex."

"You weren't very friendly. What was up with that?"

"After hearing everything you've been up to from Mamá and Enzo, I was expecting something different."

"What do you mean?" There was already an edge in my voice, but she had plenty of practice ignoring that warning.

She shrugged. "I don't know—I expected someone, like, scorching hot. And he's not *bad* to look at. But based on the photos I saw on the news, he's no Carter Landlow."

"Stop! Stop right there. Let's talk about something else." She offered me a sip, but I shook my head and pushed the bottle back. He didn't look like Carter. He looked like Alex. He looked kind and earnest. Granted he might also look tired today—a little residually puffy from missing yesterday's dialysis—but it didn't make him hard to look at. I'd looked *plenty*. If anything, he was hard to look *away* from. I scowled at her.

"Chill, Maggie. I didn't mean to make you pissy." She took a long sip and put the bottle beside me. "And maybe if I'd heard *anything* about him from *you*, then I'd have a clue what was going on." Her smile hadn't slipped, but there was pain and challenge in the tone of her voice.

I laughed. It echoed off the rafters of the barn, and Lupe clapped a hand over my mouth. "How can you be a stealth ninja when sober but a . . . a failed ninja when you drink?"

I nipped her palm, and she giggled as she moved her hand. "Oh, Loops. If *you* had a clue what was going on with Alex, that would make one of us. This isn't like Carter—I'm not keeping you in the dark on purpose. I'm still fumbling around myself."

"But with Carter—" She paused and studied my face. I

nodded my permission to continue. "I still don't get why you didn't tell me. Okay, not Lames. Not your Family—but this is *me*. I don't care what your last name is. I've always been your friend first, screw the Family. You should've told me. And I shouldn't have let you get away with playing 'mystery boyfriend' for so long. I just wanted you to *choose* to tell me the juicy details. It's less fun when I have to pry them out of you."

Every detail she could want to know—more details than even her greedy little romantic heart could desire—were sitting on the printer in the meeting room. She'd happily dig through those pages and swoon, gush, and ask all sorts of questions. She was the audience I'd thought I wanted, but the emotional cost of reliving those memories would be astronomical. The torture of nostalgia and past tense.

I handed the bottle back, suddenly no longer feeling like giggling at the roof. The sequins of Lupe's top scratched my skin. Or maybe it was the hay that was making a pincushion out of my back and thighs.

"I loved him so much, Loops."

She crawled over to kneel next to me. "I'm so, so sorry, chica."

"He made me feel like we were invincible. I know that's ridiculous now, but it was true. I felt . . . limitless when I was with him. Godly, untouchable. We were that couple that made heads turn and people say, 'I want what they have.'" My voice broke. "I want it back. I want that love that felt like being drunk, like being high on him."

"Oh, Maggie." She gripped both the hands I was wringing in my lap.

"He's *all* I wanted. He's all I ever wanted."

"I don't know what to say. I'm no good at this and I didn't know him, but you're *nineteen*. Be sad. Be mad. Be the half of a one-night stand that has the most fun. But your life isn't over. You need to find *something* new to want. Some sort of goal."

"I know." But knowing her words were true didn't make them easy. Another thing I knew—I'd left all those precious pages in the meeting room. Just abandoned them to chase down Alex. I sat up, climbed across her to the ladder. "I'm going to head in."

"It's early. Wimp! I just survived midterms—what's your excuse?"

She was trying to provoke me into playing along. I wanted to. I wished I could grip her levity with two hands and cling to sass and giggles.

"Next time," I promised.

"Fine," she grumbled. "Care if I stay here and kick the bottle while making a call I'll regret to this guy in my p-chem class?"

"Nope. I'll leave the back light on and pull out the trundle bed."

"See you in a bit. Love you, Maggie girl."

"Love you, Loops."

CHAPTER 37

I should've factored in the ladder when I let Loops pick my footwear. And I definitely shouldn't have kicked them off halfway down. But when I jumped and my bare feet hit the barn floor, there were two warm arms there to steady me.

"Hey," I whispered. Then, thinking about the giggling girl flirting into her phone not so many feet above us, I put a finger to Alex's mouth and tilted my head toward the door. He nodded and the motion made his lips drag across my skin. I shivered and pulled my hand back, banging into the ladder as I took a step away from him.

"Everything okay down there, failed ninja?"

"Fine." I hurried across the barn and flung out an excuse. "Just trying to shut the stupid door."

"Leave it stupid-open so I don't have to stupid-struggle."

"Okay," I called up, then turned to Alex, who was already

standing on the wood chips outside. Lupe was stupid-wrong about him. And maybe Mama was right, because in this light his skin glowed and his hair waved in a controlled chaos I would play with all day if it were mine. His full lips were slightly parted, and I recalled the way they'd felt firm and soft against my finger. And his eyes were full of moonlight and stars and questions as I smiled at him.

"Can I talk yet?" he asked in a deep whisper that reminded me of the hum of plugging in an amp.

I nodded.

"I was coming from the clinic and heard you laugh. You asked if I was busy—I thought . . . I didn't mean to crash your party."

"S'okay," I said. "I wanted you there." I was about to apologize for Loops; tell him her attitude earlier was targeting *me*, not him. Instead, I stumbled over a garden hose. I didn't quite fall, but he didn't even attempt to catch me. And when I straightened with a "whoops" poised on my lips; it faded in reaction to the scowl on his.

"No, you didn't," he said.

"Huh?"

"You didn't want me there. I heard you. You don't want *anything* but him."

"How much did you hear?" My stomach sank as I rewound the night—Loop's harsh comparison, our mindless gossip, my soul-deep confessions.

"Just a minute. The part about how he was a god and you're going through withdrawal now that you have to spend time with mere mortals." He shoved his hands through his hair, but with none of the playfulness I'd just imagined. "I'm never going to be able to give you that sort of 'contact high.'"

"Why would you say that?" I looked away from the sincerity on his face. Looked across the backyard, not at the pool or the entertainment room, but at the land beyond. Because I wanted out of this conversation. I wanted to escape, and my toes were curling in the wood chips as if they were preparing to run. But even if I ran, even if I ran and he stayed here, those words would chase me. The questions they were inspiring as they wriggled their way under my skin would join those already echoing in my head, floating in my veins.

"Because you're too drunk to remember; because you're going to DC and I'm going home. And it's probably the only way I'll be brave enough to say it out loud."

"I'm not drunk," I answered. "Seriously, I'm on the sober side of tipsy. We shared *one* bottle of wine. And I left before it was empty."

His eyes went wide. "But . . . You . . ."

"Heels on a ladder," I suggested. "And Loops and I are idiots when we're together."

"Great." He slapped his hands against the thighs of his jeans. "That's even better. Then you were sober, and that was all straight-up sober sincerity, and you'll remember everything I've said. I should've known—I mean, I *did* know earlier . . . *all those pictures*. But you said 'flirting' and smiled like— You said we'd go dancing. And 'later.' And I—dear God, why can't I shut up?"

"I really wish you would," I said. Then wanted to take it back. Wanted to take back the part where I'd said I wasn't drunk—not that it was lie, but it would be a convenient excuse for my no-filter honesty. It would be a kindness to him if I could pretend this conversation was lost beneath a hangover. A kindness to me if we could have a do-over tomorrow where I wasn't caught off-guard. "That came out wrong."

"No, I get it."

"You *don't* get it." I could barely get the words out between my clenched teeth. But I didn't know who I was angry at: him for asking questions I wasn't ready to answer, me for feeling things I wasn't ready to admit, Loops for demanding explanations that had scraped me raw and left me unprepared for this, or Carter. Carter, who'd understood me but still abandoned me—chosen Dead Meat and money and eleven more surgeries over us and a Vickers-Landlow, Landlow-Vickers future. *I miss you. I need you. I love you.*

For the first time, I wished I could say to him, *"How could you?"*

"You're right, I don't get it at all. I've never felt invincible. Carter had perfect health, privilege, and bodyguards. He had *you*." Alex's voice was hoarse with distress. He reached out and touched my wrist with one finger. It was a question, not a caress. I could have pulled away, but I turned to face him instead. Forced myself to look into his eyes. "And I know you're going to remember I said that in the morning, but I'm saying it anyway. He had *you*, which means he was about as lucky as any guy could ever be."

He stepped back and broke the connection between his finger and my wrist. The skin there still felt warm, but the rest of me was so, so cold. I wasn't sure if the hot spell had broken just that minute, plunging the temps down to typical late-November forties . . . or if it had been cold at night for weeks, and I'd been too self-focused to notice. I shivered as Alex looked at me with flat eyes and said, "Not that it matters. If he's all you wanted, all you *still* want, then there's no place for what I'm feeling in any of this."

He walked away, and I was left standing there. Left with the words *How are you feeling?* still on my tongue, twisted up with *How do I know if I'm ready?*

I stared at the sky and begged for answers that wouldn't ever be given to me. They would never be easy or come without pain or cost—they were answers I'd have to create for myself.

It took three trips to carry Carter's printouts from the meeting room to my bedroom. I grabbed one of the suitcases that had been dropped off earlier and opened it. Slowly, I stacked the pages inside, trailing hesitant fingers and fussing with the arrangement of the last half-ream.

When I looked down on it all, one word came to mind—but not one I'd expected. Not proof but *closure.*

Like Alex had said about his faith, I didn't need anything external to validate what I'd had with Carter. I didn't need anything on any of these pages to corroborate what I already knew. It was my relationship, my first love.

And I could honor that. I could respect that. I could let that go.

I stood up on my mattress and pulled the photos off the metal crossbars that held up my canopy. I carefully removed the tape from the back of each and placed them on top of the others.

I pressed my hand to my lips. Pressed my fingers on that top page, then closed and zipped the suitcase.

I love you. I need you. I miss you.

I grieve you.

Good-bye.

CHAPTER 38

I'd pretended to be asleep when Loops crept in to settle on my trundle bed. And again when she blew me a kiss and tiptoed out to meet Anna for breakfast. Only then did I fall into a sleep that, judging by the tangles in my hair and sheets, must've been restless. I woke around noon, still thrumming with the type of anxiety that can only be shed through miles and sweat.

I rooted in my closet for running gear and a pair of much-neglected sneakers, dressed, and double-tied my laces. I didn't let myself pause or look longingly at the door across the hall, but began my run inside, hitting my stride before I'd crossed the patio.

My endurance was gone. My stamina too. And whatever inner thing that used to say "Shut up, sore legs, this is the route I picked, and you'll run the whole dang thing."

Maybe because my mind was already fixated on something—someone—else, and all the things I would say if given a do-over of that conversation beneath the stars.

I stopped just shy of the creek and sat down on the bank. My sweat mixed with the dirt, attracting bugs and making my shirt cling as I panted.

I hadn't run as far as I'd planned, but I'd run fast. Like I was racing demons or trying to escape Alex's anguished declarations. But all of those things still clung to me like the river dust that stuck to my wet palms.

I brushed them off. Stood. My pace was slower when I restarted my run, but more purposeful. I had a destination in mind and a plan for when I got there. I'd promised not to do anything *illegal* to get Alex a kidney, but I could work around that. And maybe if I couldn't tell him with words, I could *show* him how I felt.

Dr. Ackerman was on the phone when I walked in, on a call that was definitely *not* to someone in the Family. It sounded like it was to *his* family, and I couldn't remember if he had one. My eyes darted to the hand holding the phone—wedding band.

He looked up and smiled, holding up one finger. "Pal, I've got to let you go. I'll see you at your soccer game. Can't wait. Love you, buddy."

"Son?" I asked when he hung up.

"Nephew. I've got a daughter—Gia. She loves racing up and down the sidelines, so I'm sure she'll be chasing her cousin around the field soon enough."

He flipped a frame around on his desk: him, his pretty blond wife, and a beautiful round-cheeked baby with deep-brown skin.

I had a vague memory of Mama talking adoption, but didn't remember any of the details. It could've been *him* that got arrested—he deserved for me to at least know the name of his daughter, to have a picture of her in my mind when I asked him to gamble with his future.

"You have a lovely family. Gia looks so happy."

"She has her moments, but the twos aren't terrible and she's made us about as happy as any parents have a right to be. Happier, even." He grinned at the picture before putting it back down. "So what brings you out here?"

"I'm going to ask something about Alex's kidney." I wasn't looking for permission; I was psyching myself up. "It's not illegal. I promised him."

"Is it confidential? Because I can't—"

"I want you to test me." I yanked up my sleeve. "I want to know if I'm a match. If so, can't I give one of mine altruistically? Isn't that legal—as long as no money's exchanged? Test me."

Just looking at the blue lines in the crook of my elbow and knowing . . . needles. Blood. I breathed slowly in and out of my nose. It didn't help.

Blood. Blood in a vial. In tubing. Flowing in and out of the dialysis machines. All over the ground around Carter. And if there was a match—surgery. Knives. Cutting me. Cutting Alex. *They'd cut Carter.*

I shut my eyes and tipped my head back on the chair. Sweatier now than when I'd finished my run.

"Magnolia." Dr. Ackerman's voice sounded farther than just across the desk. Like the keystrokes I was hearing, the chair pushing back, his footsteps were all in another room. "I'm not going to take any of your blood. Let's calm down about that."

"But—" The word was thick in my tight throat. I cracked my eyes to find him kneeling by my chair. "You have to."

"I already know your blood type." He pointed to the computer monitor he'd spun around and the medical records displayed there. "You're AB. Do you remember what I told you Alex was?"

"A. Is that good? That's not good, is it?"

"Without needing additional treatments, his blood type is compatible only with kidneys from another A or an O. You, you're what's called the 'universal recipient.' You could get an A, B, AB, or O."

"So, I could get his kidney, but not the other way around?" Dr. Ackerman nodded. And I laughed bitterly. "Of course. Of course it plays out like this."

"For what it's worth, Magnolia Grace, I think you coming in here and asking was a noble gesture."

"Yeah," I said. "For what it's worth . . ." Which wasn't much, since it had been useless. "Thank you."

He nodded, then called my name as I reached for the doorknob. "Even if you were a perfect match, he wouldn't have taken it. Not from you."

"I know." And all the stubbornness in the world wouldn't have changed his mind. "But I had to try."

Just like I had to call Penny once I was squinting in the sun on the clinic's porch.

"Guess what? I'm learning," she said when she picked up.

"Learning what?" Certainly it wasn't how to answer the phone without plunging into the middle of a conversation.

"Well, last week I learned the right answer to 'What'd you do this weekend?' is not 'Worked on political polling.'"

"If the answer they were looking for was 'got wasted at so-and-so's party,' then I'm pretty sure you're the one who's too cool for them."

"I was thinking I'd go with a half-truth. 'Hung out in my boyfriend's dorm,' but leave out the part about us working on Organ Act mailings. Sound good?"

I laughed. "Add 'hung out at *Georgetown* in my boyfriend's dorm.' You'll get bonus points for dating an older guy. Though I bet they know from the media coverage."

"True. I've gotten a few comments like 'Is he that hot in person?'"

Char chuckled in the background and asked, "What do you tell them?"

"The truth—you're hotter."

I heard his laughter. Her responding squeal was muffled.

God, I hated how much I envied them.

I cleared my throat. "Penny?"

"Oh, right. Um. *Hi.* I hear you're coming to be our third Musketeer."

"Yeah, about that—" I bit my lip. "I have a favor to ask."

"Sure. What can we do?"

"Ask the vice president to get Alex back on the government transplant list."

"Oh." Her pause stretched so long, I wondered if I'd accidentally hung up because I was pressing the phone so tightly to my ear. "That's . . . that's the boy who was at the center of all the problems this week? Alex?"

"Alejandro Cooper," I said. "He's the only reason you get me as a third amigo, so isn't one lousy kidney a fair compromise?"

"I . . . we can't. I know your father already asked Bob. And Nolan gave a *lengthy* speech about it when I brought it up. There's already opposition to the idea of involving the Families—they can't grant us any favors and still look impartial."

"He's Char's age. How would you feel if it was *him*, Penny?"

Except, if I completed that analogy: *Char is to Penny as Alex is to Maggie*, then where was the spot for Carter?

I sat down hard on a chair by the pool, squinting at everything around me that was still sunny, bright, normal. Which it shouldn't be. If my world was going to change so dramatically with the slip of a tongue, with a zip of a suitcase, then shouldn't there be something tangible to reflect it? A gaping chasm in the ground, a seismic rattling of the earth? Not hummingbirds hovering around Mama's feeders and a gentle breeze that lifted the drowsy heads of her fall flowers.

Penny hadn't even noticed. His own sister didn't realize the betrayal I was teetering toward. "I wish I could think of a way to help him," she said with a sigh.

James appeared on the edge of the patio making wrap-it-up gestures as he tapped his foot. I nodded. "Thanks. I've got to go, Penny. But thanks. Talk soon."

CHAPTER 39

I jogged across the pool deck to where James was waiting. "Everyone okay? Your family?"

"We're hanging in there." He must've noticed I was still tense, because he added, "Alex is fine too—though he's looking similarly keyed up. I missed something, didn't I? Want to fill me in?"

"Not even a little."

"Fair enough." He turned toward the house. "So, stinky, you getting back in shape in case you have to outrun an angry Family mob?"

"Maybe." I opened the door. "They giving *you* grief?"

"Not so much. I think it's arrested-father sympathy."

"You missed seeing Loops." I grinned. "Remember Naggie?"

He laughed. "Yeah. Is that better than 'stinky'? And either way, I'm not giving you permission to revive 'Lames.'"

"Revive," I scoffed. "You make it sound like Loops and I ever *stopped* calling you that."

He snorted. "So, you gonna go shower at some point? Because your dad's been asking for you for the past hour. He's got big plans to lock you, me, and Alex in the meeting room and not let us out until you're the Organ Act's best spokesperson."

"All three of us?" I swallowed and started up the stairs. "Together?"

James nodded. "I know I can't think of anywhere I'd rather spend my day than locked up with two people who—"

"Don't even finish that sentence." I rubbed my temples and remembered Alex's face as he'd looked at those photos, as he'd stood by the pool and repeated what he'd overheard.

James and I had reached my bedroom door and I could've escaped behind the excuse of soap and water, but I owed our friendship more than that. And maybe *this* hard conversation would help me practice for the one I needed to have with Alex.

"Those things you said about the Family the other day— were they a reaction to your dad's arrest?"

He could've said "What things?" and I would've had my answer. He could've said "Maybe" and postponed the discussion until he felt more certain. But he raised his chin and said, "No."

"You really want out?" I tried not to take it personally, but the idea hurt. I'd just gotten his friendship back. I'd need people like him if I ever made it to the other side of Daddy's desk. No, not people *like* him—him.

"It's not a decision I've made lightly. Once you're out of the Family, you're *out.*"

The way he said it gave me shivers. "Why the finality? It's not like your dad's going to disown you. He still talks about Baby all the time. He shows me pictures of your nephew."

"But have you met Sam? When was the last time you saw Baby?"

"Wasn't she at—" Except, no, she wasn't at our high school graduation. Or our going-off-to-college party. Or any other holidays or events I could think of. "She *can't* come back?"

"There's not a rule book, but she wouldn't be welcome. I won't be either. I'm not saying I won't miss things, but I just—I need to forge my own path."

"Let me know what I can do to help." If I thought of this as good for him instead of bad for me, I could force a smile. "I know I sometimes suck at this friends thing, but I'm here for you, Lames. Anytime."

"Thank you." He leaned in like he might hug me, then wrinkled his nose. "For now, just get your stinky self in the shower and get downstairs before your dad blows a gasket."

I didn't have time to dry my hair or grab lunch before I found myself ensconced in the meeting room with James, Alex, and an arsenal of office supplies and tech.

"That's a bound-up copy of the act's current wording," Daddy said from the doorway. "Let me know if you need anything else, but don't come out until Maggie Grace is prepped to support the Organ Act like she wrote it. Understood? James?"

He saluted. "I'm on it."

"Alex?"

"Yes, sir." He glanced up to meet my daddy's eyes, but he'd been doing everything he could to avoid acknowledging me since I came downstairs.

"Magnolia?"

The weight of Daddy's expectations and disappointment pressed on my spine, but I stood tall. "I understand."

"Good. You're leaving soon. They want to get your face and voice noticed before the senators head home for Thanksgiving."

"How soon?" I narrowed my eyes—Thanksgiving was only nine days away.

"Anytime in the next seventy-two hours. I'm waiting on a call. The current plan's for you to stay three days. You'll attend a few parties, meet with influential vote makers, speak at a hospital with Penelope and Char, and do some 'pool spray'— that's DC talk for staged photo opportunities. Then you'll come home. If we're lucky, they'll squeak in this vote before they adjourn to eat turkey."

"The vice president's having duck," I said.

"Now that's just un-American." Daddy looked around the room one more time and gave a satisfied nod, saying "Y'all play nice" as he left and shut the door.

Alex was the first to sit, but he chose a seat at the far end of the table and was fidgeting with a stack of pens and notebooks like they were the most interesting things in the room.

I couldn't decide if it was better to claim the chair beside his or give him space. I wavered and paced a few seats in either direction.

James leaned against the wall on the other side of the table and watched us both. "Since we're clearly not rocking group work mojo today, how do you propose we get this done? Should we start with some trust falls? Would you rather? Never have I ever?" His levity clashed with the tension in the room. I studied the way he was tossing a whiteboard marker from hand to hand, trying to gauge if he was truly amused or just trying to lighten the mood.

If so, it wasn't working.

I had no doubt Daddy had designed this task as punishment for James and me—but did he have any idea how truly punishing it was? Or how much of that punishment also landed on Alex's slumped shoulders? His feet were braced on the floor; one hand gripped an armrest while the other continued to fiddle with the office supplies.

If I was stuck in here with one boy pretending I didn't exist and the other campaigning to make Lames the most apt nickname ever, I would scream.

I crossed the room, leaned over Alex's shoulder, and placed my hand on top of his around the pens. I doubt Medusa ever turned anyone to stone as quickly as he froze at my touch. I hovered there a beat too long, struggling to come up with something concise and relevant I could whisper in his ear.

I'm sorry for—

Please don't—

Alex, I—

Throat dry with frustration, I gave up and pried the pens from his grip.

"We'll each write out what we already know." I spun a notepad across the table to James and flung a pen after it. I grabbed myself a set and retreated to a seat closer to the door. "Then we'll compare."

"Okay," said Alex. His voice made me exhale. It was just one word, but it was the first he'd said to me today.

In the quiet of their pens scratching paper, I stared at my own blank page. I wasn't ignorant about the act—in fact, with all the research I'd been doing lately to play all the roles to all the people—I could quote portions of it verbatim. It was more of the *But what do I believe?* that tripped me up. Not what did Daddy want to hear? Not what would make it easier for Alex to get a kidney? Not what would make Penny smile or win over some crotchety old senator? Not what was my position six months ago, when Carter was alive?

But what did I believe *now*?

And, as much as I wanted to fill this notepad with a letter of apology and explanation for Alex, I *needed* to spend this time figuring out my own opinion, so when I came back home and got off my soapbox, I could still look myself in the eye.

I picked up my pen and got to work—adding my own scribbling, crossing out, pen tapping to the room's symphony of tension.

Many pages later, when my head felt empty and my hand felt cramped, I set down my pen and studied the boys. James was marking a page of the act with his finger as he copied out a passage. Alex's face was hidden by his shoulder and hair, but his notepad was covered in words, circles, arrows, things underlined and crossed out. I'm sure the logic was there. I'm sure the ideas were passionate and important—but, like the guy who wrote them, they'd take some time to figure out. You might not realize they'd won you over until after you'd pieced them together and seen their beauty, their brilliance, and their bravery.

"Alex, Maggie looks ready to tear that notepad from your hands." This was pretty accurate—I'd been daydreaming about taking his pen and holding it hostage so he was forced to talk to me. I shot James a death glare and used the second it took Alex to finish scrawling his thought to sit back in my seat and pretend I hadn't been pining. "You about done?"

"Yeah. Just about. Another minute or two. Five?"

"Take your time," I said.

James stood and dropped his notebook on top of mine. "Take as long as you like—but I'm going to mosey. Three hours in this room's about all I can handle. Plus, I'm getting the sense I'm in the middle of something—so I'll get out of y'all's way."

Alex looked up just in time to catch my panicked expression. Our eye contact lasted through several slow blinks. His eyes darkened as they lingered on mine, falling to rest on my mouth. I studied the pen cap in his.

James cleared his throat for the third or fourth time.

I licked my dry lips and the pen cap fell from between Alex's. I watched the muscles of his throat and jaw as he swallowed.

"So . . . I'll just be going," James called. "Not that I expect you to care—or notice. I could probably even lock you in without—"

"What?" I whirled toward where he was laughing in the door. He winked.

But when I glanced over my shoulder, Alex was already back to writing.

The door clicked *loudly* when it closed. I sprang from my seat. "If you actually locked that, James Byrd, so help me, I will fill your boots with fire ants and—" But the knob twisted in my hand, and I stepped out to where he was waiting in the hall.

"Traitor," I accused, after closing the door behind me. "I can't believe you said that."

"Coward," he countered. "Which isn't a good look for you."

Coward? It may be true, but it was also a fighting word. I tilted my chin up defiantly. But when I opened my mouth to argue, what came out was a pathetically quiet, "He won't even look at me."

James snorted. "Oh, he's looking plenty."

"Yeah, at everything *but* me."

"I did a project on body language last year, and I seriously wish I could redo my case study just to write about the insane avoidance-awareness displays you two are putting on. I don't know what went down between y'all since the other day at the creek, but here's your chance to fix it before you leave."

"Thanks." I turned back to open the door, then paused with my hand on the knob, a selfish request on my lips. "Come with me to DC?"

"Can't." He ducked his head and toed the floor.

"Just wanted to ask—I knew with your dad and everything you probably couldn't, and might not even want to, but . . ." I was scared, and I wanted him there—knew I had the power to insist on it. Power I'd never use because his free will mattered more to me than my fear. "I'll be fine."

"Should I expect a hayloft summons tonight?" he asked.

I shook my head. "No. You're busy with your family."

He palmed his keys. "I'll keep my phone on."

"Me too. It works both ways, you know."

"I do." He paired his wave with a smile so precious and genuine that if I'd been able to capture it, capture the emotion of this moment in a way that could be shared, it would be the only explanation I'd ever need for why I loved being part of my Family. It was this loyalty. This *I got your back,* and respect, and *I know you true and through.*

It was why I hated for the Family to lose him. And why I'd never ask him to stay.

CHAPTER 40

Alex wasn't writing when I walked back in the meeting room. His notepad was pushed aside, and he had mine and James's in front of him. "His is just facts—helpful for you to know and filler for speeches. But yours . . . This is good." He looked at me over the top of the page. "Do you mean any of it?"

I opened my mouth to answer, but he shook his head. "Let me finish reading first. Here's mine." He nudged his notepad toward me.

I slid into the chair beside him and picked it up. Even in a room without distractions I don't think I would've been able to follow his chaotic scribblings. With Alex sitting a few inches away and making little noises of "hmm" and "eh"—jotting down notes along the margins of my pages—I was a short attention span divided against itself.

"You know how you said your life stopped and started because of risks?" I asked. "Like, the risk of drag racing and then the risk of blackmailing me?"

He nodded.

"My version of that is technology, I guess. It was a virus that brought you into my life. And some automatic computer whatever that sent the photos and files that drove you away."

"I'm right here." Alex said it quietly. He dropped the notepad and turned to me. "I'm *right here*. At least for another two hours—then I've got to get myself on the machine because I start overnight dialyzing today. But, Maggie, I've lost count of the number of times I've made a fool of myself over you, and there's probably only so many ways I can be wrong. Last night—"

"You're not." I swallowed. "Not wrong."

His hands inched to the edges of his armrests and flipped palm up; a clear invitation for me to slide mine inside. And, God, I wanted to. My heart was pounding, and I couldn't decide where to look, those hands, his lips, his eyes. I dropped my gaze to my lap, where I was tying my fingers in anxious knots in an attempt to keep them from reaching for him.

"I feel like . . . the conversation we need to have is one we're not coming back from." I pointed between us, waving my finger through air that felt lit up with electricity. "If we can . . . , we should finish the DC prep then have *that* talk in your room once you're set up."

"But I'm not wrong?"

I shook my head, and Alex closed his eyes for a few seconds. When he opened them, they glowed with relief, hope, expectation.

"And I'll try not to do the whole panic-and-shut-down thing. I *want* to talk. Promise."

He nodded solemnly, like he knew how hard that promise was for me to make and would be for me to keep. "All right, then let's do this—work now, talk later."

I turned back toward the table, using the motion as an excuse to shut my eyes and exhale my relief. Then I tapped his pages. "I'm sure this is all brilliant, but between the Spanish and the crossing out . . . or is that underlining? Anyway, I'm lost."

He grinned and reached for the notepad. Our fingers brushed as I handed it over and neither of us jerked away, we let the contact linger for an extra beat while he swallowed and I bit my lip. Sweet Lord and all things holy, it was going to be hard to focus.

"Ready?" he asked.

Nope. Not at all.

Ninety-eight minutes later we'd devoured dinner trays, eating one-handed and talking around mouthfuls as we debated and discussed and looked up facts. It was everything I loved about spending time with Alex—the conversation, the way he challenged me, the way he could point out I had barbecue sauce on my cheek and I didn't feel self-conscious . . . at least not until he reached over, his palm cupping my face as his thumb brushed it off.

My "oh, thanks," was breathless.

His "anytime" was a growl.

We both smiled tightly, averted our eyes, and rolled our chairs an inch or so apart. It'd been a *long* ninety-eight minutes, and my only real comfort was that he seemed as affected, distracted, and impatient as I did. "Um, could you repeat what you were saying?" I asked. "About answering the question I *want*, not necessarily the one that's asked?"

I'd covered five more pages with notes. Alex had played reporter by lobbing questions at me, and then he was a PR consultant, critiquing my responses. I'd laughed at his reporter voice, which was just as deep as his regular one, but slower, and full of over enunciation.

"C'mon. Just one 'In a world where anything can be bought and sold . . . *including human organs*,'" I teased. "You were born to do movie voice-overs."

He lifted one eyebrow and made his voice even lower as he said, "Focus."

I grinned and turned back to my notebook and the answers I was polishing—one set for in-Family, one set for DC.

"In a world where Magnolia Grace Vickers—" I lost the rest of his sentence because I was laughing so loud the sound reverberated off the glass light fixtures. And he was laughing too, bumping his chair against mine. "I think we've been trapped in this room too long. I'm starting to lose it."

"I just need—" I held a finger to my lips and made final

tweaks on what I was writing, then flipped my notebook around to show him. "I might actually be able to pull this off."

"What's this?" He tapped my calculations on the opposite page, the laughter disappearing from his eyes. "Bottom lines? Net income? The senators won't care about your profits—you're supposed to be focused on helping *people*."

My posture straightened automatically in response to the challenge in his voice. "I need to have a platform ready for DC, but I've also got to sort matters out *here*. The Family want to know where I stand and why they should stand with me. That's my answer. And I'm sorry if mentioning profits offends you, but it's the language that's going to speak to the men here whose jobs are on the line. They need to know that if we can't keep them we'll be able to, at the very least, give them a generous severance package. But I'm hoping we can find new roles for everyone in the post–Organ Act reorganization."

"It's kinda hot when you talk business." Alex was tilting his head and staring at me in that way that made my cheeks flush.

"Um . . ." I swallowed. "Thanks." I was at the end of my resistance, but the finish line was so close. If we could keep it together for two more minutes, then we could do all sorts of mutual admiration. I shoved my notebook at him again. "Now, if you'll look *here*, where I was actually pointing, these are my sound bite answers for DC. Do you approve?"

It took him far too long to read the three answers I'd written on the page. They were succinct and legible—so as time and silence stretched, my patience did not. I worried over the angle of his eyebrows, the way his lips moved as he mouthed my words, as if trying them out. I watched his eyes track back and forth across the paper, scooting over so I could figure out where he was and why the holdup.

He put the notepad down and swiveled his chair toward mine—I'd moved so close our knees touched, but he didn't back up and I didn't either. And my question, "So, what do I need to fix?" died on my lips, because his face was . . . wonderment. It was bright eyes and lightly flushed cheeks, and lips parted into a wide smile.

"Yeah," he said quietly, his voice a deep rumble. "I approve."

His dark-eyed gaze conveyed that he meant more than just what was written on the paper. It hit low in my stomach in a way that made me shivery. I inhaled a breath that stuttered its way to my lungs and turned away from him.

"Good. Because Daddy's going to need to hear how amazingly well-prepared I am and you've only got about ten minutes until you need to get all needle-y on yourself."

"Maggie—" He breathed my name against my neck, and I couldn't decide if I wanted to lean back against him or bolt forward out the door.

I didn't turn around or stop stacking notebooks and gathering pens. "I'm not panicking, Alex. I just need a minute to—I need a minute. I'll go talk to Daddy and then meet you in your room. Text me when you're done with the scary part."

"Okay," he said. "But *you're* the scary part right now."

I glanced back over my shoulder, at his mouth so close to my skin. "I'm not."

"I'll text you. You'll be there."

It wasn't quite a question, that last statement of his. But it wasn't a declaration of fact either. Neither was mine when I echoed him. "I'll be there."

CHAPTER 41

Over the next thirty-four minutes, I packed for DC, sweet-talked Daddy ("This is some fine work, sport"), and typed up and sent my mission statement memo/apology to the Family. I did it all without putting down my phone, which *finally* chirped with a message from the guy across the hall.

Ready.

Each step was a decision, a choice to move forward. I took a deep breath and pulled open his door, went inside, and shut it behind me. My heart was hammering, and my hands were so sweaty I didn't so much put down my phone as let it slip from my fingers onto his bedside table.

"Hey there." He smiled—it wasn't a grin, it was on the timid side of the spectrum—but it was a start.

"Hi." I threw myself forward and sat down on his bed, because I'd promised not to panic, but I swear I'd left my stomach back in my own room. I pulled a throw pillow into my lap and began to knead the heck out of its stuffing.

"I'm proud of you, you know. For what you're doing for the Organ Act. And for listening when I asked you to stop looking for a kidney for me."

"*Illegal* kidney," I corrected. But it didn't make sense to tell him about the legal routes I'd tried today. Not when both had been dead ends. "Now all that's left is to persuade some senators and win the vote. Then I'm going to find you a perfectly legal six-out-of-six match."

"Thank you. I know you hate waiting, but it's better for everyone that way."

"No. It's better for everyone but *you*." And I was having a hard time remembering the "greater good" and "long run," when I considered the personal risk to *him*. I gripped the pillow tighter in hands that were suddenly shaky. "And I swear on all things electronic and wired, Alex, if you get so much as a cold before that transplant, you're in so much trouble. The first time you sneeze, you'd better call me."

"So you can come play nurse?" He was looking at his tubes, which meant I was looking at them too. I swallowed—nope, I hadn't left my stomach in my bedroom. It was here, and it was churning.

"Maybe you should stay here on the ranch. So you'd be close to the clinic. Just in case."

"I'm not moving into your house permanently, Maggie." He laughed and shook his head. "It already feels weird bringing this dialysis machine home."

"I know you need to go, but . . . I'm used to having you here. I like having you across the hall." It took me a moment to realize how entitled that sounded and while Alex laughed first, I beat him to the punch line. "Yes, I'm a *princesa* and I know you're not a plaything, but . . ."

"Go on." His eyes were hooded and his voice gravely as he shifted to face me as much as possible, which wasn't all that much with his arm connected to the machine. "I'm not a *plaything*, but . . . ?"

But there was nothing stopping me from turning. I tucked my feet up on the bed so my knees were pressed against the outside of his thigh. "I want to be able to look across the table on Thanksgiving and say the thing I'm most thankful for is the computer virus that brought you into my life."

"But what about . . . ?" He didn't need to finish the statement; the residue of yesterday was all over the tense lines of his posture. It was pushing hope off his face and hardening the feelings left behind.

"I'm allowed to want more than one thing, Alex. If that makes me a princesa, then get me a tiara and I'll find a spot to put the throne. But"—I put a hand on his knee—"I'm pretty sure it just makes me human. I shouldn't have said Carter was *all* I ever wanted. It's not true. Right now I'm wanting chocolate ice cream, and cozy pajamas, and a kidney for you, and Byrd home from jail, and to not have to go to DC, and—"

For you to shut me up by kissing me. That was the next thing I'd planned on saying, and he did shut me up, but not with a kiss.

"But you want *him*. And I'll never be him."

"Nope. You won't." When he looked up at me with stormy eyes, I shrugged. "Get over it. No, you're not Carter. You'll never get to be my first love."

"Yeah, I've noticed." His voice was as bitter and weak as coffee made from twice-brewed grinds.

"But who says I want you to be? Why is my first love the only one that has value?"

He sat up on the edge of the bed so his back was to me. "I'm supposed to be happy I'm your second pick? Your consolation prize?"

"There was no *picking*."

"Because he's dead."

My arguments dried up in a mouth that tasted like ash. "Yes, he is."

"And if he were still alive, you'd never be sitting with me having this conversation. I saw all the pictures, Maggie. I've heard the way you talk about him."

"I'm not going to say I'm happy he's dead. I'm *never* going to say those words. If that's what you want to hear—that I'm glad he was murdered so you could take his place—then walk out that door and don't ever, *ever* come back." The tinkling of the throw pillow's beaded fringe gave away my trembling hands, but my shaking voice had already betrayed me. "That's not fair. He was a good person."

"I can't walk out the door right now." Alex lifted his hand with the tubing attached. "And I don't want to. I just need to know . . ."

"*Yes.*" I stood up and walked around the bed, knelt in front of where he was sitting. "Yes, I want *you*. But enough with the competition. I won't play that game. I'm not going to denigrate Carter to make you feel special. You *are* special. And my heart is not a one-time-use item. If so, I gave it away to a horse when I was six. Sorry, you're thirteen years too late."

He reached out a hand and I took it, climbed up beside him.

"What was the horse's name?"

"Mama wanted to name her Princess Sparkles or something like that, but Daddy said it was my horse, my choice. I picked Conniption."

Alex laughed. "Because?"

"Because I loved the word. Mama said it every time I had a tantrum, and I thought it was pretty fabulous."

His chin skimmed my shoulder as he turned to me. "Well, I suppose I can share you with Conniption."

I leaned in. "You don't have to share me with anybody."

I would've thought our first kiss would be all maneuvering and caution . . . all me being hyperaware of the machine and the tubing.

It wasn't. It wasn't. It soooo wasn't.

Mostly because our first kiss was a brush of lips on lips. Smile on smile, really. Sitting side by side and meeting in the middle—giving, taking, gliding, breathing.

Then he pulled back, lay back. And raised his eyebrows in an invitation I was all too willing to accept.

The dialysis machine whirred quietly by the bedside, cleaning his blood, making him stronger—but I forgot all about it when he tugged me down beside him, slanted his head, and deepened our kiss. We felt like our own cycle—as his confidence grew, as he groaned and touched his tongue to mine, I was absorbing all the fear and uncertainty. Gripping his shoulders tighter like holding on to him, holding on to this moment could keep him safe.

He moved his mouth to my neck and I wanted to shut my eyes, but I couldn't stop staring down at this guy who'd conquered every corner of my heart—despite my best efforts to fight him off. Despite the tremendous energy I'd spent telling myself I couldn't feel anything, *shouldn't* feel anything.

"Please be safe." I whispered it like a prayer. And maybe I would start praying again, because I needed Someone to tell these fears to. I wanted to believe in Someone looking over him and me and guiding our lives—Someone benevolent who wouldn't have led me to Alex if He was only going to snatch him away.

I tugged his mouth back to mine and this next kiss felt a lot like a leap of faith. The expression on Alex's face looked a lot like worship.

But that was as far as I let my thoughts drift—because the feeling of Alex's body against mine was deliciously sinful.

He pulled back first, sinking into his pillow, but tugging me close in the crook of his arm, and leaning over to press a breathless kiss to the top of my head. His jaw was clenched, his eyes dark and intense, but soft in a way that made me glow. "¡Estoy loca por ti!—I'm crazy about you. Do you know how hard it is to not be able to hold you in *both* arms?"

I glanced down at where he was clenching the blanket. And even though there were tubes—and *blood!*—only a few inches higher up that arm, I touched my fingers to my lips and caressed them across the back of his hand until his fingers relaxed and intertwined with mine. I brushed my mouth across the skin above his collar, then nestled against his chest, yawning.

"Next time we'll plan better so you can use both arms. Maybe. If you're being good. I wouldn't want to make it too easy on you."

"Easy?" He laughed. The sound still gave me the best kind of shivers, especially now when I could feel the rumble of his chest beneath my ear. "I don't think that word's even in your vocabulary."

"Hush," I murmured drowsily. "Because you're crazy about me, and I'm so sleepy."

His lips brushed across my forehead, and his arm tightened around my shoulder. I *mmm*'d at the sensation and shut my eyes.

"Maggie, shouldn't you head back to your own room?"

"You follow too many rules," I mumble-protested, then drifted into the vibrations of the encore of his laughter.

CHAPTER 42

"What do you *mean*, Magnolia is missing?"

My eyes blinked open at the roar of Daddy's voice. I wasn't looking at gray canopy curtains, but the blue walls of the guest room. The tousled hair of the guy I'd nestled so close to, I was sharing his pillow.

"How the blazes could she be missing? Where have you looked?"

The door flew open, and my first instinct was to brace Alex so he wouldn't jerk upright and strain the arm attached to the machine. He rubbed his eyes, the fear of God on his face. Once I was satisfied he was alert enough to be safe, I turned to face the wrath that had put it there.

"Magnolia Grace Vickers!" Daddy bellowed, grabbing my arm and pulling me off the bed.

I meekly smoothed down the wrinkled skirt of my dress. "Hi, Daddy."

"You're not too big for me to tan your hide—but I don't even have time to give you a proper hollering." He turned back to whoever was lingering in the hall. "Damned poor search party y'all are—go on now and get ready."

He'd never so much as swatted my hand, so I knew my "hide" was safe, but the non-sticks-and-stones parts of me were cringing. "I—I fell asleep. We were talking and—"

"And *you*," Daddy thundered at Alex. "In *my* house. Under *my* roof—you dare—"

"I'm sorry, sir. We were just sleeping."

It was hard to look contrite when I was hearing Alex's extra-rumbly morning voice for the first time. And bed head. He did superb bed head. I wanted to get my fingers caught in those rumpled tangles.

"She was on you like a tick on a dog," accused Daddy. "*That's* how you repay my hospitality?"

The dialysis machine started beeping—the heart rate alarm lit up *and* the bell that meant his cycle was over. Why couldn't *that* have happened five minutes sooner? Given me time to slip back into my own room before all this commotion.

"As lovely as that thought is, Daddy, it's just not true." I put a hand on the one he still had around my arm and pushed him a step back from the bed. "We were talking, and I fell asleep. End of story."

"*My* house, Magnolia Grace. Not in my house."

Alex was hitting buttons, and his movements were frantic,

jerky. I needed him to calm down before he hurt himself getting off the machine. I needed Daddy to calm down too—but since that wasn't likely anytime soon, I needed him out of this room.

"What did you want?" I asked.

"You. On a plane. You're leaving this morning."

"Today?" Alex and I asked in unison. Daddy shot him another glare.

"Today. I need you downstairs, Magnolia. *Now*."

"Okay, I just—"

"Now!"

I met Alex's eyes. I wanted a kiss. I wanted a do-over where our morning was soft and slow and smiles and whispers.

"Calm down before you . . ." I pointed at his machine. "And sorry. And . . . I'll see you downstairs."

"See you downstairs," he echoed.

"So help me, Magnolia Grace, if you are not out of this boy's bedroom in two seconds . . ."

One last look. Summer-grass eyes that smiled despite the circumstances, lips I wished were against mine.

Daddy slammed the door after me. "Tell me you're packed."

"I am." There were two suitcases on my bed. The heavier one—the one full of memories—I tucked away in the back corner of my closet. The other I handed to Daddy. "What time do I leave for the airport?"

"Now. Twenty minutes ago if you'd been sleeping in your own bed and I hadn't had to hunt you down. A truck is waiting out front."

"Now?" I gaped at him. "But—"

"The only butt that's even close to acceptable at this moment is yours in that vehicle. I e-mailed you the itinerary last night, right after you sent out that memo." Left unspoken but clearly communicated was that I should've been paying more attention to my in-box than getting *in bed*.

"Don't I get to say good-bye—" When his face turned a darker shade of murderous red, I finished, "to Mama?"

"Call her from the road." His hand was on my back, and I barely had time to snag my purse, boots, and a cardigan before we were out of my room.

He propelled me down the stairs at practically a run. "But— won't the plane wait?" I asked as Brooks took the items from my hands and carried them out the door and Anna refilled them with a cup of coffee and a plate of something.

"You're not taking our plane. So no, it won't. Get in the truck." Daddy stamped a hasty kiss on my forehead and took my plate. I snatched the toast off it and stubbornly refused to give up my coffee mug. "And we're having a talk about this morning, a right big one, when you get home."

Enzo grabbed my coffee mug, holding it in front of me like a lure while Daddy pressed a hand on my back and Brooks called from the truck, "Ask if she has her wallet— she'll need ID."

"I do." I slapped away the hands herding me. "And I can buckle myself." Then the door was shutting and the tires were turning and I hadn't gotten to say good-bye.

I hadn't even gotten to say good morning.

I smoothed out the skirt of my rumpled sundress and slid on the boots Brooks had dumped on the floor of the backseat.

My phone. My phone was on the bedside table in Alex's room.

"Brooks, can I have your cell?" I asked him. "I forgot mine, and I assume Enzo won't be turning around so I can get it."

He handed it over, but I paused before hitting any buttons. "Is it the two of y'all coming with me—or do I have triple-quadruple coverage now?"

"Just me," said Brooks.

"Oh." My stomach sank as I considered the possibility that no one else would work with me . . . or him. I owed him a different kind of apology than the ones I'd given in the foyer or e-mailed out last night. "Brooks, I'm real sorry for whatever trouble you got in on my behalf. Let me know if—"

"Dangit, Magnolia, why do you got to go and make it so hard to be mad at you?" Enzo slapped a hand against the steering wheel.

"Thanks? I think? Though no one else seems to be struggling." None of the men had greeted me this morning as I was rushed past. And they hadn't looked too hard before letting Daddy find me in Alex's bed.

Brooks smacked Enzo. "Stop hijacking my apology. And you"—he pointed at me. "Stop apologizing. I knew what I was agreeing to. As for the men—give 'em time. You being away on this trip, and Alex leaving your place—that'll help."

"This trip where Daddy couldn't even get two-guard coverage for me?" I pressed my lips together and nodded. "It seems real promising."

"I'm not gonna lie—I wasn't his first choice to come with you." Brooks gave me a minute to absorb that blow. "But the plan was always you plus one. Your goal is to make the Family look wholesome. A mess of bodyguards wouldn't. The vice president's got Secret Service. I'm pretty much along to open doors and call your daddy if you cause trouble."

He and Enzo both gave me raised-eyebrow looks of warning and anticipation that felt so close to normal I wanted to sob in relief.

"I'll try and behave," I managed, before turning to the phone and texting James.

It's Maggie. On my way to DC. Forgot cell. Please check on Alex ASAP. Talk soon.

"Do you have Penny Landlow's number?" I asked.

"Can't say I do," said Brooks. "But they'll be sending a motorcade to meet us at the airport."

"And what about . . . Alex?" It was supposed to sound nonchalant, but came out as a mumble, which Enzo greeted with a chuckle and Brooks a grin.

"Nope. Haven't ever needed to call that boy."

I shrugged like this was no big deal—fooling absolutely no one—then handed back the phone. "Let me know as soon as James responds."

I could feel my panic creeping back in—fear about Alex and Daddy, concern for James and Byrd, insecurity about my ability to do my Family and the Organ Act proud.

I exhaled a quavery breath and tried to push it all aside. Tried to find some of Alex's calm and faith.

I leaned my head against the window, stared past the strip malls and developments, then laughed so loudly at a church billboard that both guys startled, until I pointed and they joined in too. BE AN ORGAN DONOR: GIVE YOUR HEART TO JESUS.

CHAPTER 43

Brooks slept the whole flight. I spent it refining my sound bites in the margins of the airline magazine. I woke him at landing, waited for him to yawn and stretch, then prompted, "Any news from James?"

"If we were going to be here longer than three days, I'd say our first stop should be a cell phone store."

"Think we *can* make unexpected stops in a motorcade?" Taking in the exasperation on his face, I added, "Well, can you blame me for being keyed up? Daddy was furious when we left."

"He's not going to take the kid out back and castrate him. He'll bluster a bit, then remember he *likes* Alex and you still had your clothes on—" He paused, waiting for me to affirm this.

I rolled my eyes and nodded. *"I'm* the one who should be getting yelled at. Not him."

"Beg to differ." Brooks was drawling extra slow. It made the woman waiting in front of us to deplane turn around to check him out. "If your daddy had known what you were up to before, the Landlow boy would've been—"

"You can beg to differ all you want, but last I checked I'm nineteen years old. I'm not asking permission or forgiveness for any of my choices."

One of my favorite things about Brooks was he knew when to shut up. He wisely did so now. Nodding like he was mulling my words over and then holding out his phone. "Nothing new. I'll keep you posted."

"Thank you." It was time for me to stop asking. James would get back to me when he could. And while Daddy's anger might not rank in Alex's top ten memories, I had to give him a little credit and acknowledge that compared to everything else he'd gone through, it wouldn't be in his bottom ten either. He'd be fine. We'd laugh about this later.

Maybe *a lot* later, but eventually we'd laugh.

When we got outside the airport, a five-foot-three-inch ball of energy shot out of a car and danced around me. "You're here! I can't believe you're here! Finally."

If Pen's expression was pure sunshine, then the man who'd fallen over himself trying to contain her was a storm cloud.

"Hi, Penny."

"Right. 'Hi' should come first." She hugged me gently, then turned to Brooks. "Hi, I'm Penny Landlow, and we should probably get back in the car. Right, Mason?"

"Yes, ma'am. Back in the vehicle. As quickly as possible."

"I'm not very good at the whole Secret Service thing," she confided once we were all inside. As expected, Char had come with Penny to pick us up and was waiting when we got in the SUV. He laughed at her statement. So did the man and woman in the front seat.

"It's good to see you, Maggie," Char said.

"Likewise." I went through introductions with Brooks, watched the guys shake hands and then fall into conversation about the agenda for our trip. And maybe Pen was right to call Ming "Char," because the heat between them was palpable. It was the simple things—the way he had his arm around the back of her seat and rubbed her bare shoulder with his thumb—so even when he was talking to Brooks, his attention was also on her.

Penny had done good things for Char's confidence. I'd thought he was attractive, but kind of schlubby. Not anymore. He met my eyes now. He had his shoulders back and carried himself in a way that commanded and steered the conversation instead of just following.

It made me miss Alex—made it tempting to ask Brooks if there was any chance he'd missed a call or text from home in the five minutes since I last asked. Instead I turned to Penny and let myself absorb the true joy in her smile.

I'd complained about the timing of this trip. Complained about its purpose and its interruption to my life. But I hadn't stopped to think about the positives too. Among all the devastation of this spring and summer, Pen was a high point and an anchor.

"Hi," she said. "Figured I'd get in an extra greeting now because the rest of your visit is probably going to be a whirlwind. And who wants to waste time on pleasantries?"

I laughed. My mama lived for pleasantries. She could spin them into a whole conversation so you walked away feeling like you'd gorged on cotton candy—full, sweet-sick, but not satisfied. God love a girl who believed the opposite.

"It is good to see you, Penelope Maeve. So, besides failing Secret Service 101, what have you been up to?"

"Oh, I'm awful at Secret Service. My first agent quit without even saying good-bye. Which was hard—I really liked Whitaker. Didn't you, Char?"

And . . . he was Ming again. In that instant, all confidence slipped away and he was making the dodgiest eye contact when he said, "Um, yeah. He was nice."

I narrowed my gaze. "You have no idea what happened to him?"

"Bob told me Whitaker requested a reassignment—I really can't blame him," Penny said.

Char looked like he was going to slink off the seat or climb out the window. I'd be asking him about that later, because if Whitaker was a threat to Penny I wanted to know. And if Char was threatened *by* Whitaker and had had him reassigned, well, he better put on some big-boy pants and deal with his issues—because her safety was not secondary to his jealousy.

Penny sighed. "I'm trying to be better, especially when I'm out with any of the Formans, because security is *crazy* then. But I've only ever had no freedom on the estate or no limits in New York. This in between is impossible. Gate me and put me in lockdown, or let me go wherever I please . . . but don't show me new places, then tell me to stay in the car." She shook her head. "I'm sure Mason and Louise want to quit daily."

"Only once a week, ma'am," said the woman behind the wheel.

"You'll figure it out," I said. "Give it some time."

"So they say. Anyway, ready for this lunch?"

"Key players plus public place, so be persuasive and look photogenic. Does that sum it up?"

Char nodded. "I've put together dossiers on the three senators who'll be joining us. Would you like to review?" He held out a tablet, but I shook my head.

"Thanks, but I've got this."

"You sure?"

"Very. I had some help preparing. I'm good."

"The trip was so last minute—I hope that didn't keep you up all night," Penny said.

Brooks snorted. I elbowed him and blushed.

She gave me a curious smile before adding, "So glad you're here."

I waited to corner Char until after our lunch with the senators. Until after we were at One Observatory Circle and finished the meet-and-greet with the vice-presidential family—quietly-serene Mrs. Forman, infectiously friendly Kelly, catalog-perfect Caleigh, and the artfully charming veep.

I waited until Brooks had gone off with Mason and Louise to go over security plans.

Until Penny had bemoaned an English paper she had due.

Then I said, "I'll walk Char out so you can get started."

Even though they'd probably planned on some farewell kisses at the gate, he said "Sure," and Penny gave me an I'm-so-glad-my-people-are-getting-along smile.

I grinned right back and held it in place until Char and I were out the front door. Then I spun on him, "Let's talk."

"Oh, okay." He swallowed. "About something in particular?"

"Why did Penny's agent Whitaker quit?"

He almost stumbled down the stairs, but grabbed the railing and made a show of studying it. Like walking suddenly took all his concentration. "How would I know?"

"You're full of it. I saw your reaction in the limo. But, fine, next topic: artificial organs." Because when it came down to it, Whitaker was already gone. He wasn't a problem I could fix.

"What about them?"

"I know your Family has them; I want to know how safe they are. How comfortable you are implanting them."

We were in the middle of a green lawn—in front of us, the security fence where Char's guard was waiting, the vice-presidential residence behind us. But he halted like a kid playing freeze tag. His skin was gray. He put down his man-bag and focused his lost brown eyes on me. "How long have you known? Are you going to tell her about Garrett?"

"Garrett? What are you—" My eyes went wide. "You know! You know where he is, and she's driving herself sick with worry about it and ragged with guilt because she knows talking about him upsets you."

Now he was slack-jawed and bug-eyed. "You didn't—"

"No. I didn't. But now I will, because you're going to tell me." I picked up his bag and carried it to a gazebo. Char hesitated so long I thought he might abandon his stuff, but he finally followed and sat down beside me.

"I can't—I can't talk about this."

"Is she safe? That's really all I need to know."

"Of course." He shot back to his feet. "You think I'd put her in danger? Never!"

"Is he?" I asked. "Safe. And/or a danger to her?"

"I'm not supposed to talk about it."

"But you want to." It was clear in the pinched lines between his eyes, in the way "I can't" had become "I'm not supposed to."

"I didn't ask for this secret," he said, sitting back down. "Your questions—Whitaker, artificial organs—I thought you knew. Whitaker didn't leave Penny because she had too many conversations with strangers on the way from school to the car. He volunteered to be Garrett's contact when he went into witness protection."

"I thought as much—not the Whitaker part—but that after testifying against his family, Garrett might have to go into witness protection. Why can't she know?"

"He was shot—at my house. He was shot protecting *her*, and as much as I want to hate him, and I really, really want to hate him—I can't forget the way he put himself in front of that bullet." Char shut his eyes. "I was too far away . . ."

I gave him a few seconds to breathe deeply, then touched his arm. "I can hate him enough for both of us while still being glad he saved her. Go on."

"The bullet lacerated his liver. He was in hypovolemic shock by the time we got him to our clinic—already acidotic. We couldn't stop the bleeding. My father was getting prepped for his artificial heart transplant. He ordered the doctors to prep a prototype for Garrett too—for an artificial liver. There wasn't time to get them to the hospital—the house was locked down. I thought he'd bleed to death, and—she was unconscious. Maybe I should've paid more attention to what was going on in the other clinic rooms, but I couldn't make myself care while Penny was unresponsive. Her blood wouldn't even register a platelet count."

I knew the bones of this story—I knew the outcomes, but hearing the way his breath was catching, his chest heaving, seeing that unfocused, haunted look in his eyes—I knew he couldn't remember the end while he was stuck in the middle. Sometimes the journey matters more than the outcome, but sometimes the scars or joys from the voyage supersede the final destination.

"My dad stroked out on the table . . . He's—he's not doing well. I don't expect him to last until the New Year." Char shut his eyes and pinched the bridge of his nose. "But he chose that. He knew the risks, and he chose it. Garrett didn't."

"But Garrett *isn't* in a coma." I'd seen him on TV. I'd read his testimony. I'd cursed the image of him walking in and out of the courthouse.

"No. But it's a prototype. There's so much we don't know about how it's going to work or react to different factors. He became a human guinea pig without his consent."

"And Penny doesn't know?"

He shook his head. "When I go home every month to visit my dad—they bring Garrett in too. The head of our research division was killed in the raid, but I worked closely with him. The clinic doctors check Garrett—and then I check the liver's function."

I leaned forward and practically squeaked my next question, *"You've seen Garrett every month and haven't told Penny?"*

"I'm not allowed to. That was part of the deal—the whole witness protection thing. I had to sign all sorts of confidentiality agreements."

"I think Penny is the exception to that rule. Do you know how she's going to feel when she finds out?"

"She *can't* find out. I know she stresses about him. I know she's hurt by my refusal to talk about him. You think I *like* lying to her? You think I *enjoy* spending time with *him*? Hearing him ask about her? Seeing that he *cares*?" Char's hands were fists, and he was digging them into his legs. "But she'd want him to have the best possible care—I know the prototype better than anyone. And every time a level comes back off, every time *anything* looks suspect . . . What will she think if anything happens to him and it's *my* fault?"

"She'll think you didn't trust her." I turned to stare out the tall fence around the property. Did it bother her as much as the one on her estate? She'd traded one guardhouse for another. How would she handle another person she loved keeping secrets? Because Carter had had so many. "She'll wonder what else you hid from her. And if it would have made a difference if you'd told her. She'll have so many doubts."

"Are we still talking about Penny and me? Because I don't think she'll wonder if she could've made a difference—she has no medical expertise in this area."

I laughed bitterly. No. No, we definitely weren't. And on the spectrum of voyages to outcomes, mine was definitely enjoy it up front and pay for it later. I'd paid. I'd be damned if she had to pay too.

"Take it from someone who knows—tell her. Don't let this Ward bastard steal anyone else from her—and if she finds out later, it will. It'll destroy you guys."

"I love her."

"I know." My mouth was metallic, coated with all the truths

I didn't want to keep swallowing. "But do you trust that *she* loves *you* enough to be able to deal with this?"

If Carter had told me he had doubts about Dead Meat, that he was tossing and turning on a bed of morality and questions. Tangled up in a spiderweb of loyalty and obligation and fear it was too late to stop. *If* he had confided any of the things he'd confessed in his last letter—a letter I didn't read until it was weeks too late—would I have listened? Would I have given good advice?

Could I have saved him?

Could I save the boy I'd left back home?

I gritted my teeth. "Kidneys—where are you in the process of developing those?"

"Artificial? We're not. I'm out of the research race. Right now, with freshman year, the Organ Act, my dad, Garrett, Penny . . . I'm spread too thin."

"But surely your people—"

"Is this about the guy from the kidney arrest the other day? He's why you're here, right?"

I nodded.

Char studied me a moment, and I felt my cheeks start to flush. He shook his head. "I wouldn't put a prototype in anyone I loved—they're just not safe. I'm sure he's getting good care—great care—from your Family doctors. Trust them." He reached over and squeezed my shoulder. "The best thing you can do to help him is be effective here—and you were already amazing with those senators at lunch."

I lifted my chin. "Well, get ready, because that was just the warm-up."

"Good. And I know Penny's said this a dozen times, but we're glad you're here."

"Me too." I held his eyes for a few long seconds. "But *tell her.*"

CHAPTER 44

After dinner, I borrowed Brooks's phone again. When James didn't answer, I tried Daddy. Then Enzo.

And, as a last resort—Mama.

"Hello, honey. Did you have a nice flight?"

"Mama—did the zombie apocalypse hit Texas? Because I can't think of any other reason everyone's gone MIA."

"I have no idea where everyone is—well, your daddy's in his office, but the rest . . ."

Of course she didn't. She reveled in not knowing. "Why isn't Daddy calling me back?"

"He says you need to be focused on your task *there* and less concerned about what's going on *here*." She paused. "Though, between you and me, sugar, I think he's still calming down from this morning. You may be nearly a woman, but you'll always be his little girl. There was a great big row about it before they left. Lots of screaming and fuss and that vase in the front hall got broken—you know the one Suetta gave me for my wedding? It was crystal! Baccarat. And then they *left*."

"Who left? Dangit, Mama." Two minutes about a vase and nothing about what I needed to know.

"Magnolia Grace Vickers, that is not how a lady talks."

Then she would've enjoyed the words dropping like bombs in my head. "Where. Is. Alex?"

"I. Don't. Know." She copied my slow, overarticulated speech, and just before I threw Brooks's phone across the floral-printed guest room, she added, "But . . . there was an ambulance here this morning. It's all been terribly stressful."

"I'vegottogoMama." I blurred it together like one word. There wasn't time to waste on her runaround. I dialed James as I threw my suitcase on the bed and began to shove shoes and dresses inside. "Answer, answer. Please, answer." But he didn't, so I texted.

Coming home.

I busted out of my guest room yelling "Brooks!" because I couldn't remember which room was his.

"Maggie?" Pen popped out from the door beside mine. "Everything okay?"

I shook my head. "How long to the airport? What's the fastest I could get through security?"

"Magnolia?" Brooks leaned out of a guest room down the hall, his hair still wet from the shower, his chest bare, and his jeans clinging to damp skin.

"Get a shirt on. We have to go home. Alex. Mama said—" My chest was crushed beneath the weight of the next word, my knees loose with the uncertainty. "Ambulance."

Had he messed up the dialysis last night? Had I done something or bumped something while kissing or cuddling? Or this morning—when he'd been shouted into alertness and had to unhook himself from that machine under Daddy's angry glare?

I leaned against the wall, sliding down the velvet paper. Brooks's phone fell from my hand, and I stared at it lying on the golden carpet. He was asking me questions. Penny too. But theirs weren't as pressing as the ones I was asking myself.

And then I shook them off. Picked up the phone. Picked myself up. "We need flights. You need clothes. James needs to stop doing whatever the heck he's doing and call me back."

The phone rang in my hand, and Brooks grinned at the name on the screen. *James.* "Maggie Grace Vickers, apparently the universe is yours to command."

I glared at him while punching the Accept button. "Ambulance? What's wrong with Alex?"

"Breathe, Maggie. Nothing. There's no need for you to come home. The ambulance was for Manuel. He cut himself when a vase fell. Sliced his leg up good. Twenty stitches— but an actual ambulance? Total overkill. Dr. Ackerman wasn't here, but we could've driven him to the hospital. Anna just freaked when she saw the blood—I imagine you would've done much the same—once you were done passing out or puking."

"What's going on?" Penny put a hand on my arm and Brooks must've ducked in his room to grab a shirt, but he was back, leaning against his door, brow furrowed.

"Alex is fine," James said.

"I didn't ask how he was." Though hearing this felt like a dozen clamps had been removed from my lungs. "What's going on?"

"He went home. You knew that was the plan, and with you gone—well, I don't think he had a reason to stay."

"He's gone." It made sense—him not waiting around for me—but it hadn't occurred to me that he wouldn't be there when I got back. "Okay, give me his number, please."

"I can't."

"Why not?"

"He told me not to. He doesn't want you to have it."

"James, that's not funny."

"I know," he said solemnly. "I'm sorry."

"I—I don't understand." And I knew it wasn't the same, but all I could think of was that call from Daddy five months ago, *Magnolia, I have some sad news*—

I'd been out shopping for bikinis that I'd planned to model the following weekend in New York. I'd only half-listened to Daddy. I was distracted because I hadn't heard from Carter in over fifteen hours. Then he'd said, "Carter Landlow was killed last night"—and I'd made him repeat it over and over because it didn't make any sense. My brain kept rejecting the news that my world and heart had broken.

It wasn't the same thing at all, but it was that same sort of mental fog. That same sort of tilting and warping of walls and thoughts I'd believed to be solid. And Carter's sister was staring at me with blue eyes so similar to his. And Alex . . .

"But he . . . I—" I shook my head at Brooks, held up a palm when Penny started toward where I was backing into my room. I shut the door and sat down on the carpet. "He doesn't want me?"

"I don't know what to tell you, Maggie." James's voice was pinched. "It surprised me too. But he—he said he wanted a clean break. He doesn't want to hear from you."

"What did my daddy do?" Because that had to be the explanation, right? Daddy pointed fingers and slathered on blame and guilt in such thick layers that Alex had decided it was better to shrug them off—shrug *me* off—than bear their weight. "If I could just talk to him."

"It wasn't . . ." I could hear James swallowing and sighing. "Alex was pretty clear about what he wanted."

"You mean what he *didn't* want," I whispered. "Did I—did I do something?"

"Ah, Maggie. You're killing me right now—I want to kill *him* for hurting you."

I cringed at his word choice. "Swear to me the ambulance wasn't for him."

"It wasn't, I swear. He's fine."

Which stung, because I *wasn't*. "Is this . . . is this like a *breakup*? Did you play middleman in my first breakup? Should I come home? Do you think . . ."

"No! You can't! You've got important things you need to be doing. If you quit and come home—the Family won't get over that."

"You're right. I'll stay. Of course."

"You okay?" James asked, all soft letters and pity.

I was grinding my teeth. Sharpening the feelings between them from sorrow into something darker. Something slippery and acrid. "Why wouldn't I be? He was just a boy. Just a boy who needed a kidney. For a second I might've believed . . . but what would I know? He was a patient and my bedside manner sucks, remember?" He made a sound of protest, but I cut him off. "It's fine. I'm fine. This is nothing, James. Compared to everything that's happened this year, this is nothing at all."

"It's okay to be upset. And maybe just give him some time."

"He can take from now till judgment day for all I care. I'll be busy. Speaking of, I should go make sure Brooks isn't booking us on the next flight home. I've got work to do here. I don't have time to waste on this."

"Hang in there. And, listen, Maggie, I hate to do this—I know the timing sucks, but you're not going to be able to reach me for a couple of days. Hawk and I are going to his hunting cabin. I need to get away and do some thinking, and his clinic was shut down. So . . ."

His "so" was so close to "sorry," and he shouldn't have to apologize for not being available to be my sounding board, counselor, and human Kleenex twenty-four/seven. That wasn't friendship, that was indentureship, and I hated that our relationship always got caught in the middle of the push-pull between Family and family.

"Sounds fun." I wrapped the words in an airy tone, but they fell like hailstones. "Give my best to Hawk."

"I'll be back in a couple days. Maybe even before you."

"Not a problem. Just promise me one thing."

I wanted a cautious "What is it?" but he gave me an earnest "anything." Which meant I was right about him being worried and me needing to prove that this news wasn't going to drown me.

"Don't you shoot each other, all right?"

His laughter was thin with relief. "Promise."

"Okay. Well, if I don't get off this phone in the next ten seconds, Penny's liable to tear it from my hands." Penny wasn't even in the room, but that was my guesstimated countdown to tears. "'Bye, Lames."

"You take care, Naggie."

I was cross-legged on the floor like a kid playing tea party, wishing I could be that little again, when my biggest problem was chipping Mama's china because I was too rough with cups and saucers.

What had changed between "See you downstairs" and "Don't give her my number"?

Maybe Alex—maybe all of him and all he'd told me—maybe it was a long con. He'd played me to get access to my Family, to a kidney.

Drag racing, his parents, school, all the stories he'd shared could've been straight-up lies to get my sympathy. A seduction didn't seem like *that* high a price to pay if the end result was a transplant.

Except . . . we'd had a conversation once, when his legs were cramping during dialysis and it was such a relentlessly hot day and he'd hit his fluid-intake limit. I'd asked him what the hardest part was. The pained expression on his face when he said "hope" . . . even the best actor couldn't fake that.

He'd gone on to add, "And the side effects of dialysis—the looking ahead to the ones caused by anti-rejection meds. The cost. The treatment schedule that consumes your life. And on really bad days you have that moment—and it's just a moment— but it's so much *work* to stay alive. And sometimes . . ."

That *sometimes* had haunted me. It had kept me up at night.

One life versus how many others. I was the *one* now—the one whose voice could effect change or destroy it. I pushed up to my feet, hurt heating to anger, and anger calcifying in the spaces between my cells as I marched to the door and yanked it open.

Brooks and Penny were still waiting in the hall. "Everything okay?" she asked.

I nodded and tossed Brooks his phone. "Alex?"

"As far as I know, he's fine." My voice was brusque. "I'm tired. I'm going to bed."

They didn't stop me. I didn't fool them, but they didn't stop me. I lay in bed, and my emotions had hours of ceiling staring to fuse into an armor of confusion, guilt, fear, blame, betrayal, fury . . . detachment.

The Organ Act needed a spokesperson, and I needed a goal—DC and the media needed to be ready, 'cause I dang well was.

CHAPTER 45

Penny and Char hovered in my doorway as I finished up a phone interview. I held up one finger.

"And while our Families have always maintained high standards in donor care, this makes those things legally binding. Donors already assume the medical risks that go along with their acts of life saving, why should they face legal risks too? And if doctors are paid, insurance companies, nurses, and hospitals too—why should the donors be expected to give up a piece of their body for free? Or worse, at a loss of travel expenses, lost wages, and medical costs? The Organ Act creates support and safeguards for those willing to give the gift of an organ. It provides compensation, health care, paid medical leave. It prioritizes donors should *they* ever be in need of a transplant. And it does this for less than the cost of Medicare maintaining the would-be recipient on dialysis or other life-prolonging measures."

"Magnolia, you've certainly given us a lot to think about, and like many people, I'm anxiously awaiting the Senate's vote for H.R. 197. Once that happens, we hope to have you back on the show."

"I'd like that too. Thank you, Cooper." I waited the five count like I'd been instructed, then disconnected and turned to the couple in party clothes.

"Has anyone ever told you you're a force of nature?" Char asked.

"Yes." For three days I'd been relentlessly pursuing opportunities to push our agenda. If James thought I fixated before, he should have seen me now. I'd doubled the events on my schedule and stayed up until all hours responding to written requests. I'd practically snarled when Bob told us the Senate wouldn't be calling for a vote before they recessed for Thanksgiving.

It was my last night here. Only twenty hours until my flight. If I was lucky, I wouldn't be spending more than three at this party. Since I hadn't thought to pack a cocktail dress, I was wearing one of Penny's. It made the five-inch difference in our height extra apparent. If I dropped anything tonight, it was going to have to stay on the floor.

I chugged what remained of my sixth cup of coffee. "Let's go mingle. Then pool splash? Is that the right term?"

"Pool spray," corrected Char. "It's a quick photo op. We don't even have to answer questions."

Except, sometimes questions were so darn tempting. Especially since I had answers prepped and ready, way too much caffeine, too little sleep, and no fondness for silence or space to think. So after a minute of "Look here" and "Let's see a smile," I didn't hesitate to answer the first one called out by a reporter.

"What do you three say to people who call your Families 'butchers' or 'body thieves'?"

There wasn't a microphone, but I'd always hollered better than I whispered. "I'm well aware some people think what my Family did was wrong, but I can't agree. We filled a need the government created by rejecting people from its transplant lists. For those patients, their options were find the organ they needed elsewhere, or *die*. That's not much of a choice. And now, with bill H.R. 197 up for a Senate vote, there's so much at stake for the hundred and fifty thousand Americans currently waiting for organs."

"You're saying the government transplant list is wrong?"

I took a breath before answering that one, because I was about to go *way* off-script. "There's so much subjectivity in deciding who deserves a place on the transplant list. It's not right or wrong. I get that. I get that even if this act passes, the government's not going to be able to say yes to everyone. But at least we could help some people who would have formerly been noes . . . the people who may have secondary health issues or chromosomal disorders, who might have learning delays or no family nearby—all these things can equal rejection from the transplant committee.

"A high schooler's truancy record shouldn't be considered, nor should misdemeanor crimes. Last I checked, getting caught sexting your girlfriend has no relevance to a lung transplant—yet there was a boy who died, drowning in fluid filling his lungs because his record wasn't virginal white. And should I even open the can of worms that's the rate at which *minority* patients are rejected compared to affluent, Caucasian males? Because those are some ugly facts. Same with mental health—depression can be used as a disqualifier—but isn't depression a natural reaction to the environmental and physiological realities these patients face?

"My point is, I know there need to be some noes. I know there are plenty of people who hear 'Hang in there, you're not sick enough yet,' or, 'Wow, you're really, really sick, and we've found you worthy—now let's hope you don't die while waiting for someone else to, so we can give you their parts.' I don't envy the transplant committees when they have to decide between a fifty-year-old and a twelve-year-old. I know for every yes and good news call they make, there are many more people waiting for their phones to ring. But let's address the underlying problem—there aren't enough organs. Let's open up the field. Legalizing this industry revolutionizes the supply. Let's make there be fewer noes because we have the capacity to say more yeses. Because these patients—*my* patients, your neighbors and teachers and the people in all our communities—they deserve a better chance."

The beat of silence after I finished was long enough to make me swallow self-consciously before it was broken with, "Magnolia, what about artificial organs?"

Barreling on felt so much better than standing still, drumming my fingers on my conspicuously bare legs, replaying what

I'd said—and worrying whether anything could be viewed as anti–Organ Act.

But even if it was, it was *real*, it was how I felt.

"Artificial organs? Are we developing them? Yes, us and a zillion other countries and companies. Surely you don't mean to stop medical research?" It was a bit of an exaggeration—my Family had made some progress with skin, but nothing internal. Nothing like the Zhus had accomplished.

"What about the rumors they're being used in humans without FDA approval?"

"Rumors are for schoolkids and Hollywood tabloids," I snapped, suddenly wary about this odd line of questioning.

"Penelope, what do you think?"

"Innovation is scary, but it's also important. I'm excited to see the sorts of advancements that happen throughout the medical community over the next few years, but like Maggie said earlier—people waiting for organs can't cross their fingers that they'll live long enough to see artificial ones. We need to get them better access to transplants *today*. And that's where the Organ Act comes in."

"And Mr. Zhu, you agree? Artificial organ testing on humans isn't happening illegally?"

Char cleared his throat and smiled nervously. "Oh, you've noticed me here? I'm more than willing to let these smart, beautiful ladies field all the questions. They're doing fine so far."

Penny blushed and reached for his hand. I clasped mine together. I needed to wrestle back control of this conversation before Char slipped and incriminated himself. That question was a little too on the nose, and *this* was not the stage on which Penny should learn about Garrett.

I cleared my throat. "Artificial organs are neither here nor there. They're not mentioned in the Organ Act at all."

A new figure joined our group, and I saw Penny stiffen as she noticed her former tutor edging closer. Nolan was angling to get into any last pictures. She didn't frown, but her eyes hardened as she gave the reporters a gracious wave. "Thank you all for coming, but we should get back to the party."

"One last question," a reporter begged.

"All right, but *last* one." She smiled and pointed to Char. "This one gets cranky if he misses dessert."

"Were you and Garrett Ward romantically involved?"

The pause that followed wasn't silent, but it sure felt that way. It took me a beat and several flashbulbs before I swallowed and stepped forward. "No. Not at all. Uh-uh."

"That was a question for Ms. Landlow. Penelope, I have a source—"

Her eyes were as wide and round as quarters, her mouth a similarly shaped O.

"I'm sorry, we've got to go get this boy some chocolate cake." I flashed a smile that would've made Mama pageant-proud then gestured for Penny to precede me back across the flagstone. She bypassed the doors leading into the party and took the next set over, taking us all into a half-lit library.

"How could they—how could they know?" she whispered.

"I mean, we weren't—but how could they . . . Do you think *he*? Did *he* give an interview or something?"

She looked from Char to me and back to Char. The one person she *didn't* look at was the one who answered. The one who had followed us into the library uninvited.

"This is why you're not supposed to allow questions during a pool spray," said Nolan. "If you ignore the established parameters, you encourage the press to disregard them at future ventures. And by *not* answering, you've made *that* the most interesting fact in what would've been a really innocuous pool report."

"Oh, shut up, Nolan," I said. "If you want to be helpful, go away."

I hadn't noticed Caleigh Forman until she laughed—which made Nolan's neck turn even redder as he smacked his lips together, mumbled something about "insolent," then marched out of the room. Because why would he stay when he'd done his damage, and the press and important people were elsewhere?

Caleigh was sitting in a high-backed chair in the corner of the room. She had her shoes off and her phone in her lap. "That was pretty epic. Can you stick around and do that *every* time he becomes obnoxious?"

"Which is *always*," said Penny softly. "I shouldn't have taken the question. I shouldn't have frozen."

"We've all done it," said Caleigh, earning herself an esteem bump in my book. "If you want proof, google how I answered 'What's your *least* favorite class?' I've apologized to the National

Council of Teachers of Mathematics—*twice*—and I'm still convinced that some rogue geometry teacher is going to take me out with a protractor and compass."

"Thanks," said Penny shyly. "I always feel so bad at all this."

"If you are, I am too." Which, based on the press's adoring coverage of Caleigh's preppy red curls and winsome smile, was a lie. At least it was a kind one. She sighed and slipped her phone in her pocket. "I should get back in there before anyone notices I'm missing. But I can cover for you if you need a few minutes."

"Thanks," said Char. He poured a glass of water from a pitcher on a side table, delivering it to Penny with a kiss on her cheek. "That would be great."

"Of course." Her smile was a tad wry as she slipped on heels and added, "Can you believe Nolan weaseled his way into a Thanksgiving invite?"

"I can't," Pen said once the three of us were alone in the room, "I can't eat *duck* in the same room with that man. Char, can I come home with you?"

I was all set to exit and give them privacy to plan their first holiday together, but Char shook his head. "No. Sorry, love. It's not a good idea."

"I promise I won't get in the way. If you want to spend the whole trip with your father, I'll just . . . not get in the way. But please don't let Nolan be the only thing that reminds me of home on Thanksgiving."

He hung his head. "Sorry."

Just before I gave in to the urge to ask what the heck was wrong with him, I got it. If Pen went to California, she'd encounter a much stronger reminder of home: *Garrett*.

Though she had tears collecting on her eyelashes, she pressed her lips together. "Fine. I apologize for asking. I wouldn't want to intrude."

"I'm really sorry."

"I said it was *fine*." I'd never seen Penny angry. Even after everything she'd endured, she'd kept this airy innocence. And she was such a small thing, with a circle of space always around her. It made her look aloof, even though I knew that wasn't why. But she was full Landlow right now. Boy, was she full Landlow. I wanted to tell Char to pluck the water glass from her hand, because Carter had smashed more than a few during his thunderstorm arguments—a habit he'd inherited from his father, and from the way she'd cocked her hand back, I guessed she had too.

She looked at it for a long moment, then put it down on a table and stepped away.

Char, bless his heart, was in completely over his head. I *almost* wanted to intervene on his behalf, but not quite. I'd warned him that not telling her about Garrett was inviting disaster. If he'd listened to me, his girlfriend wouldn't be coiling like a rattler and readying her venom to strike.

"It was presumptuous to invite myself," she snapped in an icy Miss Manners voice. "I shouldn't have put you in a situation where you had to tell me I'm not welcome."

"Guess what?" I stepped forward—between the boy who looked like he was being stuck with twelve hot pokers and the girl on the verge of an explosion of temper or tears. "I'm about to do the same thing—invite myself. Penny, can I stay? Please? I don't think I'll like duck either, but I promise to continue to tell Nolan to shut up."

"Really?" she asked. "You want to?"

A month ago it might've been an obligation, but not anymore. "It's been such a fast trip, and we've had next to no time that wasn't scheduled. Can I stay?"

Going home meant facing Family members who may or may not have cooled down yet. Sitting at a holiday table where Alex *wasn't* there to be the thing I was most thankful for. Facing an empty room across the hall from mine. Dealing with a whole new relationship that had collapsed without warning or proof it existed in the first place. Not that it made sense to call what I'd had with Alex "a relationship." It couldn't be. A few kisses, some hand-holding, some soul sharing.

I thought we were building something. But I was wrong. It was nothing like what I'd had with Carter.

His sister—my friend—was currently dabbing at her eyes and smiling. "Yes! Yes, *please!*"

Char caught my gaze and mouthed the words "thank you," but he was the last person I'd done this for. I'd done this for her. I'd done it for me.

CHAPTER 46

"Mama, I'm going to stay here for Thanksgiving."

"Pardon?"

"I'm going to stay here—with the vice president. Well, with Penny."

"Want to run that by me one more time?"

"I'm not done here."

"Maggie Grace, this was meant to be a three-day trip, not the Crusades."

"It's Penny's first holiday since she lost her family. It's *my* first Thanksgiving where I won't be sneaking away to talk to Carter."

"I used to wonder if we needed to have you checked for a UTI—all those bathroom breaks."

I snorted then softened my voice. "I need to be here, Mama. Not for anything Business-related, but because she's a friend."

"Alrighty then, you'll stay."

"Really?" It couldn't possibly be that easy. I'd expected to get my way eventually, but not until she'd invented twelve new ways to aggravate me.

"It'll be a quiet holiday." She sighed. "But, yes, of course. Didn't you ever wonder *why* I insist on no Business talk at the table?"

"Because it bores you?"

"No. Well, yes, but that's not why. It's because I hoped to keep you away from it. That was clearly impossible—you've been chasing after your daddy since you before you had all your baby teeth. But I wanted to show you there's a work-life balance. It's not easy—especially not in this Family—but you need parts of you, parts of your life, that aren't related to the Business. That's why I supported you on every running thing you ever wanted. It's why I keep asking you to do book clubs, photography, pottery—anything I can think of. I want you to have things that aren't about the Business. It's why I pushed you to go back to school this fall when it was clear to the Lord in heaven and everyone beneath that you were bad off. I hoped . . . I hoped getting away from here would help. So, make your relationship with Penelope about friendship, not about the Families you grew up in. Make your romantic relationships about the ways the boy makes you feel . . . Don't let what your Daddy does for a living destroy something that could be good."

"Do you think he's okay?" I whispered.

"He was fine when he left, so I can't see why he wouldn't be." Mama's voice was soothing. "I'm holding on to that when I say my prayers."

"You're—you're praying for Alex?" I thought prayer was just something she talked about with her church ladies. Something they bandied about self-righteously—"I'll pray for you to see the error of your ways"—or a means to spread church gossip via the prayer chain whenever anyone was sick, laid off, or left a spouse. But there was no audience for this call, and there was no judgment in her voice.

"I like him," she said softly. "He's a good boy. I liked—I liked how he made you better."

"I made myself better, Mama."

"That's true. I didn't mean to undercut your efforts. You climbed out of that dark place, and you're standing on your feet again. I'm proud as can be about that." She paused, and I used the opportunity to put the phone on mute, because I was sniffling, dangit, and I wasn't okay with her hearing it. "But, sugar pie, I like the balance he gave you. The way he softened your prickly edges. I've never seen you care *for* someone before. You care *about* people, but I've never seen you *do* for them. You were never a baby doll girl, and except for that horse of yours, you weren't one for pets. You think I didn't notice you watching out for Alex? How he was feeling, what he was eating, when he entered and exited a room. If he yawned, you were suddenly tired and ready for bed. If he was sweating, you adjusted the air-conditioning."

She made it sound like I was a sunflower, orienting myself around his light. And maybe it wasn't inaccurate, but the words stung and picked at wounds that hadn't begun to scab.

I clicked the phone off mute. "I'm glad you're praying for him." And maybe I would too, if I could figure out words that didn't sound so much like blame and *How could You?*

"Don't give up on him just yet. Maybe he's taking some space to make sense of all this—this Family is a lot to swallow. And you, chickpea, are a handful too."

"I wouldn't want anyone who wanted me to be less."

"You can be mighty intimidating—I don't know if you realize that. And men don't fight for ladies who fight their own battles . . . so maybe sit this round out and see if he makes his way back to you."

I wanted to hit her in the head with a feminist manifesto. Sit back and wait to see if he decided I was too much trouble? Act helpless so he could rescue me? Not in six cats' worth of lifetimes. "Is that a less catchy way of saying 'Guys don't make passes at chicks who kick—'"

"Magnolia Grace!" I could picture Mama straightening her collar and both sleeves before she added, "You are not a 'chick.' Don't refer to yourself as one."

I sighed. This conversation was a giant step forward and then a landslide back to where we started. But maybe that wasn't fair. She was trying to meet me halfway, and I was refusing to take even a step toward the center. "I've got to go. Give Daddy my love and tell him I'll check in later."

"Will do, sugar pie. We love you too."

"And, Mama?" I took a deep breath and pushed the rest of the thought out right before hanging up. "Pottery sounds fun. You know I've always loved getting muddy. Sign us up."

"Brooks, how do you feel about duck?"

He was zipping up his suitcase when I leaned in his room. "Hunting?"

"Eating."

He shrugged and ran his hand across his head, scratching at his buzzed hair. It was something I noticed him doing in almost every conversation here. I bet he was missing his ball caps. I'd seen more of the top of his head these past three days than the previous three years combined. "Can't say I care for it. It's real greasy."

"Okay." I shrugged. "Then it makes sense for you to head back this afternoon."

He hooked his thumbs in his belt loops. "Am I to take that to mean you're *not*?"

"I'm staying another week. For Thanksgiving. The menu is duck. And Grandmama Landlow's famous cranberry-apple relish—but don't tell Penny, because I want it to be a surprise." And after the ten phone calls it'd taken to find Miles Banks so I could ask him to go to the Landlow Estate and hunt down the recipe—she'd better enjoy every bite. I was still disappointed he hadn't found her dang bear.

"Now, Maggie—"

"I've already gotten the boss to sign off on it." Technically I'd gone through Mama and let *her* have the pleasure of persuading Daddy. "I'll have Penny's Secret Service detail, and I've practically taken a blood oath that I'm not fixing to cause trouble."

"A *blood* oath? Now I know you're lying." He tilted his head. "You want me to stay?"

"Nah. Just have an extra serving of turkey for me."

"Can do. Want me to leave my phone? I know how attached you've become."

I laughed. "Mama overnighted mine. It should be here tomorrow. But thank you." I lifted my shoulders and fidgeted like a toddler who's got to go to the bathroom. It was either that or hug him. And I had a reputation as a non-hugger to uphold. "For everything."

He nodded and squeezed my shoulder. A small gesture, a small bob of his Adam's apple—but for a guy who wasn't big on words, it said all he needed.

CHAPTER 47

I passed Caleigh heading upstairs on my way down to raid the pantry for some late-night cereal. "You okay?" I asked. The girl practically woke up media-ready, but now she was all disheveled hair and flared nostrils.

"Penny and my dad are talking Business in the kitchen, so I'm not welcome. Not even to grab an apple. I'm sure *you* can go in though. And let's call her boyfriend and invite him over, because Dad always has time for *him* too."

"Oh." I'd been expecting an answer like "headache," or "cramps," or "annoying math homework," so it took me a second to process. "That's not cool. I'm sorry."

"It's fine. I'm used to it—just, sometimes . . . no, it's fine. Sorry." As Caleigh talked, she spun her hair into a neat bun. By the time she had it secured, she had her smile back in place, but for the first time, I could see the cracks in her mask. "See you in the morning, Maggie. Sleep well."

"You too." Though I planned to see her in five minutes when I dropped off an apple on my way back upstairs. And to say something to Penny when we had a moment alone.

But Caleigh was wrong—I wasn't welcome in the kitchen. This was obvious from the way Penny and the veep stopped talking as soon as I rounded the corner from the pantry, my fingers clamped around a box of Frosted Flakes. Didn't matter though, because based on what I'd overheard while cereal browsing, I wasn't going anywhere.

"Can we have a few minutes?" Penny asked.

"Offal with an 'O'?" I asked. "*They* were the ones who broke into your clinic?"

"How do you know about them?" asked the veep. "*What* do you know about them?"

Penny had nodded and looked at a piece of paper on the table. I picked it up and scanned as I answered. "They've been targeting our network—trying to get in and retrieve information. They managed to get access to some of our records, but have failed all subsequent attempts to breach our security." These were the words I'd heard Alex use to explain this to Daddy. I could recite them without thinking, which was good because my mind was reeling with what was on the page. "Is this a client list, Penny?"

The names were blacked out, but the spreadsheet listed transplant dates, organs, medical reasons.

"It's part of my Family's VIP list. I guess the intruders

weren't looking for pills after all." Her smile was grim, and the veep's expression was grimmer.

I stared at it. A column of livers, kidneys, corneas, lungs, hearts, ligaments . . . and behind each organ or tissue, behind each blacked-out name, a very powerful person. "How did they get this to you?"

Penny pointed to an envelope addressed to her and Bob Forman. *Offal* was written as the return address. "There are no fingerprints."

"Is it postmarked Vermont?"

"No, California," he said. "What made you think Vermont?"

"It's where the IP address was located." I flipped the envelope over. "Did they send anything else?"

Penny looked at him, and he said, "Take a seat, Magnolia. We're about to tell you something only three people outside this room know."

"Well, it looks like at least *four* now." Penny slid a folded piece of paper across the table. "This was in the envelope too."

I unfolded it. In capital letters it said: *I KNOW ABOUT KELLY.*

"What about her?" I looked from their tight faces to the printout to the line that said **08–14–2006, kidney, Female, 10, w/DS approaching ESRD.**

End-stage renal disease, I knew that one from Alex, and *DS—Down syndrome.*

"Holy—"

"It's a secret, Maggie."

"Of course it is. Crap, if this comes out before the vote . . ."

"I didn't have a choice," said the veep—no, screw it, I was calling him Bob from now on. "She was just a kid, and she'd been rejected from the transplant list, and—"

I narrowed my eyes. "And your loved one deserved to be an exception when my—when Alex did not?"

"No, of course not." But he wouldn't meet my gaze.

No wonder Pen had been so quick to move in here last summer; Bob *wasn't* a stranger. No wonder he'd reacted badly to Caleigh calling it the "Forgan Act." I wanted to ball up the list and make him eat it, along with all his sanctimonious words about *access for all.* "Since they didn't make demands, I don't see that we *do* anything different," I said. "We push for the vote ASAP and pray that Offal—whoever they are—doesn't reveal this before then."

"That's the best we could come up with too," said Penny. "And that's helpful about Vermont."

I stood up. They didn't need me for their strategy session, and I no longer had any desire for cereal. I palmed an apple from the fruit bowl and offered the reassurances I knew Bob would demand. "Don't worry, I won't tell anyone. Your hypocrisy is safe with me. Good night."

Offal had infiltrated *my* network, and Penny's. Plus there were those pointed questions at the last party—artificial organs and Garrett—so maybe they'd gotten in Char's too. But he wasn't here to ask, and I couldn't ask Penny without disclosing his stupid, stupid secrets.

I don't know that I even gave Caleigh a smile along with her apple, because my mind was already ten steps ahead, behind my bedroom door, using the perfect excuse to call Alex and get his take on this new information about Offal.

Except he didn't answer.

And then I was wishing Mama hadn't sent my phone so I couldn't have caved and dialed and looked like a lovesick fool on his caller ID.

After all, Bob had the whole NSA at his disposal—did I really think he needed Alex?

Maybe not, but I'd needed to hear his voice on that message. I'd listened all the way to the beep before hanging up.

CHAPTER 48

Turns out apple-cranberry relish wasn't my favorite. Neither was duck, and I wasn't currently a fan of the man carving it either. But Caleigh made a fantastic pumpkin pie, and Kelly had done an impressive job of burying my piece under whipped cream. Each time she smiled at me or we shared a chat or a giggle, my stomach twisted with bitterness and guilt. It *wasn't* that I begrudged Kelly her kidney . . . It was that I resented the heck out of Bob being "organs for all" only *after* going black market for her. If he'd been willing to risk *her* the way I was expected to risk Alex, then maybe the Organ Act would've passed nine years ago and Carter and his parents would still be alive . . . along with who knows how many other people who died waiting for transplants.

But I'd managed cordial smiles over the candlesticks, been fiendishly happy that Nolan snagged the seat next to Bob's and monopolized his attention during the meal. And I could think of no better ending to the holiday than sitting next to Penny on a couch—sugar-high and duck-drowsy—while Christmas movies played on the TV.

"Can't you just stay?" she asked.

"Well, we've already gotten to the point where your closet is *my* closet. That's halfway to moving in." I'd planned for three days and would be staying eleven—there was no way even the most efficient packer could've managed that—and my suitcase was always more Jenga than Tetris.

"I raided your apartment closet all summer, so it's only fair. Though your clothes are way more interesting than mine."

"True." I burrowed deeper under a throw blanket, trying to tuck in my feet. The post-meal sweatpants I'd borrowed from Pen fit me like capris. "Have you talked to Char?"

"Of course! He volunteered to smuggle back turkey leftovers . . . but I don't know if those will travel well. So—" She turned sideways on the couch, scrunching her nose as she braided the fringe on my blanket and peeked up at me. "Is it time for boy talk? Because we're running out of days, and I want to know about *yours*."

"Mine?" It wouldn't be hard to log into Carter's account and show her picture after picture, story after story. And I knew we'd do that someday. Me asking about the memories I wasn't in, offering her some of mine—so that together we could construct the whole picture of this boy we'd loved and shared and lost. But not yet.

"Would Carter like him? The new guy you're seeing?" Her

fingers were still nimble on the blanket, but mine had gone stiff beneath it. "Alex? Was that his name?"

It was *a* name. A name I'd forbidden myself from thinking this past week because it hadn't shown up on my caller ID. It hadn't appeared in my in-box or in any of my conversations with James. Maybe it was more of a land mine than a name, since I felt like getting any closer to it would mean splaying my guts across the room.

"He's . . . I thought . . ." What had blunted the edges of my tongue? Where were the quicksilver comebacks that carved out a space where anything personal could be hidden? "He's not interested."

"Then he's an idiot." She dragged her fingers through the braid she'd just finished, separating the fringe back into individual strands. "Guys. You think you know them, then . . ."

"Yeah." I didn't know if her frown was introspective or sympathetic. Whether she was thinking about Alex changing his mind or Char's secretive trips home. Or both. I reached over and gave her a careful hug. "Any chance I can persuade you to come enjoy a Longhorn Christmas?"

Even though no one had asked at dinner, I had my answer ready. The thing I was most thankful for this year was Penny's friendship—and that my invitation chased the melancholy from her face, replacing it with a smile as she said, "Yes! That sounds perfect."

CHAPTER 49

It's not that Daddy and I had been flat out ignoring each other, but our calls over the past eleven days had been infrequent and succinct. We kept them focused on Family news—the date for Byrd's arraignment, the doctor at the Tucson clinic who'd decided to retire, and the reaction to the mission statement/ apology e-mail I'd sent the night before I left.

It seemed I was slowly winning back the men. The e-mail had been a start, but my success in DC was a bigger catalyst. "Manuel was quoting your C-SPAN interview in this morning's meeting," Daddy said when I called him from the DC airport before my flight.

"Mockingly?"

"Approvingly. And your mama said to tell you she liked your dress."

Which made me snort, because it was one of Penny's dull-as-dirt pastels. And while I was glad to hear the men were coming around, I didn't live or die by their opinion anymore.

I'd heard Daddy's farewell of "Have a good flight. See you soon, sport," but I was a mite surprised to see him behind the wheel of the SUV waiting for me at the airport. More surprising? That Mama was riding shotgun, and until I climbed in, the backseat had been empty.

I couldn't remember the last time the three of us had been alone in a vehicle, or anywhere off-estate without a team of security.

"Hey, sport" and "Welcome home, honeybee" drifted from the front seat, but the only response I could think of was "Are we safe?"

"Oh, come on now. My driving's not that bad." Daddy flipped a blinker and pulled away from the curb.

"I just mean, where's Manuel? Brooks?"

"Probably back at our place watching football. We figured family time would be a good thing to practice."

I could hear the lowercase "f" on that word. "Any reason?"

"They're calling for the vote Monday. Vice President Forman said there's more than a comfortable margin—it'll pass."

So nice of Bob to tell *me* this morning when we were exchanging tense good-byes. Now if Offal could just sit on the VIP list for another forty-eight hours . . .

"Isn't that *good* news?" Mama asked. "You don't look too happy about it."

I rearranged my expression to something more pleasant. "They had to wait until right after I left. Dangit, I'm going to miss all the celebration."

"Language, Magnolia Grace." But she was smiling.

"We can have our own celebration here," said Daddy. "Your mama's been giving me an earful on work-life balance. So, once this vote is in, I think we should go somewhere as a family—on a *vacation*, not a Business trip. How's that sound?"

Potentially good, but there was probably an equal likelihood we'd strangle each other on day one.

"The Caribbean or Europe?" asked Mama. "I'd like to go before you head back to UT in January."

"Either." I wasn't sure when my returning to school had gone from "We'll talk about that later, pumpkin" to something she spoke about as gospel, but I'd lobbied hard for it during our phone calls this past week and I was glad to see she'd yielded.

Even more glad to see a text from James pop up on my phone: **Landed yet?**

Yup. Miss me?

"Who're you typing with that's got you so smiley, sugar?" Mama asked.

"James."

Daddy snorted. "Figures. Now that *you're* back, he is too.

We haven't seen a trace of him since he and I traded words about Alex the morning you left."

"Well, he was right, you were wrong. And—" My phone buzzed again and the sass died on my lips. I whispered a curse so bad Mama was too shocked to even scold.

"What's the matter, Magnolia?"

I stared at the phone. "James says I need to get to the hospital. Can you drop me there? Please?"

"Alex?" Mama asked as Daddy took an exit, his posture and speed changing from languid to aggressive.

"I'm asking." And those four letters plus a question mark were absurdly hard to type.

James's response of three letters was harder to read.
Yes.

"Holt, did he seem sicker to you that morning?" asked Mama. "I assumed he was just upset because you were scaring him to death, but was he paler? Now I'm second-guessing. The poor boy."

Daddy didn't answer, just swore and accelerated.

Mama turned around and grabbed the hands I was tying into knots. "Maggie Grace, now you listen here. There's no sense in telling you not to worry, because you will until you've seen him. But God made you strong for a reason— and no matter what's going on, you're going to be fine. I'm here with you and you can lean on my strength, just like Alex can lean on yours. And if that boy needs anything— *anything*, Holt—that we can get him, baby girl, I promise you we will."

I'd never imagined a moment where *Mama* issued impossible Business edicts, but I was starting to realize how often I'd underestimated and pushed her away.

I squeezed her hands. "You like him that much?"

"I *love you* that much," she answered. "And if it came down to it, you'd come visit me in prison, right?" It wasn't a glib line; she was serious. This was all so serious, and Daddy kept shifting his hands on the wheel. He was sweating through his shirt.

"Darlin', I'm sorry. If I did anything that caused Alex harm, I'm sorry." He swerved into the hospital drive and jerked to a stop by the curb. "I'll park and find you. Go on."

But I froze. Getting out of this car meant hearing news I might not be able to handle. Facing grief again. And regret . . .

"You can do this," said Mama. She opened her door and then mine. "I'm right here with you."

I hadn't held her hand since I was a toddler and even then only under duress, but I reached for it as we walked through the hospital's automatic door. Clung to it. Realized it'd probably been there for me to cling to all along. I'd been too wrapped up in my foolhardy need to prove I *wasn't* like her. To define her type of strength as lesser than mine and the men's. I hoped I *wasn't* a hundred percent Daddy and zero percent Mama—because that would be a real shame.

James was sitting on a couch in the lobby. He looked pale, his face pinched as he stood slowly. My bottom lip began to quiver, my voice broke when I asked, "Alex?"

"Room 413. You go on. I need to talk to your parents, but I'll be up in a minute. Okay?"

No, it wasn't okay. I didn't want to do this alone, but I also couldn't wait a single second longer. So I nodded, gritted my teeth, and ran for the elevator.

CHAPTER 50

I'm pretty sure God, who I was working my way back to believing in, was willing to forgive me for the language I used while waiting for the elevator to reach the fourth floor. I might have been willing to forgive Him, if things weren't awful when I got there.

I found room 413 and burst through the door with Alex's name on my lips, startling a woman sitting in the chair beside a bed. The boy on it was facing the window. He had short hair, a short-sleeved gown.

"Alex?"

"Maggie?" The low voice rumbled through my veins, setting my blood on fire. "You finally back from DC?"

He rolled over, but I couldn't see those warm eyes I'd dreamed about because my own were brimming with tears and blurring everything. "I would've— I didn't know— Are you—"

"Mamá, can we have a minute?"

"Claro." She kissed his cheek, touched my arm, and shut the door behind her.

"Come here." Alex patted the bed beside him.

"What's wrong?" I didn't know what the machines meant or what was in his IV line, but everything about him *here* made me woozy. All I wanted was to hold him, but I could barely hold myself upright. Just crossing the room had me shaking, and I don't think I've ever sat so carefully in my life. I was stiff as plaster and breathing in quick, shallow pants.

"Shh," he soothed, wiping my face with his non-IV arm, which was the arm with his fistula, but I was too overwhelmed to even react. Or maybe it didn't bother me anymore—it was a part of him, a part of what kept him *healthy*. "I'm okay."

I nodded. If he was okay right now, we could figure out the rest. On Monday, there'd be a vote, then we'd petition for some sort of license or exception or waiver that allowed us to do his transplant immediately.

"This looks like more than a sneeze, and you were supposed to call me if . . ." I couldn't help but lean toward him, but the memory of what had happened between his nurse joke and now made me pull back. And maybe I should've cared about my reputation or dignity or saving my battered heart from more rejection, but instead I whispered, "I missed you. So much."

"Oh, Maggie." He lifted my hand and pressed his lips to my palm. "I missed you too. I'm sorry for telling James not to—"

"Oh, thank God." I threw my arms around him.

He winced and stiffened. But his arm held me in place as he gave a short, tight laugh. "Hey there, be gentle with me. I've had major surgery."

"What?" I scrambled off the bed so I could see all of him. "What do you mean?"

"I *didn't* mean go away. Get back where I can reach you." He held up his IV and grinned wryly. "One of these days I'm going to have both hands free to hold you."

"Surgery?" I asked.

There was a knock on the door, and James entered. My parents stayed outside, it looked like they were talking to Alex's, wiping their eyes and hugging. The guys nodded at each other, then both looked at me. I was gripping my sides and trembling with fear, confusion, relief, and impatience.

"What the heck is going on?" I demanded. "What *kind* of surgery?"

James smiled. "You're not the only one who can keep a secret, you know." He slowly reached for the hem of his shirt and all I could think was *If he went and got a tattoo without me . . .*

But it wasn't flames, or a steer, or a tribal band, or a butterfly. It was a series of partially healed cuts along his left side. I flinched from the red and black wounds, but it wasn't until I saw the larger incision spanning the bottom of his abdomen that I started to comprehend. Those weren't from stray buck-shot. Or a broken vase. Or any other sort of accident. He care-fully lowered his shirt.

"Scars are sexy, right?" Alex asked. "Because I've got a set too."

I blinked and breathed, looked from one boy to the other and back again, and tried to find words because facts were spin-ning, gathering, assembling into a gorgeous truth that left me awed and overwhelmed.

"You're not going to pass out on me, are you?" asked James. "Because I don't think I can catch you right now."

I shook my head and tears spilled down my cheeks. "Oh, Lames, what did you do?" I could barely get the words out between sobs and because I'd thrown my arms around him and my mouth was full of T-shirt and shoulder blade.

"Careful there, Maggie Grace. I'm a mite fragile right now."

I loosened my grip and attempted to wipe my face on the back of my hand. It was entirely ineffective. James laughed and offered a tissue.

I let go of him and ran to Alex.

"Shh, Maggie. It's okay. *I'm* okay."

I nodded. And cried. I couldn't stop crying. And if I couldn't hold *him* tight, it didn't mean I couldn't squeeze the heck out of his shirt with my shaking hands.

Alex whispered "shh" against my neck. He rubbed my back. "Is this the part where I'm supposed to pretend not to see you crying? Should I call your mama?"

I wiped my face and honked out a laugh. "No. This is the part where you kiss me."

"Yes, ma'am."

James cleared his throat. "You know I'm still here, right? The donor requests you wait until he leaves the room before making out."

"Shut up." I laughed. And smiled. And held out a hand so he'd walk closer. "I want to know everything. How did you— you didn't go hunting! You liar! How long have you been planning this?"

"That day by the creek you mentioned getting yourself tested. It was a good idea. If a recipient finds their own altruistic donor, they get to skip the list."

"And you matched." I nodded, shook my head, laughed.

"Yes, ma'am. Not a six-for-six match, but I figured you might not hold that against me. Especially after you hear about the *hours* of questioning the hospital put me through to make sure it was *really* an altruistic donation. We're talking intensive screening interviews and extra meetings with the ethics board. But I stand before you—the first Family member to have ever *legally* donated an organ."

I—gently—hugged him again, and then—extra gently— smacked his shoulder. "I can't believe you didn't tell me."

"He didn't even tell *me*," said Alex.

"I couldn't." James held up his hands. "Dr. Ackerman said it was the only way I'd be approved as a donor—it needed to be irrefutably clear no one had asked, influenced, or paid me."

Alex rubbed his cheek against my shoulder. "It was like the reverse of that urban legend. Instead of waking up in a bathtub of ice missing a kidney, they woke me up and forced me to accept one."

"Technically, you were already awake and in the middle of having it out with her daddy," said James. "Remind me I want to hear about that at some point, Maggie, because I'm guessing Enzo's exaggerating about the particulars of what went down in a certain bedroom across from yours. But once we got Alex alone and told him, he wasn't too hard to convince. Then it was off to the hospital, one last round of questions, tests, calling you, and being cut open." His mouth turned down, and he squeezed my other shoulder. "For what it's worth, that call was almost more excruciating than the surgery."

Just the memory of it was enough to make me wince. They both hung their heads and looked sheepish.

"You needed to be in DC," said Alex. "You'd have been on the next flight home—and you were needed there."

I sniffled. "I really thought you . . ."

"I'm so sorry." He squeezed my hand. "Can you forgive me?"

I took a deep breath and shook off the painful memory. "You could both get away with pretty much anything right now."

"In that case, Naggie . . ." James's face stayed somber. "I've left the Family. I just told your daddy. I know you said I didn't owe anyone anything, but I didn't agree. I needed to leave on my terms, and in a way that felt honorable. Giving a kidney to Alex—helping *him*, helping *you*, after all the times I let you down—it was the closure I needed." James cracked a tentative smile. "Besides, you're gonna be lost without me around, and he does a darn good job of distracting you."

"Thank you." Such insignificant words for all my gratitude. "If you ever need anything, *ever*, you call me first."

"Back atcha, Magnolia Grace." He kissed my cheek. "I'm going to stay with Baby and her family for now, but hopefully I'll see you back on campus?"

I nodded. "Yup. And I'm taking a psych seminar this spring, so you can be my tutor. And ceramics and Russian literature." James raised his eyebrows. "And some econ and accounting too."

"Sounds . . . eclectic," said Alex. "But it might help your *Quiz Show* skills."

"I don't want to 'fixate' so much. My whole life has been the Business. I want to know what I'm missing out on."

James grinned. "I like everything about this plan. Especially the part where you agree I'm right and admit you fixate. But all right, lovebirds. I'll get out of your way now."

"Thank you," said Alex, and the vibrations of his voice were thick with emotion. "For everything."

James nodded. "You take good care of her—and *you*, Maggie girl, take it easy on him."

"I'll call you later," I said. "Be prepared for epic poems of gratitude, maybe some ballads in your honor."

"Boy, give a girl a kidney and she goes all sappy on you." He waved from the door and shut it behind him.

I turned back to copper-green eyes and a waiting smile.

"You're okay?" I wanted to hear it—*needed* to hear it—over and over and over.

"I'm okay. I'm even being discharged today. They would've sent me home days ago, but I had a little infection." My eyes went wide, but I didn't even have time to go full-panic before Alex was touching my cheek and shaking his head. "*Little* infection, Maggie. I'm fine. I promise. Me, my new kidney, and my arsenal of anti-rejection meds will be home before bedtime."

I studied him again—measuring the honesty and hope in his eyes, and letting some seep beneath my skin. "I know James did the heavy lifting, but . . . what can I do? Do you need *anything*?"

"You," he said. "This—" He leaned in and I leaned too, but at the last second I turned my head and he ended up with a mouthful of hair.

"First, Alejandro Cooper, don't you ever, ever, ever break my heart like that again. I mean, it's *yours* to break, but . . . don't. Please."

"It's mine?"

I nodded.

His lips skipped across my cheek, tracing kisses up my jaw to my ear. He nipped at my earlobe, and I shivered. "What's with your Family throwing their organs at me lately? James's kidney, your heart—what's next?"

"This." I pressed my mouth against his. My fingers traced up his cheekbones and instead of hitting the soft curls I remembered, brushed stubble at the back of his neck. I pulled away to study him. To reassure myself he was here, this was real.

"So, what's this about?" His hair still flopped on top, just reaching his forehead, but on the side and back it was clipped short. It rasped against my fingertips in a way that made me want to giggle and do it all day long.

He shrugged. "Your mama said a 'suitor' shouldn't have hair longer than the girl he was hoping to pursue."

"Of course she did." I rested my head on his shoulder. His arm came around my waist and I may have been in a hospital room, but it felt like coming home.

"She said it the morning you left for DC, in the middle of your dad giving me what-for . . . and it pretty much shut him up. It sounded like her endorsement, and I wasn't going to take any chances."

"I'm pretty confident you've got her approval," I said.

"What about yours?"

I rubbed the short hair around his ears like I was tucking back a lock that didn't exist anymore. "I like it. You look older. And I can see your face. I like seeing your face."

"Want to see it up close and personal?" His voice was a toe-curling rumble.

There'd be a Business-changing vote Monday. I'd have to figure out how to prepare for Offal's next attack and their nebulous threats. How to set things all the way right with my

Family and my family. There were college classes and so many challenges in my future. But all that was okay, because Alex would be there too.

"Yes, please," I whispered against his lips. "Forever and ever after."

ACKNOWLEDGMENTS

Similar to *Hold Me Like a Breath,* the inspiration for this novel came from a fairy tale. In this case, the Brothers Grimm's *Frog Prince.* As a child I was fascinated by the princess's motivations for making and breaking her promise and the feelings that must have been involved—the prince's when he realized he'd been lied to, the princess's when she realized the significance of her lies. These emotional and motivational elements of the fairy tale are echoed in Magnolia's narrative—despite its shocking lack of golden balls and lily pads.

And, speaking of emotions . . . I've lost track of how many times I said, "*Break Me* is going to be the book that *breaks* me." This statement wore out its cleverness, but it hasn't stopped being true. *Break Me Like a Promise* is the most challenging book I've written.

I am so proud of the end result and eternally grateful for all the people who held my hand, poured me coffee, and cheered me on along the way.

From the Spanish teachers who vetted my lingo, to the Texans who weighed in on the Lone Star state, to those who shared their stories and experiences with kidney disease. I especially want to thank Lauren Strohecker, Mary Hinson, and Jared Hassler. I am so grateful to you for reading *Break Me* at a breakneck pace and sharing your insights, experiences, and wisdom. I also learned so much from the lovely folks at the IHateDialysis.com forum, arpkdchf.org, pkdcure.org, and the National Kidney Foundation. And I need to thank Dr. Southard—J-bean, little did we know way back in freshman year that your med school expertise was going to end up so helpful to *me*.

Heather Anastasiu not only gave me valuable early feedback, but her husband, Dragos, was my go-to for all things technological. Thank you to them both. And thank you to Annie Gaughen, Anne Greenwood Brown, Elisa Ludwig, Kate Walton, Robin Talley, Miranda Kenneally, Andrea Lepley, Katie Foucart, and Jessica Spotswood for retreat brainstorming and hot tub/boat deck pep talks. Eugene—our discussion about "Google Death" was a game changer.

I'm blessed with an amazing online and local book community. Mad love to Jonathan Maberry, Nancy Keim Comley, Tiff Emerick, Heather Hebert, Mitali Dave, Gaby Salpeter, Erica Haglund, Jen Calonita, Jen Zelesko, Victoria Schwab, Scott Tracey, Susan Adrian, Linda Grimes, Gail Yates, Eve

Mont, Claire LeGrand, Kelly Jensen, Joe Monti, and so many more.

And I'm not sure what I did to deserve Courtney Summers and Emily Hainsworth, but I am grateful every day for their brains and their friendship. I'm likewise lucky to have landed in such a supportive literary agency—thank you to Barry, Tricia, and everyone in BG Literary for being a community I'm so darn proud to be part of.

To my Bloomsbuddies at Bloomsbury—thank you all! Each of you has contributed so much to this story and my career. Emily Easton—for your enthusiastic response to what has to be the most ridiculous combination of words: "organ trafficking fairy tales." Laura Whitaker—for making each of my heroines your new favorite. Sarah Shumway—for pushing me to grow. To Cat Onder, Cindy Loh, Lizzy Mason, Courtney Griffin, Cristina Gilbert, Erica Barmash, Emily Ritter, Hali Baumstein, Claire Stetzer, Linette Kim, Beth Eller, Amanda Bartlett, Kerry Johnson, Jill Amack, and everyone else whose fingerprints are on this book—I can't imagine a better team!

My parents, thank you for everything, but especially for letting me bring the Schmidtlets to your house for the last week before I turned in the manuscript. Water is my thinking place—I'm not sure I would've figured out that third act if it weren't for their pool, and thank you to Emily Hainsworth for being willing to brainstorm while I paced the shallow end.

To every reader, blogger, librarian, teacher, friend, family member, and human who has spent time in the pages of any of my books—thank you! Each of your Tweets, Tumblrs, photos, e-mails, and letters makes me want to pinch myself. Many of them hang on the wall beside my desk as I write this. You are THE BEST.

St. Matt—there is no happily ever after without you! Thank you for being my safe place to land. Schmidtlets—you started reading while I was writing this book. It'll be a while until you've worked your way up to this level, but watching you fall in love with letters and words has been one of my greatest joys. *You* are my greatest job. I love you.

And finally, huge thanks to Taylor Swift for title inspiration and for songs that dominate every one of my writing playlists. If you ever want to be IRL BFFs, I'm totally game.